DARK SIDE
OF THE
MOON

The Works of Alan Jacobson

Novels

False Accusations

Karen Vail Series

The 7th Victim

Crush

Velocity

Inmate 1577

No Way Out

Spectrum

The Darkness of Evil

OPSIG Team Black Series

The Hunted

Hard Target

The Lost Codex

Dark Side of the Moon

Essays

"The Seductress"

(*Hollywood vs. the Author*, Rare Bird Books)

Short Stories

"Fatal Twist"

(*featuring Karen Vail*)

"Double Take"

(*featuring Carmine Russo & Ben Dyer*)

For up-to-date information on Alan Jacobson's current and future novels, please visit www.AlanJacobson.com.

DARK SIDE OF THE MOON

AN OPSIG TEAM BLACK NOVEL

ALAN JACOBSON

Cover design by Ian Koviak

Author photograph by Corey Jacobson

978-1-5040-5009-8

Published in 2018 by Open Road Integrated Media, Inc.
180 Maiden Lane
New York, NY 10038
www.openroadmedia.com

For the astronauts, engineers, and scientists who pioneered manned space travel, to those who gave their lives, and to those who risked them to reach beyond our limits and expand our horizons.

AUTHOR'S NOTE

When the idea for *Dark Side of the Moon* came to me, I had the ridiculous thought that my research load for this novel would be lighter than normal because I would not have to travel to locations all over the world. My most significant setting was going to be otherworldly—literally. However, I realized I needed to get my characters *to* the Moon, and as I would soon learn, I knew what the average person knows about this—at best not much and at worst *a lot* less than I needed to know.

Moreover, I had no intention of writing science fiction—not because I don't enjoy it (I grew up on *Star Trek*), but because that is not my genre, it's not what my readers expect, and that's not the world in which my characters live. That meant I needed to make this story believable and grounded in reality while using technology and methodology that currently exist. And *that* meant I needed to work with engineers and scientists far outside my usual realm of research contacts.

It was an enormous undertaking. But I learned a hell of a lot, and I truly appreciate the time and effort these experts gave me—both anonymous and named—in helping me understand how it all works. They enabled me to tell the story that I got so excited about when it first leaped into my thoughts.

My readers know that I always strive to show them new perspectives, using fresh ideas, in an effort to take them behind the scenes to places they wouldn't ordinarily be able to go—in this case, where few have gone before.

One important note: I revisit events that occurred during the Apollo 17 Moon landing in 1972. Some of the dialogue is real, taken from mission transcripts, though I summarized some of the exchanges because actual conversations are often boring—and make for poor reading. However, I depicted one event that did not actually occur and thus the dialogue spoken by the astronauts regarding it is fictional—meaning Gene Cernan and Jack Schmitt did not really say and do all these things. (If it smells like a legal disclaimer and sounds like a legal disclaimer . . .)

I trust you'll enjoy the journey and hope it'll give you a few things to think about.

DARK SIDE
OF THE
MOON

"The eyes of the world now look into space, to the Moon and to the planets beyond, and we have vowed that we shall not see it governed by a hostile flag of conquest, but by a banner of freedom and peace. We have vowed that we shall not see space filled with weapons of mass destruction, but with instruments of knowledge and understanding." —PRESIDENT JOHN F. KENNEDY

September 12, 1962

"Space appears to be the great wave of the future, and certainly military uses would be found for it. The Russians, with their lead, had probably already learned to put bombs up there, and . . . we should have our men—if not bombs—up there too. . . . Space was the new high ground, and the Air Force had best prepare to occupy it." —MICHAEL COLLINS

Gemini 10 and Apollo 11 astronaut, *Carrying the Fire*, 1974

"China and Russia . . . have hacked into every agency in the federal government including the Pentagon . . . the espionage, the stealing of military secrets, satellite technology, rocket technology out of NASA, it's prevalent. It's everywhere."

—REP. MICHAEL MCCAUL

Chairman, House Homeland Security Subcommittee on Oversight, Investigations, and Management

"Be polite, be professional, but have a plan to kill everybody you meet." —GEN. JAMES MATTIS, USMC

Apollo 17 Landing Site
Taurus-Littrow Valley
Mare Serenitatis
The Moon
December 13, 1972

Houston, we're getting some unusual radiation readings here."

"Say again? Where are you and what kind of readings are you getting?"

Apollo 17 commander Gene Cernan kept his gaze fixed on the Geiger counter. "We're on the southeast side of Bear Mountain and—"

"You're supposed to be on your way back to base," said flight director Denny Driscoll.

"Uh, this is Jack," geologist Harrison "Jack" Schmitt said. "This could be an important find. I think we should stretch our safety margin and stay out here a bit longer to—"

"Negative, Seventeen. You two told us ten minutes ago you were drop-dead exhausted from three days of climbing and digging—not to mention hauling Moon rocks for six hours today. You said your hands were tired and chafed raw from wearing those gloves and you were returning to Challenger."

"This is a once in a lifetime opportunity," Schmitt said. "Who knows when we'll get back here?"

In fact, they all knew it was going to be awhile—a *long* while. President Kennedy's very public challenge for Americans to land on the Moon before the Soviets had been accomplished—and on time. With budgets strained and the public's enthusiasm for the space program waning, Apollo 18, 19, and 20 were canceled. The writing was in NASA's budget—and as good as etched in the basalt of Moon rock: the agency was turning its attention to Skylab and something else they had been discussing: a low Earth orbit space shuttle.

There was a long moment of silence. Cernan figured Driscoll and his mission control specialists were discussing, if not debating, the timing of all they had left to do before liftoff.

Then: "Uh, Seventeen, what readings are you getting?"

Cernan looked to Schmitt. As the only scientist to walk the Moon's surface, this was his argument to make.

"Exceptionally high CPM on the Geiger. Everything here, so far, is the tan-gray subfloor gabbro that I've seen. But the rover's shadow is making it impossible to see. I think the rock I'm getting the radiation reading from is darker, slicker, graphite-colored."

"Apollo 14 found uranium and thorium."

"This is not that." Schmitt carefully leaned forward, his left hand keeping the heavy pressure suit from tipping him over as he tried to get a better look through his glass helmet visor. "This is . . . different. And I'm starting to think that maybe the gray, relatively nonvesicular subfloor may be the deeper fraction."

"Boy," Cernan said, glancing around beyond them to his left and right, "these rock fields are something else."

"Dandy," Driscoll said. "That's terrific, Seventeen. And I'm glad you're enjoying the view, Geno. But we're short on time so tell me about those radiation readings. Can you explain what you're getting, Jack?"

"I can't, Houston. I—I um, I don't know what to make of it."

"I'm gonna get a picture," Cernan said as he maneuvered the Hasselblad camera into position and snapped off several exposures. "Got it, I think."

"Seventeen, Houston. We want you to collect a small, representative rock sample, record its location, and lock it away in the lead-lined box when you get back to the LM," he said, pronouncing it "lem" and referring to the lunar module. "We'll analyze it back here."

"But—"

"You've had twenty-two hours of EVAs the past three days," Driscoll said, using the acronym for extravehicular activities. "But time's up. You need to park the rover and get your weight balanced for liftoff. Full checklist ahead of you. Go directly back to Challenger and get to it. Houston out."

Schmitt sighed, the moisture causing a slight fogging of his helmet visor. "A geologist's dream. And I—"

"You've *lived* the dream, Jack. The only scientist in human history to land on another planetary body. Get your hammer out. Let's chisel off a piece, take a core sample directly below it, and head back."

After securing the specimens, they got back in the rover and drove toward the Challenger. Upon arriving, they off-loaded the cases of rocks they had collected, taking care to use the radiation shielded container as directed. They weighed each box and placed them in precise locations to ensure that the ascent stage—which would deliver them into orbit to rendezvous with the command service module—was properly balanced. Every ounce had to be accounted for so they could be certain the engines had enough thrust to lift them off the surface.

"You good with this?" Cernan asked. "I need to go park the rover."

"Yeah," Schmitt said. "I've got some cleaning to do. This Moon dust is like cat hair—it's everywhere."

Cernan drove the LRV, or lunar roving vehicle, several hundred feet from the lunar module and turned in a circle, orienting the front so that it faced the spacecraft. He checked the movie camera mount to be certain it was framing the shot properly. Mission control wanted to film the liftoff, and this distance would give them a good view and enough perspective relative to the surface—as well as a safety margin to prevent the equipment from being incinerated by the rocket engine's burn.

Cernan climbed out of the rover and stood there a moment, pondering the fact that they had stayed on the Moon longer, and traveled farther, than any other crew had.

He knelt beside the rover and, scraping the stiff right index finger of his glove against the lunar soil, carved the initials TDC, after his daughter. He chuckled, knowing that with the Apollo program now ending, his inscription would remain undisturbed for many decades to come . . . perhaps for eternity.

He hopped and bounced back to Challenger—the lunar module's call sign—marveling at what he and Schmitt, and the hundreds of engineers at NASA and its contractors, had accomplished.

Upon reaching Challenger, he grabbed the handles to hoist himself up the ladder. This moment had haunted him for weeks. He had wanted to prepare remarks to read but he never had the time to formalize something. Just as Neil Armstrong's words of mankind's first steps on the lunar surface had become famous, the last man making his final boot prints on the Moon might likewise be remembered.

He had jotted down some notes on his sleeve over the past three days, but now, as he stood there, found that he did not need them. Instead, he spoke from the heart.

"As we leave the Moon and Taurus-Littrow, we leave as we came, and God willing, as we shall return, with peace and hope for all mankind. As I take these last steps from the surface for some time to come, I'd just like to record that America's challenge of today has forged man's destiny of tomorrow. Godspeed the crew of Apollo 17."

He lifted his left foot from the soil and climbed aboard Challenger.

AFTER ASCENDING THE TEN STEPS into the lunar module, Cernan was informed that they were over their weight limit by 210 pounds. They had anticipated this would be the case, and like some of the Apollo missions before them, they pulled out a fish scale and began weighing items they no longer needed.

Out the door went a bevy of expensive equipment: lab instruments, pouches of uneaten food, unneeded pairs of extravehicular activity/EVA gloves, two PLSS primary life support system backpacks, a Leica camera, and, last, the handheld scale.

They finished going through their written checklists and reported in to Denny Driscoll in Houston.

"We're just about on schedule," Cernan said.

"Roger, Geno. All systems are go."

"I'm gonna miss this place," Schmitt said. He sat back in his couch. "Someday, some way, mankind has to find its way back here."

"Roger that," Driscoll said. "Someday, some way, I'm sure we will."

1

NASA
Neutral Buoyancy Lab
Underwater Training Facility
Houston, Texas
Present Day

The two former Navy SEALs broke through the surface of the 40-foot deep, 200- by 100-foot 6-million-gallon pool that NASA used for training astronauts. Although neutral buoyancy diving did not perfectly duplicate the effects of a zero gravity environment, it provided the best way to simulate weightlessness for EVAs, or extravehicular activities, in space or on a planetary surface.

Astronauts who had trained at the Neutral Buoyancy Lab, or NBL, as it was known, and then went on to do EVAs outside the shuttle or International Space Station reported that it was effective in helping them prepare.

Standing on the edge of the expansive pool were FBI director Douglas Knox and secretary of defense Richard McNamara.

As the metal platform rose out of the water, two astronauts wearing modified pressure suits with leg weights strapped to their ankles stood rigidly, back to back.

Harris Welding rotated his head inside the large helmet and waited for the assistant dive operations training officer to help him out of his gear.

Two training support personnel began removing the breathing apparatus from Welding's partner, Darren Norris, while another unhooked the tank that supplied nitrox.

Once their helmets were detached from the suit, Secretary McNamara stepped forward, remaining behind the yellow and black striped safety line at the pool's edge. "You're both doing exceptionally well. We want to personally congratulate you on your progress."

Welding laughed. "Thank you, sir. But all due respect, the two of you didn't fly out to Houston just to give us a pat on the back."

"No," Director Knox said. "I know it takes forever to get out of those suits, but meet us in the briefing room in forty-five minutes. We've got some classified information to share regarding your mis—"

"Daddy! Daddy!"

Three children, two girls and a boy, came running toward Knox and McNamara, with a woman in her late thirties trailing twenty feet behind them.

"Wesley-Ann and Nicki," their mother shouted. "Stop. Michael, get your little sister!"

Knox stuck out his right arm and corralled the children. "Whoa, it's dangerous by the edge of the p—"

"Hi Daddy," the older girl, about seven, said.

A broad grin spread over Welding's lips. "Hey sweetie. What are you doing here?"

"You're s'posed to eat dinner with us, remember?"

"Oh. Uh, yeah, sweet pea. But you're way early." Welding was still sheathed in his suit and standing rigidly on the platform with a few inches of water from the humongous pool sloshing violently at his boot tops.

The woman reached Knox and gathered up her kids. "Sorry. They get so excited visiting Harris. He's been training all over the country for a year and a half, so when he's right in our backyard we try to spend as much time as possible with him." She held the three children with her left arm and stuck out her right hand. "Tanya Welding."

"Douglas Knox. You have great kids. They're adorable."

"Thank you. Are you— I know your name. But . . . sorry, I can't place it."

"No apologies necessary." The corners of Knox's mouth lifted ever so slightly. "I'm with the FBI. I try to stay out of the news as much as possible. It's not always possible."

"Sir," Welding said. "Mind if I take a little time with my family?"

"Absolutely," Knox said. "Take whatever you need. Just be in the briefing room in forty-five minutes."

DRESSED IN NASA T-SHIRTS AND CARGO PANTS, Welding and Norris sat down at the oval table. Joining Knox and McNamara were CIA assistant director Denard Ford and Brig. Gen. Klaus Eisenbach from USSTRATCOM, the United States Strategic Command.

"The time has come," Ford said, "to brief you on certain classified aspects of your mission." He turned to Eisenbach. "General."

Eisenbach's uniform was heavily decorated. He tugged it into place as he rose and walked over to the tabletop podium.

"Are Carson and Stroud getting this briefing too?" Welding asked.

"They are," Eisenbach said. "But you two are not due back at Vandenberg for a couple of weeks and it couldn't wait."

Welding and Norris shared a look, then leaned forward in their seats.

"You've spent time studying the Apollo missions," Knox said, "because they served as the basis for how you'll be approaching your op."

Eisenbach picked up the remote control from the table. "The knowledge we gained, the data we collected, the technology we developed, rank among the most important scientific achievements of humankind. But there's something that came out of Apollo that's never been publicized or published. Anywhere. Seventeen was the last Apollo, but the first to include a scientist, geologist Jack Schmitt."

"If I remember right, they brought back hundreds of pounds of lunar rock," Norris said.

"Yes. Including some odd orange, titanium-laced soil from Shorty Crater that contained the radioactive elements thorium and uranium, which are also found on Earth." Eisenbach clicked the controller, and the screen behind him lit up with a chemical diagram. "But they also found a *new* element. Like thorium, it's radioactive. But we believe it goes far beyond thorium's capabilities."

"How so?" Welding asked.

"We only had a few micrograms to work with so we couldn't be sure of what we were seeing. We couldn't produce it in the lab so a lot of our analysis required extrapolation and, more recently, computer modeling. I don't want to get into molecular physics—I'm not an expert so it'd be a short conversation—but this is one of the heaviest elements to be discovered, at the far reaches of the periodic table. Typically such elements are very unstable and highly radioactive. Elements heavier than uranium aren't usually found in nature. They're manufactured, so to speak, in linear accelerators in a laboratory. They only exist for thousandths of a second."

"What's it called?" Norris said. "This new element."

Eisenbach cocked his head. "Like everything in science, there are naming conventions and protocols. The name's unofficial since, to the rest of the scientific world, this element doesn't exist. But because it could be a great deal more powerful—and dangerous—than anything we've discovered on Earth, we've named it caesarium after Rome's emperors for the potential dominance it can provide a country that has it."

"You mentioned dominance," Norris said. "Can you be a little more specific?"

"It increases the yield of a nuclear explosion by almost a factor of ten. There are lots of variables with nuclear weapons—the two biggest being how large the warhead is and the height at which it's detonated. But if you're looking to cause maximum mayhem and civilian and economic devastation, anything that improves the explosion's strength and radius by such a magnitude is a major concern."

"It gives new meaning to the term weapon of *mass* destruction," McNamara added.

Eisenbach flicked a speck of dust off his uniform. "It could take out an entire major metropolitan city in the United States with a single nuclear-tipped ballistic missile, the kind Iran and North Korea have been testing. And if they launch multiple warheads and we're able to neutralize all but one or two—which is likely to be the case—major American cities will cease to exist. And they'll remain uninhabitable for decades."

Knox folded his hands on the desk in front of him. "They hit DC? The seat of our government—as well as the strategic planning nerve center of our armed forces—will be gone. Think about that."

They did.

Welding had a wife and three young children; Norris, ten-year-old twins. Knox knew this factored into their calculus as the seconds of silence passed.

"So what's our mission?" Welding finally asked.

"We have some HUMINT," Ford said, referring to human intelligence—spy work. "China is training for a Moon shot. From what we can ascertain—and some of this is unconfirmed—they're planning to send up a robotic lander and rover to collect rock samples."

Norris sat forward in his seat. "Are they looking to bring back caesarium?"

"We don't know. Not yet. We're working to find out. But we have to assume they are. Even if they're not, they may find it. We can't take that chance."

"So that's why we're going up?" Welding said. "I don't see how—"

"For now," Knox said, "that's all you need to know. Once we have more information, we'll lay down a specific mission plan and explain in more detail what your objectives are."

Norris held out both hands, palms up. "I can't believe no one's ever thought of this being a problem. Isn't there some sort of agreement that prevents the mining of another planet?"

"They have and there is," Eisenbach said. "The Outer Space Treaty was adopted in 1967. It basically says that the exploration and use of outer space—including the Moon—is for the benefit of all countries. It's the province of all mankind. If China's not planning to share their samples with everyone, their mission would be a clear violation of that treaty. That's the US position. Of course, if they *do* bring caesarium back, we wouldn't want them to share it with *anyone*. Except us."

"So it's a no-win scenario. Once they have it—"

"That's not all," Ford said. "The Republic of China ratified the treaty before the United Nations General Assembly's vote to transfer China's UN seat to the *People's* Republic of China in 1971. The *People's* Republic of China described the defunct Republic of China's treaty ratification as illegal, but the US considers China to be bound by its former government's obligations. So far, China's agreed to adhere to the treaty's requirements."

"There's also the Moon Treaty," Knox said.

"Which no space-faring country ever signed," Eisenbach said. "Its purpose was to prevent the militarization and resource mining of the Moon without sharing all findings with the international community, through the UN. Like the sea floor treaty."

"And then there's the SPACE Act of 2015," Eisenbach said, "which muddied the water because it gave US citizens the right to commercially explore and exploit space resources, including water and minerals. The only thing excluded was biological life. It specifically states that America is not asserting sovereignty or jurisdiction over any celestial body. But some have argued that the US recognizing ownership of space resources is an act of sovereignty that violates the Outer Space Treaty."

"So nothing's really clear," Ford said. "It also hasn't been tested—although it sure looks like that's on the verge of changing."

"But if China's getting ready to launch a Moon shot," Norris said, "and if they're going there to bring back caesarium, the bell's been rung. No way to unring it. Regardless of whatever treaties exist."

"That's pretty much it in a nutshell," Knox said. "Which is one reason why you've been training for this mission."

"The other reasons?" Welding asked.

"Reasons two, three, four, and five," McNamara said with a steely stare, "are . . . because those are your orders."

"We'll give you more as soon as we're able to." Ford folded his hands in front of him. "That's all we've got for you, gentlemen. The possibility exists that we'll be launching sooner rather than later. We just wanted you to be mentally prepared. The rocket was moved to the launch pad several weeks ago and is being prepped. Just in case."

"Questions?" Knox asked.

"Just one," Norris said with a shrug. "How will us going to the Moon stop China from launching their mission?"

"That'll be addressed at the appropriate time," Eisenbach said. "Anything else?"

A moment later, McNamara rose from his chair. "Dismissed."

FORD CAME UP BEHIND THE MEN as they entered the suit room to prepare for the afternoon dive.

"Sir," Norris said. "Something we can help you find?"

"No, no. I just—I think you two are the best of the best and we owe you a better explanation of what's going on than just the standard need-to-know bullshit."

"Appreciate that," Welding said.

"For what it's worth, I was in favor of telling you more, but there's considerable . . . debate about how to move forward. So even if we laid out the approach, things could change. If China forces our hand, I personally don't think there's a choice, but for the moment, it's classified. I know that's not what you want to hear."

"I always butted heads with my CO," Welding said with a chuckle. "I wanted all the info we had so I could be thinking about it, working it through. Just how my brain works. Getting piecemeal info, it's inefficient. For me, at least. I can be a creative part of the *solution*, not just a lethal tool who can execute a mission plan."

Ford laughed. "Then you should've stayed in the SEALs and worked your way up to—"

That was the last any of them heard as a powerful explosion rocked the room and the cinder block walls tumbled down on top of them.

2

NASA
Johnson Space Center
Mission Control
Houston, Texas
4:49 am

The mission control specialist leaned forward and studied his screen. "Hey Sam, check this out."

Sam blinked his eyes clear and reseated his headset. His oversize coffee mug was empty and he had been caught napping at his station. He glanced at Jamie, who was hunched over his keyboard a few seats to his left in the expansive high-tech monitoring center. Thankfully, Jamie was focused on his station instrumentation. "Whaddya got?"

Jamie made eye contact with Sam. "I'm putting it on the main screen right now."

An aerial view of what appeared to be a massive rocket filled the wall-size display, an intense magnesium-bright flame trailing beneath it.

"Where's this coming from?" Jamie asked as he studied the trajectory.

"China, Sichuan province. From what I remember, they've got a launch center there, so that makes sense."

"Switching satellites to get us a better look," Jamie said. He pushed a button and a three-quarter angle came up alongside the other view.

"Heavy lift vehicle of some kind," Sam said. "Four liquid boosters mounted to the first stage." He watched the image another few seconds as the startlingly white flame below the rocket turned orange. "I'd say something on the order of . . ." He scrawled a stylus across his monitor, finished his calculations, and brought his gaze back up to the screen. "Holy shit."

"That's one big mother," Jamie said.

"Big isn't the word. If I'm right, that thing is 6 *million* pounds. About 7 million pounds of thrust. Almost as big as the Saturn V." Saturn V, the powerful multistage rocket that sent the Apollo astronauts to the Moon, was one of the largest ever to successfully fly.

"Even if you've missed the mark by 20 percent . . ." Jamie's voice trailed off.

"If I had to guess, it's bigger than their Long March 3B/E."

"But China doesn't have a rocket bigger than the 3B/E."

Sam swallowed. "Obviously they do."

"We need to report this."

"Agreed."

Jamie got up from his terminal and walked briskly to the back of the large mission control center. He knocked on the glass window of his superior's office, assistant chief of operations, Zenzō Aoki. Aoki looked up from his desk and waved Jamie in.

He stepped inside, his hands now clammy. Jamie had been assigned to ops only three months ago, but he had worked at NASA for fourteen years. When he requested the transfer, his colleagues told him he was crazy because the work tended to be tedious in between launches. He was about to make them eat their words.

"Sir, we've got something you need to see. Main screen." Jamie cocked his head toward the front of the room.

Aoki craned his neck, then gave up and walked over to the windowed wall behind Jamie. Together they watched the rocket continue its ascent.

"Who?" Aoki said. "Where?"

"Chinese. Sichuan province."

Aoki crinkled his brow as he processed that. "Mass?"

"Six million pounds."

Aoki's left eye twitched.

"It's bigger than the Long March 3B/E. They were rumored to be developing something called Chang Zheng 5, but I didn't know they built it, let alone tested it."

Aoki's gaze was fixed on the screen. "Yeah."

"And a vehicle that large would be sitting on the pad for days, if not weeks. How could our satellites have missed something that big?"

"Unless China hid it," Aoki said under his breath. "Okay, Jamie. I'll take it from here. Go back to your station. Keep monitoring it until further notice. And get me a trajectory."

"Yes sir."

As Jamie put his hand on the doorknob to leave, he turned back and saw Aoki lift the red telephone handset.

"This is Assistant Chief Aoki." He looked up and locked gazes with Jamie's reflection off the window. "Get me the Pentagon."

3

Naval Air Station Patuxent River
Chesapeake Bay
St. Mary's County, Maryland
7:59 AM

Hector DeSantos, senior operative for OPSIG, the Operations Support Intelligence Group, steadied himself in the front seat of the F/A-18 Super Hornet's cockpit. The sky was generally overcast with patches of thick cloud cover mixed with an occasional glimpse of a baby blue ceiling, morning rays of sun slicing through the cottony puffs. However, with the fighter jet effortlessly piercing the air at a leisurely .69 Mach—6.9 miles per minute—grayness appeared to dominate.

Although DeSantos only caught glimpses of it, below him sat a picturesque landscape, parts of it yellow from the young sun as it rose in the east and cast a glow over the forest of broccoli-like treetops and the flowing Patuxent River.

Strapped into "the pit" behind DeSantos, supervisory special agent Aaron Uziel, head of the FBI's Joint Terrorism Task Force and occasional OPSIG Team Black member, looked up through the cockpit canopy. "This is the best part of the job."

"Flying an F-18?"

"Hell yeah. I mean, I know this is training, but are we the luckiest guys in the world, or what?"

DeSantos looked at his surroundings, then brought his gaze down to the forward instruments. "Can't argue, Boychick," DeSantos said, using his nickname for Uzi—Yiddish for buddy. "Right now, I'm on cloud nine. And ten." He craned his neck and watched the passing clumps of cotton. "And eleven."

"I think we should do this more often," Uzi said.

DeSantos laughed. "I had to pull strings to get us this sortie. Enjoy it while you can."

After doing an afterburner takeoff from Pax River, a large military proving grounds that housed a US Navy test pilot school, they rotated, sucked up the landing gear, and started a 10 degree nose-high climb, then turned left to 180 degrees. They leveled off in the "soup," or clouds, at 3,000 feet.

After making contact with Washington Center, they were cleared for an unrestricted climb and given permission to operate from 14,000 feet "mean sea level" up to a flight level of 36,000 feet.

"Awesome!" Uzi said. "Just awesome."

DeSantos lit the afterburner and pulled his nose up 20 degrees, then popped out of the altostratus clouds at 9,000 feet. "Woohoo!" He looked around, creamy blue above and a sheet of gray to cerulean cotton below stretching miles into the distance.

"Never gets old, does it?"

After they made several maneuvers and "pulled Gs," they got down to business. Uzi checked beyond line of sight communications gear that OPSIG planned to deploy on future missions.

"I keyed in a ZAP," Uzi said, referring to a text message, "and I just got a response from the ops center. The kit is working beautifully."

"Roger that. The SecDef will be very happy his $30 million equipment purchase actually works. So far so g—"

"Caution. Caution."

"Bitching Betty," as fighter pilots called the audio fault system, started blaring in their headsets.

Red lights lit up on DeSantos's panel. "Ah, shit."

"This our first training exercise?"

"Not sure." DeSantos examined his instrumentation and pecked away at the up-front touch screen control display. "Navigation and EGI/GPS system just shit the bed."

"You're kidding."

"I wouldn't joke about that."

"Exercise or not, we should play it straight." Uzi keyed his mic. "Washington Center, this is X-ray Bravo 69. We need to RTB," he said, using the abbreviation for "return to base."

The response came back immediately: "X-Ray Bravo 69, Washington Center, squawk 4322."

Uzi did as instructed, identifying them on the air traffic controller's radar display.

"X-Ray Bravo 69," Washington Center continued. "Radar contact turn left direct to HELEM and descend to 16,000. Pax River altimeter is 29.90."

DeSantos acknowledged the instructions and entered the altimeter setting, starting a left hand turn and a descent to 16,000 feet. As the aircraft responded with the required G for the turn, DeSantos controlled the airspeed by pulling the throttles back from mil, or military power, to idle.

As he finished the maneuver, the jet noticeably decelerated.

"What the hell was that?" Uzi asked.

DeSantos scanned his instrumentation. "Nothing good, I can tell you that."

Another Bitching Betty alarm interrupted their moment of fate-pondering silence.

"Warning. Warning."

DeSantos took a deep breath as his eyes swept the panel. "Left engine just flamed out."

They both knew that it was not abnormal for these advanced fighter jets to experience a single simple problem that compounded itself and cascaded into a mass of catastrophic system failures. A fire or flameout, even when controlled quickly, often caused unseen damage: those seconds when it was burning destroyed wiring to a hydraulic or fuel line, resulting in escalating leaks and irreversible damage.

"Boychick, squawk 7700," DeSantos said, dividing the cockpit task and referring to the emergency code. "Call Ops. Let 'em know we're single engine."

"Washington Center," Uzi said, "X-ray Bravo 69 declaring an emergency. We've lost an engine."

DeSantos knew the center should respond back immediately. But the radio remained silent.

"I don't think we're transmitting," Uzi said.

"Great. Any luck with Ops?"

Before Uzi could answer, Washington Center said, "X-ray Bravo 69, plan on holding at HELEM for five minutes due to weather and traffic."

"Center," Uzi said, "X-ray Bravo 69 declaring an emergency, request immediate vectors to final at Pax River."

Nothing. The radios remained silent except for the incoming communications from the center to other aircraft.

"They're not receiving us." After continued radio silence, Uzi said, "Do we hold? Or start the return to base?"

"X-ray Bravo 69, Center. Descend and maintain 10,000. You have traffic ten miles ahead, left ten o'clock at 16,000."

"Center," Uzi said, "X-ray Bravo. How do you r—"

"This is Washington Center on Guard. X-Ray Bravo 69, contact me on 133.900," the controller said, referring to a commonly used East Coast frequency.

"Flat-out interrupted me," Uzi said. "We're definitely radio out. So we can receive but can't transmit. Our twenty-ton $65 million tactical fighter jet can't navigate and can't communicate. Just a guess here, but this isn't a training exercise to see how we handle a catastrophic failure of multiple systems."

"Definitely not," DeSantos said. "Can you fix comms?"

"My tech knowledge is a bit limited in a machine like this—I can't tap into the operating system flying at 400 KCAS. Not to mention I don't have a direct—" Uzi was interrupted by audio coming through their headsets:

"Brave 01 and 02 airborne."

"They're scrambling F-16s from Andrews to intercept," DeSantos said.

"Intercept? You mean assist."

"No, Boychick. Intercept. I have a feeling we're pointed at the NCR."

The NCR, or national capital region, comprised restricted and prohibited areas above and around Washington, DC, that extended out to thirty nautical miles. Created after 9/11 to ensure the safety of the federal government, it was a controlled region that governed all aircraft—including that of the military. If a jet or plane wandered toward the sensitive security zone, it would be intercepted. If it was noncompliant or presented a threat, it was shot down.

"We need to return to base," Uzi said.

"And which way would that be?"

"Let's try to get a location, do a ground-to-map navigation."

"In this soup?"

"Hopefully the cloud cover'll break soon and we'll be able to see some landmarks. Or in a matter of minutes, two F-16s are gonna pull up alongside us and tell us to get our asses away from the capital."

"Oh man. Perez is gonna be one pissed colonel. When he gave us this sortie, he specifically said, 'Just don't crash the damn thing.' He said it tongue-in-cheek, but in retrospect the comment seems a little too prophetic for my taste."

"So let's try to make sure we don't have to crash this thing."

"All right," DeSantos said, "here's the plan. When the 16s show up, we'll signal them what our situation is and ask them to guide us through the weather to a drop-off landing at Andrews." Once they were around 1,200 feet and below the clouds, Brave 01 would give the lead back to DeSantos, who would land their F-18.

"Break in the soup," Uzi said. "Got us a landmark. We're headed northwest, over the Potomac. Let's use our whiskey compass to confirm we're headed northwest. Turning right at least 90 degrees should point us southeast of Nottingham, away from the NCR and toward Annapolis. Need be, we can set her down in the Chesapeake."

"If we make it that far. Hate to say it, but I don't think this bird is gonna live to see the boneyard," DeSantos said, referring to the military base in Arizona where planes go in their old age to retire.

"I'm not giving up yet," Uzi said, "are you?"

"Hell no. But we've got another issue to deal with."

"Fuel."

"Roger that. We've been up here too long." F/A-18s did not have a big fuel tank to begin with—and with the addition of a second seat for training, it meant less room on the jet for gas.

"How bad?"

"Bad enough," DeSantos said. "Wish we hadn't done that last afterburner loop and kept more fuel in reserve. We've only got 1,600 pounds left. And we're burning 4,000 pounds an hour."

"So no matter what, one way or another, in twenty to thirty minutes, this flight's gonna be over."

They were well aware that F-18s had no backup hydraulics or electrical. If they lost the second engine, they could not glide to find a good place to put her down.

"That second engine goes," DeSantos said, "we'll have to jump out. And one huge drawback to flying on the East Coast is—"

"Population density. Yeah, I know. We may not be able to see what's below us, but I think we both have a pretty damn good idea."

Houses. Businesses. Apartment buildings. Highways and expressways. Lots of people.

DeSantos checked the instrument panel and MFD displays. "There's a limit to what we can do. If our checklist can't solve the problems with our redundant systems—and it obviously can't—if we need to ditch this thing, we'll be dropping twenty tons of metal and flaming jet fuel on innocent people. Hopefully we won't kill anyone."

"Including us. What was I saying about being the luckiest guys in the world?"

"For what it's worth, there's no one I'd rather have in the backseat."

Uzi chuckled. "You're just saying that."

"I am. But we may not survive this. We should be generous with the bro praise, don't you think?"

"We *are* gonna survive this, Santa. We'll stay with this ailing bird for as long as we can, but if she gets too sick, we'll just have to ride the rails and give her back to the taxpayer."

DeSantos knew Uzi was talking about ejection, the absolute worst flight experience next to exploding a plane into the ground—and those who had been through ejections argued that the latter was still a more pleasurable experience.

The sequence was complex yet simple: after pulling the lever, the canopy exploded open and the cockpit filled with flames from the ejector rockets. They would then blast up and out, experiencing 20Gs—intense pressure that was bad enough if it were not for simultaneously getting hit in the face with winds of 300 miles per hour. Many pilots ejecting at high speed blacked out immediately, the force whipping their hands back behind the seat, dislocating their shoulders and breaking bones.

That was if everything went well. Then there were potential ejection *malfunctions.*

"Cloud deck clear," Uzi said. "We're—shit, just like we thought. Lots of houses and buildings all around us."

DeSantos glanced down at the network of humanity below. "Just be ready. Hydraulics fail, second engine goes, there's nothing we can do. Copy?"

"Copy."

As he spoke, the clouds returned, obscuring their view.

DeSantos clenched his jaw. "Dammit."

"X-Ray Bravo 69, this is the United States Air Force on Guard. You have been intercepted by armed fighters. If you hear this transmission, rock your wings and contact Brave 01 on 243.0."

"I'd love to respond, buddy, but you're gonna have to meet me halfway." DeSantos rocked the F/A-18 as requested and saw the nose of the NORAD F-16, call sign Brave 01, edge up parallel to them, about five to ten feet off his left wing. DeSantos knew that the other F-16, Brave 02, was maintaining a mile trail with a radar lock on his jet, ready to fire, in case he and Uzi had gone rogue and intended to wreak havoc.

"Uzi, you remember your HEFOE signals?" DeSantos asked, referring to the emergency procedure used by pilots to visually communicate problems they were experiencing with their plane: a fist held at the top of the canopy, followed by hand gestures, indicated a failure of one or more systems: hydraulic, electrical, fuel, oxygen, or engine.

"Passing them now." Uzi gave the Brave pilot a one, two, and five, then a hand waving up and down across the face mask with a thumbs down, telling him that they could not transmit. He then tapped his helmet on his left side with a thumbs up, indicating that "receive is good."

"X-ray Bravo 69, Brave 01 understands," came the response. "Hydraulic, electrical, and engine problems. No transmit but can receive. If correct rock your wings."

DeSantos gently pivoted the F/A-18's body left to right a couple of times.

"Hallelujah," Uzi said. "Kind of like sign language in the sky." He passed additional signals, telling the Braves to take the lead in guiding them down through the soup.

The F-16 moved out in front and DeSantos lined himself up on Brave 01's right wing as they descended into the thick cloud cover, grayness enveloping the canopy above and around them, drops of precipitation streaking across the glass.

DeSantos glanced down at the fuel—so far so good. He figured they were about twenty miles south of Andrews Air Force Base, so they should make it without—

"Warning. Warning."

Uzi groaned. "I think I've heard enough out of Bitching Betty."

"Looks like I was right about this baby," DeSantos said, seeing a flame through the window. "Second engine's gone."

Caution alarms started blaring. Their airspeed dropped, as if they had applied their brakes while riding downhill on a ten-speed bike.

"Get ready," DeSantos said, tension elevating the volume of his voice. "We're goin' for a ride."

"Roger that," Uzi said as he grabbed onto the handle. "Good luck, Santa."

"Back at you," DeSantos said, his finger joints aching from holding the ejection handle so tightly. Nothing was going to knock it off—or make him pull it prematurely. "We're at 9,200 feet. Stand by, I want to get us down a bit lower—6,000 or even 8,000 would be better."

"Standing by," Uzi said.

DeSantos kept his eyes on the altimeter as the numbers tumbled lower. "Remember, we pull on three. Watch your arms and shoulders." He waited a beat, then said, "Bail out, bail out, bail out!" He yanked the grip with both hands toward his abdomen and the canopy covering both pilots flew back as smoke filled the cockpit. With a sudden burst, the two rockets under Uzi's seat exploded.

A second later, DeSantos shot skyward.

"WASHINGTON CENTER, BRAVE 01 on scene. I'm picking up a large fireball on the ground, breaking through the clouds, North 38 35, West 76 40."

The pilot knew the media would be listening in and high-tailing it to those coordinates—but he hoped the NORAD team would get there first to cordon off the scene because of the airborne fibers and toxins given off by the explosion of a modern day fighter jet.

"Copy, we confirm. Any sign of the X-ray Bravo 69 crew?"

"Negative. Weather precluding visual confirmation. We're staying above their last known punch-out altitude."

"Brave 01, we need to find our men."

"Roger. All eyes on alert."

THE OPENING SHOCK HIT DESANTOS with an aggressive tug, like being hit on the leg straps and harness by a 240-pound linebacker.

The emergency locater transmitter, or ELT, an iPhone-size radio buried in the kit below his seat, started blaring an alarm heard by everyone on the frequency.

The early April air was a chilly fifty-five degrees, meaning it was about thirty-seven at their altitude. DeSantos swore he felt every single degree as it sliced through the thin Nomex flight suit.

The parachute had deployed from the ejection seat and was slowing him down, moisture beading up on his helmet's visor.

As DeSantos descended to about 1,200 feet, the cloud deck broke and he could finally see the ground. He figured they had about a minute before touchdown.

With the round type of chute on their backs, they had very little control over where they landed—they were largely at the mercy of where the wind blew them. About all they could do was pull the risers to slip/turn to gain some gross maneuverability while trying to avoid getting caught in power lines or large trees. The former could decapitate them and the latter could hang them. Neither was appealing.

DeSantos was attempting to avoid obstacles and Uzi was trying to follow his lead and get as close to DeSantos's landing site as he could.

As the grassy field accelerated beneath him, DeSantos's training came back to him: ground impact . . . eyes open and on the horizon . . . feet and knees together, knees slightly bent, elbows tight to his side, chin on his chest.

He was only going to get one shot at this. He would be striking the ground at thirty-two feet per second; if he did it wrong or hesitated, he would end up a human pancake, severely injured—or dead.

THE COSPAS-SARSAT SEARCH AND RESCUE SATELLITE, a distress alert detection system in low Earth orbit, picked up the signal from DeSantos's and Uzi's seat kits hanging thirty-five feet below their boots as they descended through the clouds.

Until the NORAD team arrived, the two F-16 Braves were the on-scene commanders tasked with coordinating search and rescue. Using GPS, they narrowed DeSantos's and Uzi's twenty to within 1.24 miles—but depending on the terrain, it would still require a meticulously plotted effort to find them.

◆ ◆ ◆

AS DESANTOS'S BOOTS HIT THE GRASS, he became a rag doll and went with the fall, as his instructors had drilled into his brain: the "parachute landing fall," touching down on the balls of the feet, then the side of the calf, thigh, and buttocks, and lastly the back.

He caught his breath and immediately disconnected the chute risers to keep from getting dragged to death by the gusting wind. After rolling to his knees, he dug out the ELT, which he knew was still transmitting its endlessly repeating alarm.

After turning it off, DeSantos removed his helmet and got to his feet to look for Uzi. He swung his sore torso around and saw his buddy about a hundred yards away, walking toward him and waving an arm above his head.

"You okay?" Uzi said over the radio.

"Sore but in one piece. Good to see your ugly face." DeSantos pulled out his survival radio. "I'm gonna contact Brave 01 and have him push over to 2828," he said, referring to the secondary 282.8 channel that would allow them to communicate with one another.

As Uzi trudged toward him, Brave 01 came back on the radio. "X-ray Bravo 69, I have your location."

DeSantos glanced around. "We're in a clearing about two football fields in diameter, just west of what looks like two nuclear smoke stacks, those huge cooling towers that are part of a reactor."

"Affirmative on that," Brave 01 said. "You look to be located inside the Calvert Cliffs nuclear power plant. Don't breathe too deeply. Risk of exposure to, and inhalation of, airborne radioactive contamination. Rescue helicopters are en route and should be on your position in ten minutes."

"Roger that, Brave 01." DeSantos turned back in time to receive a bear hug from Uzi.

"Can you believe this, Santa? We landed inside a—"

They both spun around at the rumbling sound of an approaching truck. DeSantos knew the vehicle: a Bearcat used by tactical teams. It skidded to a stop and six men poured out of the rear, semiautomatic rifles at the ready.

"Hands on your heads! Don't move."

DeSantos and Uzi did as instructed.

"Everyone keep a cool head," Uzi said. "We're law enforcement. If you let me—"

"Law enforcement officers don't parachute into a secure nuclear power facility. Wearing flight suits."

"We're on a training mission out of Pax River. I can dig out my ID—"

"I don't think so," the commander said. "You two clowns are with me. We'll straighten it out later."

DeSantos figured the men, clad in their black turnout gear, were a hired security team bored with its monotonous drill routines and itching for some genuine action—and a fight.

"I think we're screwed," Uzi said.

DeSantos shook his head. "We'll get it sorted out. A few hours in custody, a couple calls, and we'll be headed to the base hospital."

"Or maybe not."

The low rumble of an approaching helicopter vibrated in DeSantos's chest. "Here comes the cavalry."

Uzi kept his hands on his head but craned his neck toward the sky where an orange red HH-65 Dolphin Coast Guard rescue helicopter descended in the clearing a few hundred feet to their east, its single main rotor flattening the grass as if the fine green blades were being crushed down by a massive invisible weight.

A second later, a Black Hawk appeared over the treetops and landed a few dozen yards from the Dolphin.

Everyone remained where they were, the security team no doubt beginning to wonder what the hell was going on.

Two Coast Guard personnel in khaki flight suits hopped out of the Dolphin and joined four soldiers in BDUs—battle dress fatigues—from the Black Hawk, in addition to a large African American man wearing tactical gear. The contingent advanced with purpose on the knot of personnel.

DeSantos recognized the gait of the lone non-uniformed individual as his OPSIG colleague, Troy Rodman.

The security officers kept their weapons raised as Rodman strode up to the commander. "I'm here on orders of the secretary of defense. Looks like you're holding our men. Is there a problem?"

"They're trespassing on a secure facility. We're taking them into custody."

"No," Rodman said, his deep voice devoid of emotion. "You will stand down and release them to us."

"All due respect, I don't know who you are, if you're legit or some guys dressed in uniform who hired a couple of fancy helicopters. I don't have any orders—"

The commander's radio crackled. He clenched his jaw then lifted the mic off the hook on his shirt. "Repeat." He stuck his index finger against the left earpiece and listened, then frowned. "You two are free to go. Next time get clearance before you conduct your training exercises in our backyard."

Uzi frowned. "Thanks for the tip, buddy. Dumbshit clowns like us never think of those things."

4

Joint Base Andrews
Air and Space Expeditionary Forces
Camp Springs, Maryland

FBI director Douglas Knox pressed a button on the conference room desk and glanced at the attendees: Hector DeSantos and his fellow OPSIG covert operatives Troy Rodman and Alexandra Rusakov, Uzi, CIA director Earl Tasset, Secretary McNamara, and General Eisenbach.

"I need to confirm that you left your phones at the door," Knox said.

This meeting was above top secret, the highest level of security classification, and any potential for electronic eavesdropping had to be eliminated.

DeSantos and Uzi, looking a bit rough around the edges with facial scrapes and superficial burns, nodded affirmatively, as did Rodman and Rusakov.

"I was briefed on your flight test maneuvers at PAX," Knox said. "I'm glad you two rose to the occasion—for more reasons than you can imagine."

"We didn't rise to the occasion," DeSantos said. "We fell back to our training." It was a saying common among Navy SEALs and understood by all Special Forces operators.

Knox uncharacteristically broke a slight smile. "Take your seats."

McNamara dragged a hand across his cheek. "At 0500 hours a mission control specialist at Johnson Space Center detected the launch of an unidentified heavy lift multistage rocket from China's old Base 27 at the Xichang satellite launch center in the Sichuan province. We determined it was carrying a large payload." He paused, cleared his throat. "And it's headed to the Moon."

"So?" Uzi shrugged. "Russia's Project Luna spanned, what, fifteen years?"

Knox turned to Uzi. "Those were a very long time ago and were legit scientific missions to study the lunar surface, measure radiation exposure, search for water ice. That type of thing. This is different."

"Russia's sending a specialized module to the International Space Station next month," Tasset said. "The Agency believes Russia's going to use it to build their own space station, which will then make it possible for them to construct a lunar base—and use *that* base to colonize Mars. Both China and Russia are ahead of us in long-term planning and execution."

"Are we concerned about that?" Rodman asked.

CIA director Tasset pushed the tortoise shell glasses back up the bridge of his nose. "We're *concerned* about Russia's aggression. We're *concerned* about its unprofessional and aggressive behavior in the air, in space, and in cyberspace, not to mention its nuclear saber rattling. We believe one of Russia's ambitions is to erode the principled international order—including our own democracy."

"The Pentagon," McNamara said, "is also deeply concerned about Russia's SSC-8 cruise missiles. Bluntly stated, we've got no defense against them. None. And they can be fitted with nuclear warheads. That's a real worry. As if that's not enough, China presents a whole other set of problems."

"Since we're all sitting here," DeSantos said, "I'm guessing that China's Moon mission is not in our best interests."

Tasset smiled sardonically. "General Eisenbach from USSTRATCOM will answer that."

The slightly built man rose from his seat. Uzi thought his uniform must weigh twenty pounds with all the ribbons and badges hanging from it.

Eisenbach adjusted his wire-rimmed glasses. "In 1962, President Kennedy pledged that the US would win the space race and put a man on the Moon within eight years. Everyone thought he was crazy—the first car was mass-produced in 1908. The first commercial jet in 1952. But the Moon was 240,000 miles away and we needed to build a rocket the length of a football field, made of metal alloys that hadn't been invented. And it had to return to Earth by reentering the atmosphere at 25,000 miles per hour while withstanding heat half the temperature of the sun.

"But we did it. We landed on the Moon in 1969. Nine Apollo missions went there. Twelve men walked its surface—a huge accomplishment. Eventually the public stopped caring about the Moon shots, NASA took heat for spending lots of money to go back to a place we'd already gone, and the last three Apollos were scrubbed. NASA moved on to Skylab."

"But the last one, Apollo 17, discovered something in 1972 that's causing a major upheaval decades later." Eisenbach told them about caesarium and the magnitude of destruction a weapon produced with caesarium would wield compared to currently available nuclear fissile material.

"I'm not an expert by any stretch," Uzi said, "but I've got a background in molecular science. There's something called an island of stability. Are you saying caesarium exists on that island?"

"According to the briefing we had," Eisenbach said, "it's right at the cusp. These superheavy magic nuclei have some kind of new shape to them that prevents them from rapidly decaying. Because of that, they've got important military applications, including the development of compact nuclear weapons."

"So that's why China launched this rocket?" Rodman asked. "To bring back caesarium?"

"Yes," Tasset said. "In the last couple of days we secured some additional HUMINT. Comes with a high degree of confidence."

Knox brushed back a lock of gray hair that had settled over his forehead. "In December 2014 China launched the Chang'e 3 spacecraft, which was the first soft-landing mission to reach the Moon's surface in thirty-eight years. It deployed the Yutu rover to examine the Moon's geological makeup and subsurface layers."

"The China National Space Administration doesn't release full information about its missions," Tasset said, "so we've had to fill in the blanks using HUMINT and what we've been able to determine by the CIA's targeted hacks into the administration's servers."

Eisenbach nodded at Knox, who pressed a button on the table. An image of the rover appeared onscreen. "The Yutu carried ground-penetrating radar and spectrometers to inspect the composition of the soil and the structure of the lunar crust. We were very concerned that if they didn't already know about caesarium, they would—as soon as they began drilling.

"Our planetary scientists feel that if caesarium was deposited on the Moon millions of years ago by an asteroid or meteor strike, it'll only be present in a specific area. Most of them thought the Yutu wasn't anywhere near where we thought caesarium would be. But where it is, and how deep, we just don't know.

"So we interfered with the Yutu's communication array—not easy because the European Space Agency deep-space ground stations were assisting with communications. By the time we got a handle on it, the rover went into sleep mode for two weeks to weather the extreme cold of the lunar night. We couldn't take any action until it woke up. Even if we figured out how to wake it, we would've drawn the attention of Chinese National Space Administration's mission control. So we waited.

"Our efforts paid off. China's state-run media announced that the rover had suffered a mechanical control abnormality from the brutal lunar temperatures and didn't wake up completely because of frostbite-like damage."

"Were they able to get any data from the Yutu before you disabled it?" Rusakov asked.

"Yes," Tasset said. "They found some new minerals, but if they located caesarium, they weren't saying and we weren't asking. Our HUMINT tells us they didn't. And it wasn't until recently that they announced plans to return."

"So here we are," Eisenbach said. "The launch we observed was the Chang'e 5—two years earlier than planned. They may've moved it up because Russia and the European Space Agency have been talking about lunar bases and China didn't want to get left behind. Or they got wind of our plans and wanted to get there before we could act."

"What plans?" Uzi asked.

"We'll get to that," McNamara said.

"The Chang'e 5," Eisenbach said, "is a robotic ship and rover equipped with optical cameras, mineral spectrometer, instruments for analyzing soil composition, a thermodetector, Geiger counter, and a new kind of autonomous coring drill. Officially, the mission goal is to return samples of lunar regolith from a depth of two meters. It was supposed to land in the northeastern Oceanus Procellarum region, but we now believe the target site was changed."

"Or," Tasset said, "the location was disinformation for cover. The Chang'e has everything they need to mine caesarium, but even if they only bring back half a kilogram, it'd be enough to substantially alter the balance of power. It could be the biggest threat to peace the human race has ever faced. That's not hyperbole."

"So you want us to steal the caesarium after they bring it back?" DeSantos said with a scoff. "They'll be guarding that stuff in a facility as secure as Fort Knox."

"We can't let them bring this element back to Earth," McNamara said. "Period."

"Step one was successfully severing their communications with the Chang'e 5," McNamara said. "But the craft itself is still operational. Their mission control is blind and deaf, but sample recovery is automated. It can still secure caesarium and return to Earth without human input."

"Have we been able to send the Chang'e off-course, into deep space?" Rodman asked. "Or can we crash it into the lunar surface?"

"We tried," Eisenbach said, "but so far we haven't been successful. We've got to be careful because certain types of interventions on our part can be traced back to us."

"Any chance the Chinese can regain control of their ship?"

"We're working to prevent that," Eisenbach said, "but yes, it's possible."

Uzi spread his hands. "So what are we thinking? Some kind of negotiated agreement to not mine the element?"

McNamara shook his head. "Treaty discussions, diplomacy move slowly. To give it urgency, we'd have to disclose that caesarium exists. To everyone. Including the Russians, who happen to be looking to expand their territory. And who have strategic alliances with Iran."

"There's another consideration," Eisenbach said. "The US is the leader in space-based military technology, which gives us tremendous advantages—we can look down on the world with high resolution to monitor our adversaries, communicate and move troops and military assets globally, and so on. But it leaves us open to attack and catastrophic losses."

Uzi unscrewed the top of his water bottle. "Because our satellites are vulnerable. They follow known and consistent movements, so they're easy to locate and target."

Eisenbach nodded slowly. "All our orbital assets are sitting ducks for a nation with the know-how to disrupt our ability to defend against an attack or launch a counterattack. Even just jamming our signals, hacking their firmware or operating system, taking out their sensors, or blinding them would have a catastrophic effect on our ability to move troops in the field, navigate, collect intelligence, target, and communicate."

"Both China and Russia have been working on these kinds of weapons," Tasset said. "They have, or will soon have, the capability to take out our orbiting assets." He let that hang in the air a moment. "We need to act while we still have these advantages."

"But the Chang'e 5 is on its way to the Moon," Rusakov said.

"We've put together a plan that should prevent anyone from getting their hands on caesarium," McNamara said, rising from his seat. "NASA's been developing a spacecraft called Orion, part of the space launch system, or SLS. It's been undergoing extensive testing and has performed well during test flights.

"The Pentagon has been working alongside NASA and its contractors to develop the super heavy lift rocket that makes up the SLS. DOD calls it the Hercules II. Every pound of weight, every piece of equipment we put on that spacecraft, has to be accounted for. The ability of the rocket to lift that weight is of paramount importance. The Hercules is up to the task."

"Have we confirmed China's intentions?" Rusakov asked. "What if we're making wrong assumptions? We're risking an international incid—"

"We have confirmation," Tasset said. Instead of elaborating, he reached over and took a drink from his water bottle.

"In the eighties," McNamara said, "the Department of Defense built a space shuttle launch pad at Vandenberg Air Force Base in southern California. It was designed for space-based military missions and saw a lot of action for covert launches of rockets, satellites, and other secret payloads. Given everything we've discussed, our only viable option is to send a team up to the Moon to disable the Chang'e so it can't return to Earth. Hector, you and Uzi will be part of that crew."

DeSantos's jaw went slack.

Knox leaned forward and folded his hands on the table. "Your two crewmates are NASA-trained astronauts originally from the Orion program. They're also former Air Force test pilots and ex–Special Operational Forces. There are multiple avenues open to us for disabling the Chang'e. We'll discuss mission specifics later."

"When do we report for duty?" Uzi asked.

"Soon as we're done here, you'll board a cross-country transport to Vandenberg Air Force Base," McNamara said. "You'll be living at Vandy from the moment your plane touches down until you lift off. A month's worth of training will be compressed into ten days. We'll make up time by limiting you to twenty minutes for meals, thirty minutes of down time per day, six hours of sleep. The other seventeen and a half hours will be intensive instruction, training, and repetition. That starts as soon as you board the jet. We'll put those five cross-country hours to use."

"I don't have to tell you how important this mission is," Tasset said. "A lot depends on your success."

"How do we know that we'll get to the surface before the Chang'e collects its samples and lifts off?" Uzi asked.

"We don't," Knox said. "We believe their mission can last up to 120 days—meaning the Chang'e stays on the Moon until its onboard laboratory determines the rover's found what it came for."

"So," Uzi said, "if they hit pay dirt right away—no pun intended—we've got a problem."

Tasset stood up and moved behind his chair. "At that point we'll have to decide, first, do we shoot down the Change before it reenters Earth atmosphere and trigger World War III, or, second, do we let them return with the caesarium and risk being obliterated at a future date?" Tasset grabbed the seat back with both hands and squeezed. "That's why you two cannot fail."

"One final note." Eisenbach looked down at the table, composed his thoughts, and said, "Science and technology are sometimes unpredictable. We think we have the physics defined. We think we have the engineering laid out."

"But you're not sure," Rusakov said.

Eisenbach looked up. "We've done our best to put these things through the motions, testing tolerances and systems, and we've even flown two test flights. But . . ."

"Something always goes wrong with tech this sophisticated," Uzi said.

"Unfortunately, that's one of the unofficial laws of physics."

DeSantos grunted. "I never took physics."

Uzi tossed his pen onto the desk. "In plain English? Despite expert engineering, technology sometimes does unexpected things. Like our F-18, systems fail. Shit happens."

5

Leesburg, Virginia

FBI profiler Karen Vail followed the SWAT team through the door of the Leesburg, Virginia, home, Det. Paul Bledsoe at her side. Normally she and Bledsoe would hang back and wait for the tactical team to clear the house and apprehend the suspect—a process that could take hours.

Even though this would have been proper procedure, Vail and Bledsoe did not have time to wait. The life of nineteen-year-old Nadine Palma depended on it.

Bobby Ray Jackson, the man who had kidnapped Nadine, was here. Vail was certain of that. Six dead women, strangled to death before he sexually assaulted them, were notches on Jackson's belt. But they had reason to believe Nadine was still alive because that was Jackson's ritual behavior. He did not kill them right away. He "played" with them, torturing them for five days before taking their lives.

This was day five in their search for Nadine.

The two month pursuit of Jackson had thus far been an exercise in futility—until an anonymous tip led them to this heart-pounding moment.

A noise in the other room—and they both converged on the door, standing on either side of it, before Bledsoe smashed it open with his oxford. It was another first-class breach of procedure, but Vail knew he was determined to act first and answer questions later.

"Don't move!" Vail said, squaring her Glock 9-millimeter on the head of the man they had been looking for. He was in his boxer shorts and a sweatshirt, trying to wedge himself into a closet.

"Bobby Ray Jackson," Bledsoe said, "you're under arrest for murder."

He stepped back and slowly lifted his open-palmed hands above his head. "Murder?" Jackson laughed. "I'm just a software coder. A game designer. I mean, I make killer games"—he chuckled again—"but murder? Me?"

"Keep your hands where they are," Bledsoe said.

Vail holstered her Glock, handcuffed the man, and patted him down without finding any weapons.

Bledsoe took the search warrant from one of the cops behind him. "Everything. Every inch. Don't leave anything untouched. You hear me?"

"Yes sir."

Bledsoe holstered his pistol, then tossed the folded document on the bed to Jackson's left. "You'll have plenty of time to read that over in prison."

"I don't know what you think I've done, but you got the wrong guy."

"I hear you," Vail said. "Happens to us all the time."

"Really?"

"No, asshole. Not really." Vail pulled a desk chair over and gestured for Jackson to have a seat. "So tell us where Nadine is."

"Nadine who?"

"Look," Vail said, "we can play this game if you want. But I've played it so many times I already know how it's gonna end.

I've questioned people like you for over twenty years. You really think you can dodge my questions? Fool me somehow? I'm an expert in behavior and body language."

"Read all you want." Jackson shrugged. "You're wasting your time." He bent to the right, peered around Vail at the cops in the other room who were executing their search. "You're not gonna find anything."

"You might be right. But we're still gonna look."

Jackson made eye contact. "I'm not who you think I am."

"So you'd rather play the game, huh?" She shook her head. She wanted to pull out one of the guy's fingernails. Make him tell the truth. But she was here as an agent of the FBI, not an operator for OPSIG. Not that long ago, Vail had been recruited into OPSIG, a part-time assignment she begrudgingly accepted—as if she had a choice, which she did not. So no fingernail pulling today, as tempting as it was.

"Is Nadine still alive?"

Jackson twisted his mouth. "Why wouldn't she be?"

"Because you keep your victims alive for five days before killing them. This is day five."

"Oh, I read about this case. The Virginia Strangler, right?"

"Right." Vail sat on the edge of the mattress. "Now personally, I respect the Strangler because he's, well, he's famous. And *really* good at what he does. He's been killing for three years and the cops haven't been able to find him."

Jackson smiled. "I know. Pretty sweet, eh?"

"I bet they're going to make a movie about him someday. And you know, when they do that, the media always wants to do interviews with the real offender. Because to get away with it so long, he's gotta be much smarter than other killers."

"I'm sure he'd enjoy the attention."

"So hypothetically, Bobby, where do you think the Strangler would be keeping the women before he kills them?"

"Wow. Who knows? I mean, the Strangler knows. But how on Earth would you find out where he's got this Nadine woman without finding the Strangler?"

I'd like to strangle you, you pissant—

There was a commotion outside the house. Muffled shouting. Vail glanced at Bledsoe, who was peering out the bedroom window.

Wait, I know that voice.

"Can't see anything." Bledsoe pulled his handgun.

"You can put that away," Vail said, raising a hand. "I know who it is." *And I hope he's not here for me.* "Friend of mine. He's not a threat."

"Stand down," a deep male voice shouted from the other room.

The door burst open and Troy Rodman was standing there, clad in a black tactical uniform.

"What the hell do you thi—"

"Your services are needed." His expression was cold, icy. And his imposing stature made Vail think of an offensive lineman on a football team who had not eaten in days: he possessed a hard expression and slightly bent hands, dangling at his sides as if ready to rip someone's head off for looking at him the wrong way.

"I'm in the middle of a case," Vail said. "An interview." Her eyes flicked over to Bobby Ray Jackson.

"An interview." Rodman laughed. "Why don't you people just call it what it is—an interrogation?"

This isn't happening. "Seriously. You need to get out of here. Now."

"My orders are to not leave without you."

"And I'm not leaving until this scumbag tells me what I need to know."

Rodman stepped forward, all 280 pounds of him. "Does this scumbag have a name?"

"Bobby Ray Jackson. Serial killer who kidnapped a young woman."

"*Accused* serial killer," Jackson said. "I've admitted nothing."

"And he's not telling you where this woman is?" Rodman asked.

"Look," Vail said, "I know you're trying to be helpful, but—"

"Just answer the question."

Vail folded her arms across her chest. "Correct. We think she's still alive—but not for long."

Rodman stepped back and closed the door—as best he could, given the poor treatment it had received from Bledsoe's shoe. He then walked over to Jackson, who weighed about 165 pounds fully clothed. Rodman stood in front of him and looked down on the man's greasy hair. "You need to answer Agent Vail's question so she can leave."

Jackson laughed. "I don't know who you think I am, but I've got rights."

"Answer the damn question."

"Already answered it. I have no idea what she's talking about."

Rodman turned to Vail. "You're sure this is your guy? And that he's holding the woman you're looking for?"

"Yes. No question whatsoever."

Rodman puckered his lips and nodded slowly. Then, with the swiftness of a tiger, he struck the man in the throat with the knife edge of his hand.

Jackson's eyes bulged. He gasped for breath and his chair tipped backward onto the dusty wood floor.

Vail grabbed Rodman's arm. "What the hell are you doing?"

Bledsoe rushed to Rodman's side as the big man shrugged Vail aside and then kicked the chair out of the way.

He knelt atop the squirming Jackson, who was still trying to suck air into his lungs. "I don't have time to fuck around," Rodman said calmly. "I have my orders to take Agent Vail with me.

So you're going to cooperate. Right now. Tell her where you're keeping that woman."

Jackson coughed violently once, twice, three times. Rodman grabbed the man's throat. And squeezed.

"Hey!" Bledsoe lifted his pistol. "Let him go."

Jesus Christ. Is this really happening? "Bledsoe, lower the weapon." She whispered in his ear: "Block the door, make sure no one comes in." He started to object but she gave him a hard look and he complied, albeit with a frown. Vail then turned back to Rodman and softened her voice. "Please. You can't . . . you can't just barge in here and do this. He's right. He's got rights. You know that. There are rules."

But unlike the FBI, OPSIG followed no rules. It was all about the successful completion of the mission. And Rodman was an OPSIG operator.

"I'm not law enforcement," Rodman said, his large leg pinning down the thighs of Jackson, who had stopped choking—but the man's face was red, wet with perspiration. "Answer me. Where's the woman? Or I'm gonna close my fist and crush your goddamn windpipe. I've done it. More than once."

"Leithtown," Jackson squeaked, followed by a cough as Rodman released his hold.

"Where in Leithtown?"

"Ranch house . . . 4502 Setter Lane."

Bledsoe rushed out of the room. The information had not been obtained legally, so their case against Jackson would not be able to include Nadine's testimony—but weighed against the young woman's life, Vail knew he was not likely to complain too loudly.

Rodman pushed himself up and adjusted his shirt. "Vail, you're with me." He marched out, not waiting for her—but knowing she would be following close behind.

6

Gulfstream V Jet
West Virginia Airspace

General Klaus Eisenbach handed DeSantos and Uzi a glass topped up with orange liquid, then settled himself in the tan glove leather seat.

"I'm a former NASA flight engineer. Before that I flew F-16s in the Air Force, the First Gulf War. I remember watching Apollo 11 land on the Moon—which is why I ended up at NASA. Needless to say, I'm thoroughly familiar with your dossiers."

The ice cubes clinked as Uzi took a sip and made a face. "This is orange juice."

"No more alcohol, processed sugar, refined carbohydrates, fried or fatty foods. Your diets will be tightly controlled from here on out, your health monitored on an ongoing basis. Your weight will be watched as well."

"There's no substitute for efficiency," Uzi said as he glanced around the Gulfstream's interior.

"Efficiency is the name of this mission. With one exception, all seven Moon missions were successful, thanks to the engineers who designed the rockets, the engines, the computers, and the spacecraft—as well as the hours of testing and training to ensure we did everything possible to bring our people home safely. We tried to anticipate every contingency. We didn't always succeed—shit happened—but when things went wrong, we had systems in place to deal with them. So, efficiency? Yes. We want to carry out our mission and get you home safely."

"Point taken."

"The typical astronaut course," Eisenbach said, "involves astronomy, aerodynamics, rocket propulsion, communications, medical testing, meteorology, physics of the upper atmosphere, navigation, flight mechanics, and geology. We'd like at least a month to prep you for the mission. We don't even have two weeks. But you're not going to be piloting or navigating the spacecraft, and you're already highly trained in some of those skills, so we've got a strong foundation to work from. For the most part, you'll be glorified passengers until you get to the lunar surface."

"I think we can handle that," DeSantos said.

Eisenbach reached across the table and gathered up two Surface tablets. He handed one to Uzi and the other to DeSantos. "These contain your study materials, including schematics, photos, and video tutorials. The hard drives are encrypted. That's the password on the Post-it. Memorize it, then give it back to me."

They both looked at it a moment, then passed the notes to Eisenbach.

"Your backgrounds and skill sets are similar yet different, so we've assembled the course material to fit your individual strengths. Additional content will be pushed to the devices when you're at the base."

They turned on the tablets and entered the password.

"Spaceflight today, like flying a jumbo jet, is automated. There's very little a pilot needs to do other than monitor his or her equipment—and know what to do if something goes wrong. I've scheduled a lot of simulator time so you can get a sense of what it'll feel like maneuvering in zero-G in the crew module and walking in one-sixth gravity on the lunar surface. You also need to learn how to use your pressure suit and you'll get some basic training on the operations of the crew module." He looked from DeSantos to Uzi. "Any questions? No?"

Eisenbach pressed on. "Redundancy is the mantra at NASA. Backups to backups. So while the plan is for you to just enjoy the ride there, we'd rather you have an idea of what's going on. Uzi, you'll huddle with the flight engineers and rocket scientists to get some instruction on the computer systems, rockets, and engines. Given your engineering background at Intel, that material will be a good fit for you.

"Hector, you'll work with the pilots to get simulator time flying the crew module and even the lunar descent and ascent vehicles. If we're ahead of schedule, we'll do some cross training."

"You think we'll have enough time to get a handle on this stuff?" DeSantos asked.

Eisenbach lifted his heavy whiskey glass from the table in front of him. "Not even close. But you'll be *familiar* with each task. Something comes up, we'll be able to talk you through it. Only your previous experience and knowledge base make it remotely possible we could pull this off."

"If this mission was being planned for years, why bring us in at the last minute?" DeSantos asked. "With all due respect, sir, it doesn't really add up."

Eisenbach swirled his drink, the ice cubes rattling against the sides. DeSantos had a feeling his clear liquid was not water.

"We had a team of four ready to go," Eisenbach said. "The two astronauts you'll be flying with and two SEAL team operators, Welding and Norris, who'd been training for the mission. Five days ago, Welding and Norris were at NASA's Neutral Buoyancy Lab underwater training facility when an explosion ripped through a part of the facility. We lost our men—and five others.

Two of them were our backup team. One was the assistant director of the CIA."

DeSantos narrowed his eyes. "What kind of explosion?"

Eisenbach stared into his glass. "A bomb. And no, we haven't caught the bastard. FBI's working on it." He took a sip. "We launched a selection process to replace our fallen operators, but when they gave me the list of names the SecDef strongly suggested I give the two of you a hard look."

"That's encouraging," Uzi said.

"Starting from scratch, and now facing a hard deadline, it made the most sense to insert you two into the team and, well, hope for the best."

DeSantos turned to Uzi. "So much for the vote of confidence."

"From what I'm told, you two are very good. I heard two of OPSIG's best. But flattery doesn't get anyone anywhere. You're operators and this is a mission. Nothing else matters. I know you'll give it your all."

"During the briefing," Uzi said, "you mentioned that the plan would prevent a country from getting caesarium."

"We believe so, yes."

"But let's say we accomplish our mission and we disable the Chang'e so they can't bring it back. What's stopping them from launching another Chang'e six months from now?"

Eisenbach removed his glasses. "Tomorrow morning we're launching the OLEC, an unmanned spacecraft carrying three satellite-based laser-emitting cannons. OLEC will reach a lunar orbit in ninety-six hours and release the satellites at strategic intervals. Officially, it'll be NASA's long-planned Lunar Atmosphere and Dust Environment Explorer—LADDEE. Its design is roughly the same size and shape so we should be able to get away with that explanation."

"Laser-emitting cannons?" DeSantos asked.

"For the past thirty-five years," McNamara said, "the DOD and the Army's Space and Missile Defense Command have been developing directed-energy weapons at the White Sands test range in New Mexico. *Lasers.* And high-powered microwaves and particle beams. The Navy's LaWS, or Laser Weapon System, is now operating in the Arabian Gulf and can be deployed for ground, air, and space-based warfare."

DeSantos inched forward in his seat. "Instead of sending us to the Moon, why not just use a laser to shoot down the Chang'e?"

"Our high-power, deuterium fluoride chemical laser can heat rocket warheads, literally blasting them to bits. The Chang'e isn't a warhead, but it'd probably detonate if hit by a laser because of the onboard fuel. Problem is, the Chinese would know we did it. No deniability. They'd have to respond. It'd be an act of provocation at best, and really an act of war."

Uzi chuckled. "One that Russia would be all too happy to back them over."

"And you're right—it wouldn't solve anything because they could just launch another Chang'e."

"So what's the laser for?" DeSantos asked.

Eisenbach refreshed his drink and squeezed in a section of lime. "To prevent future attempts to mine caesarium, we're deploying an array of optical lasers around the Moon. Anything entering lunar orbit will be destroyed. The US will keep these satellite lasers in orbit until a treaty is signed. All missions to the Moon's surface will need to be preapproved by a UN body and enforced by UN troops. The mining and recovery of caesarium and any as-yet undiscovered elements or minerals that have the potential to be used in weapons of mass destruction would be prohibited."

"Interesting," Uzi said.

"Moon shots would need to be submitted for review to the international body. And to keep everyone honest, all spacecraft returning from the Moon will be subject to forensic inspection. Once an agreement and infrastructure are in place, the laser array will be deactivated."

"I like it," DeSantos said. "Incentive to reach an agreement."

Eisenbach gestured toward their Surface tablets. "You've got five hours to study before we land. It's all arranged in the order you should be reading this data. My staff has been updating it and expanding on it to reflect what the engineers have been telling us. So some of it might be a bit rough around the edges. Some of it is incomplete. Some of it is still being worked out."

DeSantos harrumphed. "Sounds like a lot of our missions. We plan and train, but sometimes we have to ship out without all the i's dotted."

"That's the bottom line of what we do, isn't it? We do whatever it takes. Sometimes we mission plan on the fly when things don't go the way they've been drawn up, when the unexpected gets in the way and the fog of war inserts itself—as it always does. SecDef McNamara tells me you're used to this and that you always find a way to make it work."

Uzi snorted. "My wife used to do this thing where she'd add 'in bed' to the end of every fortune cookie fortune. 'You're going to have the time of your life today *in bed*.'"

Eisenbach furrowed his brow. "Your point?"

"Maybe we should add 'in space' to the assurances you're giving us for this mission. 'OPSIG always finds a way to make it work *in space*.' Those two simple words change the equation, and risk, dramatically." He got serious. "I don't think we can apply the benefit of confidence and experience with prior mission success to this because there are too many unknowns *in space*. *That's* my point."

"At West Point," Eisenbach said, "I had a subcourse instructor on special operations forces who pulled me aside after I made a similar point in class about prior mission success." He leaned back in the lounger and looked at the ceiling, as if reliving the memory. "Had me take a walk with him. Told me that when the bell rings you have your orders. Your sole focus is to carry out those orders. And if you have doubts, there are two words you should always remember." He cast his gaze to Uzi. "You know what they are?"

"Tough shit."

"That's what I want you to remember on this mission. Tough shit. You have a job to do and a dozen reasons to have doubts. Doubts are normal. But they need to be controlled so they don't interfere with your performance. Because your two other teammates are depending on you to perform without hesitation. With confidence. With intelligence and good judgment. And with unselfish motives."

"I got it sir," Uzi said. "No worries."

"We'd be robots if we didn't have any worries," Eisenbach said. "We have to channel these fears and rise above them. That's what good operators do. That's what good soldiers do. And that's what you four are going to do. *In space.*"

7

The Pentagon

Ten minutes after pulling into the Pentagon parking lot, Karen Vail was getting out of the basement elevator. She made her way through the biometric scanners and was heading down the hall to the conference center when Douglas Knox stepped into the corridor.

"Glad you could make it on short notice."

"Hot Rod was . . . quite persuasive. The serial killer I was in the middle of questioning didn't know what hit him." *Literally.*

"That's why I sent him."

"So what's going on?" Vail asked as they walked. "Am I working this as an FBI agent with the Bureau's resources behind me?"

"No," Knox said, "this is an OPSIG matter, which will become clear in a minute. Your investigation is top secret, with far-reaching diplomatic, foreign policy, military, counterterrorism, and global security implications."

"So nothing too terribly important."

Knox frowned. "I've recommended you for this mission because we need your investigative skills. And assuming we're successful and find a person of interest, we'll need your interview skills. A majority of OPSIG operators are, well, operators. For obvious reasons. This mission has many tentacles, but this part of it plays to your abilities."

"I would think that Uzi—"

"Agent Uziel *is* involved."

"In another one of those tentacles."

Knox made a noise—Vail thought it was a cross between a grunt and a groan. "Let's get in there. You need to get up to speed."

Seated around the table were director of central intelligence Laurence Bolten, CIA director Earl Tasset, director of the National Security Agency Elliot Stern, and Secretary McNamara. Knox and Vail took their places at the head of the room.

"Anyone here not know Special Agent Vail?"

Stern raised an index finger. He was tall and thin, with closely cropped gray hair and thick-framed bifocals. The two made introductions and shook hands.

After ten minutes, Vail had been brought up to date on pertinent aspects of the mission, the properties of caesarium and the danger of it falling into the hands of aggressive and rogue nations. The attack on the Neutral Buoyancy Laboratory was outlined in detail—as much detail as they had at the moment. Lastly, she was briefed on the assignment DeSantos and Uzi had been given.

Tasset got up and pulled the lid off his paper coffee cup. "We have reason to believe that we've got a leak, and probable theft, of information from NASA and/or the Pentagon."

"The NSA and US Cyber Command are running a parallel investigation," Stern said. "They're focused on a potential cyberattack. That might bear fruit because these breaches occur on a daily basis in one form or another. But based on the information we've gotten from foreign entities, we believe there's something more expansive at play."

"Such as?" Vail asked.

"Such as one or more moles." Tasset spoke with his back to the room as he stirred some sugar into his cup. "A full-blown spy operation. Worst possible scenario. And it also wouldn't be the first time—not by a long shot." He turned to Knox, who stood up and started pacing.

"In the seventies, when NASA started designing the space shuttle, they discovered, too late, there'd been a leak. Ten years later, Russia launched its own shuttle, the Buran, that looked just like ours." Knox pressed the remote and a photo of Discovery appeared, the room lights dimming automatically. He stopped by the edge of the screen and hit the controller again. The shuttle picture slid left and another image, bearing the USSR's "CCCP" designation, appeared beside it. Aside from the rocket boosters, the Russian and US spacecraft looked identical.

"Our designs were sold to the Russians," Tasset said. "The Buran only flew once, in 1988. It was successful, but the Soviet Union collapsed several months later and the program was mothballed."

"We're not aware of a cyber breach at NASA," Knox said, "so we could have another spy who alerted the Chinese about caesarium. China's been working on their space program aggressively. Before Chang'e 3 they sent several unmanned craft to the Moon, so it's hard to say when they found out about it. He turned to face them. "But we have to assume we've got a mole until proven otherwise. There's too much at stake."

"We've got high confidence that the mission they just launched is intended to bring back caesarium," McNamara said. "It takes a long time to plan this kind of thing, select the best weather patterns for a launch, build and equip the lander, and so on. The US military's Future Combat Systems program estimates China would only need eighteen to thirty-six months if they had equipment and systems already built for follow-on Chang'e missions. The breach, if there was one, likely occurred within this eighteen- to thirty-six-month window."

Bolten set his pen down. "I've asked the NASA administrator, Nora Peabody, to join us." He pressed a button and told the receptionist to show her in. "She's been briefed on certain aspects of the operation and obviously knows about the OPSIG component, though not the operational specifics—so let's keep all that under wraps."

The door swung inward and a short, middle-aged woman walked in, walnut tinted hair tied back into a bun and wearing a formfitting business suit.

Vail nodded and the men stood.

"Major General Peabody," Knox said, "glad you could join us on such short notice."

She nodded and took a seat between Vail and Stern, near the head of the table. "NASA takes these breaches very seriously—and I don't mind telling you I've been sick to my stomach since we hung up the phone."

Vail introduced herself, then said, "Can you assemble a list of employees who could've supplied information to a foreign country?"

"Right now the administration has roughly 23,000 employees. The list could include nearly all of them. I assume you'd want to narrow that down somehow."

"First and foremost, it's about access," Vail said. "If we can eliminate those who don't have access to the sensitive information, whoever's left had the ability to steal, and pass on, that data. I'm guessing that'll slice a large group off our list."

"Of course." Peabody took a deep breath. "Well, as you know, a federal agency like ours, which deals in sensitive science, research, and engineering with potential military applications, has several levels of compartmentalized security clearances."

"Right. The higher the level, the more sensitive the information he or she has access to."

"It's not that simple, Agent Vail. We've got some engineers who work on multiple aspects within a single project. Orion/SLS is an incredibly complex endeavor that's been in development in various forms for over a dozen years. It's being designed and tested at multiple NASA centers all over the country. So an engineer in California might've worked on propulsion and guidance, then also consulted with the engineers at the Florida or Texas centers. Not to mention the work they've done with contractors who were building out the hardware and software that were integrated into our mission objectives."

"Contractors," Vail said. "How many are we talking about?"

"Five majors. Two aren't even in the United States. But there are hundreds of others. About 3,000 people work on Orion—contractors, civil servants, subcontractors, suppliers, and small businesses.

"NASA engineers meet regularly with the engineers at these companies. But everyone undergoes vetting depending on what they're working on. There are also some contract employees who work at NASA centers doing jobs that are virtually the same as their civil servant counterparts in the adjacent cubicle. Others work at aerospace companies building hardware on contract to NASA. So you can see this isn't a simple question."

I can see *is that this is a fucked up system as far as security is concerned.*

"NASA employees—and our contractors—get background checks, depending on their level. Level 4 positions are 'special sensitive' jobs involving top secret information. Level 3 positions are 'critical sensitive' jobs involving secret information. Level 2 positions are 'noncritical sensitive' positions.

"Like any federal agency dealing with these kinds of things, access to the most sensitive information is granted on a need-to-know basis to individuals considered mission critical for a particular task. It's a good system. I don't see how anyone could subvert it."

Vail cleared her throat. "I don't have to remind anyone in this room that Edward Snowden was an NSA contractor with extremely high classified clearance. And we all know how that turned out."

Everyone was silent. Mentioning Snowden in this room was like a nuclear strike on the Pentagon.

"Okay," Vail said, realizing she had made her point. "This is a daunting task, so we have to filter out as many people as we can to make this manageable." *And possible.* "As I said, access is key, so we'll first eliminate everyone we can based on access to the type of information that could be compromised. Once we've done that, we'll carve off another group of people."

Peabody cocked her head dubiously. "It'll take some time to do that."

"After that," Vail said, pressing forward, "we'll see if any of the remaining people have, or had, any kind of ties to Russia or China—relatives, friends, phone calls. And financial or investment deals. Always follow the money, right? This obviously might not mean anything, but it could be significant and it could also help chop away at the list."

"We have to be careful with paring it back too aggressively," Tasset said. "I'd highlight those people who get flagged but I wouldn't remove anyone from the list based solely on known ties to a country. Some spies purposely have no obvious connections to their employer."

"Good point." Vail faced Tasset. "What countries are we talking about?"

"The usual bad actors—North Korea and Iran now have to be in that basket, even though the likelihood of spies coming from North Korea is a great deal lower than China or Russia. They just don't have the sophistication or infrastructure to pull off something like this. Yet."

"Let's not leave out social networking hits, friends, photos." Vail turned to Stern. "I assume that's NSA territory?"

"I can get my people on that," Stern said. "We'll have something for you within an hour of getting the full employee list from Administrator Peabody. I think it'd be best for us to work from the complete database without any filters. We've got very complex systems that can pick up things you may inadvertently eliminate. And I don't want to miss anything."

"There's something else you should know about," Peabody said. "Three years ago, the deputy administrator's laptop was stolen from his car. The media focused on the confidential information lifted from the hard drive—tens of thousands of social security numbers, names, and birthdates. We initiated a review to determine how something like this could've happened and what procedures needed to be changed so it wouldn't happen again."

"What was *not* publicized," Knox said, "was that the laptop also contained info on employees' personal lives from their background checks. Like the OPM hacks a year or so later, it exposed sensitive information on key people. Opened them up to potential extortion."

"If you've got something on somebody," Bolten said, "details of their life they don't want released, you can leverage them. Blackmail them. 'I need you to get some information for me. Oh, you don't want to help us out? Fine, we'll let the world know you had a rape expunged from your record when you were a minor.' Or that he's got a child by another woman he's paying support to."

Stern nodded. "The kind of stuff that could be extremely embarrassing on social media or damaging to your marriage, your family, your career."

"Oldest trick in the spy book for turning someone in a key position," Tasset said. "We've used it more times than I care to count."

"And that could be exactly what happened here," Bolten said.

"Do we know who was behind the theft?" Vail asked.

Stern adjusted his glasses. "No. It's not like a hack where there may be a trail or fragment of code we can trace or identify. The info taken off that hard drive was probably sold on the dark net—a secret overlay network that requires certain nonstandard encryption protocols to communicate. It's where cyber criminals sell and share pilfered data."

"If that's the case," Vail said, "if it's a key person with clearance who's been leveraged, info on caesarium may not be the only thing he or she has passed on to the Chinese."

"We've discussed that," Peabody said. "And we're looking into it, a review of all systems. We'll let you know if we find something."

"About that," Knox said. "Your people are not moving fast enough. A USCYBERCOM team is en route. Make sure they get all the cooperation they need."

"Would've been nice if I was informed."

"You just were."

Peabody scribbled a note on her pad. "Terrific," she said under her breath.

"And a reminder—the OPSIG part of this is not to be mentioned. To anyone outside this room. Are we clear?"

"Clear," Peabody said.

Knox and Bolten rose. The others followed.

"When can you get that employee list together?" Vail asked.

Peabody picked up her purse. "We'll get started on it immediately."

8

Astronaut Training
Vandenberg Air Force Base
Lompoc, California

The jet landed and a black SUV ferried Eisenbach, DeSantos, and Uzi across the Air Force base.

"Can you walk us through the space-based part of the mission?" Uzi asked. "Overview."

Eisenbach looked out the windows at the passing buildings. "The Orion follows the original Apollo concept: the Hercules II, a thirty-story rocket, has multiple stages, each one with engines designed to propel you to the next point in your journey. As the fuel burns out in one stage, the engines on the next stage kick in and start their burn. After getting into low Earth orbit—like where the space shuttle flew—you'll make one or two revolutions around the Earth until conditions are right. Then we'll fire the engines again in translunar injection, or TLI."

"And that blasts us out of Earth orbit," Uzi said.

"Right. Once you escape orbit, you'll fly at 30,000 miles per hour on a trajectory toward the Moon. The onboard computer will make minute course corrections, if needed, to keep you on target. This is vital, because if you're off by even a few degrees you could miss the Moon and go off into outer space."

"And that'd be a bad thing," DeSantos said.

"No," Eisenbach said. He took a sip of his drink. "That'd be a *very* bad thing. Because of weight and space constraints, you'll only be carrying enough fuel, oxygen, water, and food for this mission. Nothing extra. You could ration and buy some time, but there's not going to be a rescue party. We don't have that capability."

DeSantos did not need to have it spelled out: they would have no way to get back. They would die in space without food. Without water. Without oxygen. Basically," Eisenbach continued, "Orion seats four astronauts, two stacked atop the other two. It's bigger and a whole lot more advanced than Apollo. Our engineers and scientists have had decades to fine-tune, research and develop technology, gather data, brainstorm, think, learn from mistakes, and debate. But basic physics and current rocket science dictate that it'll still take about three days to travel the quarter-million miles between here and there.

"About 225,000 miles into your journey, you'll enter the sphere of the Moon's influence and you'll start to accelerate because its gravity will pull you toward it. When you get within eighty miles of the Moon, your rockets will fire and you'll enter lunar orbit on the dark, or far, side. Because the Moon will be between you and us, we'll lose radio contact with you.

"You'll move into the lunar lander and it'll separate from the Orion crew module. For Apollo, the pilot stayed aboard the command module, which orbited until his two crewmembers returned from the surface. But Orion is fully automated. The crew module remains in orbit while all four astronauts make the landing.

"After you finish your mission, you'll lift off from the Moon in the ascent stage, leaving the descent portion of the lander behind.

You'll dock with the Orion crew module then fire your rockets and begin your journey back to Earth, where you'll splash down in the Atlantic just north of the equator."

"Splash down?" Uzi said. "That's so . . . 1970s."

Eisenbach laughed. "Vertical landings are all the rage now. But they require tons more fuel, which you'd have to haul all the way to the Moon and back—and your launch vehicle would need to be a whole lot bigger. Didn't make sense for this type of mission.

"NASA, Lockheed, Aerojet Rocketdyne—and hundreds of other contractors—have had dozens of design team engineers testing parts, fairings, avionics, and rockets to make sure that their analyses matched up with how the systems would actually work in space. Based on the test results, they made changes and additions—because that system has *got* to do its job when the computer tells it to. Your lives, and this mission, depend on it. Most of the systems have undergone significant infrastructure testing and an exhaustive design validation process."

"*Most* of the systems?" Uzi asked.

"Most of the systems."

DeSantos knew there were substantial risks, and because of the sophisticated and complex technology involved, more hazards than he cared to think about. He chose to focus on the things he had control over.

"How reliable is this thing?" DeSantos asked. "Level with us."

"I'm not gonna give you odds. The military's been involved with testing and validating Orion, its rockets and engines, reentry, and recovery. NASA has run vacuum chamber simulations and dozens of trials on the ground and in the lab, as well as a number of in-flight tests. They blew the pyrobolts on the fairings and ran a full suite of vibration and acoustic evaluations. They stressed it at the system level in a variety of environments. Parachutes were tested at Davis Monthan Air Force Base, avionics at Holloman

Air Force Base, and splashdowns at the Kennedy Space Center. They placed a thousand sensors all over the crew module then blasted it into space and monitored everything. Changes were made as necessary.

"Bottom line, we've got teams all over the country maturing the design of the vehicle to make sure, as best we can, that it'll function as intended and designed."

The van slowed and DeSantos took a moment to glance outside. The number of armed personnel in the area had increased exponentially: they were in a busier—or more sensitive—part of the base.

"Hercules was built in stages at different locations," Eisenbach said, "including NASA's vehicle assembly building. The stages were then transported by ocean barge to Vandenberg. An advantage of Vandy is that it's located right on the coast. Perfect for a covert mission. But it also creates logistical issues because the launch trajectory will be north-south instead of east-west, which you'll need for a lunar parking orbit."

"And the fix was?" Uzi asked.

Eisenbach laughed. "I wouldn't understand the details if they tried to explain them to me. All I needed to know was that the computer will make a major course correction to line things up."

"When do all the stages get put together?" DeSantos asked.

"Already done. Hercules was erected vertically into its final launch configuration several weeks ago. It's gone through rounds of checkouts of all subsystems, including propulsion, guidance, navigation and control, and structures."

The transport pulled up to the front of a nondescript building that had a large "U" painted on the side. They filed in and were met by a dark-complected man in combat fatigues. "Klaus," he said, giving Eisenbach a shoulder hug. "Good to see you again."

"Delivering the rest of our crew. Hector DeSantos and Aaron Uziel."

"Bansi Kirmani." He shook their hands. "I'm going to be your instructor and drill sergeant. I'll be assisting the flight director once you four lift off, so you won't be rid of me once you climb on board that rocket. Even though you may want to be."

Eisenbach laughed—with a hint of nervous energy.

"Ex-military?" DeSantos asked.

"Captain," Kirmani said. "Naval intelligence. Assistant flight director on the last two shuttle missions. And I already know about you two." He started walking down a long corridor. "We're on a very tight schedule, so let's get to it. The two astronauts who'll be flying this mission are doing some training in the EVA simulator. We had been working on it at the Sonny Carter training facility at Johnson," he said, referring to the Neutral Buoyancy Lab in Houston. "But I'm sure you heard about what happened."

"We did," Uzi said. "Sorry for your loss."

Kirmani stopped at a door and pushed through it. "Because of the explosion we've had to turn back the clock several decades. This is how we trained for Apollo. But it worked for them, so it'll work for all of you."

A crane-like apparatus was attached to a handle on the two astronauts' pressure suits, suspending them slightly as they walked—more like hopped—in a large circle.

"Simulates one-sixth gravity. You'll be suiting up and doing this too. It's one of those things you can't just read about—you have to do it to get the hang of it."

Five minutes later, the two astronauts were being unhooked from the apparatus. They were helped off with their gloves and then their helmets were unlatched and removed.

DeSantos and Uzi walked over, taking in the machinery as they neared. "Interesting contraption," DeSantos said.

"Not as good as the NBL," the black-haired man said, "but it's not bad for what it is."

"Neutral buoyancy isn't the same as weightlessness, but it's the next best thing to being in zero-G."

"This is Digger Carson and Gavin Stroud," Kirmani said as the two men approached. "Stroud was with SEAL Team 10. You hear of Operation Silver Fox?"

"That was you?" DeSantos asked.

Stroud, a shade over five-ten and sporting the beginnings of crow's feet, nodded. "Yes sir."

"What was Silver Fox?" Uzi asked.

"Afghanistan," DeSantos said. "Outside Asadabad, 2005. Two members of the team were killed in an ambush." He gestured at Stroud. "You saved your buddy's life, hid him out in the mountains until SOAR(A) could get to you."

"Pretty cool, what you did," Uzi said.

"Loyalty to country and team." Stroud shrugged. "I served with honor, placed the welfare and security of others before my own. And I never quit."

"The SEAL creed," DeSantos said.

"You know it."

"Don't let that serious facade fool you," Kirmani said. "We call him Cowboy."

"Cowboy?" Uzi asked with more than a hint of skepticism.

"In BUD/s training. Had an asshole as a CO," Stroud said, referring to a commanding officer. "Didn't like the way I wore my hat, said I looked like a cowboy. Nickname stuck."

Uzi looked at Stroud's blond-haired companion. "He telling the truth?"

"About *this* he is."

"Aaron Uziel," he said as he shook the other man's hand. "Obvious nickname: Uzi. After the machine gun."

"Because you shoot your mouth off?"

DeSantos chuckled. "Because he shoots his mouth off about all sorts of shit and most of it isn't very accurate."

They laughed.

"I'm Digger Carson."

Uzi nodded at him. "What's your story? How'd you get the nickname Digger?"

"Pops worked for thirty-one years as a Caterpillar machinist. Loved those machines. And what do they do?"

"Dig," Uzi said. "A lot."

"Exactly. He also loved digging as a kid, so he named his first son Digger."

"So Digger's not a nickname?"

"Nope. And you shoulda seen what they did to me for it in the SEALs."

"Former SEAL, too?" DeSantos asked.

"DEVGRU," he said, using the acronym for the Naval Special Warfare Development Group.

DeSantos raised his brow. "The storied Team 6." He did some quick math. "When'd you leave?"

"Last mission was May 2, 2011."

"Six did the bin Laden kill on that date."

"Sharp memory," Carson said.

"You were on that op? Neptune Spear?"

Carson nodded. "And no, I got nothing to say about it."

"Because?"

"Because it's not about us, it's about the country. The Team—long live the Brotherhood. And obviously the mission." He shook his head. "Those guys who wrote books. Not what we're about. I was disappointed in them. Good men. My brothers. But they shouldn't a done that. You know?"

"I do." DeSantos looked at Carson a long moment. "You're okay, Digger."

"I know."

They all laughed again.

"Obviously you two have already met Ridgid."

"Who?" DeSantos asked.

"That'd be me," Kirmani said.

"Should we ask how you got that name?"

"Not what you think."

"Bullshit," Carson said. "It's exactly what you think. He's a rigid son of a bitch. And he fancies himself a drill sergeant. So we named him after the Ridgid line of drills and power tools."

"Ridgid was opposed to this mission and how it came about," Stroud said. "But I think he's come around."

DeSantos cocked his head. "I sense there's more to that story, but it doesn't really matter, does it? We have our orders and we're all sworn to carry them out."

Kirmani nodded slowly. "That's not just the company line. You two don't cut it, if you can't carry out those orders—in my estimation and my estimation alone—this mission will not happen." He paused, let his gaze linger on their faces. "Got it?"

DeSantos did not reply. He was caught off guard at the sudden shift of tone from good-hearted banter to serious threat. "Ridgid" suddenly made sense.

"Got it," Uzi said, filling the awkward silence.

"Good. We've spent enough time on introductions. You can talk more during dinner. Cowboy, Digger, get out of your suits. DeSantos, Uzi, you two are with me."

They gave a nod to Carson and Stroud and followed Kirmani down the brightly lit tan-tiled corridor to a room off to the right.

Kirmani shoved the door open and gestured inside, where the décor featured gray industrial carpet, two metal-framed beds, and a wood dresser on each side. A single closet stretched the length of the far wall.

"You two will be bunking together. We'll start every morning at 0600. You'll have fifteen minutes for breakfast, twenty for lunch and dinner. Then there'll be an evening session starting at 2100 for ninety minutes, at which point you'll come back here to hit the sack. You've been issued clothing and shoes in your sizes." He turned and led them farther down the hall into the kitchen.

A balding man with a ladle in his hand was leaning over a pot.

"Bernie!" Kirmani said. "A minute."

Bernie set the utensil down and dragged his fingers across the apron that was once white and now streaked with whatever had been adorning his hands.

"This is Bernie Anderson. Your cook. He's under strict orders to follow the diet set forth by the nutrition department. So don't ask him to make you something that's not on the menu because you're not going to get it."

"And what diet is that?" DeSantos asked.

"High protein, low carb. No refined sugars. Whole grains, nuts, fruit. We want you to drop five pounds each."

"Does it look like either of us needs to lose five pounds?" DeSantos asked.

Kirmani shook his head in disapproval. "This has nothing to do with fitness but weight. Your education starts now. Everything that goes on that goddamn spacecraft has mass, and every ounce of that mass gets weighed, recorded, and logged. Know why?"

"I'm sure we'll find out."

He gave DeSantos a quick frown. "Because the rocket that's going to be lit underneath your asses has to be able to lift you, your crewmates, all the equipment you'll have onboard, the rocket itself and crew module, lunar module, and rover. The Hercules II is among the most powerful rockets ever built but there are limits. So the goal is to save ten pounds by putting you two on a nutritious, restricted calorie diet."

Kirmani started walking down the hall as Anderson returned to his cooking duties.

"The two guys you're replacing, combined, weighed ten pounds less than you two. So one way or another, we have to make up that mass. Rather than dumping equipment, we'll dump some fat."

DeSantos made a mental note not to invite this guy to his annual Christmas party.

"Your two team members have been training for this mission for a year and a half. They're more than just competent pilots. They're the best we've got."

Kirmani continued down the corridor, Uzi and DeSantos striding to keep up with the man's rapid pace.

"I'll be giving you two a crash course on particular aspects of the mission as a means of support to Cowboy and Digger. But you'll still need to be intimately familiar with things like putting on and taking off your pressure suits, how to walk in a low gravity environment, how to operate the rover, and so on. General Eisenbach gave you those tablets, correct?"

"Already had five hours to digest the first lesson," Uzi said.

"Good. My assistant and I will quiz you later."

"Quiz us?" DeSantos asked. "What is this, high school?"

Kirmani stopped suddenly and faced him. "I need to be certain you two grasp the concepts behind what you'll be doing and know how to do it. This is serious business. You screw up, there's not gonna be a rescue team parachuting in."

Uzi cleared his throat. "All due respect, sir, you know who we are. And you know we're accustomed to operating in situations like that."

"This is different. It's . . . there's something about being in space, being on the Moon, where there are no other life forms, where it'll only be the four of you. Closest human will be a quarter million miles away. Something happens, you're going to have to figure it out. We'll be here to help, to offer solutions, but it's all on your shoulders. You may've done that in the mountains of Timbuktu, but there's always the potential for someone in a Black Hawk to swoop in and drop you a line, some food, extra ammo.

Up there, it's just you. You can't really relate to what I'm saying. But you will."

"How do *you* know?" DeSantos asked.

Kirmani resumed his quick pace. "Because I was on shuttle mission ST-128. I did three EVAs—extravehicular activities—space walks. And I've spoken with Aldrin and Collins and Cernan and Armstrong. The Moon walkers can tell you what it's like on the surface. What it's like hurtling through space with nothing around you but the stars. Knowing there's a chance you might not make it back alive. We'll do everything to make sure you do—that's the most important part of my job."

Kirmani stopped in front of a room. "Let's get something clear. I'm not being a hard ass because I enjoy it. I'm trying to prepare you best I can to make sure you complete your mission successfully and make it back to Earth in one piece. Either of you got a problem with that?"

"No sir," they said in unison.

Kirmani checked his watch. "We're right on time." He pushed open the door. "Let's get started."

9

OPSIG Situation Room
The Pentagon

Vail, Rodman, and an OPSIG analyst were hunched over their laptops when a tall man with blond-highlighted hair entered.

"Hot Rod, got something for you."

Rodman swiveled in his seat. "Karen, you ever meet Lincoln Dykstra?"

Vail shook her head.

"Link, this is Karen Vail. Karen, Link. Good guy, hell of a marksman, deadly fighter. Hands, knife, doesn't matter—just plain lethal. And great with a garrote."

"Oh," Vail said as Dykstra shook her hand. She felt like pulling it away and wiping it on her 5.11s. "That's just . . . Wow. Impressive." *Sooner or later, Robby's gonna start objecting to the company I'm now keeping.*

"Good to meet you," Dykstra said. "Haven't seen you around here before."

"I'm . . . part-time."

Rodman gestured at the piece of paper in Dykstra's hand. "That for me?"

“Got something on that explosion at the Neutral Buoyancy Lab. You wanted everything coming through you.”

“Whaddya got?”

“Potential hit on the keycard and biometrics used to access the lab. Apparently one of the guys who'd called in sick wasn't sick at all. He was dead. Killed. Head shot, no sign of a struggle. His access credentials were used to enter the facility the afternoon before the blast. We've got cameras showing an unknown male in his thirties carrying a messenger bag. He walked into the area where the locker room is located. *Was* located.”

“What do we know about him?” Vail asked.

Dykstra chuckled. “For one thing, it wasn't the guy whose credentials were used to enter the lab. We ID'd him from facial recognition—cross-referenced with DMV databases. Name's Alec Hayder. Other than that, not a whole lot worth discussing. No known connections to terror groups. Hasn't ventured outside the country. Ever, it seems. No weird online posts. No significant run-ins with law enforcement. Misdemeanor drug arrest as a minor but he paid a fine, did a few hours of community service, and that was that. He's kept his nose clean as an adult. No phone calls to anyone on a watch list. Doesn't own a gun—not legally, at least. Really, he's pretty unremarkable.”

“Work?”

“Drives a local delivery truck.”

“What was he doing in Houston?” Rodman asked.

Dykstra laughed. “You mean other than planting a bomb that killed a bunch of people? No idea. Nothing seems to indicate he had a reason for being there.”

“Money trail?” Vail asked.

“No unusual deposits into his local checking or savings account at Cleveland Bank & Trust. If he was paid for a job in cash and he's stashed it somewhere, no way for us to know. Doesn't look to be in debt. His mom rents her house, been there twenty-one years. Never late on payments. We're looking to see if Hayder's social comes up in connection with any other financial institution or unusual transactions, but so far we're only finding the local accounts."

Vail scratched her forehead. "So he's pretty close to a model middle-class citizen. Except that he decided one day to drive to Texas, kill a guy, and set off a bomb that killed several others. That makes no sense."

Rodman took the document. "This all we have? A fuzzy screen grab?"

"We got lucky. A traffic stop for running a red in Ohio. Cop didn't realize it at the time, but he saw the alert on the FBI's Most Wanted list tonight when he got back to the station and recognized the guy from his stop earlier in the day."

"And?" Vail asked. "He just called the FBI?"

"He did. We've got an ID and address. Mother lives and works a few miles from the Rock & Roll Hall of Fame. Pretty sure that's where he was headed. His mother's place, not the Rock Hall."

"Thanks, Link." Rodman tapped Vail's shoulder. "We'll get a late dinner on the run. Let's go get the bastard."

VAIL AND RODMAN ATE SANDWICHES on the short flight to Cleveland. Two agents from the local FBI field office picked them up from the airport and brought them to the SWAT staging area three-quarters of a mile from the Hayder house on Whitman Avenue.

It was nearing 11:00 PM and the quiet, mature neighborhood was busier than usual—the presence of the tactical trucks on the street had everyone peering through their windows into the darkness.

In the back of their Bearcat vehicle, SWAT commander Fredericks outlined the preliminary work his team had done on the house where their suspect was located. He poked a finger at a map in a three-ring binder and showed them where they would be initiating the action.

"We've had eyes on the place and quietly evacuated the residences on both sides, as well as across the street," Fredericks said. "Neither he nor his mother has gone anywhere."

Vail glanced out the small rectangular windows. "What's the plan?"

"We'll do a knock and notice. I doubt Hayder wants a shootout with his mom in the house. But if he does, we're ready. And where there's one bomb there could be others. We'll have vests for you two but we'd obviously like you to hang back and let us do our thing."

Vail figured Rodman would bristle at that, but Fredericks did not know his skill set—or hers—and it was best to let their team execute without interference.

"So this guy set off a bomb at a NASA laboratory in Houston?" the commander asked.

"Unfortunately," Vail said. "Yeah. More than that, we can't say."

"You know anything about why he did it?" Fredericks asked. "Disgruntled former employee?"

"Everything we know says he's a pretty ordinary guy," Rodman said. "No known beefs. No connection to NASA or the government. No motive at all as to why he'd do this."

"Since he used explosives once, we'll be sure to check for signs of booby traps and IEDs around the exterior." Fredericks stood up. "Okay, well, we've got a job to do and we're gonna do it. Hopefully in an hour you two will get a crack at asking him the why's."

They loaded up their trucks and drove to the Hayder house. They deployed around the periphery, Vail and Rodman camping out across the way behind a sedan.

The area was filled with mature, gnarled trees. Picket fences lined the street, with wide, grassy terraces between the curb and the sidewalks that fronted the homes. The Hayder residence reminded her of the shotgun homes in New Orleans: long and narrow, with a Victorian style roof.

"I don't like hiding behind a car while someone else does the dirty work for me."

"Figured you wouldn't," Vail said. "I don't either. But these guys have had hours to prep. And we haven't. This is what they're paid to do, what they spend day after day *training* to do. Most important thing is we get this asshole somewhere quiet where we can question him."

Rodman did not respond but she knew he had to realize she was right.

After finding no explosives, the SWAT officer knocked on the door and announced himself. Seconds later, a middle-aged woman answered. She looked surprised and—as any innocent citizen would—appeared scared by the presence of a group of armed men surrounding her house.

Vail could not make out what was being said, but the woman stepped aside and the officers entered. As the fourth one cleared the threshold, someone jumped from the second floor into the side yard.

"You see that? Hayder, the window—" Vail blurted, starting across the street. She had the Glock in her hands, Rodman behind her.

A shadow flashed to her left. Vail stutter-stepped toward the adjacent house, then ran forward. *There he is.*

"Police! Don't move."

Hayder turned toward her, appeared to raise his hands above his head in surrender—and then brought them down quickly.

Rodman fired. Hayder's torso bucked, then dropped to the ground.

"WELL THAT SUCKS," Rodman said. "Sorry. Didn't see a choice."

"I know," Vail said as they approached the stilled body. "If you hadn't fired, I would have. But it does suck. Big time."

Fredericks came upon them at a gallop. "What the hell?"

"He jumped from the second floor window and ran," Vail said as she hooked a gloved index finger around the trigger guard and lifted Hayder's gun from the hard-packed dirt.

The commander spoke into his radio and updated his team.

"You find anything in there? Bomb-making materials? Weapons?"

Fredericks shook his head. "We're still clearing, so it'll take awhile, but nothing so far. Just a plain old middle-class home."

"And a typical middle-class family," Rodman said.

"With a murderous son who sets off bombs and murders NASA personnel for no reason," Vail said.

"Lots of cash under the mattress," a voice said over the two-way.

Sounds like we just found the reason.

"Ten-four. How much we talkin' 'bout?"

Seconds passed. "Looks like about fifty grand, give or take."

"Under the mattress?" Rodman said. "Do criminals really do that?"

"They do," Vail said. "Harder to steal what's under you while you're sleeping. Apparently with a gun stashed in your night table. Some bury cash underground, but that's not always possible if the dirt's frozen with snow or ice. And sometimes the cash gets wet or eaten by bugs. Shit happens."

"So what's going on here?" Rodman asked. "Someone paid him to set the bomb?"

Fredericks jerked a thumb over his shoulder. "Gotta get back to my team. Your forensic people can look around in . . . maybe a couple hours, give or take."

Vail watched Fredericks jog back toward the house. "Yeah, given everything we know about Hayder—which is obviously a little lacking—it does look like someone paid him to do this."

"But who?"

"Who is right," Vail repeated, looking down at Hayder. "But if we figure out 'why him,' we may have the answer as to 'who.'"

"He's got no connection to anything or anyone," Rodman said.

"And that right there could be the reason. No one would ever suspect him. He's not on anyone's radar. Law-abiding citizen, responsible, working hard to make a living and not doing such a great job of it. Still living with his mom."

Vail crouched and let her gaze run the length of Hayder's body. "We should get away from here. Media's gonna be by any minute."

"So this was all about money?" Rodman asked as they headed away from the house. "That's it? He was willing to kill for fifty grand?"

"People have killed for far less." She chuckled. "You don't want to know the going rate—but it ain't much, my friend."

They crossed over to the next block, away from the knot of law enforcement personnel.

"We can't assume he was the one who killed the NASA worker," Vail said. "Most likely someone else did the murder, then handed off the key card to Hayder. My guess is Hayder had no idea what was going on. Probably had no clue the backpack he was bringing into the NBL had a bomb inside."

"How can we know for sure?"

Vail blew some air from her lips. "Could take years to solve. We may *never* know. Our best shot is boots on the ground police work. It's a public case and until we prove otherwise, it was an act of terrorism. The FBI will investigate Hayder. Knox will feed us anything we need to know."

Vail called the director to report in while Rodman arranged for a ride to a nearby motel.

Thirty minutes later they were getting a room at the local Holiday Inn. Ten minutes after that, Vail was fast asleep.

10

ASTRONAUT TRAINING
VANDENBERG AIR FORCE BASE

The alarm blared from the small device on his night table, a no-frills wood cabinet beside a no-frills twin mattress pushed against one wall of the room where Aaron Uziel slept.

Hector DeSantos opened one eye. "Shut that thing off."

Uzi wind-milled an arm around and slapped the buzzer with his fist, quieting the noise. But five seconds later, bright ceiling lights lit up and the double groan that emerged from their mouths sounded like a backup chorus for a B-side of a failed '80s rock band.

Uzi swung his legs off the bed and trudged toward the bathroom, a few steps ahead of DeSantos.

Fifteen minutes later they were sitting down at the breakfast table. Carson and Stroud were already there, appearing chipper and focused.

"You guys sleep okay?" Stroud asked.

"Oh yeah," DeSantos said sardonically. "Fantastic."

"Good morning, good morning, good morning!" A smiling Bernie Anderson appeared from behind a wall wheeling a stainless steel cart with several plates. He went about setting them out in front of each of the four men.

Uzi and DeSantos sat there a second studying the spread.

"Nonfat Greek yogurt with walnuts, honey, cinnamon, blackberries, blueberries, and chia seeds," Anderson said as he poured coffee into their empty mugs.

"Bagel?" DeSantos asked. "Toast?"

"No sir," Anderson said. "We'll be limiting carbs. My orders are—"

"Yeah, yeah, yeah." DeSantos pursed his lips, resigned to forgoing his usual eggs, bacon, and home fries.

"You guys feeling good about the mission?" Uzi asked.

"Hell yeah," Carson said. "We've been at this a year and a half. We've been itching to go for a few months now. We figured it'd be soon, but the Chinese launch lit a fire under the brass's asses."

Stroud chuckled. "And pretty soon they'll light the biggest fire of all under ours."

THEY SPLIT INTO TWO TEAMS, Stroud and Carson assigned to their final tune-up simulations in the Orion crew module while Uzi and DeSantos met Kirmani in a classroom three doors down from the dining hall.

When they walked in, Kirmani was huddled with a cadre of men and women who were wearing large earmuff protectors. They were fussing over orange uniforms and bulky white garments, all of which were draped across thick hangers on a heavy-duty mobile clothing rack.

Kirmani consulted his watch and nodded approval. "We're going to spend the first fifteen minutes fitting you for your pressure suits—that's what they're called. You wanna call them space suits, fine, we'll know what you mean.

"The white, bulky ones are EVAs, or extravehicular activity suits, for when you're on the lunar surface. The orange ones are the ACES—or advanced crew escape suits—and are known around here as pumpkin suits. They're the ones you'll be wearing in the crew module for launch and reentry as well as the trips to and from the Moon. Boeing's designed a new Starliner suit, which is a lot more comfortable, but we haven't rolled it out yet. So we go with what we've got."

A man dressed in jeans and a blue work shirt pulled out a measuring tape and asked to see DeSantos's hands.

"These pressure suits are not off-the-rack sizes," Kirmani said. "They have to be fit to you individually."

"Bespoke," DeSantos said.

"Fancy term, but yes. We'll be taking over a hundred different measurements, most of which will involve your hands. The gloves have to fit well because it's hard enough working in a low gravity environment wearing an oversize pressure suit, but put on a set of bulky, stiff gloves and then try to operate equipment . . . and you'll quickly realize why we're making such a fuss over them."

DeSantos extended his right hand and the tailors went to work. "Is it cool to be talking about our mission with . . . them in the room?"

"That's why they've got the noise-cancelling headphones on. Music is being piped in, rather loudly. They're used to it. We can talk freely. Now, because of our schedule, we don't have the usual amount of time to fit these suits to you. The contractor that's been making NASA's EVA suits since Apollo designed these specifically for this mission, using their I-Suit model as a base. Your pumpkin suits will be made by the same company that makes the NASA launch and reentry suits.

"These good people are going to work all day and through the night so that when you get up tomorrow morning you'll be able to try them on. Any adjustments will be made on the spot. Two identical suits of each type will then be made in case one gets damaged during training."

While the man working on DeSantos took the measurements, his assistant was doing the same with Uzi's hands.

"So here's a quick and dirty top-down view of the white EVA suits. There's no oxygen on the Moon, so if something goes wrong with the suit, you'll lose consciousness within fifteen seconds. Your blood and body fluids will boil or freeze because there's little or no air pressure and the surface temperatures are extreme—minus 250 degrees Fahrenheit in darkness to 250 degrees in direct sunlight. Your skin, heart, and other internal organs will expand because of the boiling fluids."

"So if we take these things off," Uzi said, "we're dead."

"It really is that simple, gentlemen. You get a cut in the suit, you're dead. Your glass helmet cracks, you're dead."

"I see the pattern," DeSantos said. "We need them, and we need them to work properly, to survive."

"Thank God they didn't send me idiots." Kirmani stepped over to the rack, where tubes and a large white backpack were hanging. "Bottom line, your pressure suit must be airtight so that when it's pumped with oxygen, it doesn't leak. It'll provide a pressurized atmosphere—and remove the carbon dioxide that you breathe out. It maintains a constant and workable internal temperature. It'll also protect you from micrometeoroids and, to some degree, from radiation."

"And the radio?" Uzi asked.

"All hooked into the suit—and the backpack, which I'll get to in a moment. Once you're outside the spacecraft, the radio will enable communication with one another as well as ground controllers. One thing we've been working on, in association with DARPA," he said of the Defense Advanced Research Projects Agency, "is a heads-up display built into the helmet glass. We'll spend some time on that too, so you'll know how to use it."

Kirmani stepped over to the cart and lifted up a three foot by two foot device. "This is your primary life support system. PLSS for short. It's been refined quite a bit since Apollo, but the function's still the same: it's got air, lithium hydroxide to remove carbon dioxide, water, and electrical interfaces."

DeSantos looked at the hulking white backpack. "How much does that thing weigh?"

"About forty-five pounds," Kirmani said. "But once you put it on in the lunar module, it'll be weightless. And when you step outside onto the lunar surface, it'll tip the scale at seven pounds. The suit and the PLSS are a set. Whenever you leave the lunar module, you'll be wearing both."

Uzi nodded at the pressure suit. "Looks like we'll need help getting it on."

"It's a bit of a process. You start by putting on a diaper, which—"

"Wait—what?"

"The suit takes a long time to get into and out of. Last thing you want is to have to pee as soon as you finally get the thing on and the gloves attached." Kirmani lifted up a thin gray garment. "After the diaper you'll put on a layer of polypropylene underwear, followed by wool long johns that have tubes running through them to circulate cold water around your body to keep you cool. Next comes a G-suit, which is a giant compression stocking that inflates to keep the blood in your torso and brain. In zero or low gravity, your heart doesn't work very well."

"How much training time are we gonna get in these things?"

"Every minute we can spare. In a perfect world, your two colleagues would still be alive and getting ready to launch with Carson and Stroud. But this isn't a perfect world, so you two are it."

The person measuring DeSantos's hand turned it over and moved on to the palm.

"Tomorrow we'll be doing a simulation of zero-G and reduced-gravity atmospheres on NASA's DC-9 Weightless Wonder. Also known as the vomit comet. It's a modified cargo jet with an empty, padded fuselage."

"I know about it," DeSantos said. "They fly a parabola by climbing at a very steep angle. The pilot then sends us into a sharp dive." At that moment, anything and anyone inside the plane falls to the ground at the same rate, creating the sense of weightlessness. "I felt zero-G in my T-38 flight training."

"Not like this," Kirmani said. "The sensation's the same—you'll feel the blood rising in your chest and face—but in your training you were strapped into the jet's seat and it only lasted a couple of seconds. In space, you won't be belted down, so suddenly your feet won't be touching the ground and you'll be floating toward the ceiling. You'll need to learn how to balance and control your body, how to move and restrain yourselves in the zero-G environment. A little push can send you rocketing toward the opposite wall. And there's no up or down—you'll feel like you're upside down, as if the craft rolled 180 degrees. But in fact your body won't have moved at all."

Uzi lifted his brow. "Good thing we'll have some time to practice."

"You have to feel it to get the hang of it. When the time comes, I want you to *react* and not have to *think* about *how* to react."

11

OPSIG Situation Room
The Pentagon

After a delayed flight out of Cleveland, Vail and Rodman arrived at OPSIG headquarters at noon. Rodman briefed the other team members on what transpired with Alec Hayder while Vail checked in with the analyst who had been helping her locate the suspected mole.

Rodman walked in and sat down beside her. "Anything?"

Vail clicked and then highlighted a field in her Excel spreadsheet. "Finally got the list from Peabody while we were in Cleveland. It was beyond unmanageable, but we pared it back to 279 names. I looked at the profiles, evaluated access, motivation, connections or travel to red flagged international countries, looked at who was in debt . . . you know the drill." *Then again, he's never been a cop. Probably doesn't know the drill.*

"And?"

Vail leaned back in her chair. "I've narrowed it down to five. One's deceased, one's out on a long-term workers' comp from a failed hip surgery, one's been on maternity leave for six months because she's had complications. So that leaves two: Jason

Lansford and James Feith. If they turn out to be dead ends, we'll go back and loosen up those filters and start over."

"Of those two," Rodman said, "what does your gut say?"

"I've got some people working up Feith. So far nothing stands out. But Lansford holds a lot of promise."

"Because?"

"Both are software engineers who've worked on Orion. Neither has any connection to Alec Hayder. There were trips to Houston, but because of the Johnson Space Center and NBL, that's to be expected. Regardless, neither went there in the past nine months."

"That's it?"

Vail called up a photo of a couple in their late thirties. "Lansford's twin brother and sister-in-law live in China. And Lansford's made multiple trips to Beijing during the past couple of years. He was in danger of having his house foreclosed upon two years ago, but I'm not seeing any further notices from the bank. We still have some digging to do on that. Feith shows no connections whatsoever to any of our targets. No financial issues. And no international travel."

"NSA?"

"Putting together a dossier right now on both of them. But if Lansford's our guy, I doubt we're gonna find a smoking gun. That foreclosure situation might be our only indication of a sudden infusion of cash—and even that's circumstantial unless we can prove a direct line of payment from China to Lansford. But spies these days are careful."

"And they use encrypted comms."

"Which means NSA might not be very helpful," Vail said.

The sliding doors opened and Richard McNamara strode in. "Where are we?"

In the Pentagon, sir. "It's been tedious, but we're making our way through—"

"I need results, not excuses."

"We had to wait for NASA to get the list and then fly to Ohio to apprehend Alec Hay—"

"Sounds like another excuse."

Vail's jaw dropped. "I wasn't making excuses. I—" *Be smart. This guy is career military. You're not gonna win this argument. And he may be right.* "Yes sir. No more excuses."

"Results are all that count," McNamara said, firming his brow. "Am I being clear?"

"Yes sir."

"Then do you or do you not have someone to look at?"

"We do."

"Then what are you waiting for? Grab him up, get him in a room."

"Right," Rodman said. "We're on it."

Oops. Left out the warrant part. Probably because we'd never get one.

"Agent Vail."

Guess I've gotta work on my poker face.

McNamara stepped closer and sat on the edge of the desk. "I realize you've been a law enforcement officer all your life. And that affects how you approach your OPSIG duties. But we need to be on the same page here. We're not looking to build a legal case against the Chinese spy. It's better if we don't because it'd be embarrassing for China and at the moment, that's not in our best interests. It'd stoke an international crisis—on top of the one we're gonna come dangerously close to sparking. So the idea is to get the information we need. Quietly. We *must* assess the damage to our program, what the Chinese have gotten hold of, and take proper steps. Under the radar."

"If this is our guy," Vail said, "what happens after we get the information from him?"

"After that, we may cut him loose. Or not, depending on what he tells us. Do you understand?"

"I understand." *I understand I don't have a choice.*

"I've got Agent Zheng Wei on standby, ready to help out. He and a small team led by Agent Rodman will accompany you and pick up this guy—what's his name?"

"Jason Lansford."

"Zheng is in charge of the op to grab up this Lansford. So you'll follow his orders. Got it?"

He looked at Rodman for acknowledgment but did not need to say anything further.

"I get it," Vail said.

McNamara eyed her wearily. "Let's hope you do."

12

Falls Church, Virginia

The buzzer sounded in the study of Lukas DeSantos. He glanced at the television screens displaying closed circuit high definition video and saw several armed men dressed in black tactical gear at the front entrance to his palatial home.

They discharged high end submachine guns of some sort—MP7s from what he could tell—and his security guards returned fire. But they were outmanned and outgunned, and several difficult seconds later, his men were but dark heaps on the ground.

Jesus. What the hell is going on?

He glanced at the other set of monitors—showing the rear of his extensive property—as the same scenario played out there.

His mouth suddenly dry, he grabbed for his phone—and found the line dead. Dug out his mobile—no service.

"Of course," he said into the still air.

Whoever these guys were, they were professional, organized . . . and lethally efficient.

He had mere seconds to get to his safe room, a hardened chamber that could withstand reasonable intrusion attempts. He was a seasoned battlefield commander, career military—but the instant, massive adrenaline dump into his bloodstream sent his heart rate to dangerous levels.

As he made his way out of the study and through the walnut-paneled library, the lights went out. Because of his decades of training, he had anticipated this and was prepared. By the time he arrived at the door to the bunker, the backup generator had kicked in and restored power to the electronic keypad. He punched in the code and the magnetic lock released.

Lukas slid inside and closed the door behind him. He took a deep breath to settle his nerves, then placed his thumbprint over a sensor. A steel cabinet popped open, exposing a bevy of weapons. He set the MP5 submachine gun on the counter to his right, then took the Beretta 1301 tactical shotgun in his left hand and shoved a SIG 9-millimeter pistol in his waistband.

After activating the color LCD screens, which tapped directly into his security system, he watched as the men made their way into his home. He threw a switch and the generator powered down, maintaining electricity to only the safe room.

The cameras switched to infrared mode. Lukas tried to get an angle that would give him a clue as to who these men were—which might indicate who had sent them. He had plenty of enemies, those in foreign countries that had been on the losing end of a military offensive that he directed, high profile battlefield wins in Iraq and later Afghanistan that put his face on *Time* magazine. It was something he resisted, but ultimately agreed to, given his plans to retire and start his own defense contracting company. He knew the system and he had the contacts, political heft, and access to the massive funding to make it work.

And make it work he did. DeSantos Defense Industries was the fastest growing military contractor with a profit-to-earnings ratio more befitting a high-flying Silicon Valley tech company. When he took his company public two years ago, he pocketed

$750 million and retained control of the company. Not bad for six years of work.

But he also knew it made him even more of a target than he otherwise was—which was saying a lot.

No. Enemies were something Lukas DeSantos was not lacking.

It came with the territory, like tanks and missiles and fighter jets came with armed conflict.

Lukas watched the screens and saw the men make their way directly toward him.

That's when he realized he had made one error. And it was unfortunately a big one. He had guarded the plans for his bunker construction—but he had hired the job out to a local architectural firm. That was the mistake, because no matter how well he kept the security system blueprints under wraps, he had no control over that company's employees and computers. He thought it unlikely an enemy would know how to find out who designed and built the alarm, but sometimes the "unlikely" became reality. He played the odds as a four-star general, and it had served him well.

Not so much in this case, however.

The men stood at the door to his safe room—which was not feeling so safe about now.

He stepped back as far as he could get, the shotgun grasped firmly in both hands.

Nothing was impenetrable. No one was impervious to attack if an enemy wanted to get in badly enough. He knew this. And he was prepared.

But whoever was behind this was prepared too.

Lukas watched as they pulled something from a rucksack and appeared to be placing it on the wall.

An explosive.

Ten seconds later, the door blew and swung open, the reinforced hinges destroyed by steel-defeating charges.

"Down on the ground!" one of the ski-mask-clad men shouted.

Despite the darkness, Lukas made out half a dozen intruders. And based on what he had seen on the cameras, there were several more waiting somewhere else in his house . . . likely going through his papers and searching for his laptop. The hard drive was encrypted, so he doubted it would be of much use to them, but whoever was responsible for this knew what he was doing and had considerable resources behind him.

But Lukas was not going down without a fight. He fired his Beretta shotgun with a couple of enormous blasts. Two men recoiled and the rest withdrew.

Lukas grabbed the MP5 from the counter. Cordite hung in the air, smoke filling the small space. Then two men appeared in the opening, ballistic riot shields held out in front of them.

Lukas understood when it was time to fight and when it was time to submit. He had no clear exit route at the moment and he wanted to continue living out the rest of his life and, hopefully, find a way of reconciling with his son Hector and his wife Silvana. There was no longer a way to shoot himself out of this predicament.

"On the ground!" one of the men yelled again.

This time he did as instructed and kissed the industrial carpet, setting the MP5 down at his side.

"Who are you?"

"We're the guys who're now giving the orders, general."

Lukas thought he detected a slight accent, but it was subtle and he could not place it. Regardless, they knew who *he* was. No surprise there. They efficiently neutralized his guards and breached a high-end security system with ease. Whoever they were, he respected their skill and level of training.

"And I'm taking the orders," Lukas said. "What would you like me to do?"

"Go to sleep."

Something blunt and heavy struck Lukas in the back of the head. Searing pain erupted from his skull as everything went dark.

13

Dulles Technology Corridor
Reston, Virginia

Vail sat in the back of the Ford surveillance van with Rodman and Zheng Wei, an intense man of few words. Physically he reminded her of a friend, ATF agent Richard Prati: short in stature but imposing and built like a bulldozer.

While their colleagues continued sifting through the records of both suspects, the three of them had been camped in the parking lot of a large defense contractor, Aerospace Engineering, Jason Lansford's employer. They took a spot across, and a dozen yards away, from his late model Infiniti FX, waiting and observing.

The idea was to grab him up in an out of the way location where cameras, witnesses, and video cams were nonexistent. They had done this numerous times, mostly overseas, but the concept was the same: Lansford had to vanish without a trace of foul play. To do that effectively, it was best to wait until dark, when he was alone, and preferably on a low-traffic road. They had rigged his car with a kill switch, which would interrupt the flow of fuel into the carburetor and bring the vehicle to a halt wherever, and whenever, they wished.

"You think China's involved?" Vail asked.

Zheng pulled his eyes away from the LCD screen, which showed a wide-angle view of the parking lot, and looked at Vail. "My thoughts are unimportant. I was told that you felt Jason Lansford was worth questioning. That's all I'm concerned about."

"I'm looking for some background," Vail said. "Your name hasn't been Americanized, so I'm assuming you're originally from China."

"Correct assumption."

"Knowing the country as you do, is this something the government is capable of?"

"Capable of? Absolutely. Beyond that, I'd just be offering my opinion."

"That's what I'm asking for."

"Might as well answer her," Rodman said. "She's like a Boston terrier. Once she gets her teeth into something, it's tough to make her let go."

"I respect that." Zheng turned back to his screen. "Yes, this is something they would and could do. They've done things like this before, as I would imagine you're aware of."

"Actually, only superficially. I'm a behavioral analyst. I'm not in counterterrorism, and I don't investigate industrial espionage or international relations."

"All countries spy on one another. And industrial espionage is unfortunately a fact of doing business. But China takes it up a notch or two. Or three. So yes, it's worth looking at. I reviewed what you guys put together on Lansford and it's promising. You might be on to something."

"And you're not concerned about violating Lansford's civil rights?"

Zheng looked at Rodman, as if asking him to answer in his stead. He did not, so Zheng said, "China is a very proud country. Calling them out is deeply insulting. And the people resent it.

There's been a lot of tension the past few years because of the South China Sea, China's repeated cyberattacks on the US, and its growing military might—some of which it got from stolen US military technology."

"So if we built a case," Vail said, "arrested Lansford, and it became a huge media story, wouldn't they think twice about—"

"No. It'd only strain relations further. China would not take it well; they'd be insulted that we took such action, regardless of how reasonable it was. They would deny, deny, deny. It wouldn't make this guy talk and it wouldn't stop the government from spying on us."

"The president does not want another high profile incident with China," Rodman said. "So we do it this way. Quiet, under the radar. It also helps the US avoid another embarrassing episode of military property being stolen or hacked or leaked."

"There he is," Vail said, gesturing at the screen.

"An hour early." Rodman checked his watch. "This is not good."

Zheng leaned back in his chair. "Doing a snatch and grab in daylight is too risky."

Vail looked at Rodman, then Zheng. "But McNamara said he wants—"

"I know." Zheng continued watching the monitor as Lansford walked to his car and got in.

Rodman knocked on the wall abutting the passenger compartment. "Fire it up and follow, but at a safe distance."

"If he's going directly home for the evening," Vail said, "we're gonna have to change our approach."

Rodman pulled his seatbelt tight. "Like I said, this is not good."

LANSFORD DID NOT GO straight to his house. He stopped at a grocery store in a well-lit area then returned to his car and took side streets. The sunlight was waning, dusk not too far off.

"Another twenty minutes and we'll be able to take him," Rodman said.

Vail consulted her phone. "He's only . . . 1.2 miles from his house."

"Unless he's planning on making another stop," Rodman said, "we've gotta do this soon or—"

"Get ready to hit the kill switch," Zheng said to Rodman. "This road looks pretty secluded."

They were headed down a residential street with only a few homes and no people visible outside.

"Not a good idea," Vail said. "We're out in the open. It may look clear, but someone's bound to see us."

Rodman fingered the button on the remote. "Even if they catch our tag, the license plate won't show up in any database."

"I feel like we're desperate," Vail said, "and that's no way to run an op. We need to be smart about this. We can't delay it forever, but we can't screw it up, either. That could be a whole lot worse."

Zheng did not reply. Vail could not tell whether he agreed and did not want to acknowledge it or if he was merely ignoring her. But at that moment, Lansford pulled to a stop at the corner.

"Now," Zheng said. "Kill it."

"No!" Vail leaned closer to the surveillance screen. "Patrol car approaching. Block away."

"You kidding me?" Rodman said.

They watched as Lansford accelerated through the intersection and two streets later, hung a left onto a boulevard. The cops were now queued up behind their van.

"He's gonna take this street right to his house," Vail said, zooming in on her smartphone map.

"And that," Zheng said, "means Plan B."

VAIL, RODMAN, AND ZHENG SAT in their vehicle a block away from Jason Lansford's Herndon residence. The two-story home was gray with steel blue accents, a well-maintained structure built in the late seventies. It had an attached single-car garage—where Lansford's Infiniti was now parked. Strategically, there was decent spacing on both sides between neighboring homes and weak lighting in the area, which made their job marginally easier. In short, they should be able to operate without too much difficulty or prying eyes.

"I've got the floorplan," Vail said as she worked her laptop. "Zillow. Terrific for privacy."

"Privacy?" Rodman asked. "What the hell is that?"

Zheng grunted. "Speaking of which. Just heard from NSA. This is coming together nicely." He scrolled through the encrypted message. "Lansford's wife and kids are in Charlottesville, visiting her sister for a couple more days. She owns a winery. Hmm. Mostly reds."

"See if she'll drop by a bottle of Cabernet," Vail said. "We're gonna be here a few hours."

Zheng smirked.

"Just kidding. I never drink when I'm on the clock." *Except when I did. In Napa. Once. Or was it twice?* "So here's the floorplan." Vail swiveled the laptop to the left so both Rodman and Zheng could see. "Master is on the second floor, far right of the house."

They looked it over a minute then discussed their approach, which involved taking Lansford in the middle of the night. He had no alarm system, that much they knew from the permits, so they would make a stealth entry, inject him, bag him, and carry him out.

Rodman made a phone call and scheduled a helicopter with infrared sensors to do a flyby to confirm that Lansford was the sole occupant of the residence.

Twenty minutes later, they were notified the chopper was approaching. They were told to patch into the air unit's video feed and seconds later Vail, Rodman, and Zheng were watching as it hovered over the target house.

Vail leaned forward, studying the green-hued imagery. Because she was familiar with the home's layout she was able to roughly identify the rooms.

"How come I'm not seeing any hot spots?" she asked.

"Good question." Zheng got on the radio and confirmed that the helicopter was surveilling the correct address.

"Affirm," came the response.

"That does look like Lansford's house," Vail said, "judging by the layout."

"So why the hell's no one home?" Rodman asked, his gaze fixed on the screen. He keyed the mic. "Circle back in twenty and do another pass."

"Roger that."

"Could he have left and we didn't see him?"

Zheng's fingers played across his keyboard and he pulled up a map. "Car's in the garage."

Vail stole a look. "You put a tracking device on his car?"

"I did, when I installed the kill switch. Just in case."

"Then he's gotta be there," Vail said, "unless he went for a walk. Does he run?"

"No idea." Rodman pulled out his phone. "We're a little thin on intel, despite NSA's best efforts. We just haven't had enough time to gather a complete profile. Our kind, not your kind. I'm sending off a note to OPSIG, see if they can find out more about his habits. And I'll have them ping his cell."

Several minutes later, Rodman's phone vibrated. He answered, listened a second, then said, "You sure? How—" His shoulders rolled forward. "Got it."

Vail wiggled her fingers as he hung up. "What's the deal?"

"Phone's off. And we can't listen in through the mic because apparently he pulled the battery. A few handsets have that capability. And coincidentally—or not—he uses one of those models."

"So he's on to us," Zheng said.

"Not necessarily. According to his carrier logs, looks like he removes the battery every day after work."

Vail cocked her head. "Who does that?"

"Someone who doesn't want any chance of being tracked."

"Lansford's not a fugitive."

"But he might be a spy."

Vail started to object—she felt it was a generalization that might or might not be true. It was easy to fall into the pitfall of making the facts fit your suppositions rather than looking at the facts objectively and drawing well-reasoned conclusions.

But Zheng held up a hand. "Spies are paranoid shits by nature. And by necessity. I know. I used to be one."

The chopper returned, made another pass, and found the same result.

"Cleared to return to base," Zheng said, then tossed the radio down.

"How about we get closer, put eyes on the house?" Vail asked.

"We could do that, but if he *is* a spy, he'll be looking out for stuff like that. They're naturally paranoid, remember? For all we know, he saw us tailing him and fled."

Vail looked out into the darkening landscape. "Let's hope that's not the case. For now, I'd rather put it off for a day when we can pick our spot than take a chance on losing him forever." *Not sure how McNamara's gonna take a delay. But hey, it's not my call.*

"You agree?" Zheng was talking to Rodman, who nodded. "Fine. We'll camp out here for a few more hours, take turns walking by his house and doing a visual. If things don't look like they're in our favor, we'll be back at his office early tomorrow morning in a different van and do this all over again."

I told them we could use a bottle of Cabernet.

14

Astronaut Training
Vandenberg Air Force Base

Uzi and DeSantos had been working at breakneck speed. There was no more jesting, no more small talk, except at lunch and dinner—and sometimes even those short intervals were spent discussing the finer points of what they had learned during the day. Carson and Stroud were helpful, providing perspective and answering questions based on their own experiences during the past year and a half.

After their initial orientation to the Orion crew module, Uzi and DeSantos practiced various types of escape scenarios, including NASA's new launch abort system—designed to shoot them far and wide in an instant upon discovery of an impending catastrophe on the launch pad or shortly after liftoff.

Following lunch, they trained with Carson and Stroud for the first time, working on water-based exfil drills following splashdown.

Between them, Uzi and DeSantos would have made a complete astronaut: Uzi picked up the technical and scientific aspects of the mission and DeSantos was quicker with the strategic and pressure suit–related duties.

Uzi's first foray with the suit did not go as well as he had expected. The successive formfitting layers caused his movements to become more and more restricted. Finally, when they locked the helmet into place he had a bout of claustrophobia for the first time in his life.

He did his best to hide it—his face was, after all, not visible through the mirror-like glass. However, his blood pressure and pulse rate skyrocketed, his respiratory rate quickened to an unhealthy rate, and Kirmani ordered the helmet removed.

Although Uzi was embarrassed and felt concerned his reaction might threaten the mission, Kirmani reassured him that his response was normal and most astronauts experienced it. "But you better control it, and control it right now. Because we don't have time for you to get acclimated to it. You can either do this or you can't. Tell me now."

Uzi felt like slugging the man—if he could have controlled it, he would have—but hid his disdain and told Ridgid he would be fine.

His second attempt went better, and by the evening he had learned how to deal with the anxiety before it overtook him: he had them increase his oxygen flow rate, which helped calm him by lessening the body's autonomic response.

He suddenly understood what Karen Vail went through. Her claustrophobia was long-standing and not restricted to a pressure suit.

After dinner, Kirmani took them to the adjacent building where the Orion crew module mockup was housed. He stopped on the far side of the massive warehouse-like space in front of a rectangular machine that was the size of a large microwave oven.

"Either of you know what this is?"

"A 3D printer," Uzi said. "It's revolutionizing manufacturing."

"Gold star for you," Kirmani said.

Uzi looked at him. Was that a dig for his claustrophobic incident? He gets a gold star for answering correctly and redeeming himself?

"Never seen one," DeSantos said. "Don't quite understand why it's called a printer. What's it printing?"

"It uses a *somewhat* similar concept to the early HP and Canon inkjet printers, but instead of spraying ink, it lays down plastic or metal. Technical term is additive manufacturing. NASA has been working on 3D printing since the early 2000s. They started out making tools and replacement parts out of metal and ceramic powders, using lasers and computer-aided 3D CAD software.

"The idea is that you make items by printing layers on top of each other—additive—instead of the typical manufacturing process of carving something out of a block—subtractive. The parts produced in these 3D printers are identical to, and in some cases superior to, traditionally manufactured components."

"The advantages are obvious for spaceflight," Uzi said. "You can replace any broken part by using the printer and raw materials you bring with you—or, in some cases, use minerals from the planet you're visiting."

Kirmani was nodding.

Uzi wondered if he just earned another gold star.

"Point is," Kirmani said, "you don't have to bring a million spare parts with you—which is physically impossible. Remember what we talked about regarding mass? Every pound is accounted for, so this is a huge breakthrough in terms of the ability to colonize Mars. We've already used these printers on the space station. And the European Space Agency's propulsion engineering section has used 3D printing to build the extremely complex shapes and internal geometry required by rocket nozzles, combustion chambers, and showerhead injectors."

"I assume we'll be taking one of these with us?" Uzi asked.

"You will indeed."

15

Fairfax, Virginia

The cell phone was ringing. Vail heard it in her dream before her brain yanked her to consciousness. In the process of grabbing the Samsung, she accidentally pulled the charging cord from the device.

"Yeah," she said, too groggy to check the caller ID.

"Is that how you address the FBI director?"

Vail's eyes widened and she swung her feet over the edge of the bed. "Sir." She coughed, tried to shake the cobwebs. "Sorry."

"Are you awake?"

"I am now. I got to bed at four—"

"Good. Then I'll see you in my office in one hour."

An hour? What the hell time is it? Early. It's early. Glanced at the clock: 6:59 AM. "How about ninety minutes? Traffic—"

"This is not a negotiation."

"Um, okay. Right sir. Okay, I'll—"

"A car will be at your door in fifteen minutes. Be in it and be here by eight."

"Yes, will do." But she was talking to a dead line.

"Who was that?" Robby Hernandez, her fiancé, stepped into the bedroom as he knotted his tie. Their chocolate standard poodle, Hershey, jumped on the bed and gave Vail a big dog kiss on the cheek.

"No one important. FBI director."

"No one important." Robby laughed, but his smile faded immediately. "Are you working another OPSIG case?

"Can't say."

Robby turned back toward the bathroom. "You just did."

VAIL ARRIVED AT 7:59. She had managed to shower and dress but did not have time to dry her hair. At least she remembered her Glock and phone.

When Vail walked into Knox's office in the Hoover building, he was pacing in front of the seventh-story picture window. He did not turn to face her. "There's been a new development. A kidnapping."

Vail stood there waiting for him to elaborate. It was as if he wanted her to know—but did not want to tell her. "Who, sir?"

"Lukas DeSantos. Someone close to him contacted me directly. She reported him missing under suspicious circumstances."

So this is a brother? Father? Cousin? A son I don't know about?

"You're catching me at a disadvantage. Is Lukas—"

"Hector's father."

"And how could this person close to him contact you, the FBI director, directly? Do you know her?"

"I know Lukas DeSantos. Very well."

Um . . . okay . . . weird that Hector never mentioned that. "Do Lukas and Hector talk to each—"

"That's a story for another time. Right now, all you have to understand is that I've known Lukas for thirty years. He's a war hero, a protégé of General Schwartzkopf, another highly decorated—"

"Wait a minute. We're talking about *General* DeSantos?"

Knox stopped pacing and faced her. "Yes."

Vail worked that through her thoughts. "So for him to go missing, to have been kidnapped, if that's the case, is—"

"Disturbing. *Very* disturbing." He looked out the window into the distance. "He's due to receive the Presidential Medal of Freedom next week." He pressed a button on his keyboard and the large flatscreen on the wall lit up. "We received a proof of life video."

"Where'd it come from?"

"Support personnel found a USB drive on the steps to the Washington field office. Once they saw what was on it, they handed it over to an agent with the Joint Terrorism Task Force, Hoshi Ko. She works with Agent Uziel—"

"Yes sir. I know Hoshi."

"Ko recognized the general and gave it to her military liaison on the task force."

"Surveillance video show who dropped the flash drive?"

"Busy field office, lots of traffic. We watched it, but . . . no."

"Let's take a look."

Knox launched the video. "It's actually a gif file. Seconds long and automatically looping."

Vail saw a man on his knees, in clear contrition to his captors. His face was bruised, one eye swollen shut.

"He looks like shit," Knox said. He rapped his fist against the table. "Sons of bitches. We've gotta find him." He closed the file.

Vail eyed him a moment, trying to process everything. "Any metadata in the file?"

"Scrubbed."

"So these people are pros—or at least tech savvy."

Knox nodded but was clearly preoccupied.

"Are you thinking it's somehow related to the medal cerem— No. Operation Containment?"

"Hector is training for a mission that'll take him to the Moon on a black op to prevent China from getting its hands on a dangerous weapon that no one else has. And his father is suddenly reported missing. I think I can draw a straight line between those two statements."

"There's more to this." She wanted to add, "Isn't there?" but she knew the question would only be rhetorical.

Knox began pacing again. "Lukas DeSantos is a retired four-star general. He has a lot of enemies in the Middle East, but also two other countries whose leaders don't particularly care for him: China's president Jao Ping and Russia's president Yaroslav Pervak."

"And why is that?"

Knox stopped pacing and again turned to the window. It was unnerving staring at his back. Since she had gotten to know him—superficially, at least—she figured he probably wanted it that way. "They have unfinished business. And Lukas founded an immensely successful defense contracting outfit. DDI."

"I've heard of it. I had no idea."

"The official corporate name, which no one uses, is DeSantos Defense Industries." He spun around. "So we have something new to investigate. Where are you on the mole?"

"Going slower than we'd hoped."

"We need it to go faster."

So I've been told.

"Sir, what do you think they're after?"

"Not sure. Depends on who took him. But I doubt money is the motivator."

"Retribution then?"

"Can't rule it out."

"If it is related to Containment, I would think it's about leverage."

Knox's eyes narrowed. "If that's true, then it could be aimed at me. Because of my position, statements I've made about China's cyberattacks. China's been engaged in a widespread effort to acquire US military technology and classified information for several years. That stealth jet they now have—the Chengdu J-20—is a near-copy of our F-22 stealth fighter jet. They stole our F-22 and F-35 blueprints during a cyber breach in 2008. Not to mention industrial espionage—stealing the trade secrets of our companies, both here and those operating in China. Theft of American intellectual property has hit $1 trillion, so it's a big goddamn deal."

"I'm not plugged into the Bureau's efforts to stop the cyberattacks," Vail said. "But I've read some declassified briefings over the years."

"The Chinese government has been using this tech and information to help support its long-term military and commercial development. It's part of China's—and Russia's—national policy to identify and steal sensitive US technology, which they need for their country's development. When a large US tech firm enters the Chinese market, they're usually forced to turn over technology in exchange for the ability to set up shop in China. We're talking 2 billion consumers, so the companies don't see a choice. They give the Chinese previous-generation technology, but China's infrastructure has matured to the point where they're able to rapidly build on that foundation and turn out products that compete with, or surpass, their US counterparts. It's like making a deal with the devil. So to speak."

"And you've testified before Congress on this."

"More than once." Knox paused. "I've been the administration's most outspoken critic of the ransom companies have to pay for the right to operate in China. I've also publicly called out the Chinese for their state-run cyberattacks on US institutions—government databases and corporate networks."

"I'm told China takes such public spankings very personally."

"Yes they do." He harrumphed. "Their ambassador let the secretary of state know just how pissed they were. So Lukas's snatching could be a way of sending me a message. I'm sure their intelligence network knows all about my relationship with him."

"One possibility. Yes sir." Vail folded her arms. "But think like an interested party. Consider the context of what's going on. As you said, there's a valuable element on the Moon that'd give a foreign power a huge tactical advantage; Hector's chosen for a mission to prevent that from happening; and we're pretty sure a mole has been working for, or with, an actor or group of actors who appear to be a key contractor with access to the spacecraft that's delivering Hector to the Moon. So we have to draw that line you mentioned before. And put all resources behind the most logical explanation."

Knox pondered that. "Get over to Lukas DeSantos's house and look around. I've got men stationed there to prevent entry. You'll join a forensic team that's been onsite for a few hours. Help them figure out what went down."

"Yes sir."

"You asked me what I thought the motive was. What do you think?"

Vail leaned both hands on the back of the chair that stood in front of her. "I think Containment is the key. They take Lukas, let Hector know they've kidnapped his father, and the ransom is . . . leveraging him to allow them to gain access to the caesarium. Or to make him do something to jeopardize the mission."

"They could be thinking along those lines."

"They don't know Hector like we do. And we know Hector can't be bought."

"Yes . . ." Knox began pacing again and fell silent for a long moment. "Under normal conditions, I'd agree. Hector is as dedicated and honest as they come. But we're talking about his flesh and blood. His father. A national hero. Even if Hector can compartmentalize that and not let the personal aspect of this affect his performance, it's human nature to do the opposite." Knox stopped and turned to

Vail. "He can't know. I don't want Hector thinking about his father. He needs to be focused on his mission, which is tough enough. And without him knowing, there's no leverage. Are we clear?"

I hate this. Pitting me against my friend. "Clear." Vail curled a lock of red hair behind her right ear. "So let's take this a step further. Hector's at Vandenberg, an Air Force base. About as secure a place as there can be. But if they could find a way in, they'd go for the weak point. A way to communicate with him."

"We've restricted internet and phone access," Knox said. "They're dark."

"Then I'd look at insiders, people who can get a message to him."

Knox nodded. "Good, yes. We'll take appropriate measures. Cameras, guards throughout all areas where they're training. It's unlikely for them to be able to gain access to a secured facility like that, but . . ."

But it happened a few years ago in the run-up to the US election. And no one knew that better than Douglas Knox.

"I'll get with the SecDef. They have procedures in place to lock the facility down."

"There's another way to play this, sir." She could not shake the sense she was betraying her friend.

"Don't keep it a secret, Agent Vail. That's why you're here."

"We let them make the attempt to contact Hector, but in a way they don't actually get through to him."

Knox began to pace, absorbing her comment. "There's risk involved in that—if they succeed, that could be problematic. It could disqualify Hector from the op, and I consider him key to this mission. We're training two others as backup, but . . . losing Hector would be significant."

"But the payoff could be big on the other end."

"Convince me." Knox stopped and turned to face her. "What do you have in mind?"

"Use covert means of watching over him. Cameras, strategically placed, separate from Vandenberg's normal security apparatus. In case our bad actors try to use someone who knows about Vandy's security measures, or has access to them in some way. It doesn't have to be too elaborate, but we could use traditional CIA methods for covert surveillance. If an attempt is made to contact Hector, we get that person in a room—and he or she could lead us to whoever's behind this."

"Unless they're a compartmentalized cell."

Vail cocked her head. "That would make it a lot more difficult. It'd slow us down considerably, maybe lock us out completely. But . . . not necessarily."

Knox shoved his hands in his suit pockets and stood there for a moment, then said, "Thanks for your input. I'll take it under advisement." Knox looked off at the blank wall to his left. There was nothing to see, but it garnered his attention. "Because of your investigative skills, I want you involved in locating Lukas. I'd rather keep this within OPSIG. We don't know where this will lead and it could open some cans we don't want opened."

"If you do bring in people from outside the team, it's best if you keep the group small. And select."

"And controllable." He nodded then said, "Leave your Bureau phone here. I'll let your unit chief and ASAC know you'll be incommunicado for a while."

That'll go over real well.

"By the time you get to your car Lukas's address will be securely messaged to your OPSIG phone."

ON HER WAY DOWN TO THE PARKING GARAGE, she called Rodman and told him she was leaving a meeting with the director and was on her way to investigate something that might or might not be related to their case. She would join them in about two hours.

"At the moment, we're in a holding pattern. Our target did not show up to work today. We're looking into it, but that can't be good."

"Don't jump to conclusions just yet," Vail said as she pulled out her keys. "There could be other explanations."

"Let's hope you're right."

"Keep me posted."

She made good time to the address in Falls Church. But she was not prepared for what she encountered. She knew the area was exclusive and one of the wealthiest in the District, but this exceeded her expectations. As she drove along the winding, tree-lined road that led to the front of the residence, she estimated that the property covered several acres. *Not a house. Not a mansion. An estate.*

Vail checked in with the second layer of OPSIG personnel, who informed her that the forensic team was in the safe room. She slipped booties on and entered the large, brown slate-faced building. It was four stories tall and seemed to stretch fifty yards in both directions.

As she walked inside, she realized she had calmed considerably. She was in her environment now, standard police/detective work, possibly even some criminal investigative analysis. No covert ops with noms de plume, fake identification, and cover stories.

Vail checked in with the crime scene personnel and proceeded to do a walk-through before going over particulars with them. She wanted to form her own opinion without bias.

After spending thirty minutes outside walking the grounds to get a feel for the scope and sophistication of the attack, Vail traversed the first floor to evaluate the clues left behind by the intruders, including muddy boot tracks. By the time she rejoined the forensic team, she felt fairly confident of what had gone down.

Vail stepped back into the safe room and caught the attention of the lead technician. "Let me run my theory by you. Tell me if

I've got something wrong, something that doesn't jibe with the facts."

"Shoot."

"Armed assault. Several men overpowered the general's security personnel with a combination clandestine and brute force attack, then made their way into the house and to the safe room. Judging by the straight path that they took from the entrance to where Lukas was hiding, they must've had detailed knowledge of the estate. Access to the blueprints of the residence as well as the nuances of the bunker. Or it was an inside job.

"They got him to open the door—not an easy thing to do with a decorated general. But he tried to fight his way out." She gestured at the blood and the walls, which were pocked with bullet holes and embedded rounds. "He ultimately surrendered, either figuring the fight was over or he had enough confidence in his abilities to think he'd find a way out, a leverage point, later. At that point, submitting to them had more potential for survival than eating a pound of lead." She stopped and eyed the technician. "How'd I do?"

The man nodded. "Yeah, that looks consistent with what we're finding here."

"And judging by the drag marks in the blood, the general's shots did some damage and they had to help their fallen men out of the house."

The technician bobbed his head. "There's a small blood trail leading out the back. So I'm not sure I can say how bad the gunshot wounds were. Oh—there's a closed circuit security system installed. Cameras all over the property. But the hard drive that stored the footage is missing."

"Missing?"

"Removed." He gestured at a panel on the wall of the safe room. "These people knew what they were doing. I think you're right, they had to have had the blueprints, or some other kind of insider knowledge. I guess it's possible they got the general to tell them where the footage was being recorded, but I can't imagine him giving that to them."

"Agreed. Plus it sure looks like they made a bee line to the bunker. Nothing disturbed along the way. Judging by the boot marks and tracked-in soil, they marched in and right to the door. And the general knew to run to the room because he saw them on the cameras. Or one of his men warned him."

Vail took out a pen and wrote down her OPSIG cell number—no Bureau business cards here. "Call me if you find anything unusual, anything that contradicts what we just discussed."

"Will do."

Vail left the premises, headed to her meet with Rodman and Zheng. But by the time she reached her car, Zheng told her that there was a change in plans.

VAIL MET RODMAN AND ZHENG at her house, where she picked up her go-bag. They left her car in the garage and drove to Andrews Air Force Base for a flight to New York City.

With some circumferential questioning by an OPSIG operative posing as an agent with the FBI cyber division, the Aerospace Engineering human resources director disclosed, without realizing it, that Jason Lansford had been dispatched to their Manhattan office for a meeting with a potential customer, Space Launch Consortium, which wanted to hire them to write code for their robotic lander's operating system. The consortium had raised $50 million in funding and wanted to enter the Google Lunar XPRIZE, which could net them another $20 million.

"That explains why he disappeared from his house," Zheng said. "We checked for an Uber or Lyft account, but it doesn't look like he's got one. Either a friend or a neighbor took him to the airport or he had a car pick him up."

Vail felt the pull of the plane as it went wheels up. Two hours later, they arrived at the New York City offices of Aerospace Engineering, a sleek all-glass building on Park Avenue South. The logo, representing a planet and a rocket circumnavigating it with a vapor trail behind it, was visually striking. High profile location, high profile logo on a massive sign mounted where passersby could not help but see it.

They evaluated the physical premises—which they had previewed on Google Maps during the flight to DC—and it presented no surprises. Where proprietary secrets and billion dollar developmental contracts were concerned, security would be tight. The lobby incorporated physical barriers, armed guards, video technology, and biometrics. Trying to enter on a ruse would likely prove unsuccessful.

"According to Link," Rodman said, "Lansford's in meetings all day. We'll have to grab him up at his hotel once he's asleep. The company uses the Grand Hyatt on Forty-Second for out of town employees. Link found his booking."

After arriving at the Hyatt and staking out the building, they constructed a plan of action and observed customer flow and staff procedures.

Of prime importance was determining which room Lansford had booked and gaining key card access. He had already checked in, which provided an opportunity. Posing as Lansford, Rodman asked the bellman—Miguel according to his gold nametag—to deliver his suitcase to the room. The bag was nothing fancy, just a basic black roller Vail had purchased at a nearby storefront and stuffed with tourist sweatshirts and knickknacks.

Rodman checked his watch, expressed surprise it had gotten so late, and said he had a meeting in ten minutes. After palming Miguel a crisp twenty, he backed away as the bellman assured him he would take care of it.

◆ ◆ ◆

VAIL, WHO WAS OBSERVING THE TRANSACTION from across the large, open lobby, followed Miguel into the elevator and up to the twenty-second floor. She took note of the room he entered and kept walking, then took the stairs down.

To avoid attracting attention, Vail parked herself at various locations around the hotel with a laptop and a club soda. Rodman and Zheng came and went at different times, moving with the flow of patrons. They rode the elevators, then disappeared into Grand Central before repeating the process.

A little after nine o'clock, Lansford entered the hotel with two individuals, whom Vail identified as colleagues from Aerospace Engineering's New York office. They sat in the bar and drank for another two hours. He then bid the two men goodnight and retired to his room.

Vail called Rodman and Zheng. "He went up."

"Give it ninety minutes, then check it out."

She hung up. Once they were certain Lansford had shut off his light and fallen asleep, they would go to work.

VAIL WALKED TO THE END OF THE CORRIDOR and called Rodman. "All's quiet. Last time I checked the TV was on. He was watching some late night talk show. Went by again twenty-five minutes ago. It's off. Should be in dreamland by now."

"Copy that. We'll give it another thirty to be sure."

When the elevator doors parted and Rodman and Zheng exited, they were wearing different outfits from what they had on earlier in the evening. Rodman had a brimmed hat pulled low and Zheng a Knicks ball cap.

"No security cameras I can see," Vail said, remaining down the hall as the two men passed her en route to Lansford's room. "I think we're good."

"At two in the morning, it's gonna be fairly quiet on the floor."

"Which means you guys have to be quiet when you get into his room."

"No worries," Rodman said in a low voice. "This isn't our first abduction."

Did he have to say that? Jesus.

"Remember," Zheng said. "Any problems, three quick knocks on the door."

"I remember."

"Good." Zheng elbowed Rodman and they headed down the hallway toward Lansford's room.

RODMAN REMOVED THE TINY RFID CARD READER he had placed on Lansford's room door earlier in the day. There was a bit of a risk it would be discovered, but the "skimmer" was constructed to blend in with the most commonly used hotel room doorknob hardware, so the chances of discovery were minimal. He then called guest services and asked for an extra blanket and pillow to be delivered to the room, forcing the staff to use—and thus duplicate—the card's digital contents.

Rodman and Zheng replaced their hats with ski masks and moved into place outside the door.

They entered the room and in a few quick strides were alongside Lansford's bed. There was a woman next to him, sleeping in his arms.

She would need to be dealt with in a way to give them time to get far enough away before law enforcement was notified. Either way, short of killing her, which they preferred not to do, this was an unwelcome complication.

Zheng emptied the syringe into Lansford before the man could thrash too heavily—though his movement was enough to wake the woman. Her eyes bulged and she opened her mouth to scream.

But Rodman's large, gloved hand clamped down across her lips and muffled the cry.

It was then that he realized they had a major problem.

The man Zheng had just injected was not Jason Lansford.

16

Undisclosed Location

Lukas DeSantos awoke in the back of a van, hogtied and on his stomach. He had no idea what time it was—or even what day. The only thing he could determine was that they were traveling on some kind of secondary road that was rough and pocked with potholes.

And there were three masked men in the back with him.

"Look who's awake," one of them said.

Lukas's head ached and he still felt drowsy. "What do you people want?"

"We want you to shut up. We're not interested in conversation."

He tried to roll onto his side but he was sore—his back, his legs, his face . . . everything hurt.

"I can get you money, if that's what you want. Give me a phone and I'll have it wired right into your accounts."

They did not reply.

Lukas knew he had to get them talking. The more he could learn from them the more information he would have, information that could eventually tell him who he was dealing with, what they wanted—and if they intended to let him live.

"Weapons? You want handguns, rifles? What?"

No answer.

He craned his neck as far as he could to the left. “You guys intending to kill me?”

“Depends,” the closest one said.

“On what?”

“Whether or not you stop talking.”

“Do you know who I am?” he asked, pressing ahead.

There was no way one of these “soldiers” was going to kill him. A larger plan existed—which no doubt relied on him remaining alive, at least in the short term. He just had to figure out what it was.

“We know who you are.”

“I’ve led men into battle. I’ve faced down Taliban warlords. Iraqi commanders. Islamic terrorists who wanted nothing better than to put a bullet in my brain or cut off my head. I served to defend our country. For you. For your families. For your freedom. Doesn’t that matter to you?”

“It matters sir. But you also know it’s important to follow orders. And that’s what we’re doing right now.”

“Sometimes you have to question those orders if you know they’re blatantly wrong.”

“Really sir? I happen to know you never told that to any of the troops under your command.”

Was this one of my men?

“Son, I can tell you served. Ask yourself this: how can this possibly be helping your country? Think of the damage it’ll do if I’m kil—”

“I told you to shut up!”

Something hard struck his skull, his head bounced against the van floor . . . and once again, everything went black.

17

Grand Hyatt
Floor 22
New York City

Shit!" Rodman said, doing his best to cover the woman's mouth and simultaneously keep her body planted firmly against the mattress. "Give me something to tie her up."

Zheng shoved the man's body aside and ripped off the pillowcase.

While Zheng held her down, Rodman wrapped the material around the woman's face, forcing open the jaw and wedging it in her mouth. Rodman grabbed another and tied it around her eyes. "Get her ring. And his wallet."

Rodman pushed his thigh and leg against her body while Zheng pulled an emerald-cut diamond off her finger, found the man's the wallet, pocketed the cash, and removed the driver's license.

"Bedsheet."

Zheng ripped it off the mattress and tied the woman's legs. They set her on the desk chair and fastened her limbs to the wheelbase and armrests.

Three knocks on the door.

Fuck! Rodman was not sure if he said it aloud, but he rushed to the front of the room and let Vail in. He told her to be quiet—but she saw the woman in the chair—and gave him a look: "What the hell's going on?"

He leaned into her ear. "Not Lansford. We screwed up. We've gotta get out of here. We'll take the stairs. You take the elevator."

Rodman nodded at Zheng, who bent over in front of the woman.

"We're gonna leave now. Don't make a sound. We got what we came for. No one's gonna get hurt—unless you scream. Understand?"

She nodded.

"No sounds for fifteen minutes. Understand?"

Again, she indicated agreement.

"We'll be listening. You call for help sooner than that, we know where you live." He held up the driver's license. She nodded vigorously.

They quietly left the room and pulled the door closed then jogged down the hall. Vail pressed the elevator button as her colleagues entered the stairwell.

Forty-five minutes later they rendezvoused back at their car, which was parked a block from Bryant Park.

"Now what the hell do we do?" Vail asked as she turned over the engine.

"We get some sleep. And tomorrow we try again."

"How?" Vail asked. "How'd we get it wrong? We had his room number."

"We got it earlier in the day. He must've changed rooms. Maybe he didn't like it. Or the heater broke. Or he's not a smoker and the place reeked. Take your pick. All that matters is that the NYPD's gonna be alerted. Hopefully they'll think it's a robbery."

Vail snorted. "How many robberies do you think involve an injection of tranquilizer? Hopefully this guy is somebody, a public figure of some kind. That'll keep the detectives busy trying to figure out who has motive." She turned left on West Forty-Third Street.

"Hopefully we weren't caught on camera," Zheng said.

"We were," Vail said. "Somewhere. But unless they're looking for us, I don't see how that'll lead to anything. This is New York City. Always people on the streets, no matter what the hour is. Especially around Grand Central."

"For what it's worth, I sent the guy's name and address off to OPSIG," Zheng said, pocketing his phone. "Maybe they can do a little magic to cover our tracks."

"Our people will be monitoring the NYPD," Rodman said. "If anything weird comes up about a robbery at the Grand Hyatt, they'll deal with it. Somehow."

THE FOLLOWING MORNING, while en route to Aerospace Engineering, Rodman took a phone call from Dykstra at the Pentagon.

"Looks like Lansford will be joining their chief executive officer, Bill Lastings, and chief technology officer, Scott Durn, at Citi Field for a Mets game tonight."

Vail laughed. "I grew up a Mets fan."

"And now?" Rodman asked.

"Still a Mets fan. What can I say, I'm a masochist."

"And the Nats?"

"Nats fan too. Except when they play the Mets—which is way too often."

"I have a hard time with baseball," Zheng said. "Too slow."

"That's because you have ADHD," Rodman said.

"No, it's because I can't sit still for three minutes waiting for the pitcher to adjust his hat, spit on the mound, go through all his superstitious gyrations just to get ready to throw his next pitch. I lose interest. My mind starts to wander to other things."

"Like I said," Rodman said with a laugh.

Vail found a parking spot and fed the meter.

"Citi Field is a major sports venue," Vail said. "The Mets are competitive these days, so they fill the stands—at least 35,000 people, if not more. Not exactly an optimal place to make a covert move on someone. In fact, the words 'covert' and 'sports stadium' don't go together."

"You got another idea?" Zheng asked. "I'm open to suggestions."

Rodman looked up at the skyscraper. "We don't even know if he's in this building. He could be at a meeting five miles away."

Vail thought a moment. "Got an idea. Meet you back here in an hour, ninety minutes at the outside."

"Where you going?" Zheng asked.

"Checking out my idea."

Vail hopped the subway and took it uptown to the Lower Manhattan Security Initiative's headquarters, the brain of the city's Domain Awareness System. A marriage of software and hardware designed jointly by the NYPD and Microsoft, it was the ultimate crime-fighting tool that utilized a several thousand-strong network of closed circuit cameras, radiation sensors, audio microphones, license plate readers, and nuclear detectors. Deployed all over the city on officers' utility belts, trucks, boats, helicopters, and police cruisers, the devices took air samples, used video with facial recognition and audio to find problems—or to help locate a perpetrator if a crime had been committed.

One of the chief operators of the system—Vail knew him only by his first name, Isamu—was a trim man who spoke fast and worked his keyboard faster. Vail wondered about his name, as he did not look Japanese.

Vail used her faux Department of Defense identification to get Isamu to the security window. He saw her and did a double-take, then had her buzzed in.

"Department of Defense? I thought you were with—"

"Still am," Vail said. "Long story. And even if I had the time, I couldn't tell you."

He gave her a sideways glance as he led her back to his ops center. "Okay. That's weird. But whatever." After a few more steps, he said, "Undercover?"

"Yes, you could say that. So you haven't seen me today."

"Right, sure. And what can I help you find?"

"Not what. Who. Name's Jason Lansford." Vail gave him a photo she had gotten from the DMV records and another they had obtained from his LinkedIn page. It looked a lot more recent than the one on his driver's license.

"Any idea where he might've been at any point in the day?" Isamu asked as he fell into his ergonomic chair at a workstation that faced large wall-size displays.

"Matter of fact, yeah. Not for sure, but probably." Vail gave him the address of Aerospace Engineering and approximate times to check.

"So how'd you get the Japanese name?"

"During World War II," Isamu said as his fingers danced across the keys, "my dad was stationed in Tokyo and met my mom. I was named after her grandfather, who was MIA at the end of the war."

They were interrupted by a beep from Isamu's computer.

"Got him! Eight-eleven. Entered the Aerospace Engineering building. I can track him into the elevator and . . . that's where I lose him. Give me a minute to see if he leaves."

"I knew you'd be able to help."

"You knew, huh?"

"I hoped."

"More like it." He laughed. "Oh, there *you* are. With two other guys." He leaned closer and looked across the room at the screen. "You're undercover, eh?"

"Save it," Vail said. "Just tell me if Lansford left the building."

A couple minutes later, Isamu sat back. "He did leave, about . . . eleven minutes before you arrived. Took an Uber cross town to this address." He jotted it down on a pad and handed it to Vail.

"Grand Central Station?"

Isamu grinned conspiratorially. "Maybe he went to the Tumi store because he needed a new suitcase. Or he bought a deli sandwich from Mendy's."

Back to his hotel room? Or maybe he took a train somewhere.

"Did he leave Grand Central?"

"You know, I have real work to do," Isamu said.

"I'll get the violin out of my car. Oh, wait. I took the subway."

Isamu laughed. "Give me a minute, I'll let you know if facial rec picks him up leaving the premises." He moved a joystick and scanned video in rapid fast forward mode—but the computer beeped again and he froze. "Got it. He did, indeed, leave. Three minutes ago."

"Headed?"

"North on Forty-Second. And . . . then he caught a cab."

"This guy is killing me."

"You look quite healthy to me. Very healthy."

The comment jarred Vail's attention. "Watch those hormones, Isamu." She gestured at his ring. "You're married."

"Yeah, so? I'm not dead."

"Keep looking at me like that and you will be." Vail straightened up. "Let me know where he goes. And if you can figure out what he did while in Grand Central, that'd help too. It's important." She pulled out a pen and jotted the number down on a pad. "When you're done, eat this piece of paper."

"Eat it?"

"Shredding it works too."

Isamu hesitated a moment, then said, "For you, anything."

Vail rolled her eyes. "Good seeing you again, Isamu. Until next time."

VAIL MET RODMAN AND ZHENG near the entrance to Aerospace Engineering thirty minutes later. She explained where she had gone and the capabilities of the Domain Awareness System. Rodman knew about it, but Zheng did not.

"Anything?" Rodman asked.

"Yeah. He's not here. He went to Grand Central and then caught a cab."

"Back to Grand Central?" Rodman asked.

"He needed a new Tumi suitcase."

"What?"

"No idea what he was doing there," Vail said. "Could've been having lunch in the food court."

Vail's phone buzzed with a text from Isamu:

reviewed gc cams

he bought a tumi ;-0

actually he met a woman

in front of apple store

no hits in system

sending you a screengrab

"Hmm. So he apparently met a woman at Grand Central."

"Do we have an ID?" Zheng asked.

"Photo's coming through but she's not on any watch list. Maybe Dykstra can get something not available to the NYPD or listed in federal databases. Could be completely meaningless. Business associate. Friend who lives in New York."

"Or another spy," Zheng said. "His handler."

"You're right. We can't deal in possibilities without facts." Vail became aware of two men who were eyeing her a couple dozen yards away. "I think we should move. We're attracting attention staying here so long."

"You're the one attracting attention," Zheng said. "That red hair of yours."

Yeah, that's it. "Then again, we are a bit of an odd trio: a red-headed Caucasian woman, a huge black dude, and a short, stocky Chinese guy."

"Hey, New York's a melting pot," Rodman said as they made their way over to their car.

"We have tickets to the game tonight?" Vail asked.

Rodman nodded as they reached the vehicle, casually keeping watch over the two men, who were now over a block away. "We do."

"We know where Lansford's going to be. Let's focus on that. Check the place out, try to determine where he's sitting and how we're going to take him."

"I agree." Zheng climbed behind the wheel and cranked the engine. "We've got time to plan it right. Let's use that to our advantage."

18

Vandenberg Air Force Base

Eisenbach walked into the multimedia room and took a seat next to Kirmani.

"Where are they?"

"Headed to rover training in the desert," Kirmani said. "What'd you find?"

Eisenbach gestured at the man seated to his right. "Play it."

They turned to the screen, where a wide-angle view showed the corridor leading to the bedroom shared by DeSantos and Uzi. A broad figure stepped into the frame, filmed from behind.

"Well that's super helpful," Kirmani said. "How about the reverse angle when he comes out of their room?"

The technician hit a button and the film fast-forwarded a few seconds to the door opening. He played it at normal speed as the man stepped through, walking toward them.

"He's turning his head," Eisenbach said, "shielding his face from the cameras."

"Where he *thinks* the cameras are—where the base cameras are. Smart move putting them in the opposite location. But . . . that hat."

A deep shadow created by the bill of a baseball cap obscured the man's features, rendering an identification near impossible.

"I'll see if our guys can take that frame and brighten it enough so we can get an ID."

"Even if you can't, analyze his gait, his clothing. Did you check for prints?"

"Couldn't," Eisenbach said. "The black powder would've made a mess and there was no time to clean it up before Hector got back. They dusted the envelope and paper but there was nothing."

Kirmani leaned in close and pointed to the man's shoes. "And check that out too."

"What do you see?"

"When I was growing up, I worked as a busboy in my uncle's restaurant. They used rock salt on the kitchen floor to absorb the liquid from the dish washers, who sprayed water all over the goddamn place. The salt kept people from slipping on the wet concrete but I hated it because it stuck to my shoes and caked up around the edges of the sole."

"So you think that's what we're seeing there?"

"Sure looks like it. Check it out. And compare the time code on the video with what the kitchen staff was doing at that time."

Eisenbach nodded. "Then we'll see who doesn't have an alibi."

Kirmani straightened up. "I'm pulling everyone off kitchen duty. Just in case I'm right. We'll keep them confined till we know who's involved. We can't have them poisoning our crew."

"They're probably safe for the moment," Eisenbach said. "They left Hector the note for a reason. He's of no use to them dead."

Kirmani looked at the frozen onscreen image. "I'm not taking any chances."

19

Citi Field
Flushing, New York

Vail entered the stadium fifteen minutes before Rodman, who had followed Zheng inside. People with business dinners at the upscale Porsche Grille, located beyond the left field wall and featuring a stories-high wall of glass, came early for a comfortable meal. Vail was hoping that Lansford would fall into that category.

"I tried to case the Porsche Grille but it's not open yet," Rodman said via cell phone to Vail and Zheng. "Might be a place where Lansford and the execs would eat."

"Still nothing on the woman he met in Grand Central," Vail said. "They're doing a general population search, which will take longer. There are what, 9 million in the city?"

"I'm sure they're being smart about it," Zheng said. "Half are men and another 20 percent are minorities, another chunk are brunette and—"

"Do we have a ping on his cell phone yet?" Rodman asked.

"No. But if he's on the company clock, I have to think he's going to turn it on soon. I'm surprised he's kept it off this long."

"Unless he swapped it out for another number. If he slipped in a new SIM card, we'd never know."

"But then the number would change. Not saying it's impossible, but he'd have to give his company a good reason."

"A guy like that could think of several," Zheng said. "Believe me."

"Because *you* could?" Vail asked.

"Could. And did."

"They're going to let me know as soon as he turns it on." Vail walked along the Shea Bridge and glanced left at the field.

"And if he never turns it on," Rodman said, "how about you get your buddy to use the Domain Awareness System, track him down that way?"

"He actually works a normal job, so he's long gone for the day. And I doubt the NYPD has cameras and sensors inside Citi Field." Her phone started rumbling in her hand. "Call you back. It's the director."

Vail switched to Knox and immediately informed him they were not on a secure line.

"Understood. Something you need to be aware of. You're going to see some breaking news very shortly that a certain person has been reported missing."

"Reported missing by whom?"

"Doesn't matter. This is a problem no matter who or where it came from."

"Sir, the media won't know what to do with it because they don't understand the connections."

"That won't last long. They know who he is, a national hero. He's been in the news because of the medal ceremony in a few days. And as soon as the press realizes this is more than just a missing persons case—which is bad enough—"

"Our response should be that the—that you're looking into it. At the moment it's nothing more than a missing persons case. There are no known motives at present and no reason for us to believe it's anything more than that."

"You don't think his captors will push the envelope?"

"Think of their motive, sir. They want to make sure our friend hears his father is missing. He'll know what's going on. He won't need the media to spell it out."

"What if we plant a false story? He's on a trip overseas, can't be disclosed because of his previous military career."

"We could piss off his . . . hosts," Vail said. "Like sticking our thumbs in their eyes. They could release a video of him there. We don't know what they've done to him, what stuff they've got on him. Either way, we shouldn't underestimate them."

"We'd just deny it, call it a fake. No way my friend would cooperate with that kind of dog and pony show."

Vail stopped and turned to face the field. "If this were a court of law, it'd be sufficient. But this is the court of public opinion. An image would be implanted in the public's mind. Even if we claim it was fake footage, they couldn't unsee it. It's like instructing a jury not to pay attention to what they just heard. It's not possible."

"Fine," Knox said, frustration evident in his voice. "I hear you."

"I'll keep you posted on what we're doing here. I hope to have something in the next couple of hours."

"I'm gonna hold you to that."

20

FBI HEADQUARTERS
WASHINGTON, DC

Douglas Knox took the phone call from Secretary McNamara in his office.

Knox switched to a private, secure line and McNamara proceeded to lay out what they had just discovered in southern California.

"A note in Hector's bed, under his top sheet."

Knox began pacing behind his desk. "What kind of note? What'd it say?"

"We've got your father. We need to communicate with you. Write down the best way to do this and stick it in the envelope. Leave it in your bed. We'll get it."

"And Hector has not seen it?"

"No. Those cameras Vail suggested tipped us off to an entry into their room at 3:10 PM. Hector's in training all day."

"You had Klaus intercept it, I take it."

"Yes. He immediately reviewed the digital file and they think they've got an idea who left it."

Knox stopped in front of his window. "Who?"

"He didn't say. Until he makes a positive ID he wanted to keep it close to the vest."

Knox rubbed his right temple, where a pulsing headache was beginning to gnaw at him. “Have your men noted any unusual behavior or unauthorized contact with Hector?”

“Nothing,” McNamara said. “I think our system worked. Hector’s doing his thing and according to Klaus, things are progressing well, more or less on schedule. They’ve picked everything up exceptionally fast.”

“Overall assessment?”

There was a long pause. “I have confidence in our men. Carson and Stroud are ready. Hector and Uzi will be fine in their supporting roles. I don’t want them piloting the spacecraft or trying to land the damn thing, but that’s not why they’re here. If we find ourselves in that situation, we’ve got a problem.”

“I wish we had more time to prep them.”

“The Chinese have pushed our hand. Just know that there’s risk in sending up *four* highly seasoned, highly trained astronauts. So keep it in perspective.”

“I don’t want perspective. We need results.”

“I know it. I think we’ll be okay, Douglas.”

Knox stretched his head forward, the sore muscles in the back of his neck going taut. “When does Klaus think he’ll have an answer for us?”

“I told him we needed something ASAP.”

Knox closed his eyes. “Keep me posted.”

21

Astronaut Training
Vandenberg Air Force Base

Uzi sat beside Gavin Stroud in the front seat of the lunar rover. The sun was tracking downward in a lazy winter descent, orange hues and lengthening shadows blanketing the desert-like terrain.

Before Uzi and DeSantos got into the vehicle, Kirmani gave them a three-hour orientation on the twelve-wheel explorer, a significantly upgraded version of the one that flew on the last three Apollo missions.

In addition to transporting the astronauts across the lunar surface, it gave them the ability to attach modular equipment depending on the task that needed to be completed, as well as work inside a pressurized cabin without the encumbrance of bulky suits and clunky gloves.

"NASA only built a couple of prototypes of the SPR, or small pressurized rover. This is one of them. It's nearly identical to the one you'll be using on the Moon."

Their exercise this afternoon was to practice emergency recovery procedures. They were in a secluded area of southern California that provided a hard-packed, rolling terrain designed to approximate that of the Moon.

DeSantos was on the "lunar surface," with an injured Digger Carson lying supine, suffering from a fractured leg.

Uzi had gotten the distress call and was driving the rover, nicknamed Spider—a mix of its abbreviation and appearance: from the exterior, it looked more like an insect than an interplanetary SUV. They were in an encapsulated cabin, in a cantilevered cockpit that sat a few feet above the wheelbase, with two large rectangular windows across the top and three smaller windows by their knees and feet.

Uzi maneuvered through a deep valley that was chock-full of NASA-constructed craters and gullies. "Hang in there, Digger, we're en route."

Stroud consulted the controller panel in front of him. "ETA seven minutes."

"Seven minutes?" DeSantos said incredulously. "You're not that far away."

"Spider only goes six miles an hour," Uzi said as he negotiated a boulder. "We're not exactly driving your 'vette here."

Stroud pointed ahead. "Watch that crater. They landscaped this test bed to mimic the lunar surface where we'll be landing. It's like an obstacle course."

"I noticed." In circumnavigating the crater, Uzi swung wide around a deep dip, then headed back toward DeSantos's position.

"That one you could've driven through. The six wheel/twelve tire setup gives you a lot of flexibility. It can handle shallower undulations and smaller-size rocks. The wheels pivot and can move vertically three inches to avoid—"

They hit a sharp depression in the terrain and the rover dove to the right and tumbled into a crater, rolled onto its side, and stopped in a cloud of dust.

"Jesus," Stroud said. "You okay?"

"Yeah, yeah. You?"

"What happened?" Carson asked over the radio.

"Not sure, b—" Before Uzi could finish his thought, a loud pop interrupted him and black vapor started filling the cabin. "Get the hell out!"

But Spider was not designed for quick ingress and egress. In fact, just the opposite: on a planet with an inhospitable "atmosphere," engineers did not want a means of quickly exposing the astronauts, who were not protected by pressure suits, to immediate death.

They started feeling their way through the dense smoke for the access door into the pressure lock.

Uzi could not hold his breath any longer as acrid smelling, chemical-laced gas choked off his lungs. He yanked open the panel—and came face-to-face with a hot wall of fire.

Two hands grabbed his uniform and yanked him backward, through the opening in the top right of the vehicle—which was now wedged against the rocky ground.

Three men surrounded Uzi and Stroud, lifting them by their armpits and dragging them clear of the crash site.

Trying to suck in as much clean air as possible—a challenge in southern California smog—Uzi and Stroud coughed violently as their heels dragged through the dry dirt.

Firefighters ran in the opposite direction, toward the upended rover, as firefighters are wont to do: head into a danger zone while civilians run out.

Having reached the designated distance, the men sat Uzi and Stroud on the ground, pulled an oxygen mask over their noses and mouths and yanked stethoscopes from their cargo pants.

"You guys all right?" one asked.

"Yes," Uzi mumbled under the clear plastic face piece.

The medics listened a moment, did a quick examination, then told them they might be coughing for a while but were going to be fine: their exposure to the smoke appeared to be minimal because they had been extracted so quickly.

"What the hell happened?"

Kirmani's voice. Uzi squinted into the low afternoon sun and saw Ridgid and Klaus Eisenbach standing over them.

Uzi pulled off the mask. "My fault, sir."

"Seriously?" Kirmani asked. "You'd better get your act together or we're gonna scrub this mission. And I don't have to tell you the damage that'll cause."

"Uzi's only trying to protect me," Stroud said. "And I don't need protecting," he said, looking sternly at Uzi. "I can stand on my own." He got to his feet and faced Kirmani. "I thought he was taking too long to get to Digger, so I pulled the wheel over and I guess I misjudged the proximity of the crater's edge."

Kirmani and Eisenbach shared a look of consternation.

"Well that's just terrific," Kirmani said. "Because you've totaled it and it takes three months and millions of dollars to build one of these things. We've only got one Spider left—and it's already packed in the fairing."

"One will be fine," Stroud said.

"It better be."

Uzi turned and watched as the crew continued to battle the flames, which did not want to die. "Lithium ion fires are tough to put out. The liquid electrolyte burns when it's exposed to air and other oxidants inside the battery. They fuel the fire from within and the cells stay really hot, continuously releasing more electrolyte in the vapor and feeding itself. So all you can do is keep the thing under control until the reactants burn up."

Kirmani frowned. "Why don't you go over there and tell the firefighters how to do their job?" He muttered something under his breath and walked off.

"Get your gear and get on the bus," Eisenbach said. "Rover's destroyed. We're done here. And we don't have time to waste."

When Eisenbach was out of earshot, Uzi turned to Stroud. "Why'd you do that?"

"Do what?"

Uzi frowned. "Cover for me. I appreciate it, but I don't need that kind of help."

"In this case you did."

Uzi tilted his head. "Come again?"

"Shit happens. To all of us. Did you hit the crater? Yeah. So what. Ridgid knows people aren't perfect—but he expects us to be. Thing is, this mission needs to launch on time. He knows that too. They've got another two guys going through the same regimen in another area of the base. But I don't want them replacing you."

"A backup."

Stroud chuckled as he headed in the direction of the bus, which was driving toward them, its headlights on. "*You're* the backup team. This is the backup to the backup. And I don't have to spell it out for you but I will anyway: this isn't just another mission. Beyond the obvious of going to the fuckin' Moon. What's at stake is something that threatens America's ability to maintain its qualitative military advantage. Not because we're the mighty USA, but because we're a benevolent country committed to doing the right thing around the world."

"C'mon, Cowboy, we've done some shitty things—and some boneheaded things—in our history."

"But never out of malice. Huge difference. We don't plot to take over the world. We don't invade or bully other countries, we don't claim or steal others' land or resources. Some countries, they don't have such benevolent goals. They want to dominate world affairs—or seize territory that's not theirs. China, Russia, Iran—you know the players. Not to mention the ones that wreak havoc through their proxies—one of which sits on the verge of being a nuclear power. In a matter of years, they throw the switch, and they're in the nuclear warhead business."

"They also happen to be the top sponsor of terror in the world."

"Then there's North Korea." Stroud stopped walking and waited as the bus approached. "This mission is designed to prevent any of that from happening."

"I get it."

"So *that's* why I took the blame for the crash." Stroud swung around and glanced at the still-billowing plume of dense black smoke. "If the bosses thought the other two guys were the best ones for the mission, *they'd* be here. Not you and Hector. So I'd rather have you watching my six than them."

"So the truth comes out. Forget that bullshit about qualitative military advantage. You did it for selfish purposes."

Stroud laughed. "You know it." He stopped walking and the smile left his lips. "It's just going to be the four of us up there. We have to depend on one another. And I do think you two give us the best chance at getting back home again."

The small bus pulled in front of them. DeSantos and Carson were already inside.

"We'll get back," Uzi said.

Stroud stepped up to the door. "You know this?"

"I do."

"Well, you know the intricacies of lithium ion fires. If you remember useless shit like that, you'll probably do well with stuff you *have* to know in order to survive."

"Just keep me away from the edges of craters."

"Oh, no worries about that. You won't be operating the rover after we land. As mission commander, I just revoked your driving privileges."

22

Vandenberg Air Force Base

Eisenbach and Kirmani entered the common area where the four astronauts had just sat down to dinner.

"How are things going?" Eisenbach asked.

DeSantos glanced at Eisenbach and Kirmani, attempting to read their expressions. Both of them suddenly showing up at a meal meant that something unusual was going down.

"Good," Uzi said. "Real good. We're slightly ahead of schedule, despite the rover . . . mishap."

"Mishap," Kirmani said with a frown that looked like he had bitten into a chunk of raw garlic. "Not my choice of words."

"Things are going very well," Carson said. "Why? What's going on?"

"We've decided to push the mission up," Eisenbach said. "And the launch."

The four men looked at one another.

"Why?" Stroud asked.

"Because," Kirmani said, "we can take advantage of the three days of travel to the Moon, when there'll be little for Uzi and Hector to do. The past week, we've been training mostly on simulators. The rest is book and classroom learning, with regular exams to ensure you're absorbing the material. All that can be done on your tablets while en route."

"When do we leave?" Uzi asked.

"Tomorrow morning," Eisenbach said.

"All due respect," Uzi said, "seems to me this has been your plan all along. You can't just turn the ignition on and leave. A rocket like this has to be prepped and tested."

"To answer your question," Kirmani said, "which I'm not obligated to do, yes, it was always our plan to launch tomorrow. Hercules and Orion were rolled out to the launch pad several weeks ago. Couple of days before you arrived, Carson and Stroud went out there to do a terminal countdown demonstration test, worked with the launch team, and practiced the countdown in their flight suits, strapped inside Orion just like they'll be doing tomorrow morning."

"But," Eisenbach said, "the actual launch date was dependent on several factors, some of which had to do with intel we were getting on the Chang'e 5 and some on how you two were progressing."

"I haven't been very pleased with Uzi's performance at times," Kirmani said, giving Stroud a long look—signaling he knew the truth about the rover—"but I think he's ready. And so do Cowboy and Digger."

A buzzer sounded and the door to the room opened. A portly man wheeled in a cart with their dinner.

"What happened to Bernie?" DeSantos asked.

"Family emergency," Kirmani said. "Had to fly back to Kansas."

DeSantos eyed Uzi, suspicion evident in his raised brow.

Kirmani and Eisenbach turned and started for the door.

"Soon as you finish eating," Kirmani said, "I suggest you get to bed. The transport that'll take you to the launch pad will be here at 0500. Wake up alarm will be at 0400. Van will depart here at 05:05." He stopped and faced them. "It won't be late. And neither will you."

23

Citi Field
Flushing, New York

Vail located Jason Lansford. She spoke with a few of the ushers until she found the one who knew where the Aerospace Engineering box was located. It was in the Hyundai Club, slightly up the third base line but extremely close to home plate.

This presented a minor problem. Entry required a special pass, electronic barcode, or a white-and-green striped wrist band. They had none of them. If they had time and local resources, OPSIG could've reproduced one or more of them. But this was an op on-the-fly, the riskiest kind.

Rodman and Zheng rendezvoused with Vail in the rear of the Mets' Hall of Fame museum, ten feet from the framed scorecard of game five of the 2015 World Series.

"We can't get into the Hyundai Club, not without attracting attention." Vail waited until a woman and her daughter moved deeper into the museum, out of earshot, headed for a display of the original Mr. Met mascot. "And he has no reason to leave the club until the game ends because they have a self-contained restaurant, restroom, and gift shop. Unless he wants to take a stroll around the stadium, we've got a problem."

"Then we have to be creative," Zheng said. "We have to lure him out somehow."

"Here's how things are going to go down from a law enforcement perspective. After he leaves his seat, once he's gone for fifteen-twenty minutes, the CEO and CTO will start to wonder what happened to him. They'll call him and get voice mail. They'll discuss what to do, then go looking for him. When they can't find him, they'll call again. When it goes to voice mail, they'll report it to stadium security, who'll alert their staff by radio—the equivalent of a 'be on the lookout.' The NYPD, which also patrols Citi Field, will be notified."

"So we don't have a lot of time once we start this," Rodman said.

Zheng looked around the museum. "We have to be ready to act as soon as we inject him."

"That's assuming we can get close to him in a secluded area," Vail said, "which I'm not sure we're going to be able to do."

"Hey! Karen. Karen Vail?"

Vail winced. Normally she would welcome a friend or acquaintance. But in a situation like this, a chance encounter was less than ideal. She turned—and saw Det. Steven Johnson standing there, a David Wright uniform jersey pulled over his svelte torso.

"What are you doing back in the city?"

"Catching a Mets game."

"That much is obvious. But—hey, who're your friends?"

Vail turned to Rodman and Zheng, who were doing their best to avoid engaging in conversation.

Rodman extended his right hand. "Terry Redmond. This is my buddy, John Cho." Zheng shook, but he looked like he could think of five hundred other places he would rather be.

"Have you seen Leslie?" Johnson asked. "She's now in your neck of the woods."

"We worked a serial killer case together several months ago. She didn't tell you?"

Johnson bobbed his head. "Well . . . we had an argument, big brother was right, she was wrong, little sister can't admit it."

Something tells me Leslie'll have a different read of that assessment.

"No biggie," Johnson continued. "She'll come around. Gotta give her some space. She fitting in?"

"I know her partner real well. He's a good guy. They seemed to be getting along fine."

"Hey, I don't mean to be rude," Rodman said, "but we've got that thing before the game starts."

"Yeah, yeah," Vail said, excusing herself and apologizing for not having more time to talk.

"That case I helped you with several months ago, you close it?"

The codex? Yeah, you could say that. "Sure did. Your info was very helpful."

"Still can't tell me what it was all about?"

"Still can't."

"Glad to hear I was at least able to help," Johnson said, not disguising his disappointment.

Rodman placed a hand around Vail's bicep.

"Gotta go, Steve. I'll tell Leslie to accept that she's wrong and that she should call you."

He laughed. "I wouldn't put it quite that way, but I'd appreciate that. She can be stubborn and this has gone on long enough."

Vail winked at him. "Leave it to me. Miss Diplomat." Before he could reply, she walked off with Rodman and Zheng.

"Nine million people and you personally still know, what, a hundred? And you run into one in the middle of an op?" Rodman shook his head. "We need to take care of business and get the hell out of here before who-knows-who-else pops up."

"At least let me have till the seventh inning stretch. Syndergaard's pitching."

Rodman gave her a look.

"Kidding."

"Okay," Zheng said, leaning in close. "We've gotta get our guy out of that club. We could have him paged, or we—"

"Wait a minute, Steve had a wrist band on. It had writing on it. Could be the Hyundai Club. Hang on a second."

She walked over to one of the stadium staff, then returned. "Hyundai Club."

Rodman snorted. "So you're just gonna tell this Johnson dude you need his ticket? And then what?"

"Then we'll figure it out. But at least I'll be in."

Zheng turned away. "Too risky."

"Anything we do here is risky. I can make this work."

"Can you trust this Steve Johnson guy?" Zheng asked.

"He won't be a problem." In truth, she did not really know him. But if he was anything like Leslie, and if her first impressions of him were correct on that case he helped her with, she had nothing to worry about. Vail pulled out her cell and realized it was her OPSIG phone. She accessed her contacts on Gmail, found Johnson's number, and texted him. He replied a moment later, her suggestion to meet her at Mr. Met in the museum getting a laughing emoticon in response. But a moment later, he showed up.

"I need a favor."

"Okay."

"And you can't ask me what it's about."

Johnson eyed her obliquely. "I'm a detective. You know that, right?"

"Obviously."

"This is weird, just like last time you asked for help. You wanted information but you couldn't tell me why or what it was for. And if I had to guess—"

"I don't want you to guess. I just want your ticket stub."

"You crazy? I paid two hundred bucks for this seat."

"I don't want your seat, just admittance to the club. So to speak." Vail gestured at his wrist band. "That'll get you in."

"And what if they ask for my ticket?"

"Show them your badge."

Johnson frowned. "Now you're trying to get me fired?"

"Make it subtle. C'mon, man, you know how to do this."

"Yeah, but *why* do I need to do this?"

Vail grinned. "That's the favor part."

Johnson sighed. "Karen, you—"

"Are a good friend of your sister's, and you asked me to help reconnect you two, smooth things over. Right?"

Johnson chewed on his bottom lip, considering her request.

He pulled out the stub and handed it to her. "Leslie told me stories about you. Don't make no trouble."

Vail recoiled animatedly. "Really? Me?"

TEN MINUTES LATER, with the game getting underway, Vail showed the ticket and was waved through the entrance to the Hyundai Club, which featured life-size photos from the 1969 and 1986 world championships. Wearing a blue hat with orange stitching that read "NEW YORK METS 1962," she passed through the lounge, catching a glimpse of the home-cooked food as steam rose from the catering dishes, the pungent smell of crushed garlic working its way into her nose. An artisanal cheese table, salads of all kinds, slow-cooked meats, grilled veggies . . . Her stomach rumbled. *Would it hurt to grab a piece of salmon and a side of sautéed mushrooms?*

Vail made her way to the doors that led to the field. She pushed through and looked around. *Damn good seats.* For a split second she was lost in the moment. There was something about night-time baseball, the grass lit up brightly, the buzz of the fans in the stands, the stadium's circle lending importance to the game that was unfolding in front of you.

Lansford was sitting a few rows away. She verified his identity, then took up a position that did not block anyone's view. She had no idea how long she would have to stand there, but now that she had eyes on Lansford, she was not about to give up her spot.

As the bottom half of the first inning began, an usher asked her if she minded taking her seat. She told him her back was bothering her and she had trouble sitting for extended periods. That would work for a while, but she would draw attention hanging out there indefinitely.

In thinking it through, she reasoned that if Lansford was here to watch the game with his colleagues, he would not be going anywhere—at least for the first two-thirds of the game—other than to get something to eat or drink or use the restroom. She hoped he was not one of those guys who ordered food at the seat and didn't get up until the last pitch was thrown.

Vail noted that the ways out of the club went through the buffet and adjoining dining areas that featured windows with views of the field. The most likely place someone would go, at least once during the game, was in here to use the bathroom or get a snack or drink.

She walked inside past the sizzling onions and stopped in front of the large framed photo of Hall of Famer Tom Seaver in full windup, then turned in a circle trying to think this through. She could wait it out in here, checking on Lansford every fifteen minutes or so, but the more unusual behavior she exhibited, and the more contact she had with people, especially as it related to Lansford, the greater the chance she would become an NYPD person of interest when he went missing. Hat aside, she was not making any concerted efforts to disguise her appearance.

The better approach was to engineer a reason for him to leave his seat. As she ruminated on that, she glanced at the wall-mounted televisions showing the action on field, then the white aproned cooks behind the buffet preparing food, the fans milling about, and the people filling their plates and heading out the doors to their seats.

She could not think of a way to compel him to come into the dining area—without attracting attention. She had to be patient, ride things out, and wait for Lansford to enter the lounge. If and when he did, she devised a plan to get him alone—and then out of the club: memorabilia, the game-used stuff, balls, broken bats, and bases the team sold.

Vail used OPSIG's secure text messaging app to share her idea with Rodman and Zheng. For now, they were to stay close and loiter around the general vicinity of the team store. Vail would wait for Lansford to emerge and then engage him.

By the fourth inning, Vail had split her time out by the seats, in different spots that afforded her a view of Lansford and the food bar. She estimated that their target had consumed two large Cokes, but he had yet to get up from his seat. Though it was a warm night, it was not by any means humid or hot, so she figured there was only one place he could be storing that liquid if he was not sweating it out. He would be making a bathroom run fairly soon.

After the fifth, she was beginning to get concerned. Robby had a large bladder and could go hours without peeing—but he was six-foot-seven. Lansford was five-ten. As she ruminated on the length of time a male could go between trips to the john, Lansford pushed through the glass doors and entered the club lounge.

Vail texted Zheng as she followed Lansford and stopped at the entrance to the men's room. She moved quickly to the exit and palmed her ticket to Zheng. "Bathroom," she said. "Through the doors, left all the way down."

◆ ◆ ◆

ZHENG HELD UP THE TICKET and continued past the usher, who stuck out a hand.

"Wrist band, sir?"

"Gave me a rash," Zheng said, not stopping to argue. "Had to cut it off." He strode by the buffet and pushed into the men's room. Lansford was not there.

He made another pass in front of the urinals, checked the sinks, and then glanced under the stalls. Three were taken. Two of the occupants were wearing tennis shoes and jeans. According to Vail's description, Lansford was wearing charcoal trousers and black wingtips—just like the remaining man two doors down.

Zheng walked out and waited by the exit. He pulled out a staff lanyard he had pilfered from a worker in a crowded elevator and hung it around his neck.

Seconds later, Lansford appeared.

"Jason."

Lansford stopped and looked up. "Huh?"

"Bill said you'd gone to the bathroom," Zheng said.

"Yeah." He squinted. "Do I know you?"

"Oh, sorry, John Cho. I'm with the PR department and the Mets want to give you a game-used ball from tonight's game."

"A ball—for me? Why?"

"Aerospace Engineering has been a very good corporate partner, and every week we draw from all our season ticket holders and award them with a gift. Your company won and Bill said I should give it to *you*. He said I should take you over to the memorabilia kiosk and let you pick out what you'd like. Most people like game-used balls, which come fully authenticated, but you're welcome to have a bat if you'd like that instead. You can have a base too, but there's an upcharge for that. It's not too bad, though, only thirty bucks. But come with me. It's right outside." He gently took Lansford's elbow and led him out of the club. "Did you see the kiosk on your way in?"

"Uh, no, we, uh . . ." Lansford glanced back over his shoulder but continued alongside Zheng without resistance. "We had dinner at the Porsche Grille. I didn't get a chance to explore before the game."

"Oh," Zheng said. "I might be able to arrange a private tour. Tomorrow maybe, if that works for you?"

"Headed back to DC in the morning, but I appreciate the offer. Maybe next time I'm in town?"

"Absolutely. Just give us twenty-four hours' notice." Zheng walked toward the team store, Rodman approaching from the opposite direction. He bumped into Lansford, knocking him backward and spinning him around. Zheng grabbed his arm to keep him from falling as Rodman drew close and pricked his abdomen with the needle.

None of the milling fans seemed to notice.

"Ow," Lansford said under his breath. His speech slurred as he whispered, "What the fuck was—"

"Jason, you okay?" Zheng helped get him erect. "You nearly took a header." Lansford was going limp—but Rodman steadied him as Zheng put his arm around the man's shoulders and helped him to, and down, the escalator thirty yards ahead, right behind Vail.

As they descended, Zheng attempted to look casual while he maintained his grip on Lansford's body. Lettered above the semicircular windows that spanned the front of the Jackie Robinson rotunda, were the namesake's immortal words: "A life is not important except in the impact it has on other lives."

Well put, Jackie, Zheng thought. *That's exactly what we're trying to do.*

"He okay?" an usher asked as they came off the escalator, headed for the stadium exit directly ahead of them.

"Too much to drink," Zheng said. "Wife left him this afternoon and . . . well, it's my fault. I should've kept a closer watch on how much he was tossing back."

"I hear ya," the usher said knowingly.

Rodman and Zheng more or less carried Lansford into the parking lot and sat him down on the stone retaining wall that rimmed the restored Shea Stadium red papier-mâché "Home Run Apple" that was displayed out front.

Rodman pulled him against his body, keeping his head from flopping forward, as Vail went to get their van.

Six minutes later they were loading him into the front seat. Once clear of prying eyes, a hundred yards from the exit, they transferred him to the back . . . where no one would see him until they arrived in DC.

24

Space Launch Complex-4 East
Vandenberg Air Force Base

The morning arrived faster than usual. DeSantos and Uzi both had difficulty shutting down their thoughts, initially lying in the dark and talking to each other like teenagers on a sleepover. They avoided the red elephant in the room—what they were about to do—and finally drifted off. But they spent the next few hours in and out of fitful dreams.

When the alarm blared and the room lights snapped on, they climbed out of bed and faced each other. Without a word, they padded into their bathrooms to get ready. It was 4:00 AM: T-minus five hours and forty-five minutes.

And counting.

THEY RODE THE ELEVATOR up the launch umbilical tower to the top level of the gantry, at which point they were led into the White Room, where several uniformed closeout crew personnel were waiting to receive them. After exchanging pleasantries, DeSantos and Uzi were helped into their orange launch-and-entry pumpkin suits as they prepared to board through the main hatch of the Orion crew module.

"We really doing this?" Uzi asked.

"We are." DeSantos adjusted the stretch material that covered his head. "Some are born great and others have greatness thrust upon them."

Uzi cocked his head as two men scurried about them, getting final preparations ready. "You're parroting Shakespeare? What's that got to do with this? Better yet, what's gotten into you?"

DeSantos shrugged. "I just like the quote."

"You're nervous. You always get goofy when you're nervous."

"If I wasn't nervous, you'd need to check me for a pulse. We're about to get into a giant tin can sitting on top of 10 million pounds of highly flammable fuel. I should be having my head examined."

"It's only 9 million. Stop exaggerating."

A voice came from behind them: "This way, guys. It's time."

"Last chance to back out," Uzi said.

"There is *nothing* that could keep me from this op."

Uzi slapped DeSantos's shoulder. "Same here."

"That's peachy," the launch tower technician said. "Because we've gotta go." He helped DeSantos seat, and then lock down, his helmet and guided him through Orion's trapezoid-shaped hatch.

He and Uzi had been inside the mockup many times during the past week, and had spent several hours in the simulator learning how to operate basic functions of the flight system software. But this was different. His heart rate had increased and the level of anxiety swelled in his chest. They *were* really doing this. They were rocketing into space.

Carson and Stroud were already strapped into their seats going through the preflight protocols on the cockpit user interface. They did not acknowledge DeSantos or Uzi, as they were engrossed in their checklists and communicating with the flight director over the radio.

DeSantos did as he had been trained, taking seat number three beside Uzi, who was in four, in the two-up and two-down stacked arrangement. A touch screen had been mounted to the lower chairs—a military variant of the standard Orion—originally designed to enable Welding and Norris to participate in crew module tasks. The displays now provided Uzi and DeSantos the ability to continue their self-paced training curriculum.

After fastening his restraints, DeSantos turned his attention to launch control and the chatter that was going on between the capsule and mission planners.

He suddenly became aware of the gentle vibration in the metal chair. He had avoided thinking about what they were about to do; they had been so absorbed in learning, and retaining, everything they needed to know for the mission that he had not wanted to engage in mind-wandering philosophical thoughts that provided perspective on the nature of the operation: unlike anything he—or any special operator—had partaken of in history.

And like everything about this mission, it would not show up in history texts . . . at least not those printed in the next few decades. Perhaps there would come a time where it, and its details, would be declassified. But that all hinged on whether or not they were successful, and at what cost.

During the next two hours, DeSantos and Uzi continued their tablet-based studies and largely ignored the radio chatter, technical conversations, questions, and answers being exchanged between Carson and Stroud, CAPCOM—capsule communications—and launch control engineers. They checked the stabilization and control systems, telemetry and radio frequencies, tracking beacons and attitude and guidance systems. They armed the pyrotechnic bolts, checked internal flight batteries and the automatic sequencer, pressurized the reaction control system, and updated the altimeter.

DeSantos had zoned out several times, the lack of sleep settling in and the adrenaline dump starting to clear his bloodstream. He was craving a double shot of espresso. He was going to miss Bernie Anderson's cooking; his healthy, calorie-controlled meals were surprisingly satisfying.

DeSantos was pulled out of his reverie to hear the update:

"All going well at this time; two hours, forty seconds and counting. This is launch control."

"Remember, guys," Stroud said, "from this point forward, the Orion crew module will be known by the call sign Patriot. Once we move into the lunar lander and undock from Patriot, we'll be known as Raptor."

"Copy that," DeSantos said.

"We're named after a bird of prey," Uzi mumbled. "Brilliant."

"Boychick, you've got a live mic."

Uzi twisted his lips: oops.

The next ninety minutes passed quickly, DeSantos's apprehension building again as the clock ticked down. Was it the humongous engines? The seventy-two-metric-ton, thirty-two-story rocket—taller than the Statue of Liberty—filled with explosive fuels exposed to searing high temperatures and extreme velocities? He found it within himself to chuckle. It was all of that—and more.

He glanced at Uzi and he could tell, even through the helmet glass, that his friend was feeling the same sense of anxiety: tense face, set jaw. And although Uzi was staring ahead at his screen, it did not look like he was absorbing any of the material.

"We are at T-minus thirty minutes and counting. Still looking at a final liftoff at 9:45 AM. This is launch control."

He and Uzi shared a look as the launch pad director gave them two thumbs up and told them all systems were go—which they already knew because the engineers were blabbering techno terms in their headsets. She uttered a nondenominational

"Godspeed" blessing, then she and a coworker swung the hatch closed and secured it.

"OKAY BOYS," Stroud said. "You ready for the ride of your lives?"

"As ready as I can be," Uzi said.

"All systems go," Carson said. "Launch control, do you show go for final launch status check?"

Uzi's shoulder muscles tightened at the mention of the phrase "final launch status check." This was it. They were starting the "go/no go poll," in which the flight controllers gave their readiness assessment for each of the systems. Go meant clear for launch, while no go meant the item needed to be examined—and a hold would be placed on the countdown.

Uzi had tried to force this moment from his mind, but his subconscious would not let him shove it aside. Instead, as each of the voices ticked off their status in his headset, he tried to take the analytical approach: scrutinizing each step of the process. Liftoff was one of the most tense, and dangerous, times of the mission. The eleven minutes it would take them to reach Earth orbit were particularly risky because of the extreme forces involved. A single malfunction could spell instant disaster.

The checks continued in his headset:

"Booster," the flight director said. The engineer's response: "Booster is go."

Retro. Retro is go.

Guidance. Guidance is go.

Surgeon. Surgeon is go . . .

But liftoff was only the first of many dicey moments, tasks, and maneuvers that awaited them. Next up was the translunar injection, when the Hercules's third stage engine ignited and literally blasted them out of Earth orbit, on course toward the Moon. Then came entering lunar orbit, followed by landing on the surface, walking on the Moon, lifting off, rendezvousing and docking with the Patriot, reentering Earth's atmosphere, and splashing down in the ocean. Mechanical failures or human errors, it did not matter. A minuscule, though critical, mishap would blow them into a million bits. The image of the Challenger space shuttle exploding in midflight looped through his thoughts.

Stop it, Uzi told himself. *First we need a successful eleven minutes. Then we'll tackle each step as it comes.*

Navigation. Navigation is go.

Control. Control is go.

Network. Network is go.

Recovery. Recovery is go . . .

He tuned out the crosstalk and tried to clear his mind. He had experienced mission jitters before. This was not uncommon with special operators, spies, and soldiers of all stripes. He knew how to deal with the anxiety and rarely had issues controlling it, but for some reason he was having a tougher time than in the past. He took a deep breath and closed his eyes.

"Vehicle's in great shape," launch control said in his ears. "Weather's a go. Um, on behalf of the launch team, we'd like to wish you guys good luck and Godspeed. We'll see you back here in nine days."

"You are clear to launch, Patriot. Launch sequencer now controlling."

"Roger that," Stroud said. "Thanks for your help, launch control."

"We are T-minus one minute. Now arming the sound suppression water system."

Uzi took another breath, let it out slowly. He knew that handoff to the onboard computers was due to occur at thirty-one seconds, assuming nothing prevented the launch from proceeding before that.

"T-minus forty-five seconds, handoff in fourteen."

"Here we go, guys," Carson said. "Hang on."

The rocket vibrated vigorously as the engines built up thrust.

"Standing by for the handoff to Patriot's onboard computers," Stroud said. "T-minus thirty-one seconds. And . . . the handoff has occurred."

"Firing chain is armed," CAPCOM said. "Go for main engine start."

Eight.

Seven.

Six.

On the bright side, Uzi thought, *someday I'll have a great story to tell my grandkids. Oh wait. No I won't.*

Three.

Two.

One.

Zero.

"And we have liftoff!" Launch control's usual dead-panned, dispassionate communication had considerable emotion behind it, the culmination of a long process of planning, practice, and execution.

The rocket's intense rumble was like being in the epicenter of the longest earthquake in history. Uzi felt the rapid, violent shake in his head, his throat, his stomach, his fingers and toes.

"You have cleared the tower," CAPCOM said. "Looking good. You're on your way, Patriot."

25

Undisclosed Industrial Park
Springfield, Virginia

Jason Lansford sat in a generous-size room containing only a couple of metal chairs and a small table. He was connected to a polygraph and his hands were handcuffed to the arms of the chair.

Psychophysiologist Terrence Jones resided in an adjacent observation chamber monitoring the results remotely, along with Vail. Although polygraph examiners often plied their trade beside their test subjects, Vail and Zheng felt it was best if Jones took his baseline readings and then communicated the responses via earpiece so he did not interfere in any way with their session.

Zheng Wei walked into the interrogation room and slammed the door behind him. Lansford did not jump. He did not react at all.

"I want an attorney," he said without making eye contact.

"There won't be any attorneys. We're not the police and you're not under arrest. So you have no rights. This is a kidnapping, pure and simple. Except it's not ransom we're after. It's information."

"I don't know what information I could possibly have that you'd want." He faced Zheng. "My shirt size?"

Zheng stared at him, his expression devoid of emotion.

Lansford looked away.

"This is not a joke. It's not a prank. You need to answer our questions truthfully."

"Or?"

"You'll find out." Zheng fixed his gaze—and his jaw—for a moment before turning and leaving.

He walked into the adjacent room where Vail and Jones were waiting.

"He's very composed," Jones said. "Almost like he's in a trance."

"The trait of a good spy," Zheng said, watching Lansford through the two-way glass. "We have to find a way of getting under his skin, breaking down his defenses. Get to him emotionally."

"I'll do my best," Vail said. "But to do this right, it could take weeks."

"I don't care if you do it right or do it wrong. Or something in between. Just get the information. And you've got hours, not weeks."

Vail chuckled.

"This is not a law enforcement operation, Karen. You got that?"

Crystal clear. "He's got no right to remain silent."

Zheng locked gazes with Vail. "No rights of any kind."

"Yeah," she said. "I got it."

VAIL ENTERED THE ROOM and walked to a spot in front of the chair where Jason Lansford was seated. She felt naked without her FBI badge and creds.

"Who are you?" Lansford asked.

"Right now, I'm the only friend you have in the world."

"Great. Then you won't mind removing these handcuffs."

She pulled over another chair and set it in front of Lansford. "Jason, right? My name is Katherine. Tell me about your work for Aerospace Engineering."

"First you tell me what this is about."

"My colleague already told you. This is about information. Information you have that we need. Like who you work for—other than AE."

"I don't know what you're talking about."

"That's not the way this is going to work," Vail said. "Telling the truth will help you immensely. Lying, however, won't get you anywhere. But it *will* get you trouble."

"I've been in trouble before."

"Okay," Vail said. "Fair enough. But don't tell me I didn't warn you. Just trying to look out for your well-being."

"I'm not lying. I don't work for anyone other than Aerospace Engineering."

"We know about your trips to China."

"I didn't realize that was a crime."

"We're not the police."

"Lots of people go to China," Lansford said with a shrug. "They're tourists, they travel. Others go there on business, some visit family."

"You appear to have done all three. Yeah, we know about your brother Brad and his family. And we know about his problems with the government. And your pledge to pay off his debt." *A bit of a guess, but if I'm right . . .*

His brow twitched, a slight contraction of the musculature. "I don't know what you're talking about."

Oh, but there's something. I see it on your face.

"So you agreed to do something for the government. Get them info on something AE's working on. Corporate espionage. You know, if that's all it is, if it's just a matter of trying to help out your family, I get that."

"Wrong tree."

"What?"

"You're barking up the wrong tree."

"We had something," Jones said in her earpiece, *"when you brought up his brother's problems. A minor response."*

"I'm just saying that if you were passing on info to the Chinese government because you were repaying Brad's debt with them, that's just being a good brother. But I need to know what it was that you gave the government."

Lansford shook his head, as if he were pitying her for her stupidity.

"Helping out your family is a whole lot different than spying for another country, which could be classified as an act of terrorism. The US government takes that very seriously these days—as I'm sure you've heard."

"But you're not the police."

"I've got debts to repay too. If I turned you over to the Feds, that'd go a long way to paying them off. Unfortunately for you," she said with a shrug, "you'd never get out of prison."

"Do what you gotta do. They'd have nothing on me."

Vail smiled. "Now we both know that's not true. But if you could explain to them that something happened *accidentally* . . . well, that's not only understandable but excusable. Is that what happened? Did something slip out during a conversation with someone?"

"Nothing slipped out. There was no accident. I didn't pass any information to anyone."

"To pay off your debt to the Chinese government. You handed over some . . . what? Blueprints? Documents?"

"No, nothing like that. Like I said, I didn't pass any info to anyone, here or in China. How many times are you gonna ask me the same thing?"

"You know, Jason, I had a friend like you. And he thought he was doing the right thing. He accepted some money, was convinced he was helping—"

"Sorry to hear about your friend. But it doesn't have any relevance to me. I'm not a spy. I didn't pass information to anyone.

I'm just a guy who goes to work every day, does his job, and goes home."

"He appears to be telling the truth," Jones said.

Bullshit. I know he's lying. And I've got hours, not weeks, to break him.

For the first time, Vail had the fleeting thought that DeSantos's interrogation techniques might be useful. Maybe even necessary—at some point, at some time. Even if it was just used as leverage or a bargaining chip.

No. Stop thinking like that. It's wrong. Immoral.

And I'm not Hector. So how do I make Jason Lansford talk?

She could not motivate him with threats of prosecution and there was no time to build trust. None of her methods would work in a situation like this, against the clock.

She wanted to put her fist through the wall.

It would not be the first time.

Her friends' lives could depend on her ability to make this guy talk. And she was no closer than she was when she started. She had come up empty.

There was a knock at the door. Vail took the interruption as an excuse to take a breather, collect her thoughts, refocus, expunge the frustration—because it would not do her any good.

She walked out. Standing there was a smartly dressed young woman with shiny brunette hair. Striking. Stunning. Only one other female she knew had such natural beauty—her friend Roxxann Dixon.

"Alexandra Rusakov." She held out a hand and Vail shook.

"We met. A few months ago, at the Pentagon. OPSIG—"

"Right," Rusakov said. "The codex case."

"What are you doing here?"

She gestured to the adjacent observation room. As they entered, Rusakov said, "I was asked to get over here, see if I could help."

"You can't insert yourself into the interrogation without knowing anything about—"

"I reviewed his file, did some . . . homework while you were in New York. I know what you know. Actually, a little more." She winked.

Vail turned to the two-way mirror. "They don't think I can get Lansford to talk?"

Rusakov tightened her mouth as if resisting the urge to smile. "Knox felt you stood the best chance. McNamara wasn't so sure and wanted me to be ready in case you—well, in case you failed."

Lovely. And here I am failing. Miserably.

"And don't take this the wrong way, but that's what appears to be happening."

Vail waved it off. "No worries. I didn't take that the wrong way." *Bitch.* "So what does McNamara think you can do that I can't?"

"I've got intelligence training. I can pick up on certain things."

"I know how people think. And I'm good at reading them, their body language."

Rusakov nodded slowly. "And I'm sure that's useful in some situations. But I can do things you may be . . . uncomfortable doing."

Vail stared at her.

"The book is out on you, Karen."

I didn't realize there was a book.

"I'm not a fan of physical torture. If that's 'the book,' then the book is right. It's not happening. Not on my watch."

Rusakov laughed. "Here's the thing. You're not in charge."

"So tell me. What makes you so qualified that McNamara thinks you're the better person for the job?"

"I was the first female Naval Special Warfare combat surgeon, part of SEAL Team 4 deployed to Afghanistan. Sometimes we took prisoners and needed to get at intel quickly. Lives were on the line. We didn't have time to play games. And since some of the mujahideen were trained to resist harsh interrogation methods, we had to devise ways of getting at the information we needed." She turned to the window and watched Lansford a moment. "I'm going in."

"Like I said. No physical torture on my watch." She tried to make it sound forceful. Intimidating. But clearly Alexandra Rusakov was not one to be pushed around.

"Think about it this way, Karen. Your friends are preparing to strap themselves into a metal capsule and get shot into the middle of freaking nowhere, hurtling through space traveling at insane speeds. With no rescue ships. Something goes wrong, they'll be dead in a matter of seconds. If they lose oxygen, it'll be a slow, emotionally and physically painful death."

"We don't know for sure that Jason Lansford has anything of value. And we don't know for sure their lives are in jeopardy. Do we?"

Rusakov stared at her a long moment. "Do we know they're not? Which is more acceptable to you? I'd rather make a mistake—and have it be nothing—than make a mistake and end up costing DeSantos and Uzi, Carson and Stroud their lives."

Vail turned her back on Rusakov and stared at Lansford.

"So you're willing to live with this? Could you look yourself in the mirror knowing you could've helped do something that saved their lives?"

Vail sighed heavily and leaned her forehead against the window. "No."

"We're on the same team here, Karen. It doesn't really matter who gets the intel, does it?"

"That's not the point. No, I don't care. I mean, to be honest, yeah, I would've liked to have gotten him to talk. But the most important thing is that we get the info. Period."

"Good. I agree. I'm going in there now."

"I was trained to not even be present when torture is taking place." *Of course, this would not be the first time I had to look the other way.* And she knew that, as a member of OPSIG, such conflicts would potentially arise from time to time. That did not mean she had to like it. But it did mean she had to accept it.

"You're not carrying your badge and quite frankly, right now you're not an FBI agent. Plus, you're making assumptions about my methodology. We can talk about it more later. Right now, time is ticking. Take a breather. Go get a coffee, a breath of fresh air." She patted Vail on the shoulder and walked out.

After watching Rusakov step into the room with Lansford, Vail pushed through the door into the hallway. A cup of coffee would do her good. That and a stiff drink.

26

Liftoff

The Hercules shook and rattled something fierce, and the noise in the cabin was loud, even with their helmets on. Despite their restraints they were tossed left and then right and left again.

And then an alarm blared.

Carson stared at his touch screen. "Uh, CAPCOM, we've got a master caution light here!"

"I see it," Stroud said. "What the hell's going on?"

The CAPCOM on duty, Bob Maddox, said calmly, "Abort? Do we need to engage the LAS?"

The launch abort system was designed to activate within milliseconds to blast the crew module away from a failing rocket toward a safe landing. Stroud's right hand moved down against the LAS manual lever that—if pulled—would end the mission in the blink of an eye.

"No," Stroud yelled. "No. It's—I just can't make sense of these readings."

As a seasoned pilot, Stroud knew to trust his instruments, not his body. But the figures on his panel were so out of sync with what was supposed to be happening that he was at a loss as to what to do.

"Everything looks good on our end," Maddox said. "What are you seeing?"

"Severe oscillation, two of five first stage engines have shut down. Imminent turbo pump structural failure. But—"

"Advanced health management shows temperatures, pressures, turbo pump speeds, and accelerometers all within normal tolerances," Maddox said. "Your readings are incorrect. Engines are functioning normally."

The massive rocket was still vibrating and shuddering violently—but Stroud knew that was not necessarily abnormal.

"No on abort," Maddox said. "Repeat, no on abort. Confirm."

"Roger, CAPCOM. No on abort." Stroud moved his hand off the LAS handle and sighed relief.

Another three seconds later the ride smoothed out and they kept rising. Stroud muted the alarm and tried to ignore it. He wanted to shut his eyes and not look at the erroneous readings on his screen but all his training told him to never, ever do that out of fear of missing a key data point.

"Good job," Uzi said.

Stroud groaned. "Bullshit. I got lucky. My hand was on the LAS lever. I was that close to fucking up this mission. *Way* too close."

DeSantos looked up at Stroud. "Close only counts in horseshoes. Right now we're still on course. All's good. Take a breath. We're on our way."

WHILE CIRCLING THE EARTH at 17,500 miles per hour, Patriot made translunar injection, a burn of their powerful rockets that blasted them out of orbit and up to a speed of 25,000 miles per hour, on a course for the Moon. It came off without a hitch or glitch—though they all admitted to having a white-knuckled grip on their armrests until confirmation from CAPCOM that they were, indeed, on the proper trajectory.

They would be coasting to the Moon now, slowing progressively as they crossed over into the Moon's area of gravitational influence, approximately 210,000 miles from Earth. Patriot would then accelerate as they were pulled toward the Moon. By the time they reached it, they would be traveling about 5,000 miles per hour, which they would reduce to 3,000 by firing their engines so they could enter lunar orbit.

Stroud adjusted his headset. "Come again?"

Bob Maddox repeated his statement, even though he most certainly knew Stroud's question was rhetorical. "Doesn't look like anything was actually malfunctioning with Hercules. All systems check out healthy. We've analyzed telemetry and all the readings were textbook."

"But the oscillation. The turbo pump speeds were cl—"

"I realize that," Maddox said. "We can't explain it, but we're still analyzing the data. We've got an engineering team ready to work 'round the clock on—"

A few seconds of silence passed.

"Uh, CAPCOM," Carson said, "can you repeat?"

"I said, we've got another team of engineers who are on their way in. We'll get them to work on it too. We'll have a report for you as soon as we've got some—"

"Some what?" Carson said. "CAPCOM, do you read?"

No response.

"Uh, we understand," Stroud said in case they were transmitting. "Comms winked out a couple of times. If you read, Patriot is standing by, awaiting your analysis."

Uzi looked at DeSantos and wondered if he was thinking the same thing he was: sometimes these complex machines experienced failures.

And sometimes those failures caused a catastrophic cascade.

But in the black void of space, there were no ejector seats. No parachutes. And no "Brave" F-16s to guide them to safety.

27

BLACK SITE

Alexandra Rusakov removed her blouse, revealing a body-hugging tank top, toned shoulders, and shapely arms.

"My name is Veronika," she said. "You're Jason." She smiled, her head cocked at an angle that let her thick brunette hair fall across her face. It was a look she had practiced and knew exuded beauty.

But Lansford held his own and did not react. "I told the other woman, I have no information for her. I didn't do whatever she thinks I did."

Rusakov slinked to his side, let her left index finger trail along Lansford's cheek.

"What are you doing?"

"I don't know who you were talking with before and I don't care." She stopped by his right side, in line with his shoulder, took his chin in her hand and tilted it up toward her eyes. "I think you're kind of cute."

He swallowed.

She moved in front of him. "Do you find me attractive?"

"I'm married."

Rusakov nodded. "Where I come from, in Russia, that does

not matter." She ran her fire engine red fingernails through his brown hair. "Does it matter to *you*? Do you want me to stop?"

Lansford's gaze dropped to Rusakov's full cleavage.

She swung a muscular leg over Lansford's lap and sat down.

"Do you need me to tell you that he's aroused?" Terrence Jones, the polygraph examiner, asked in her ear. *"Because he is. Shit, I am too. Oh sorry. I'll shut up now."*

"What—what are you doing?" Lansford asked.

Her fingers were wrapped around his belt. "I think I'm loosening your buckle." She laughed softly, then leaned forward and breathed in his right ear. Kissed his neck.

Lansford sucked in some breath. He stopped resisting, stopped moving. He was cooperating.

"Does this feel good?"

He did not speak.

Rusakov separated the belt buckle, deftly undid the button of his pants, and let her fingers trail down to his groin. Felt the firm erection. "Guess that's a yes." She leaned over to his left ear. "That's it. I *know* it feels good."

He swallowed. His breathing quickened.

"Tell me what I want to know and I'll go further."

He brought his gaze to hers, spoke at a near whisper. "That other woman—"

"Not a problem," Rusakov said. "I locked the door when I came in. So tell me, Jason, what I need to know."

"You do this first," he said. "Then I'll talk."

"Promise?" She kissed his neck lightly, massaging his penis through his underwear.

"Yes, yes," he said in a near-whisper. "I promise."

She rubbed him, kissed his forehead, then his cheek, then lightly—very lightly—on the lips. She pulled back slightly.

"Take off the handcuffs."

She giggled. "So much more fun with them on, Jason. Trust me. If you've never tried it . . ." She looked down, grabbed hold of the waistband and ripped it open with a sharp, forceful tug. Took his erection in her hand.

And he closed his eyes.

VAIL WALKED DOWN THE HALL, cup of burnt coffee in hand—there was no hard liquor in the break room, unfortunately—and an overwhelming sense of frustration threatening to make her hurl the drink at the wall.

Sometimes, no matter how hard you tried, you could not find the answers, could not get at the information you needed. Could not get where you needed to get in time to save a life. She knew it was part of the job—not just with OPSIG but with the Bureau.

But intellectually knowing something and being able to turn off the emotional spigot were two different things.

Vail entered the observation room and set her cup down next to Jones. She looked up at the two-way mirror and saw Rusakov bent forward in her chair.

"What the hell is she doing?"

Jones muted his microphone. "She's giving him a h—"

"Are you kidding me?" Vail was out the door in the next half second.

LANSFORD MOANED. His body tensed, then relaxed. Rusakov tilted her head, still holding his penis in her right hand, cradling his testicles in her left.

"Now. Jason. Tell me what I want to know."

Lansford, eyes still closed, reclining in the chair, shoulders relaxed, did not answer. Finally, he said in a low voice, "They'll kill me. And my wife."

"And how will your wife feel when I tell her what you just told me to do to you?"

Lansford opened his eyes. "She won't believe you."

"Oh, Jason," she said mockingly. "But she will. We'll show her the video."

His eyes widened. "Video?"

"Tell me what I want to know or we'll bring her in right now."

"You wouldn't."

"Trust me, Jason, you don't want to ever say that to me. You'll be sorry every time. Because I'll do whatever is necessary. *Whatever* is necessary."

"She'll understand," Lansford said. "Show her the video, see if I care."

Rusakov squeezed his testicles with a grip as strong as a metal clamp.

"Ahh!" His eyes bulged as he instinctively tried to pull away. "That hurts. Stop!"

VAIL GRABBED THE KNOB AND TWISTED. It was locked.

"Open up. Al—Veronika!" Vail jiggled it again, more forcefully. "Veronika. Let me in!"

Vail heard the scrape of metal on metal and she pulled the heavy door toward her. She gave Rusakov an angry look. "Go clean yourself up."

Rusakov looked down at her soiled top, then left the room.

Vail took a deep breath. *Remember where you are. Focus.* "Jason, you've gotta work with me here. Give me something I can use. There are people who . . . who aren't bound by the morals I'm bound by, who'll do things that—that you don't want done."

Lansford lifted his head, the tension of pain still evident on his face. "Really? Good cop, bad cop? Is that what we're doing now?"

Vail pulled out her handcuff key and unlocked him, then gestured toward his privates. “Put yourself away, please.”

He looked up at her as he sorted himself out. “Tissues?”

“Nope.” She waited a minute for him to finish, then refastened his restraints. “This is not bad cop, good cop. This is not an act. What I said is true. You don’t want to see what these people are capable of. Tell us what we want to know and it stops here.”

“Not gonna happen.”

Well at least he’s no longer denying that he knows something. “I’m going to get something to eat. You want anything?”

“No.”

“Take the time to think long and hard about what I just said. I’ve given you every chance to save yourself a whole lot of pain and heartache. And I mean that quite literally.”

28

Deep Space

Patriot, this is mission control."

Eisenbach's voice.

"Go ahead, this is Digger."

"Discussed your issues and we've identified some readings that we need to check on our end. We'd like you to run a diagnostic on the flight software. We're running simulations as well to see if we can repeat the problems you've had. But we feel it's important for you to . . ."

They waited, but Eisenbach did not continue.

"Repeat, mission control," Stroud said. "Important for us to what? Over."

Silence.

"Here we go again." Carson turned to Stroud. "Anything?"

Stroud shook his head as he tapped on his screen and opened the communication suite.

"How big a deal is this?" DeSantos asked.

"Hard to know. If mission control tells us they're running simulations and wants us to do a diagnostic," Stroud said, "it could be significant. Something didn't look right or they had a failed simulation. Or combined with what we've been experiencing, they could be . . . they're just trying to cover all the bases."

"Could it be related to the problem we had at launch?"

Stroud exhaled forcibly through his lips. "I don't think we know enough yet to say either way."

"If it is all related," Uzi said, "it could be a cascade of system failures."

That got DeSantos's attention and brought him back to their recent F-18 flight—which did not end well. "Does that happen in spacecraft?"

Carson glanced down at DeSantos. "Because of the reliance on computerized flight systems, electronics, and computer chips, Orion's got a lot of similarities to a modern-day fighter jet. Lots of differences too, but—"

"It's definitely a concern," Stroud said. "But we've got redundancies. NASA loves its backup systems, and for good reason. Remember, we've got a second flight computer if this one fails. We're gonna be fine."

"So now what?" DeSantos asked.

"We do what mission control asked," Stroud said. "Digger, see if you can restore comms."

"Roger that."

"Uzi, run the diagnostics while I try to get a message to Vandy."

"On it," Uzi said as he began working the touch screen in front of him.

A moment later, Stroud cursed under his breath. "Nothing's getting through. It's like we're enveloped in interference."

"Add it to the list," DeSantos said.

Uzi continued to work his console. "Hopefully we'll start reducing that list. Maybe it's just a few separate glitches. But if not . . . better we know sooner rather than later."

29

Black Site

Vail walked into the observation room and joined Terrence Jones, who had just stood to stretch.

"Not going very well," she said.

Jones checked his watch. "Going about as expected. If it makes you feel any better, I've seen worse."

Nope. It doesn't.

The door swung open wider as Jones walked out and Douglas Knox entered. His brow was furrowed and his jaw was tense. He glanced at her then turned to face the two-way mirror.

"Everything okay, sir?"

"I was just briefed on Hector and Uzi." He paused a moment before elaborating. "Someone tried to pass a message to Hector, like you suggested. And the cameras you recommended yielded an ID. He's been arrested and is being questioned by OPSIG personnel on base. It was the cook. So far, doesn't appear to be very promising. He's talking but he claims he was approached by someone who offered him five grand cash to put an envelope on Hector's bed. He was not told what was in it but it was suggested that he try not to get caught."

"Credible?"

Knox bobbed his head. "That's their opinion. He made a cash deposit of five grand into his bank account three days ago. He didn't think anyone would suspect him, and it doesn't look like he's done this before, so he wasn't very savvy about it. It checks out."

"Anything on the person who made the ask?"

"Claims it was a young woman he met in Starbucks. Hat, sunglasses, attractive, makeup, well-manicured nails. Great body. Description fits about 5 million women in southern California."

And not by accident. "How about Uzi and Hector? How's their training going?"

"They launched early. There was a malfunction of the rocket on liftoff, but it's all good."

"What kind of malfunction?"

"Don't know yet. But I'm told these things happen. We had glitches of all kinds on Apollo. They've been a part of spaceflight since the early days. Most weren't deadly, but some were."

"How do we know it wasn't intentional?"

Knox rocked back on his heels. "We don't. But I suggest you get to the bottom of what this guy isn't telling us. Given his job and where he works, it could be related. Where are we?"

Should I tell him we're nowhere? "Working on it."

Knox read her face, then said, "Where's Rusakov?"

"Restroom."

"She helping?"

Vail hesitated. "We'll see. Her methods are . . . unorthodox."

"But she gets results."

Oh, yeah she does. And those results were all over her clothing.

"Thank you for having my back, sir. With McNamara."

"I believe in you, Agent Vail. You've proven your worth in a range of situations. Don't think I haven't noticed. I also know you've been a key part of the BAU. And I wouldn't want to disrupt that dynamic. Still, there are times when OPSIG work trumps a serial killer. A dozen lives against thousands, hundreds of thousands. Millions. You're a good tool to have in our kit. No offense."

"I've been called worse, sir."

Knox allowed a slight smile to tickle the corners of his mouth. "I know."

He knows? What's that supposed to mean?

The door opened and Rusakov stuck her head in. "Ready to go—oh, sir. Didn't realize you were here."

"Just catching up with Agent Vail." He turned and headed for the exit. "I don't have to tell you we need answers. *Now*. Not later. Keep me posted on your progress."

RUSAKOV WALKED BACK into the interrogation room. She wore none of the anger she exhibited before. This was, after all, just business. Except that in this case, the 'profit' was national security—and the only currency was actionable information.

She stepped in front of Lansford and leaned against the table's edge. "Let's talk about your son and daughter, Jason."

Lansford rolled his eyes.

"Your daughter's six and your son's nine." Rusakov paused and read his face. When she mentioned their ages, his left eye narrowed slightly but otherwise he kept his composure. Rusakov filed this away. His lack of reaction told her this guy was no ordinary worker bee. Very few fathers, under threat and significant duress, would not flinch—if not freak out—when the adversary brought up his kids and mentioned key information on them. Lansford had some degree of training in interrogation methods—no doubt the reason why Vail had been unsuccessful in eliciting the information they were seeking.

"You've had some time to think. And I know you're a smart guy, so you've put two and two together. We've got your family. And what you're involved in with the Chinese, well, the stakes are very high. You need to tell us what we want to know. No more bullshit."

"How many times are you gonna ask me the same thing and I'm gonna tell you the same thing? I don't know what you're talking about. I have no relationship at all with the Chinese government."

"You've been very calm, cool, and reserved. Well-trained. I respect that. But will you remain so calm and cool when we involve your kids? You'll have no one to blame for what happens to them—but yourself. Because you can stop everything. Right now."

He studied her face, then said, "You're a woman, maybe one day you'll even be a mother. You don't have it in you to kill, let alone harm young children and an innocent woman."

Rusakov got in his face. "Maybe I'm giving you too much credit, Jason. The very fact that I'm sitting in a room here with you should tell you all you need to know about me. Do you think they'd send some lackey to do this? I'm not playing games. And *you* should stop playing them too. Because your family's life is at stake."

Lansford's eyes flicked back and forth. He was thinking.

"Nothing can be that important, Jason. Whoever you're protecting, it can't be as important to you as your family. Because I make one call, and you'll never see them again. Their bodies will never be found. And when we get the info we need—and we will—we'll make sure your 'employers' know you gave them up. Even if you didn't. You know what will happen next. I don't have to spell it out for you."

"I don't believe you."

Rusakov kept her expression impassive. "How does Kathy like first grade?" No response. "I hear Mrs. Clerk has taken quite a liking to her. And I have to say, Kathy has beautiful penmanship. It's quickly becoming a lost art, you know. Most kids these days aren't taught cursive, can't even sign their names on a financial document."

Lansford looked up at her. "Is there a point to this?"

Yes, Rusakov thought, *this guy has definitely been coached.* "Looks like Zach is having trouble with math. Funny thing is, when I asked him about it, he said that he likes it, that you've been a big help in showing him shortcuts for multiplication."

This got Lansford's attention. His mouth opened slightly. He was beginning to realize that Rusakov was not bluffing. Such details about their families often rattled even the best spies.

"Looking good," Jones said in her ear. *"Spikes all over the place."*

"So you know about my children," Lansford said. "Kathy likes blue dresses. Did she tell you that too?"

Rusakov tilted her head. "Actually, she said she hates dresses. The breeze blowing on her legs makes her uncomfortable."

A fine layer of perspiration formed on Lansford's forehead.

"Oh, yeah," Jones said. *"You've got him."*

Lansford cleared his throat. "Why are you so interested in my kids?"

"I thought I made that clear." She folded her arms across her chest. "Because you keep lying to us, Jason. And we need leverage. You're obviously a very skilled spy, so I'm sure you understand."

Rusakov grabbed a remote and aimed it at a screen on the right wall. A dark, dilapidated room appeared. Two large beefy men dressed in black with baklavas over their faces held submachine guns in their hands. The camera panned left, revealing a woman in her thirties. Her face was etched with terror, a fact not lost on Lansford, who leaned forward in his seat.

To her left, as the image shifted, a young girl came into focus, tears sliding down her cheek and reflecting the dim light that swung gently from side to side. A boy, a year or two her junior, clung to her.

Rusakov pressed another button and the monitor went black. "Now." She knelt in front of him. "Jason. I think we understand each other better."

Lansford's eyes found hers. "But you're a woman," he whispered. "How could you do this?"

Rusakov had to stifle the smile. "You may've miscalculated on this one, Jason. You have no idea who I am. What I've done." She pulled out her phone and snuck a look. "In two minutes Renata, Kathy, and Zach will be on their way to a secure location. It'll take about three hours for them to get there. That gives you some time to think, which is always a good thing."

Lansford's eyes narrowed.

"I know. Your mind's working this through. What's within three hours of Washington, DC? A lot of places, I guess. Are they flying or driving?" She faked a laugh. "So many variables to consider. Well, I don't mind telling you we've got a number of safe houses in that radius. Including Cuba, our new friend." She paused, let that sink in. "Do you know what that means, Jason? If we're taking them to Cuba, it means that we're using a black site."

Lansford turned away. "I don't know that term."

Rusakov chuckled softly, mocking him. "I think you do." She threw a thigh across his lap and sat down, placed a hand on each of his shoulders, his nose inches from her breasts. "You're being ungrateful, Jason. I did a nice thing for you before. When was the last time your wife did that for you? I made you feel good. And you did feel good. That much was obvious." She grinned, then placed a finger under his chin and raised it to her face. "Yet you continue to treat me with disrespect. I really don't appreciate that. That will work against you."

"I don't know what you're getting at."

"See?" Rusakov got up, then leaned forward and rested both hands on her thighs. "That's what I mean. You *do* know what I'm talking about. In fact, you're really good at this. You've been trained well. But I've got friends all over the world. We're analyzing your DNA right now. I'm sure you remember where I got the sample from." She paused for effect. "It's being run through CODIS and the profile is being sent to Interpol. We will find out who you're working with. And why."

"That'll be a waste of time."

"And I know that you didn't start in the spy business yesterday. Your craft is too refined. Did someone mentor you?" She studied his face a moment. "Who was it?"

Lansford narrowed his eyes but did not reply.

"Do your wife and kids know what you've been doing? Who you really are?" Rusakov waited a beat for an answer, though she did not expect one. She leaned in closer. "No, I didn't think so. And now they're on their way, on a terrifying journey, whisked off by big men in black tactical gear with scary-looking submachine guns, into a private jet. Oh!" she stopped, cocked her head. "I gave it away, didn't I?"

Lansford tensed his jaw.

"They'll enjoy Cuba. Lots of very colorful cars from the 1950s. You know, they have a hell of a time finding parts for those things. Sometimes they have to jerry rig them with custom-made contraptions to keep them running. Pretty cool, actually—it's like a scene out of an old movie, only it's real. But Renata, Kathy, Zach . . . they won't see any of it. Because they're blindfolded. Your wife is scared. Kathy was screaming when they pulled her from her bedroom. Zach peed in his pants."

She stopped, watched for a reaction. This was all conjecture, but it served to tighten the screws. However, she saw only a slight twitch in the skin around his eyes.

"Not getting much," Jones said. *"His heart rate's still elevated but he's doing a damn good job at controlling it."*

"I know," Rusakov said. "Your handlers taught you to accept it. Your wife, your kids, are collateral damage. Maybe you figured that one day it'd be inevitable something like this would happen. Or maybe you deluded yourself into believing you'd never get caught."

Lansford spit in her face.

Rusakov did not move. "The shame of it all is that they're innocent in this whole thing. You're using them as pawns."

"*I'm* using them as pawns? I've done nothing wrong. You can't prove anything. And yet you've kidnapped my family."

"Yes. We did." Rusakov stood up and used her sleeve to clean off her cheek. "But that's the least that'll be happening to them."

VAIL NEARLY ASSAULTED RUSAKOV when she walked through the door. "Are you out of your mind? You kidnapped his wife and kids?"

"I don't owe you an explanation. But you *did* hear me tell him we were going to bring his fam—"

"I thought you were bluffing."

"We've got a job to do and that guy in there has critical information we need. And he's not providing it. We had to motivate him."

"By psychologically damaging his children?"

Rusakov looked away. "I realize you don't know me. You think I'm some unfeeling bitch." She turned to Vail and met her gaze with sparkling clear gold-brown eyes. "Truth is, it bothers me. A lot. But I'm a good actor. I have to be, doing what I do. And you know what? He is too. You see how calm he is? He's not some fly-by-night mole who was paid to do a one-and-done job. He's a legit spy."

"And his family gets to suffer because of that? I doubt they know what he is, what he does."

"You tried to reason with him. I tried too. You wanted to stay away from enhanced interrogation. Despite what you think, I'm not crazy about it, either. A lot of times it doesn't work. But I'm also trained to do what needs to be done. I don't take that responsibility lightly. So what's left? There's no time to spend months building a rapport with him—which, if I'm right about him being a trained spy, wouldn't work anyway."

"I know."

"We had one thing, and only one thing, as leverage on the guy."

Vail clenched her jaw. "I still don't like it."

"The United States has four operatives risking their lives to prevent an aggressive country from getting hold of an extremely dangerous weapon of mass destruction. And our—your—friends are hurtling through space with no lifeline, no rescue team. Lansford may have information we need to help them—or keep them from blowing themselves up."

Vail turned toward the two-way glass and watched as Lansford fidgeted in his restraints. Likely agonizing over what to do. How difficult a decision could this be for him? "I've been running this through my mind, trying to reason it out. It's not adding up."

"Why?"

Yes, why. Vail sighed. "I don't know. I can't explain it, but we're missing something. We've got something wrong."

"You think he's innocent?"

"Not at all," Vail said. "He so much as admitted it to you. 'They'll kill me,' he said, if he talked to us. No, I think he's exactly what we think he is, but something . . . there's something about those trips to China. Or his connection to China, his family." She shook her head. "I'll keep on it. Meanwhile, let's give him some time to think about this."

"Time is not on our side."

"Sometimes you can't rush these things." *And sometimes you have to accept you've come up empty.* "What if we can't get him to open up? What will they do to him?"

"I honestly don't know." Rusakov glanced at Vail. "But I think we can make an educated guess."

30

Deep Space

The alarm took them by surprise.

The words "O2 tank #2 failure" were flashing across Uzi's glass display. He tapped the screen and tried to ascertain where the problem was located.

Stroud was doing likewise. "I'm seeing a main B bus undervolt."

"CAPCOM," Carson said, "this is Patriot. Bob, do you read?"

Nothing.

"Uzi," Stroud said, "look out the port window and let me know if you see any vapor venting into space."

Uzi craned his neck but did not see anything unusual, let alone a gaseous release. "Everything looks fine. Santa, you see anything out starboard?"

"Crystal clear blackness. What's the deal, Cowboy?"

"Looks like we've lost oxygen tank number two. And number one went almost immediately after that."

"Switching to exterior cameras," Uzi said. He studied the screen, which showed various angles of the ship's exterior. "Everything looks good."

"How can that be?" Carson asked. "Cowboy, what are our O2 levels?"

"Tank one's empty. Two still has 200 PSI, but it's falling. But we've also lost three fuel cells."

"Hang on a second," Uzi said. "What could cause such a complete failure of the O2 tanks?"

"On Apollo 13," Stroud said, "an explosion took out number two, which then caused number one to fail by rupturing a line or damaging a valve. Something like that."

"Sounds like the issue we're having is exactly what happened on Apollo 13," Uzi said.

"Sure does," Stroud said.

DeSantos shifted in his seat, an easy task in zero gravity. "That's kind of odd, don't you think? Almost like it was designed to mimic a previous problem."

Uzi threw a switch on his panel. "And according to CAPCOM—and from what we were able to determine from our own readings—our rocket malfunction on launch was not a malfunction at all."

"As far as we know," DeSantos said. "They were still analyzing the data."

"How much longer to go on that diagnostic?" Carson asked.

"No idea," Uzi said. "It's going system by system. So far it hasn't found any problems."

"Digger, see if you can raise CAPCOM," Stroud said.

Carson tapped his display. "CAPCOM, this is Patriot. Please respond."

No static—but no response, either.

"Looks like we're gonna have to solve this ourselves," DeSantos said, "at least until comms comes back online . . . assuming it does."

"Soon as that diagnostic finishes," Uzi said, "we'll have a better handle on what we're dealing with. We've had four distinct failures. We need to know if they're related, and how. And why."

31

Flight Operations
Vandenberg Air Force Base

The flight control engineer studied his screen, zoomed in, and turned to the adjacent monitor on his left. “Sir. A moment.”

Kirmani walked toward the man’s workstation. “Problem?”

“NORAD picked up a launch from Russia.”

“A Soyuz headed for the ISS?”

“No launches scheduled for the space station,” the engineer said. “Not for another six weeks. And this is a much larger rocket.” He rattled off the specs from the readings he had taken.

“What the hell? Put it up on the main screen.”

The man worked his keyboard and looked to the front of the room, where the rocket was shown via satellite image. It was climbing higher, a trail of fire-like exhaust burning from its bottom. “Obviously that’s a super heavy lift vehicle, sir. And given what’s been going on—”

“We have to assume this is headed to the Moon.” A phone began ringing. Kirmani walked back to his desk and answered the red handset. He listened a moment, then hung up as Eisenbach entered mission control.

"Should we have NASA contact their counterparts at Roscosmos?" Kirmani asked, referring to the Russian Federal Space Agency.

Eisenbach shrugged. "We do have a relationship with them because of the space station. They know the US monitors this stuff, so I think it'd be strange if NASA—or NORAD—doesn't contact them and ask what they're doing."

"Not that Russia will give them a truthful answer."

Eisenbach laughed. "With Russia, if there's one thing we can count on, it's subterfuge."

32

Black Site

Vail returned to the interrogation room four hours and three minutes after they showed Lansford the video of his family. They had been watching him and felt he had reached the point where he would be most pliable and open to cutting a deal for his wife and kids.

He was sweating and his shirt was punctuated by perspiration stains. His hair was greasy and his eyes were red. He had repeatedly refused food and drink.

The room was warm, humid, and musty and reeked of the kind of body odor that came with anxiety.

"I think you've had enough time to think," Vail said. "Tell us what we want to know and we'll release Renata, Kathy, and Zach."

He wearily lifted his head. "And if I don't? You'll harm my family?"

"If you don't, I leave and turn you over to Veronika and she makes the call. As you probably surmised, she's a ruthless bitch. I don't like her. I don't trust her. And I work with her. Take my advice and give us the information."

Lansford bit the inside of his lip and locked gazes with Vail—who did not blink. He closed his eyes.

The seconds became a minute. Then two.

"You're testing our patience, Jason." She turned to face the two-way mirror, where she knew Rusakov was observing. "Make it easy on yourself. And us. You make it easy on us—" she shrugged—"we'll make it easy on you. Simple. Everyone wins."

He laughed sardonically. "Without effort, you can't pull a fish out of a pond."

Vail spun around. "What did you say?"

Lansford shook his head, as if annoyed that she did not understand. "Nothing's easy. Or simple. Nothing."

"No, that's not what you said. You said, 'Without effort, you can't pull a fish out of a pond.'"

Lansford swallowed. "So?"

"I knew someone who used to say that. A guy in Brooklyn. Brighton Beach." In truth, the crime group Vail was surveilling with a wire used that phrase repeatedly. After a while, it became an idiom ingrained in her lexicon. "You know Brighton Beach, Jason?"

"Heard of it. So what?"

"It's a predominantly Russian area of Brooklyn. A lot of Russian immigrants. The Russian mafia operates there."

Lansford's forehead spotted with sweat. "And why are you telling me this?"

Vail stared at him. Watching him squirm, giving him the opportunity to say something that would implicate himself—or the person who was directing this operation. "I think you know."

"You're fishing," he said with a chuckle, trying to recover his composure.

"Oh, I'm fishing all right. Just not in a pond." She studied his face.

"Heart's galloping," Jones said. *"Bingo. You did it."*

Maybe. Not yet. "So it's not China you're working for, it's Russia. Tell me who your Russian handler is."

She saw the worry settle anew on his face like a mask: knitting brow, taut lips. Perspiration bled out from his armpits. His right knee began bouncing.

"Most significant response he's had thus far," Jones said. *"Well, except when she gave him the hand job. Stay with this line of questioning."*

"We know you met with her when you were at Grand Central." It was a bit of a gamble—if she was wrong, it would weaken her hand. But she was fairly certain that, if true, it would unnerve him. "Light brown hair, mid-thirties. You met her in front of the Apple store."

He cast his gaze toward the ground. More tellingly, he did not deny it.

"How many times have you been to Russia?"

"Never been there," he said, his voice low, less confident.

"We can find out, Jason."

The door swung open and a man Vail did not know wheeled in a crude-looking device perched on a stainless steel cart. It took a second for Vail to realize that it was a greasy car battery with cables hooked up to the positive and negative poles. *I hope that's just a threat.*

"What's that for?"

Vail knew she had to play it straight. "C'mon, Jason. You don't need me to spell it out. I tried to warn you. See, you're the only one in this room who's been lying."

Lansford squirmed in his seat, bent his torso forward a few degrees.

"What's your handler's name?" When he did not answer, Vail pressed forward. "How long have you been working with her?"

His gaze flitted over to the car battery. "I don't know anyone from Russia. I'm not working with anyone."

"Karen," Zheng Wei's voice said in her ear. "Got something for you. Come into Room A5. Just down the hall."

Vail rose from her chair and walked over to the stainless steel cart, where she set her right hand on the copper alligator clamp. "I don't believe you, Jason. And I'm going to give you five minutes to reconsider your answer."

Vail headed down the barren hallway, passing the breakroom on the left, and found A5. Zheng was seated at a table with two other men hunched over military-style laptops.

"We've gotten hold of Lansford's credit card bills," Zheng said. "He made six trips to China over a two-year period—we knew his brother lives there, so that in itself isn't a smoking gun. But I looked at his latest visit because it was easiest to get those records, and there are charges in Beijing at a number of restaurants, markets, electronics stores, coffee shops."

"That's what we'd expect to see if he went to Beijing. Not very helpf—"

"It *is* exactly what we'd expect, which makes it suspect."

"That's ridicul—"

"Hear me out. I looked at the actual receipts, at the signatures I was able to get hold of. And they don't match Lansford's."

Vail nodded slowly. "So someone used his charge card and signed for the merchandise. As cover for him because he was somewhere else?"

"That's what I'm thinking."

"And that goes right to my theory."

"Want to share it?"

"You're familiar with Beijing?"

"Very. Why?"

Vail turned and opened the door. "Walk me through what questions to ask." She explained what she was looking for, then stepped back into the interrogation room.

"Let's try this again, Jason. You say you're not working for Russia. I'll accept that as the truth—for now. So let's go back to China. We know you've been there a number of times. And we know you've got family in Beijing. So tell me. What's your favorite place to eat when you go there?"

"We never go out to eat."

"Never?"

Lansford shook his head.

"You've never gone out to eat in a restaurant in Beijing."

"I don't know how else to answer that question. No. Never."

"Where do you go when you visit?"

Lansford shrugged. "Around."

"These are bullshit answers," Zheng said in her ear. *"And it doesn't match the receipts."*

"Ever go sightseeing?"

"I'm there to visit with my brother and his family, not play tourist."

"So you just sit in the apartment all day? Every day?"

"Pretty much."

"You've never gone out, not once in all your trips?"

"Went to the Great Wall once."

"Tell me about it."

"Big. Long. Very old."

"I could've told you that and I've never been to China."

Lansford shrugged. "I'm not big on adjectives."

"So other than a visit to the Great Wall, you've never left the apartment? How am I supposed to believe that?"

"That's your problem."

"Actually, it's yours. Because we've got your credit card receipts." Zheng coached her on the places that appeared on the charge log. "We've got one from Capital M restaurant for 880 yuan. And one from Shoulashou Electronics City for 915 yuan. Ring a bell?"

"Oh, yeah. Forgot about that."

"When were those charges?

"I, uh . . . I can't remember."

"Last trip or the one from three years ago?"

"Look, who the hell remembers when they buy stuff or go out to eat?"

"Especially when you didn't make those charges. I thought you said you never leave the apartment. And that you don't eat out."

"As I said, I forgot."

"I don't think so. I think your brother had a nice dinner at Capital M and bought a flat screen TV. On your dime, as a cover. Because you were somewhere else. Weren't you?"

"I don't know what you're talking about."

"The signatures don't match. The signatures on the charge slips have your name but they don't match the ones you signed for recently in DC."

"I had an identity theft. Someone stole—"

"No. You didn't. We checked."

Lansford clenched his jaw.

Vail watched him a moment as she worked it through her brain, trying to fit the disparate facts together.

"This is Alex," Rusakov said. *"Just spoke with Hot Rod. Lansford's last trip to China, a day after he arrived, there's surveillance footage of him in Adolfo Suárez Madrid-Barajas airport in Spain boarding an Air Europa flight to Paris. And another flight on Vueling Airlines three hours later to Moscow."*

Vail grinned. *That's it, the missing piece.* "While we've been sitting here, Jason, my people have been combing through your phone, piecing together your online activity, watching surveillance video, analyzing your credit card activity, comparing facial recognition and biometric data. There's not much we do these days that can be kept off the grid—especially when you've got our resources and reach. We've succeeded in recreating your movements throughout China. And you know what we found?"

He shook his head but did not speak. His eyes canted toward the floor.

"Sure you do. You want to level with me now or do I need to spell it out?"

"I honestly don't know what you're talking about."

"We know you used your flights to China as a cover to fly on to Russia under an alias. We've got you on video, confirmed by biometric data."

Lansford looked up and squared his shoulders.

Time to test my theory. "You're working for the Russians. They approached you because of your brother and his family. They live in China, which connects you to the Chinese. And your brother's been in trouble with the authorities for things he's done with his business. They were on the verge of accusing him of fraud, and let's face it, sometimes when people are accused of things by that government, they disappear."

"So?"

"So anyone looks at you, they'll suspect you're spying for China, paying off a debt for your brother. You cut a deal: spy for them and they don't kill him. But truth is, that's not what's happening at all. *That's* why they selected you. The trips to China are just a ruse, a cover for your real work. With the Russians. That's very clever."

Lansford did not say a word. Did not move.

"This is good," Jones said. *"GSR is off the charts. Heart rate too."*

"I'm giving you one last chance before I walk out and Veronika comes in again. But instead of another hand job, she's gonna shock your balls." Vail leaned in close. "And it's not gonna feel near as good." She leaned back. "At least, that's what the last guy said."

"Nice work," Jones said. *"He's fucking freaking out. Go in for the kill."*

Vail counted to three, then stood up. "I'll now be able to sleep. Because I gave you every opportunity to help yourself—and Renata. And Kathy. And Zach. Good-bye, Jason."

She headed for the door and had her hand on the knob when he mumbled something.

Vail turned. "What?"

"I was given lines of code to insert."

She headed back to the chair. "What kind of code?"

"All spacecraft are run by computers. Even Apollo used computers—rudimentary by today's standards, but computers. And computers are run by software programs."

"Go on."

He licked his lips. "Programs are lines of code, instructions, that do everything, run everything, control everything. Computers are getting the ability to think, but only in certain situations. We still have to tell them to execute certain actions using commands. If *this* happens, do *that*. Line after line of computer code. Instructions."

"And where did this code go?"

"In the flight software. It runs on a real-time, multi-tasking operating system."

"What spacecraft?"

Lansford sucked in a deep breath. "Orion."

Shit, shit, shit. That's the one Uzi and DeSantos are in. "When did you do this? When's it going to be used?"

"Four months ago." He looked away. "I heard it was going to be used very soon."

"How soon?"

"For all I know, the rocket may've already launched. I got the sense it was being prepped. They wanted a final update to the program. We compiled it about six weeks ago."

Ten-four. That's the one carrying Uzi and DeSantos. Operation Containment.

"What's the operating system software used for?"

Lansford chuckled. "Everything. The avionics consists of the flight computers, software, sensors, effectors, displays, controls, radios, and navigation sensors. They control fuel venting, instrumentation, fuel levels, navigation, environmental control systems, communications. Everything."

Alex was right. This could be disastrous.

She could sense Rusakov glaring at the back of her head through the two-way mirror. "The lines of code you inserted. Specifically, what's it supposed to do?"

"No idea."

Vail set her hands on her knees, her face a foot from Lansford's. "Don't insult me, Jason. I've had enough of your fucking lies. You're a software engineer. You know what those instructions were designed to do."

"I—I didn't look at them. I just inserted them where I was told to put them."

Bullshit. "Look," Vail said. "If that code does something bad, causes something to happen to that rocket, or the spacecraft, it's as if you did it yourself . . . as if you pressed a button to make it happen. You put that code into the operating system. Whether or not you knew what it was going to do—which I don't believe—is irrelevant."

Lansford closed his eyes. "It was designed to make the crew think something was wrong with the ship when it wasn't. So they'd get false readings. That's it."

"That's it? I'm not a rocket scientist, but I'm pretty smart. If the astronauts get false readings, they're gonna take action to correct what they're seeing. Right? And I'm guessing here, but if they do the wrong thing, that rocket could explode."

"They could get some readings that would indicate something different is happening from what's actually happening."

"Could get or will get?"

Lansford stared straight through her, as if she were not there. "Will."

Vail frowned. "And who gave you these instructions on where to insert this code? Who gave the code to you?"

"I want a deal."

A deal? "I told you. We're not the cops. But how's this: you tell me who's working with you and Veronika doesn't put a bullet in your brain. You have my word on that."

"So *they'll* put a bullet in my brain. Or my family's."

Vail knew this was his pressure point—and her leverage. "Fair enough. Here's my best offer. And you have thirty seconds to accept it: I know a couple of Feds. I turn you over to them, they'll make sure your wife and kids are placed in the federal witness security program. Renata, Kathy, Zach, they'll be safe. And they'll be given a monthly stipend and protection."

"And me?"

"My guess is that you're going to prison. But I'll make sure they put in a good word for you with the sentencing judge." *And I'll leave out Rusakov's hand job*. "Best I can do." She wiggled her fingers. "Now. Tell me."

"I want to meet with the Feds. I need to hear it from them."

"Not gonna happen. Because if you lie to us—and your track record is pretty sketchy so far—there'll be no deal. You're just gonna have to trust me on this, Jason. And I think I've proven that I tell you the truth. Everything I've told you so far has been spot-on."

He sighed, closed his eyes tightly. "A woman approached me about three years ago. She said she had some information about me. Some . . . things I wouldn't want people to know about."

"People?"

"They'd start with Renata. And my parents. Friends. Then the *Washington Post*."

"And this information was legitimate?"

Lansford dropped his chin and nodded.

"Did she say where she got this information from?"

"Didn't matter. She told me what she had. It was true. I didn't care who gave it to her."

"Was this something you disclosed on your NASA background check?"

He looked to his left. "I wanted the job and they do a pretty thorough job when security clearances are involved. The stuff they had on me wouldn't have kept me from getting the job. But if I didn't tell them about it, if I lied, they never would've hired me. So yeah, I disclosed it. Some of it. Enough to cause a lot of personal problems for me."

Had to be from that stolen laptop.

"She offered me money, $100,000 that they put into an offshore account every year. And all I had to do was periodically get them information."

He's not telling me everything. "What kind of information did they want?"

"Projects we're working on for NASA. And the military."

"We want to know exactly what you gave to them. And we need to know *now*. No more games."

Lansford swallowed deeply. "Design plans for the operating system. And the hash algorithm, a private key of sorts. The machine, or the astronauts, holds the corresponding public key used to verify the algorithm's signature." He hesitated. "Eventually the Russians wanted the code too, when testing had been completed. I only gave it to them once."

Only once. That's comforting. "What else did you give them?"

"Information about certain things that were at my security level."

"Who'd you meet with in Russia?"

"No idea."

Vail frowned.

"Honestly. I don't know. He doesn't say, 'Hi Jason. My name's Vladimir.' Just someone I meet in a park. We're not friends. I just get them what they ask for. When I can. If I can."

"You had to go all the way to Russia to give them info?"

He sucked on the side of his cheek a moment, then said, "First time I went for training."

"Training on what?"

"How to be an effective conduit for them without getting caught."

Translation: how to be a spy. "What else?"

"Training on how to make sure the code they gave me went undetected."

"So you did know what the code was supposed to do."

He bent his head left. "Yeah."

"We'll need a full list of everything you gave them—and what that code was designed to do."

Lansford sighed. "Can I have a moment with my family to, you know, explain what's going on before you turn me in? I wanna try to make them understand."

Vail clenched her jaw. Everything in her told her not to do that because there was too much risk. He could pass a coded message to his wife. Or it could simply be an innocent apology. And a heartfelt good-bye. "It's not my decision. Very least, you could record a message to them." *Perhaps that could serve as evidence of admission because this interrogation sure can't ever be used in court.*

The door opened and Rusakov entered with a yellow legal pad and pen. She handed it to Vail and gave Lansford an icy stare before leaving. *Was that because he's a spy? What he'd done to Orion? Or because I'd gotten the info and she didn't?*

As he started to write, Vail said, "If there's one thing you gave them, something that'd be the most valuable to them, what was it?"

"I'd need to know what they intended to do with this stuff. I really have no idea."

"Bullshit!" Vail kicked her chair aside. "Lives are at stake. And given the nature of what they wanted from you, you have a pretty damn good idea."

Lansford chewed on that a moment, then returned to moving the pen across the page. He stopped and lifted his gaze from the pad. "The hash algorithm was obviously important. But the element that was discovered from the soil samples brought back on Apollo 17, I think that's what they were really after."

"What?"

"You asked what would be most valuable to them. I'm just guessing, but . . . they asked for that before they wanted the private key."

"Before?"

"It's like once they knew about that element, they shifted gears and started asking me about the operating system. And . . ."

"And what?"

"I think it was the most sensitive thing I gave them. That element supposedly increases the yield on nuclear weapons. Had a weird name, something like Caesar."

Vail had to fight to keep her expression impassive. *How would he get hold of classified documents? He did more than just insert code into an operating system. He used his security clearance to get into NASA's internal systems. He's in deeper than he's saying.*

He turned his attention back to the pad.

"You're not telling me everything, Jason. That information was not at your level of classification."

He nodded. "They wanted me to hack into the secure system. They showed me how to get into it. I tried a few times and finally penetrated the firewall one night and searched around until I found some things I thought would interest them. That element was one of them. There was a bolded sentence in one of the top secret reports." He put his head down and continued writing.

"I want the name of your handler."

He stopped his pen. "Not until my family's safe."

"You're not understanding where we're at here, Jason. You're not calling the shots. You've proven over and over that most of what you've told me are lies. So you *will* tell me what I want to know—right now—or I'll personally make sure nothing I've agreed to will be honored."

Lansford closed his eyes again. "Her name's Jessie Kerwin."

"Jessie Kerwin. A Russian handler? Give me a break. What's her real name?"

"If you know how this works, you know she didn't give me her real name—and never will."

"How do you contact her?"

"She contacts me. If I have something for them, I use a DLB."

DLB—a dead letter box, a "drop" in plain sight that both parties know about. They insert information then leave a signal that indicates something is waiting there for them: a chalk mark, a certain kind of flag hanging, a colored rag, a piece of duct tape. Standard espionage tradecraft.

"Where?"

"The northeast, near Union Market. I'll have to show you."

"You'll do better than that. You'll put something in there for her. No one knows we have you, so if you leave a note for them they won't be suspicious."

"They're suspicious by nature. And very careful."

"So are we." She gestured at the pad. "Keep writing."

Vail walked out and met up with Rusakov in the observation room. "We need to get on this before they start to wonder about him. In case they've got someone watching his home. Or office."

"We've had teams at both locations. They haven't seen anyone who could be surveilling him or his house. They haven't gone inside in case the premises were being watched remotely."

Vail looked at the two-way glass where Lansford was still hunched over the table. "Soon as he's done, let's put him in a car and get him over to the DLB. Put a tracker on him and someone in the backseat, on the floor. Can't afford to lose this guy."

"We've got his family. I don't think he'll be going anywhere."

Vail tilted her head. "People do irrational things, take extreme risks, when their backs are up against the wall. Assume nothing."

Rusakov nodded. "Point taken."

33

Deep Space

Stroud dropped his hand from the display. “Anyone find anything?”

“Everything looks good,” Uzi said. “Just like CAPCOM found. Ship’s healthy. Except that it’s not.”

Stroud sighed. “I know. But that doesn’t make sense. So where does this leave us?”

“Let’s first deal with the oxygen tank and fuel cell failure. My honest assessment is that it wasn’t a failure at all.”

“I agree with Uzi,” Carson said. “Apollo 13 saw gas escaping from the tank into space. We didn’t see anything. The exterior cameras didn’t show anything either. So . . . what? Computer error?”

Stroud flipped a switch. “The systems were tested rigorously for months. No such glitch showed up. None of these did.”

“No they didn’t,” Uzi said. “And that’s where I was going with my comment. These issues we’ve been having. They’re not errors in the computer code—a glitch, as you called it. That would’ve shown up on all the rigorous validation and testing the engineers have been doing. This was done on purpose. Malware. Inserted into the flight software.”

They were silent a moment as they absorbed that.

"Malware works on personal computers," DeSantos finally said. "Someone clicks on a file and it installs a malicious program on their PCs. But how can it infect a . . . a spacecraft?"

Uzi chuckled. "Malware is computer code written to carry out specific tasks. In this case, it's designed to infiltrate an OS, or operating system—which is exactly what our flight software is. The avionics, which includes the OS, controls our sensors, effectors, displays, controls, radios, navigation—everything that happens onboard, every reading we get, every engine burn and for how long.

"You're right, Santa. Typical routes of infection involve tricking a worker or the average Jack husband or Jill wife into clicking on a file sent through email that they think is legit. It surreptitiously installs a program on their server or computer and that malware runs and does whatever it's been designed to do—steal passwords or corporate intellectual property like blueprints or secret sauce ingredients, and so on."

"Yeah," Stroud said, "but how can it affect the operating system of a rocket, of a spacecraft? Not to mention one operated by the military."

Uzi shifted in his seat so he could face Stroud. "Most obvious explanation is that someone had access to the OS code."

"*Lots* of people had access to it. Software engineers have been working on it for years."

"It was built by a contractor," DeSantos said, "right?"

"Aerospace Engineering," Carson said. "But they've all been vetted, they've all got clearance."

"There are ways to bury errant commands amidst a hundred million lines of code," Uzi said. "If the malware was created by one or more software developers in the program, they could hide the functionality by making the code so it passes static analysis and proves nonharmful during normal dynamic analysis.

"There are also attacks generated from hardware sources like multi-layer circuit boards and chips, which are difficult to fully validate—making it a feasible place for an attack if you can get someone on the inside to pull it off."

"So we have a spy or spies at Aerospace Engineering?" Carson asked.

"I think that's the most likely scenario," Uzi said. "But it could also be at NASA. And that answers your other question, about it being a military operation. The Defense Department has piggybacked on NASA's SLS and Orion project. They've codeveloped certain aspects of it. But SLS/Orion cost billions of dollars and took over a decade to design, build, and test, so there's no way the Pentagon would duplicate those efforts, especially when it'd only fill, at best, a very infrequent need."

"I get that," Stroud said. "Our defense budget has been under fire for years. But malware in a military operation . . . Jesus, the implications."

"Malware's never been an issue on a spacecraft," Uzi said. "I'm sure it wasn't something anyone was checking for. Until a few years ago, the concept of putting malware in, or hacking into, medical devices wasn't even considered. The engineers didn't plan for it. Pacemakers and insulin pumps had little to no security controls. As with so many things, whether it's technology or government or human nature in general, it's not a problem until it becomes a problem. Then you fix it."

"Well," DeSantos said, "it's become a problem."

"Military drones have been hacked," Stroud said. "I guess this is something that was bound to happen sooner or later."

"We've got to get word to Kirmani and Eisenbach."

"Assuming we'll be able to talk with them again," Stroud said, "that'll be the first words out of our mouths."

34

Opsig Mission Control
Space Flight Operations Facility
Vandenberg Air Force Base

Status on that Russian launch?" Kirmani asked, examining the wall-size screens.

"Definitely a super heavy lift rocket," Eisenbach said, standing behind the chair of a mission control technician and peering over his shoulder. "Took off from Vostochny Cosmodrome, not their usual Soyuz facility at Baikonur. All we know so far."

"And the Russians say it's a mapping mission of the lunar surface."

Eisenbach shook his head derisively. "You don't need a rocket taller than the Statue of Liberty to map the lunar surface."

"Yeah, no shit," Kirmani said. "We knew we weren't going to get the truth. But this is China's ballgame. Why is Russia involved?"

"Maybe for the same reason," Eisenbach said. "Caesarium. Do we have any intel about recent activity in their space program?"

"I'll check with Geospatial. And NSA."

"I'll notify McNamara." Eisenbach picked up the handset of the secure phone.

"I may have an explanation," McNamara said after hearing the news. "We finally got Jason Lansford to talk. He placed malware in the Orion operating system. It could explain that malfunction you had on launch. Worth looking into."

"Who's he working for?" Eisenbach asked.

"Russia. We don't have independent verification so it's unconfirmed. But given what we've been told, it makes sense. It also explains why they were able to launch so quickly after seeing Patriot lift off. They've been planning this for a while because they knew *we* were readying a mission."

"We can't wait for verification," Eisenbach said. "We need to find a way to get word to Patriot. Its comms are being interfered with."

"How?" McNamara asked. "By who?"

"We're working on it," Eisenbach said.

"What the hell does that mean? Uplink jamming is very difficult because the jamming platform has to be within the footprint of the antenna to Patriot's location. And once the jamming starts it's not covert by any means. We should've been able to geolocate the jamming source."

"Right. Except that we haven't been able to," Eisenbach said. "We're not sure what's going on. If I had to guess—and you know I hate to guess—it's not jamming but whatever's infected the spacecraft operating system is also affecting the comms."

There was a long silence as McNamara digested that. "Keep us posted," he finally said.

Eisenbach hung up and briefed Kirmani on what McNamara had told him.

"You think our guys have figured it out?"

"Uzi has an extremely strong background in computer science," Eisenbach said. "He's done some hacking, too. If any of them are going to key in on this, it'd be him. But I have no idea what they're thinking or how they're approaching it."

"We told them to run diagnostics."

"Will that show anything?"

Kirmani scratched his forehead. "Probably not. NASA and DOD ran all sorts of verification tests before deploying the software, as did our contractor."

"But our contractor is the one who employs the spy who planted this stuff."

"Exactly. He knows the system intimately, knows how it's tested, what we're looking for and how we do it. The fuckers pulled a good one on us." Eisenbach yanked off his headset. "Bastards."

"So they covered their tracks well enough for NASA and DOD engineers not to catch it. That said, I'm sure they weren't looking for it. Malware on spacecraft operating systems is—it's just not something that ever happens."

"Past tense."

"I feel so goddamn helpless." Kirmani looked down at the control panel. "Have you heard anything about us launching a counterattack?"

Eisenbach drew back. "What are you talking about?"

"This is an act of war."

Eisenbach glanced around. "Obviously the Russians are being very aggressive. But so are we. We've destroyed communications between China and its own spacecraft, for Christ's sake. You don't think *that's* an attack?" He shook his head. "We need to ride this out, see where it leads. We have the laser satellites ready to deploy. But we've got to give our team a chance to do their thing."

"Their thing?" Kirmani scoffed. "When Russia launched that rocket, everything went out the goddamn window."

Eisenbach clenched his jaw. "Don't you think I know that?"

"This isn't going the way we'd hoped."

"Doesn't matter. None of this is our call. Our only job is to get our men through this and provide intel and analysis to the SecDef and the Joint Chiefs."

Kirmani leaned over and pressed a button on the panel. “I’ll keep trying to get a message through to Patriot. We’ve gotta somehow find a way of letting ’em know what’s going on. They’re flying into a fucking war. And they have no goddamn clue.”

35

Southeast Washington, DC

The dead letter box was in an industrial area in northeastern DC, in the neighborhood of the Union Market, a valiant attempt to gentrify the dilapidated, high crime area. There were indications that the effort was working.

The crumbling, graffiti-covered brick wall of a local tile manufacturer contained a metal handled mailbox-style door. And Jason Lansford, with Karen Vail lying prone across the rear floorboards of Lansford's Infiniti, was approaching the drop.

"Remember, Jason, we've got men stationed all over the neighborhood. You try to run and we'll have you back in that interrogation room—hooked up to that battery, just for trying to escape. And we've got other measures in place as well. Even if you get away, we'll know where you are."

"Jessie's very paranoid. And always *very* well prepared—the ultimate Boy Scout, so to speak. What if she sees your people? If this goes to shit, I want you to promise you'll honor the deal."

"We're paranoid too. This isn't our first kidnapping," Vail said, parroting Rodman. "But you already know that."

"What about your promise? No matter what happens, I kept up my end."

"You keep your end of the deal, we'll keep ours."

Lansford pulled over and shoved the gearshift into Park.

"Put the envelope inside and mark the box, then come directly back to the car."

"I thought I'd head over to the market and do some shopping. They've got some great Korean food."

And he still retains his sense of humor. Gotta admire that. "Remember, you're being watched."

In her ear, she heard Rusakov say, "We have eyes on him."

"Roger," Vail said into her headset. "Go on, Jason. Make the drop."

She felt the car rock as he got out and slammed the door shut.

"Talk to me, Alex."

"He's glancing around, heading straight for the box . . . he pulled it open . . . and he made an X with the chalk we gave him. He's heading back to the car."

"Good," Vail said, the hump in the floor starting to bother her ribcage. "I really thought he'd try to make a run for it."

"We've got his family."

"We'll have *them* regardless of whether we have *him*. But without him, having them is useless to us. They're our leverage. But we've gotta have him in custody for it to matter. Another reason to run is he may not believe we're going to honor our pledge to him. He's got no idea who we really are. He has no reason to trust us."

The door opened and the car sagged with Lansford's weight. She looked up and saw the back of his head hit the seat rest.

"Okay, let's go. Back to Union Station. We'll transfer cars and head back."

He pulled the Infiniti into gear and drove off.

They had a dozen operatives in place prepared to watch the drop for days—construction workers, homeless men and women with canine companions—with two other shifts due to take over in succession throughout the evening and overnight hours. They had no idea how long it would take; it depended on how often Jessie Kerwin checked the box for the mark. Lansford said she generally responded within two days, so they had reason to believe it would be fairly soon.

But until they had her in custody, they had no way of knowing if this lead would in fact *lead* anywhere.

FOUR HOURS LATER, Vail got an encrypted group message:

> woman late thirties at box
>
> walked by looking around
>
> bundled up but looks a match to NYC pic
>
> i think this is kerwin
>
> passed dlb 3 times in 30 min
>
> 1 careful sob

Vail was parked only a block and a half away from the drop. An hour ago, she called Robby and told him she might not make dinner—something he was anticipating since she had not joined him for a meal since the case began.

Vail brought the night vision binoculars up to her face and peered into the darkness.

RUSAKOV SAT IN THE CAR beside Troy Rodman. The sky had gone charcoal an hour ago, all remaining light eventually bleeding away and leaving inky blackness.

She let her gaze roam until it found the Moon, bright and glowing. And somewhere between here and there, four of her colleagues were racing through space at ungodly speeds, their lives potentially hanging on the actions she and her team were about to take.

Rusakov turned her attention back to the area in front of her.

"You're thinking about them," Rodman said.

"I am. Can't help it. Can't even fathom what it must be like, what they're doing. I mean, they weren't trained for this. It's not what they signed on for."

"Isn't it? They're doing what needs to be done, what they're told to do to protect the national security of the country. In the air, at sea, on land—in space, or on a planetary body—doesn't matter. Risk is always there. Just different this time around. Probably no worse than some of the stuff our spec ops did in Iraq, Afghanistan, Libya, Syria, Iran . . . the list is long. As to what they were trained for, shit, teachers blasted into space on the shuttle. Our guys are infinitely more qualified than they were. I'm not worried about them—at least the things they can control. What the Russians are doing, that's what's got me concerned."

Rusakov could not argue. She glanced around and noted that most of the vehicles had disappeared from the streets—which spelled potential problems for them. Being an industrial area, it was harder to remain inconspicuous sitting in a car once most of the workers had gone home.

They watched from a couple blocks away through infrared binoculars as the woman once again circled back and, satisfied she was alone, pulled open the metal door and extracted the envelope. With her left hand she wiped away the chalk mark Lansford had made.

VAIL STARTED THE ENGINE and drove slowly toward the target. Over the radio, she heard the team: "Converge, converge, converge!"

"Hello Jessie," Vail said under her breath.

As Kerwin settled into her car, two black SUVs careened around the corner and blocked her path: one in front and one in back. Four operatives were approaching from the sides when the woman flung her door open and ran.

"Goddamn it," Vail said as she stopped and got out of her Ford.

She legged it across the street and joined the pursuit as Kerwin, faster than Vail would have given her credit for—she was likely an athlete of some kind—fired blindly behind her, forcing her pursuers to dive for cover.

Vail, approaching obliquely, saw Kerwin squeeze between two buildings a block away, disappearing into the darkness.

Out of the corner of her eye, Vail saw Rusakov and Rodman. "Go around to the right," she yelled at Rusakov. "Hot Rod, go left, make sure she doesn't get into a car on the other side of the alley."

Vail pursued Kerwin into the area where she was last seen. Her OPSIG sidearm in hand—a Glock like hers but untraceable with a special coating that reduced the likelihood of leaving behind errant fingerprints—she proceeded into the crevice. She turned on her pistol's green laser and white LED light and sucked in her gut as she sidled into the tight space.

She did not see Kerwin, but garbage strewn about blocked her view to some degree. In her ear, the team was calling out their positions and providing SITREPS—situation reports—but thus far, no one had located her.

Vail came out the other side, but before she could right herself after emerging from the cramped gap between the buildings, she felt a sharp blow to her wrist—and the Glock went flying.

Vail dropped and rolled, got to her feet—and came face-to-face with Jessie Kerwin training a handgun on her. But Kerwin lurched forward, her head whipping backward violently into extension. She dropped to the ground, revealing Rusakov holding her HK P2000 around the barrel.

"Looks like that thing is capable of landing an incapacitating blow without firing a shot."

"It's real metal," Rusakov said, "not like your plastic toy. Packs a punch."

And in fact, the woman's scalp was bleeding profusely. Vail knelt down and handcuffed Kerwin, who was unconscious. Vail checked for a pulse and then radioed in their position.

Rodman came running up to them, followed a few seconds later by the other team members, who arrived in a dark, windowless van. They loaded Kerwin into the back while another brought a bucket over and quickly bleached away the blood evidence that had spattered on the cement.

Rusakov glanced around. There were no bystanders, but smartphones—and their video cameras—were prevalent. Because of the lack of light it would not be of much use to anyone—but it was still safer not to hang around unnecessarily.

They jumped into the vehicle and were dropped off at their abandoned cars. Moments later, they were on their way to the black site.

UPON THEIR ARRIVAL, the facility was a mass of activity. The sense was that they were about to get a major break. After removing Kerwin's jacket and wanding her, a medic stitched her scalp wound.

Vail was directed into the briefing room down the hall. When she entered, Rusakov, Zheng, and Rodman were seated around the no-frills oval laminate table. Knox, CIA director Tasset, and McNamara joined them a moment later.

"Strategy?" McNamara asked.

"We can take a number of approaches," Zheng said. "Being Russian, Alex can try to establish a common understanding, a relationship based on inherent trust—although at the moment we can't be certain Kerwin is a native countryman. I also don't think she'd be amenable to that. I can talk spy to spy, which may be more to her liking—comrades who respect each other. Hot Rod can intimidate her. And Karen can be more nuanced about it, feel her out and help us determine which tactic would be most effective."

"We can always intimidate later," Tasset said. "And going the colleague-leveling-with-colleague method is a good follow-on if we can't get her cooperation with honey. Vail goes first." He looked to McNamara and Knox, who both nodded agreement.

"Name of Jessie Kerwin checks out," Knox said. "On the surface, thirty-six years old, an employee of a custom tennis shoe manufacturer in Maryland. Works out five days a week in the evenings at a gym a mile from the DLB. She's into Krav Maga. By the time we're done, I'm determined to know everything there is to know about her—even her favorite food." He handed an iPad to Rodman, seated next to him, and Rodman gave it to Vail. "Soon as we have more, we'll pass it along. This is everything we've got. It's not much."

Vail read the two-paragraph summary, then slid the device to Rusakov. "Okay, let's do this." Vail rose from her chair and walked down the corridor into the interrogation room.

"I have nothing to say," Kerwin said as the door clicked shut behind Vail.

"That's okay." Vail paced back and forth in front of her. "I'll do the talking—and I'll get right to the point. We're not the police. But we *are* after some information. And we'll go to great lengths to make sure we get it."

"I still have nothing to say."

"We know you're a spy. We know you're Jason Lansford's handler."

Kerwin glanced at the ceiling.

"Would you like something to eat?"

"No."

"How long have you been spying for Russia?"

"I don't know what you're talking about."

"Jessie." Vail stopped in front of her. "Give me a little professional courtesy here. I know you're a spy. You know you're a spy. I'm not a cop, so you're not gaining anything by refusing to acknowledge what we both know."

Kerwin looked down and kept her gaze on the ground in front of her, as if Vail were not even present.

"We know about the DLB. Obviously. Jason left an envelope there for you. You saw his mark and retrieved it."

"So what?"

"We know about the software code you gave him to insert into the operating system. So let's just stipulate that you're a spy and move on from there, okay?"

Kerwin brought her eyes up to Vail's and tilted her head to the side. "Fine. I'm his handler. Again, so what?"

"We work for a defense contractor who has a lot of business to lose if anything happens to that spacecraft. We need to know why Russia is involved in this."

"Ask *them*."

"Jessie, just tell us what we want to know and we'll release you. We don't care that you're a spy. We only want to know who's pulling the strings and why, see if we can get them to back off."

"I don't know the answers to your questions. There's a guy I've never met. He tells me what he needs and I get it for him. And he pays me. Very well."

"His name?"

"Vladimir."

That narrows it down to a few million. Then again, she could be telling the truth. "Vladimir's last name?"

"Don't know. But I wouldn't get too excited. No way Vladimir's his real name."

We finally agree on something. "How are you paid?"

"Money is wired into an offshore account."

"How long has this been going on?"

"Why do you need to know that?"

"Anything you tell me helps us identify who Vladimir is—and how we can get in touch with him, make things right."

"Eleven years."

"Ever been to Russia?"

"When he recruited me. And no, I don't remember any of the people who trained me. It was all done in generic office buildings with no markings. Haven't been back since."

"What's your real name?" Vail asked.

"No reason for you to know that."

"Can you set up a meet with Vladimir?"

"I don't think he's who you think he is."

"You mean the Russian Federation?"

"Just saying. You might be headed down the wrong road. I can't arrange a meet for you but I can deliver a message and if he wants to contact you . . ." Kerwin shrugged. "That's up to him."

"Vail," McNamara said in her ear. "Come back into the briefing room."

Vail did as ordered.

"She appears to be telling us the truth," Knox said. "But it's also likely she's a trained liar."

Tasset removed his glasses and rubbed his eyes. "We can continue interrogating her or we can plant a tracking device and see where she goes, who she meets with. I don't think surveillance teams will work because these people are highly trained to spot that. She may even suspect the tracker and ditch it."

"We'd have to put her under, then inject the chip into her rear end," McNamara said. "But when she comes to, her butt'll be sore and she'll know what we've done."

"We'd have to keep her sedated for a couple of days," Knox said. "But we don't have a couple of days."

"So let Alex go in," Zheng said, "see if she can draw something out of her. Now that she admitted she's spying for Russia, maybe having a Russian question her will scare the shit out of her."

"I agree," McNamara said. "Keep at her awhile, see if she knows more than she's telling us. Sending Alex in seems like the right move. We can fall back on the tracking chip anytime we want."

Tasset nodded. "That also gives us some time to assemble a more comprehensive backgrounder." He turned to Rodman. "Anything yet?"

"Nothing's come in from the Agency or Interpol. OPSIG's digging. NSA said they'll need an hour to get us something—if there's something to get."

"What do we make of this Vladimir guy?" Vail said. "Or her training in Russia?"

Rusakov shifted in her seat. "That's the part I'm most skeptical about. If she went to Russia, that's a huge commitment on someone's part. And hers. Like she said, she's likely being paid very well, and the most obvious party is the government. But private enterprise can't be ruled out."

An alarm sounded. Zheng was first to the door but the knob would not budge.

"We're in lockdown," McNamara said.

Knox came up alongside Zheng. "Lockdown? Why? What the hell's going on?"

McNamara grabbed the telephone handset off the wall. "This is SecDef McNamara. Open the conference room door . . . I know we're in lockdown . . . No, goddammit, just do it n—"

A loud blast shook the floor. Vail almost fell to her knees but righted herself as the lock released and Zheng yanked on the handle.

Rusakov followed Vail and Zheng into the hallway, where a fine mist and smoky cloud fogged the air. The alarm klaxon was louder, piercing and nearly deafening.

"Suspect has escaped," Rodman yelled into a wall-mounted intercom. He slammed his fist against it, apparently realizing it was no longer operational. He took off into the smoke.

Vail figured the exits had been secured at the same time as the conference room door—which meant Kerwin could still be in the building, unless the explosion was designed to give her a way out. Vail was not taking any chances: she pulled her Glock as made her way down the corridor.

A guard was lying supine a couple dozen feet away. Vail ran to his side. His nose was viciously broken and his right elbow was fractured, bent into an unnatural angle. He had no pulse.

Kerwin's proficient in Krav Maga.

The man's watch was on the right, so he was probably left-handed.

Must've grabbed the wrist of his gun hand and yanked downward, then fractured his arm with a sharp left thrust through the joint. She swung her right palm up and into his nose, driving it into his brain.

Vail glanced around but did not see his handgun.

Her phone vibrated with a message:

bomb blew hole in back door

looks like high order explosive prob c4

kerwin gone

setting up a radius

Son of a bitch.

Vail replied:

hallway guard dead

she has his gun

Vail holstered both her phone and Glock as she entered the interrogation room. The chair Kerwin had been sitting in was askew, the handcuffs unlocked and lying on the floor.

Out in the hallway, armed men in black tactical uniforms ran by.

As Vail knelt to examine the cuffs she heard footsteps behind her. She reached for her Glock and pivoted in one motion—but saw Rusakov standing there, forearms tense, the HK in her right hand.

"She had to have that bomb on her," Rusakov said.

"That and a handcuff key. My guess is, when she got loose, whoever was watching her hit the alarm. When the guard pulled the door open, she blitz-attacked him. I don't think he knew what hit him."

"Krav Maga."

"Yeah."

"But what about the handcuff key?" Rusakov asked. "Let's get the surveillance tape, see if we can figure out what went down."

"Possible to miss a small key like that on a pat-down, but they wanded her. The magnetometer would've picked it up."

"Not if it was ceramic."

It was Zheng. He pushed past Rusakov and entered the room.

"A ceramic handcuff key?" Vail asked.

"Small, narrow, very strong. Probably concealed in the cuff of her blouse sleeve."

"But a block of C-4?" Vail asked.

Rusakov glanced around the room. "C-4 can be molded. So don't think 'block.' Think small and cylindrical, like a thin cigar or—"

"A tampon." Vail winced. "That's just . . . gross."

Rusakov shrugged. "I did it once. Good place for concealment. Very convenient if not very comfortable. Not saying that's what she did, but it's possible."

"And the detonator? Blasting cap has wires, a little bit of metal. How'd the wand not pick that up?"

"Maybe it did," Zheng said. "They're small, like the size and shape of a pen—but only half its size. She could've hidden it in her jeans with Velcro, right by the zipper. Wand goes off at the zipper, guy thinks it's a normal false positive."

"Still, whoever frisked and wanded her has some explaining to do."

Rusakov looked into the corridor. "Worse than that. This happened in front of the brass. None of us are gonna come out of this without some bruises."

Vail stood up. "I wish the same could be said about Jessie Kerwin."

36

Deep Space
En Route to the Moon

So what do you think is going on?" DeSantos asked. "This can't be jamming. I mean, if someone jams your comms, you know about it—and you know who's doing it."

"Yeah," Stroud said.

"From what I know, there are different kinds of jamming—obvious or subtle. China goes the obvious route—they play a loop of Chinese music—you know you're being jammed and you know China's behind it. But Russia is more stealthy in everything they do, so their style is subtle. And that fits with what we've been experiencing with Patriot. We don't hear anything—no noise, distorted speech, pulses. Just quiet."

"This is not jamming," Uzi said. "You have to break the line of sight communication. To jam an uplink type signal, they'd have to overpower the sending unit by creating significant noise on the frequency that was being transmitted."

"True," Carson said, "but there's more to it because NASA and the DOD use the Deep Space Network for spacecraft."

"Which is?" DeSantos asked.

"The DSN has three main sites, spaced equally across the

Earth—about 120 degrees apart—the Goldstone Deep Space Communications Complex at Fort Irwin in southern California, the one in Madrid, and the third in Canberra, Australia. Humongous antenna dishes—that's how mission control sends commands to the Patriot if/when needed. It also receives telemetry data from the Patriot."

"And once we got 18,000 miles away from Earth, we're always in view of at least one of the antenna stations," Stroud said. "Even if they wanted to risk that kind of aggressive act, after about eight hours we'd switch to the other array and reestablish comms. And there's no way they could jam the Goldstone location because—"

"It's at Fort Irwin," DeSantos said. "So what are you saying?"

Uzi sighed. "It's malware. There's code written to cut out our comms."

"Have you made any progress?" Stroud asked.

"Look at it this way," Uzi said. "The average iPhone app has about 30,000 lines of code. The space shuttle had about 400,000. A Boeing 787, over 5 million. The F-35 fighter jet, our most advanced, has well over 10 million. Facebook has around 70 million lines of code. Orion? Hundreds of millions. Once you get past 100,000, it doesn't really matter, does it? I have to take shortcuts to check it."

No one spoke. DeSantos, for one, was trying to absorb the enormity of the task—and the chances of Uzi successfully rooting out the malware. "So you're saying we're fucked."

"I'm doing my best."

"I've always found that your best gets the job done, Boychick."

"All I'm saying . . . keep your expectations in check. You'll never hear me admit this back on Earth . . . but I'm not Superman."

"Well then," DeSantos said, "it's a good thing we're no longer on Earth. Because we really need the Man of Steel to come through."

37

Fairfax, Virginia

I've got a problem," Vail said. She gripped the phone tightly, unsure of what kind of response she was going to get.

Deputy Marshal Lewis Hurdle laughed. "Something tells me you want to make this my problem too."

"That's half accurate."

"We didn't exactly leave things on a good note, Karen."

She could not dispute that. But they had worked successfully together to secure a highly dangerous fugitive—and cracked a serial killer case in the process. It was a win all the way around. But clearly Hurdle did not see it that way.

"Look," Vail said, "we did our jobs on a very difficult case and the good guys won."

"And the FBI took credit. Like you people always do."

Let it go, Karen. You need his help. Setting the record straight isn't important.

"Then on behalf of the entire Federal Bureau of Investigation, I apologize."

"And you still need my help," Hurdle said.

"Nothing's changed in the last thirty seconds."

Vail heard an audible groan over the line.

"Fine," Hurdle said with a sigh. "What do you need?"

"I need you to meet me. Name the place."

"Can't we just discuss it over the phone? I'm in the middle of two cases."

"No. This is sensitive."

"Starbucks in Fairfax on Main. Half an hour."

Truth was, Vail was in no mood to have a sit-down with anyone, let alone a law enforcement officer who would prefer to do just about anything other than help her. But she knew he was good at what he did—and right now, she needed his talents.

She arrived five minutes after their appointed time.

"You have a lot of nerve being late to an appointment you just about begged to have."

Vail sat down. "I didn't beg." There was a jacketed tall coffee at her seat. "This for me?"

"It is."

"That's very sweet of you. Thanks."

He gestured at the cup. "I hope the strychnine isn't too acidic. It'd kill the wonderful taste of the premium coffee beans."

Funny. "Nice to see you're in good spirits."

"Yeah, well . . ." He cleared his throat. "Despite how things ended, I did enjoy working with you."

"Same here. Which is why I called you. I respect your abilities."

"Is this business or personal?"

Vail lifted her coffee. "Business. But not Bureau business."

Hurdle tilted his head. "Okay, you got me. What the hell are you talking about?"

"I can't say."

Hurdle squinted. "What?"

"Look," Vail said, leaning forward and lowering her voice, "I need to locate this woman." She slid a small photo forward. "Name's Jessie Kerwin. She went fugitive a little over an hour ago."

"What else do you have?"

Vail took a drink of her coffee. "Not a whole lot. Half-page bio. Bottom line . . ." Vail spoke more softly. "She's a person of international interest. Lethal in hand-to-hand combat. We had just . . . arrested her and she escaped custody. She's very smart, paranoid, well-prepared, skilled in Krav Maga, armed—and very dangerous."

"And why can't the FBI find her?"

"Because you guys are the best at finding fugitives."

"This you talking or the Bureau?"

Vail frowned. "The Bureau. But I know it to be true."

"So if it's a Bureau case, why all the hush-hush? This counterterrorism related?"

Why didn't I think of that? "You could say that."

Hurdle accepted that and picked up the photo. "This may take awhile. I'm not even sure how many LEOs I can put on this," he said, using the abbreviation for law enforcement officers. "I wasn't kidding when I said I was in the middle of two cases."

"Glad you brought that up. You can't involve anyone else on your task force. Just you."

"Just me. You're not serious. What the hell are you drinking?"

"Coffee laced with strychnine."

"Karen, you saw firsthand how the fugitive task force works, how we track down these knuckleheads. One person can't do it on his own. Not if there's urgency."

"There is. Urgency. Lives depend on it."

Hurdle sat back and took a sip from his cup. "And who would I be working for?"

"I don't know how to answer that. Take some sick time."

"Sick time? What the hell are you talking about?"

"This is unofficial. Off the books. I'll find a way of getting you paid your normal salary for the time you work the case. But you can't tell anyone what you're doing. Not even your boss."

"Karen." He examined her face, shook his head, then stood up. "I don't think this is a good idea. Good luck wit—"

"Sit down."

"No. We're done here."

"Hurdle. Sit down. I'll—" She glanced around. "You'll be working for a federal agency. I just can't tell you which one."

He pushed his chair in. "Good seeing you, Karen."

As Hurdle left, Vail dug out her OPSIG phone and made a call. Ten minutes later someone was calling someone else—and twenty minutes after that Hurdle walked back in.

He leaned his palms on the table, putting his face a foot from Vail's, the look on his face a mixture of anger and astonishment and fear. "Who the hell are you involved with?"

"I can't say."

Hurdle looked at her long and hard.

If he had a problem with me before, I certainly didn't score any points with this maneuver.

"If there was another way, I'd do it. But you're the best I know. And this is important."

Truth was, there were others in OPSIG working on locating Jessie Kerwin. But catching fugitives was the bread and butter of the US Marshals Service. It was in their DNA. And Hurdle had proved his worth. It was risky involving someone outside the group, but Vail made the case that it was necessary. She hoped it did not backfire on her—and OPSIG.

"I can't believe I'm doing this." Hurdle kicked the chair away from the table and sat down heavily. "Tell me everything you know about Kerwin."

VAIL HAD DIFFICULTY CONCENTRATING. Her feet felt heavy and her brain had shut down halfway to her house. It was dark out and drizzling.

She had not had a good night's sleep in . . . well, too long . . . and she just wanted to crawl into Robby's arms and saw wood for a few days.

When Vail walked in, Hershey bounded over and jumped up to greet her. But Robby was engrossed in his phone. She waited a moment for him to react, to say something—anything—to her. Instead he continued to fiddle with the handset.

"Your wife walks in the door and you don't even look up? Even our dog came over and gave me a kiss. Is what's on your phone more interesting than me?"

"No, no, no," Robby said, walking toward her and mouthing something at her: Look at this.

Vail read his lips and realized what he was getting at—and whatever it was, he was purposely facing away from the security camera they had recently put in the family room.

"Is that two lesbians?" She tapped his arm, letting him know that she understood something was not right.

"Not that I find *anything* more interesting than you."

She playfully elbowed him. "Liar."

Robby pointed at the screen, which was open to the app that controlled their cameras. "You into that? I think it's kind of arousing."

"Why don't you show me." She took his hand and led him into the bedroom. After stepping into their walk-in closet—Hershey squeezed in because he did not want to be left out—Robby gestured at what he had noticed: in the camera settings, the status LED was set to the default—on.

Vail knew that they had manually disabled the bright green lights so intruders would not notice that they had wireless surveillance cams.

He leaned over and touched his lips to her right ear. "I opened the app to reconfigure it—and to see how the status light could've gotten turned on. But things were tweaked, the settings were all wrong. Things I'd never do."

She put her index finger to her mouth, then texted Knox.

could be listening devices in my house so Im
texting--ok to proceed?

She silenced her phone so the reply would not arouse suspicions. Knox wrote back immediately:

yes your OPSIG phone is safe because it was
preconfigured without access rights to make changes
so your phone isnt vulnerable
its locked down against cloning and hacking
preventing remote installations

Vail showed Robby the reply and wrote back to Knox:

whats the plan

"Oh, honey, that feels so good."

Robby looked at her and chuckled.

Knox's reply rumbled in her hand:

im sending over a team

"Ohhh, Robby . . . don't stop."

"You kidding? I can go all night."

Vail shot him a look that said, "Don't oversell it, honey."

should i shut down the modem or
cut off the internet

Knox replied a moment later:

no we may be able to tap in without
them seeing and trace the signal
someone looking in on you has to
send a signal out to the ones who
are watching
we may be able to use that
sit tight play it cool

Vail showed Robby the screen and then took his hand and led him out of the closet. She playfully shoved his chest, pushing him onto the bed. "We've got about fifteen minutes," she whispered in his ear.

He undid her blouse. "More than enough time."

38

Deep Space
Moon's Gravitational Pull

Patriot was speeding through space at an accelerating rate, having entered the Moon's sphere of influence. As they got closer, the Moon's gravitational effects increased and pulled Patriot along as if a rope were attached to its nose and it was sliding along an expanse of ice.

"We're running low on time," Stroud said. "What's your status?"

Uzi focused on his screen as he worked the keyboard. "It's common for astronauts to patch code. Ground control tells them what to do and they make the changes. Or they use a JIT compiler and organize the binary into a specific memory location—embedded programming. But we don—"

"Boychick," DeSantos said. "Don't know about Cowboy and Digger, but I don't have any idea what you're saying."

"We don't have ground control engineers to help us out here, so it's just me. I've found the malware and I'm getting rid of it. But I also just found a transmit circuit with two chips that controlled broadcast. In the same circuit. So I'm thinking, maybe it's redundancy because radio is a critical system? But no other circuits were duplicated. I pulled up an online schematic for the circuit board and the two don't match. The real board doesn't have that second chip."

"How can that be?"

"Don't know," Uzi said. "But I'm gonna open it up and take a look."

"Hang on a second," Stroud said. "Open the computer? I don't think so. The vehicle management computer costs tens of millions of dollars. It's not a desktop PC where you just pop it open and swap out a stick of RAM."

"Actually," Uzi said, "cost aside, the two aren't that different. And in my prior life I was a hardware engineer for Intel." Uzi unbuckled his restraint and floated over to the stowage where the tool kit was located. He stopped and swung back to Stroud. "Permission to proceed?"

Stroud worked his jaw a moment, then said, "Do it."

Uzi selected his instruments and slid to the right using controlled movements. In zero gravity, it was easy to push off too hard and go flying into a wall. Then again, there was not a lot of extra room for him to drift before striking an obstruction.

Uzi turned four fasteners and removed the panel, exposing the computer's innards, and then did the same with the backup system. "This one also has that extra transmit chip."

Stroud came up beside him. "Before you start doing cyber surgery, are you absolutely sure this extra chip is not supposed to be there?"

Uzi looked again at the tool kit components. "I'm as sure as I can be. It's not on the schematic. Only explanation is that someone modified this board." He leaned in close and turned on his flashlight. "Do we have a magnifying glass?"

Carson bent over the tool kit and removed a small, round lens.

Uzi took it and examined the chip. "Not sure if this is significant or not, but there's a dimple in the metal portion of the capacitor."

"You got me," Stroud said. "Is that supposed to mean something?"

"Certain manufacturers have equipment that leaves behind unique marks because of the methods and machinery they use."

"And that dimple means what?"

"It's similar to the USB metal jackets that Apple uses to identify counterfeit lightning cables that are sold very inexpensively. They're not MFI certified—made for iPhone or iPad—even though they claim to be. Apple uses that dimple, among other things, to help identify a fake product."

"So you think this is a counterfeit chip?" DeSantos said.

Uzi leaned in for another look. "Not sure I'd call it counterfeit, but it's a telltale sign as to where this chip was made."

"And?" Carson asked. "Why is that important?"

Uzi sat back. "Because it tells me this extra transmit chip was probably made in China."

DeSantos came up behind both of them. "I'm sure there's a joke here about everything in the US now being made in China. But this is not funny."

"It's possible that one of the contractors outsourced some chips to one or more Chinese companies. It does happen with other systems, but it'd have to be approved. So I can't say for sure this is a problem."

"Other than the fact that it's not supposed to be there."

"Other than that."

"Maybe using Chinese components wouldn't be an issue for NASA," Carson said. "They used Russian made engines for the United Launch Alliance rockets for years. But no way is that happening in a critical system in a military vehicle. Hell, Congress goes apeshit when a Chinese company wants to buy a US company that makes sensitive government equipment. A computer chip in a military vehicle? I can't see that being approved."

"But this isn't a pure military vehicle," Stroud said. "We piggybacked on NASA hardware and software, made modifications here and there so we could carry out certain aspects of the mission."

"I'll hang onto the bad chip so DOD can examine it later. Right now, I'm removing it and swapping out the transmit chip, see if we can get comms back online." Uzi located the correct circuit, and then, using a knife, sliced the traces around the suspect chip. After removing it, he located another one with similar functionality on the redundant computer's mainboard and inserted it into the primary system. He finished it off with liquid solder. "Surgery's done."

"Let's hope you didn't kill the patient," DeSantos deadpanned.

Uzi sat back down, turned to his instrument panel, and began working the touch screen. "The avionics system uses integrated modular technology to combine various systems into one. That came in handy because I didn't have to turn off the vehicle management computer to work on the communications radio. Rebooting comms right now."

"You think we're all clear of malware now?" Carson asked.

Uzi blew air out through his lips. "Man, I wish I could say yes, but I honestly don't know. This transmit chip issue is different from the malware problem—but it could've worked in tandem with it."

"Hold on a second," DeSantos said. "The avionics system is the Patriot's brains. Everything—power, data, tracking, nav, comms, sensors—it's all controlled by this computer. I mean, it makes course corrections for us, supplies our oxygen, deploys the solar panels . . . How do we know it's not gonna change our course? Even a few degrees, we'd miss lunar orbit. We wouldn't be able to recover and we'd basically be toast."

"Good to see you were paying attention," Stroud said.

"Boychick, can we trust the computer to keep us on the correct course? To separate the Raptor from the Patriot and land us on the Moon without making us pancake on the surface?"

Uzi stared at his display as the comms module finished its boot sequence. He did not know how to answer.

"Other than the launch," Stroud said, "we're about to enter the most complicated part of the mission, which carries the most risk. We need our systems functioning properly. Is it safe to continue?"

"Do we have a choice?" Uzi asked.

"Not really. We could fly around the Moon and slingshot home. But to be so close and not at least try to complete the mission . . ."

"Then we continue," Carson said firmly. "And we complete the mission."

Uzi's panel glowed green. "We're back up."

Carson looked to Stroud. It was the commander's decision.

"We've got a job to do it and we've come 200,000 miles," Stroud said. "We're not turning around and going home. Not until we've done what we came to do."

The radio chirped to life. "Patriot, this is ground control. Do you read?"

Uzi grinned at the sound of CAPCOM Bob Maddox's scratchy voice. "Affirmative. It's a relief to hear your voice, CAPCOM."

"You took the words right out of my mouth," Maddox said.

"We've got a lot to tell you," Stroud said.

"Ten-four," Maddox said with a chuckle. "As do we."

39

FBI LABORATORY
FBI ACADEMY
QUANTICO, VIRGINIA

Vail sat down on the stool in Tim Meadows's office at the FBI's crime lab.

"So you found something?"

"Nope. Just missed my favorite redhead and her crisp wit so I thought I'd imply I had info for you. I knew you'd have to come by."

Vail gave him a toothy smile and a toss of her curly hair. "I'm your favorite redhead?"

"You nudged out Robert Redford."

Vail recoiled. "He's like eighty years old. I'm not sure how to take that."

"It's a compliment."

"Now I know why you don't have a girlfriend."

"How do you know I don't have a girlfriend?"

"Do you?"

"No."

Vail shook her head. "Do you or do you not have something for me?"

"I do. The sample I was given from your crime scene was Semtex."

"Semtex. Not C-4?"

Meadows pointed at her. "Aha! I knew you were going to ask that question. You're so predictable, my dear Karen. Although Semtex is traditionally thought of as the overseas version of C-4, they are slightly different. The chemical makeup is the same but the manufacturing process isn't. Did you know it was developed by Czechoslovakia for Vietnam in the mid-sixties in response to our development of C-4?"

"Nope, did not know that, Tim. And how does that help me with this case?"

"When you don't have relevant information to give your boss, throw that factoid at him."

"Just like you did with me."

"Sorry, I wish I had something more to give you. Bottom line, Semtex doesn't have any compulsory tagging."

"Why's that?"

"There's no way of inserting something, like a unique metallic code, into the mass of the explosive, so Semtex isn't tagged. Unfortunately, that means there's no reliable way of identifying specific characteristics that would help you ID its country of origin, manufacturer, and so on. There's no trail to trace."

"Terrific. And what about my house?"

"Ah. That I can be a little more helpful with."

"Just a little?"

"A wee exaggeration. I've got a lot to tell you about that. So you, my dear Karen, were the victim of an elaborate infiltration of enemy surveillance equipment."

"You mean someone was spying on us."

"That's what I said."

"I already knew that."

"Not exactly. There's a lot more to it. A forensics cyber team scoured your house after you left. We found a wireless router connected through the untrusted interface. In this case, it was on the external, or firewalled side, plugged into your internal LAN. Typically, very few services, if any, are available on this interface, making it difficult to detect across the network."

"Okay."

"Are you following me?"

"Not at all. Do I need to?"

Meadows stuck out his bottom lip. "Someone entered your garage using your wireless key code control panel."

"Are you serious? They—how'd they get the code?"

"Not hard, my dear. Anyway, they hooked up a small off-the-rack router—we're talking half the size of an iPhone." He swiveled around to his keyboard and after a few taps called up a photo on the screen. "This is what they hooked into your router. They then hacked the camera and configured it to send audio and video to them."

Vail wrapped her arms across her chest. "I feel . . . violated. But how'd someone get inside my house? My dog woul—"

"Your garage, not your house. But the cyber team is hard at work, trying to trace the IP address, parsing the cyber clues. But it's not as easy as it sounds."

"I didn't think it sounded easy."

"Of course you didn't. Point is, hackers can be slippery sons of bitches. They use things to divert cops in the direction of the wrong criminal entity. So you may think it's John but it's really Scott."

"So should I arrest Scott? Or John?"

"Huh? No, I meant th—"

"Just giving you a hard time. That part I understood."

Meadows gave her an annoyed look, lips twisted and left cheek lifted. "I'm not going to let you bait me. The parts are locally sourced to an electronics store. And no, they don't have security cameras. And these assholes paid with cash. So no credit card receipts to trace."

"So we're nowhere. Great." Vail got off the stool.

"Not exactly. Because *I'm* on the case."

She turned to face Meadows. "What are you talking about?"

"I was able to lift a partial latent off the antenna. They're small and round and hard to screw in with gloves because of the fine work inside a small case. So I figured he probably had to remove a glove to do it."

"You mean you were hoping he removed a glove."

"And," he said, ignoring her dig, "he didn't think it'd matter because it's a round, smooth surface—tough to get a usable print off something like that. But they didn't know Timothy Patrick Meadows would be processing the evidence."

"And Ironman came to the rescue again, did he?"

Meadows smiled. "You think I look like Ironman?"

She frowned at him.

"Hey, I can dream, right? Anyway, we haven't gotten a hit yet, but I sent it over to Interpol in case your perp's done this in other countries. And I was told there may be an international connection."

"There may be, yeah."

"So what else can you tell me about this case?"

"That's about it."

"Anything you give me can help me to—"

"Not my call," Vail said as she gave him a pat on the right shoulder. "I have my orders."

Meadows snorted. "Since when has that stopped you?"

40

Lunar Orbit

The OPSIG astronauts conferred at length with Maddox and his team of engineers. But without having the systems in front of them to examine, the ground controllers confessed it was difficult to reach definitive conclusions.

"That redundant transmit chip definitely should not be there," Maddox said. "That much we can confirm. As for what it does and why it's there, we'll have to run it through a battery of tests when you get back."

"And the marking that Uzi saw?" DeSantos asked.

"Yeah, a few of the guys here who have manufacturing backgrounds said he's right about that. And one who's familiar with the Chinese manufacturing process—he came from Apple—said it *is* a strong indicator of where it was made. So this is definitely disconcerting. But it's not something we're going to address with the Chinese. Not until we have more complete info and a thorough analysis of that chip . . . and the malware."

"I thought we're operating on the assumption it's Russian-designed malware," Stroud said.

"It's just *that*," Maddox said. "An assumption. But that's the way it's looking. I'm told that investigation is ongoing. We'll keep you posted."

"Meantime, Bob," Stroud said, the Moon is friggin' huge. I mean, humongous. It completely fills the window."

"Sun's behind it right now, so it's backlighting it," Carson said. "Like a halo."

"We've also got Earthshine," Uzi said.

"Earthshine?" DeSantos asked.

"Sunlight that's bounced off the Earth and back to the lunar surface. That whitish area in the center of the Moon. See it?"

"Glad you're enjoying the view," Maddox said. "On a mission like this, we sometimes forget where we are, what we're doing. I hope you grab a few minutes, when you can, to take a look around. Especially on the surface. I don't want to shift your focus, but this mission aside, you guys are doing something truly extraordinary. As a former astronaut, I have to admit I'm living vicariously through you four."

"Hopefully we'll give you something to get excited about," Uzi said.

"I'm showing our current velocity at 7,600 feet per second," Carson said. "We've been steadily accelerating for the last fifteen hours."

"You'll need to slow to 2,917 feet per second to be captured by the Moon's gravity," Maddox said.

Stroud tapped his screen. "Roger, CAPCOM. Getting ready for LOI1 in eight minutes, thirty-two seconds," he said, referring to the first lunar orbit insertion engine burn.

"And we are coming up on LOS comms loss in forty seconds," Maddox said. During the planned "line of sight" communications blackout when the Patriot passed behind the Moon's far side—thus blocking the radio signal—the crew would be without ground support assistance. “We’ll be back on the radio with you thirty-three minutes and fifty seconds later.”

“Hey,” DeSantos said, “you think we can rely on the computer to carry out LOI1 and LOI2?”

There was a long pause before Maddox answered. “Let’s hope so.”

41

En Route to Black Site

On the way back from the Academy, Vail swung by and picked up Rusakov at the Pentagon. She filled her in on the assistance she sought from Lewis Hurdle, the information Tim Meadows had provided regarding the explosive Kerwin used, and the clandestine router installed in Vail's garage.

"So we may still get an ID off the latent but the Semtex isn't gonna help us any."

"Not ready to concede that." Vail pulled out her phone. "Call Special Agent Richard Prati, DEA, office" she said to the Bluetooth interface.

The line rang through Vail's car speakers and was immediately answered.

"I'm sorry," the staffer said. "Agent Prati isn't with DEA anymore."

"I just spoke to him a few months ago." *I wonder if Robby knows.*

"He's gone over to ATF headquarters. I'm afraid that's all I know."

Back to ATF?

Vail thanked the man, then dialed the ATF. When constructed, the modern facility was in a less desirable northeastern neighborhood of the District, but in recent years the area had undergone—and was undergoing—a revitalization. Completed in 2007, the campus featured a 425,000 square foot futuristic spaceship-shaped blast-proof building that looked nothing like the stodgy government facilities that previously housed law enforcement agencies. Vail had been to the complex a couple of times.

"Can I ask what this is about?" asked the woman who took the call.

"He's a friend. Tell Agent Prati it's regarding a case I'm working."

"He's the assistant special agent in charge. And I'll get him on the line for you."

ASAC. At headquarters. Impressive.

"Karen. How you doin'?"

"I guess congrats is in order. ASAC? ATF?"

"Yeah, definitely not something I was planning. Just kind of fell into my lap. A guy who worked with me on a case twenty years ago was named SAC of the DC field division and he put in a good word and next thing I know someone from the office of field ops was offering me a job."

"Was it a good move?"

"Hey, I can't complain. I loved DEA. But I also loved my time at ATF. It's a little different, having a ton of guys under me, but like drugs it's a noble fight, so all's good in my world. What about you, this case you're calling about?"

"Semtex. We had an offender use it and I was hoping to trace it. But my lab guy said that's not possible."

"Well, technically that's true. But that's not the whole story. The international community agreed that Semtex should have a detection taggant added to produce a distinctive vapor signature so we could pick it up—like by airport scanners and bomb sniffing canines. Early on ethylene glycol dinitrate was used, but that was replaced with 2,3-dimethyl-2,3-dinitrobutane and then p-mononitrotoluene. Semtex made before 1990 is untagged, but no one knows how much of this stuff is still around. Today's more sophisticated scanners can detect even the untagged Semtex."

"So it can be detected, but the origin can't be determined."

"Right," Prati said. "But it's unlikely your offender got the Semtex from an overseas source. It'd be really tough to get into the country without us finding it. Not saying it's impossible, but it's difficult."

"Then where'd she get it from?"

Prati chuckled. "Unfortunately, there are recipes available online. Posted anonymously, of course. But google it, you'll find it. It's not complicated, but obviously you have to be careful. The two key ingredients are PETN and RDX, which are used in commercial blasting and demolition, and even in certain military applications."

"What's the shelf life?"

"The older stuff could last ten years. But the Semtex made during the past twenty-five years or so probably won't last more than five."

"So it's possible the people we're looking for are current or former military personnel. Or current or former construction workers. That only narrows it down to, what, several million people on the East Coast alone? Unless they cooked it up themselves."

"There are no easy answers here, Karen."

"What about the components? PETN and RDX?"

"PETN is a favorite of al-Qaeda because it's a powder about the consistency of fine salt. It won't trigger an alarm on a metal detector and it's chemically stable so it doesn't give off much vapor. It's tough to detect by bomb-sniffing dogs and those swabs TSA uses when they rub it over your stuff to look for trace bomb chemicals don't pick it up well. It's also easy to hide because it can be mixed with rubber cement or putty. Then you've got a rudimentary plastic explosive. A little bit goes a long way. Mold it into something the size of a baseball and it'll blow a nice hole in the side of an airplane fuselage."

"How easy is it to get hold of?"

"Not hard at all. Got some munitions lying around? You can scrape it from old bombs or strip it out of detonator cord."

"Which is used in road construction and mining," Vail said. "And RDX?"

"A powerful nitramide explosive, also called cyclonite or T4. It's a hard, white, crystalline solid that has about 1.5 times the explosive power of TNT per unit weight and about two times TNT per unit volume. It's sensitive to percussion and is used in construction for blasting caps. It's often mixed with other substances, like plasticizers, to decrease its volatility."

"Obviously the combination of RDX and PETN increases not only the bomb's stability but also its yield. And it's not tough to get."

"And," Prati said, "a useful feature is that it makes Semtex shapeable and moldable."

"Like C-4. We're pretty sure our offender concealed it in her vagina."

"Ouch," Prati said, drawing the word out. "I know a few agents who'd have a really good comeback for that. But I'm . . . uh . . . of course, not one of them."

"So you're saying our offender didn't need to bring the Semtex across a border or on a flight because she could've gotten hold of the materials here and found a recipe on the internet and whipped it up in her kitchen."

Prati laughed. "Not sure that's what I was saying, but more or less, for someone who knows what they're doing, yeah. That's what you're dealing with."

"Terrific." Vail glanced at Rusakov, who had done a good job of keeping her mouth shut.

"Thanks, Richard. I appreciate your help. And good luck with your new posting. Does Robby know?"

"I have an email out to him about getting together for lunch," Prati said. "Better to tell him over a meal. Maybe I'll poach him from DEA."

"I'm not getting in the middle of that, Richard. But I'll keep your secret until you're ready to tell him."

"Good luck with your case."

We'll need it.

42

Lunar Orbit

They made orbit without incident—smoothly burning their engine for LOI2, which gently pushed them into their seatbacks at less than one G. For those six minutes, Carson and Stroud intently watched their instrument panels for anomalies as the computer cycled through a myriad of readings.

Uzi kept an eye on the settings as well, though he had to rely on his colleagues' interpretation because he had not had time to fully digest all the information he was supposed to be studying during the three-day journey. Rooting out the malware—which he was still concerned about—had eaten up that time like a ravenous hawk devouring a dead carcass.

All went as anticipated and without a single hiccup—but that did not diminish the accomplishment. If nothing else, they had hit a moving target from a quarter million miles away with extreme precision. While it appeared from Earth that the Moon remained in roughly the same place, during the past few days it had moved almost 200,000 miles from its position at the time of launch. And yet NASA's Johnson Space Center computers and engineers had accurately computed its path and, with pinpoint accuracy, programmed their navigation system so that it put them right on target with near-zero variance.

Moments later, they again went into a communications blackout with ground control—only this time the inability to transmit and receive signals was a normal occurrence, as the radio waves were blocked by the Moon as they passed around its far side, which kept its back to Earth at all times.

"Look at that," DeSantos said.

Uzi shifted closer to the port window. "Beyond amazing."

The lunar surface, dark gray, light gray, charcoal, and multiple shades in between, was close—very close—and nothing like what was normally seen from Earth or in the iconic photos of the Moon circulated during the past fifty years. Rough with craters and pockmarked with sharp pimples and pointed hills erupting across the entire surface, it was like hardened lava in its irregularity and menacing in its coarseness.

"Not what I imagined," DeSantos said.

"Welcome to the dark side, gentlemen," Stroud said. "This is where Darth Vader came from."

DeSantos chuckled. "Good thing we won't be landing here. I don't think there's a flat plain anywhere to set down."

"The more classic surface geography you're accustomed to is on the near side," Carson said. "We'll be coming around in a couple hours or so."

Orbiting at a mere sixty miles up, the lack of atmosphere—and thus no clouds, smoke, or fog—brought the finer details of the ground into sharp focus.

As they circled about to the more customary cratered and smooth plains of the highlands and the darkness of the *maria*—Latin for "seas" and so named by early astronomers who mistook them for bodies of water—they sat mesmerized by the more familiar sight of the planetary body they had all grown up gazing at as kids.

"How are the Patriot's systems?" Bob Maddox asked, interrupting their reverie.

"Doing well," Stroud said. "We arrived without incident, completed the second lunar orbit insertion burn, and have been admiring the view. All readings are as expected for a change."

"Very good, Patriot. If this were a normal Moon shot, you'd go to sleep and prepare for separation from the crew module and descent in the morning. But with that Russian craft on the way, we're gonna deviate from our plan and push things up, have you initiate landing procedures on the next pass."

"Copy," Stroud said. "Sleep is overrated anyway."

"We'll help you along with all that until you pass behind the dark side again, but when you emerge you've gotta be ready to execute."

Carson poked at his instrument panel. "We'll be ready, CAPCOM."

"Roger that," Maddox said. "I know you will."

43

Alexandria, Virginia

Vail and Rusakov were a few miles from their Springfield, Virginia, destination when Rodman texted them with the results of OPSIG's review of the Jessie Kerwin surveillance video. Although the camera angle and the proximity of the table blocked their view, it looked like their theories of how things went down, and the location where she hid the Semtex, were accurate.

And she blitz-attacked the guard very much the way Vail had opined.

"So that's not gonna help us," Rusakov said.

Vail's phone vibrated again. "But this might." She answered Tim Meadows's call via Bluetooth.

"Go ahead, Tim," Vail said as she merged right on the capital beltway.

"Got a hit on that latent I lifted off the antenna."

"Really."

"Russian guy, Evgeny Kirilenko, forty-nine. Used to work for a leading cyber security firm in Moscow. But before that, his history is a little shadier. He was with the KGB in its last three years of existence and then spent twelve years in the FSB," Meadows said, referring to the Russian Federal Security Service, which replaced the KGB.

Ignoring the Springfield sign, Vail checked over her shoulder at her blind spot as she approached the 170B exit ramp. "Tim, what's a guy like that doing in the US—and in my garage?"

"Hard to say, Karen. But that's more your speed. I just ID the players. You have to figure out how they fit in the game."

Vail entered the exit ramp and slowed. "You're not kid—" Her foot went to the floor and the car continued at sixty-five miles per hour. "What the hell! I've got no brakes."

"What do you mean?" Rusakov asked, looking at the floorboard.

The inner loop single lane road took a sharp right a hundred yards ahead. Vail grabbed the gearshift and put it in low to use the transmission to reduce her speed. She felt the engine downshift—before it revved and the odometer passed sixty-five, headed toward seventy. "Shit, I've got no control!"

"Karen," Meadows said, "are you ok—"

"Ditch it," Rusakov said. "Now!"

"I can't." They were approaching an overpass and the massive concrete vertical support struts were just beyond the edge of the asphalt—no way could she go right. And the roadway had already risen about fifteen feet above the interstate, so if she swerved left and ran off the ramp, they would tumble down the sharp embankment and land wheels up atop the fast-moving traffic of I-495.

"Watch the curve," Rusakov shouted.

Vail pulled the wheel right as the hook in the ramp approached—but the car did not respond. They smashed through the steel guardrail lanes and rolled through the tree tops and brush, coming to rest against the metal stanchion supporting the Springfield exit sign.

44

Lunar Orbit

The Raptor separated from the Patriot on schedule and without any hitches. Unlike the Apollo spacecraft, which required a pilot to remain on board while the other two astronauts took the lunar lander to the surface, the Orion/Patriot counterpart was designed to be autonomous, remaining in orbit until needed by the landing party.

"I have to confess being more than a little nervous leaving the Patriot behind," Uzi said as he watched the craft move off into the distance. "We can't get back home without it. If I was a bad actor, I'd screw with the Patriot's computer so it either leaves orbit for deep space, crashes into the surface, or refuses to dock with us."

"I'm glad you aren't that bad actor, Boychick," DeSantos said, "because that'd totally suck."

"It'd be a death sentence," Stroud said.

"I'm confident you got all the malware," Carson said.

Uzi looked away. "I wish I shared that degree of confidence."

Not lost on any of them was that they were embarking on the next major phase of their mission: the journey down to the Moon in the lunar lander, which had been folded into the rocket fairing below the Patriot crew module.

Now fully deployed with Raptor's legs unfurled, they continued orbiting the Moon as the computer controlled their descent with minimal input from Stroud and Carson.

Since aerodynamics did not matter for this type of craft, it was an ugly, utilitarian conglomeration of fuel tanks, crisscrossing brass-colored pipes and large round white balls, suspended by stick legs capped off by flat landing pods, circles at the bottoms of the struts that would support the vehicle once it hit lunar dirt.

Their home away from home was a vertically oriented cylindrical habitat that sat atop the structure with an airlock—another improvement over Apollo—that enabled them to keep the main cabin pressurized. It was, essentially, a glorified mudroom that would also keep the sticky black wet-sand-like Moon dust out of the interior—a persistent problem in the Apollo days.

It was a relatively large craft, towering thirty-two feet in height—about the size of a three-story house—and twenty-five feet in diameter. It weighed in at a hefty forty-seven tons and was equipped with four engines to get them to the surface . . . but only one to lift them off and rendezvous with the Patriot. A problem with that single rocket engine would strand them on the Moon for eternity—or approximately four days, until their food, water, and oxygen ran out. Unlike all other NASA designs, there was no contingency or redundancy to get them off the Earth's rocky satellite.

That was not to say that NASA did not take care to ensure a reliable system to get them home. They designed cryogenic technologies for the descent stages and hypergolic technologies for the ascent stage. Hypergolic fuels were chemicals that combusted on contact with each other, requiring no ignition mechanism. Both systems would be force-fed fuel using high-pressure helium, eliminating the pumps utilized in other, more complicated rockets. That was important, for if there was going to be a malfunction, it would involve those finicky pumps.

The descent stage contained the majority of the fuel, power supplies, and breathable oxygen for the crew. The ascent stage, which would lift them off the surface when they were ready to leave, housed the astronauts, their life-support equipment, and fuel for the engine and steering rockets that would put them into orbit and enable them to navigate to, and rendezvous with, the Patriot before their return to Earth.

The Raptor—officially known as the lunar surface access module—was a one-off vehicle. Built as a prototype for testing during the Constellation program before the president terminated the project in favor of the space launch system, or SLS, it was constructed by Aerospace Engineering's robotics division. But when Congress directed NASA to turn its attention, and budget, to Mars, plans to return to the Moon were shelved. But because the SLS-Orion components were designed to carry out a variety of missions, a Moon shot remained in the playbook.

Likewise, the Spider multipurpose transport rover, designed to carry the astronauts wherever they needed to go after landing, was retained and both test vehicles were placed in storage. Uzi wrecked one of them.

"We've passed the hundred mile mark," Stroud said. "Looking good."

"Roger that," Maddox said.

"You still CAPCOM, Bob?" Carson asked. "I figured you'd gone home."

"And miss all the fun? No goddamn way. You guys are stuck with me."

"CAPCOM, we've got nine minutes for you guys to check systems and give us a go for the burn," Stroud said.

"Already at work on the checklists, Cowboy. Telemetry shows textbook readings. Because of your troubles, let's have you go through a few things with us."

Maddox read off various settings and Carson confirmed them. Finally, four minutes later, ground control gave them a brief countdown and Carson prepared to fire the descent engines.

"We are falling out of orbit," Stroud said, "right on schedule."

"Roger that," Maddox said. "You are go for burn."

The rocket was pointed in the direction of descent, parallel to the lunar surface, and they were moving feet first but facedown. It did not matter—there was no sense of up or down other than visual cues, which could make it a bit disorienting if the astronauts were not careful.

"Passing over the Sculptured Hills," Stroud said. "Hard to believe these things are over a mile high. Who named these giant mountains 'hills'?"

"Coming up on the North Massif," Uzi said.

"Tell Ridgid those simulators back home were awesome," Stroud said. "I see the undulating plains beneath us. The landing site's approaching in the distance and looks exactly like it did in the sim. Coming up on the highlands that separate the Sea of Tranquility from the Sea of Serenity."

"You're right on target for Taurus-Littrow," Maddox said. "Prepare to roll Raptor."

"Preparing to roll," Carson said.

The Moon rotated out of sight of their windows as they came around, still moving parallel to the surface but facing upward, looking into the sunlit black void of space.

An alarm sounded and Stroud's voice rose an octave. "Shit. What the hell's going on? Are we—"

"We're off course," Carson said, "rising out of orbit. Firing steering thrusters to compensate."

"No," Uzi said. "Hold it."

"Canceling the alarm," DeSantos said. He hit a switch on his panel and the cacophony immediately ceased.

"Too late," Carson said as he tapped at his screen. "But I think that burn—I think that we're back . . . um, wait."

"Did it work or not?" DeSantos said.

"Not sure. Stand by."

"SITREP," Maddox said, his voice uncharacteristically tense. "I'm not seeing what you're seeing."

"Uzi," DeSantos said, "you thinking what I'm thinking?"

Uzi turned to Carson. "Digger, you sure of your readings? This could be more false data. Malware."

"I . . . I don't know. A little help here, CAPCOM."

"I'm showing you're still on orbit, descending to twelve thousand feet now."

"Descending—?" Carson slammed a fist into his panel. "None of this is making sense. I—I can't trust what I'm seeing."

"CAPCOM," Stroud said, "can you talk us through this? Looks like we've got more problems with avionics."

There was a moment of silence, then Maddox said matter-of-factly, "Roger that. Less than ideal, but sounds like we've got no choice. Switch to manual. Ignore your instrument panels."

"Switch to manual and ignore the computer?" Stroud would have come out of his seat had he not been strapped down. "How the hell can we fly this thing—and land safely—without instrumentation?"

"They'll just talk us through it," DeSantos said.

"Here's the thing," Maddox said. "There's a 1.3 second delay in comms. Not real noticeable in regular conversation, but if you're relying on us to fly, not sure how that'll work. Soon as your instruments sense an attitude or speed change, that signal will get beamed to us and we've gotta send a response back to you. That's a three second lag. That's huge."

"No choice," Stroud said. "Give it your best shot."

"Roger that, Raptor. Get ready to shut down the engine. The twelve minute burn is just about done. We're gonna try to time this right, but we're winging it a bit more than usual."

Uzi had to give the guy credit: he maintained a sense of humor when things got tense.

The loud growl of the engine caused a slight but noticeable vibration in the landing craft.

"Ready to execute per your instructions," Stroud said.

"Terminate the burn on my mark . . . and . . . mark."

"Roger. Burn terminated."

"Well, what do you know," Maddox said. "Looking good."

Uzi let out an audible sigh of relief.

"You're coming up on seven thousand feet. Pitch upright so the rocket will be firing perpendicular to the surface."

"Copy." Carson followed Maddox's directions and the Raptor lowered like a roughly vibrating elevator on its way to the ground floor. "Thirty-one feet per second, going through five hundred," Carson said. "Twenty-five feet per second, through four hundred."

"A little high. Correct it."

"Corrected," Carson said.

"You're passing the edge of Sherlock," he said, referring to one of their landmarks. "The Camelot crater should be ahead."

"Roger," Stroud said. "I see it. And Trident's on the left, Lewis and Clark on the right."

"Just don't pass Camelot. Move toward the target."

"Read you loud and clear. No worries, CAPCOM." Stroud tapped away at his screen. "Passing over what looks like the Chinese craft. Yep, make that an affirmative. The Chang'e 5."

A moment later, Uzi leaned forward in his seat. "I see Camelot."

"Nine feet per second," Carson said, "down at two hundred. Going down at five. Cut the H-dot. Fuel is—" Carson cursed under his breath but everyone heard it over the radio. "We've got a problem."

Stroud leaned closer to his panel. "Fuel's critically low. Five seconds left. Get us down, Digger—quick!"

"Four," Uzi said. "Three seconds. Two. One."

"Ten feet," Carson said.

But the engines cut out abruptly and they slammed into the surface, the shock absorbers on the struts buffering much of the impact. Everything shook and rattled . . . but at least they had struck the dirt squarely and had not tipped over onto their side.

Everything was deafeningly quiet. The loud engine rumble was gone, the vibration stilled. The radio was silent.

Uzi leaned back in his seat. "Raptor has landed."

Maddox laughed nervously. "Welcome to the Moon. Bit of a rough landing, but you made it. Congratulations, gentlemen."

45

Virginia Presbyterian Hospital

The nurse recorded Vail's vitals then shook her head. "You were lucky."

"How's my friend? She okay?"

"Can't discuss another patient with you, but generally speaking, yes, she's fine. She said she'll be in to check on you in a few minutes. She had a call to make."

As the woman left the emergency room cubicle, Tim Meadows walked in.

"What are you doing here?" she asked.

"That's a great way to show your gratitude to the guy who saved your life."

Vail drew her chin back. "Come again?"

"I'd like to, but that would imply I came the first time."

Vail looked at him.

"Okay, clearly you're not in the joking mood. So I was on the phone with you when you lost control of your car. And I'm—"

"I didn't lose control."

"*And* I'm the one who called the ambulance and pinpointed your location using your open cell signal. So, you're welcome."

"Thank you. But I must've missed something. How did *you* save my life? I broke my arm but I think the airbags saved my life."

Meadows shook his head. "Shoulda known you'd be ungrateful."

A physician entered, his white lab coat displaying a blue embroidered script that read, "Gerald Farber, MD." "How's my patient doing?"

"Meet the man who saved my life," Vail said, gesturing with her chin.

"Ah. Gerald Farber." He shook Meadows's hand. "Friend?"

"Colleague. I think I'm a friend, but sometimes I'm honestly not sure."

"Tim . . ." Vail closed her eyes.

"Right." Farber looked from Vail to Meadows and back. "I think I'll stay out of that one. Ms. Vail, the orthopedist will be here in a few minutes to set that fracture. I'm going to write you a script for Ibuprofen. I don't think you'll need anything stronger. You have any questions?"

"Nope. I'm good. Well, broken arm and a totaled car aside."

Farber gave her a chuckle and walked out.

"So let me tell you what I think happened," Meadows said.

"Is this as a friend or a colleague?"

"Given what happened," Meadows said, ignoring her, "I believe your car was hacked."

"You're kidding. Couldn't it just have been a catastrophic failure of the . . . I don't know, of the—"

"Of the brakes *and* the steering—simultaneously? No, my dear. Your car is a high-tech computer, with all its separate systems now interconnected and run by onboard computers—and complex operating systems bulging with one hundred to two hundred *million* lines of code. Add internet connectivity, infotainment entertainment systems, Bluetooth, and real-time monitoring like OnStar, and you've got a problem waiting to be exploited. Actually, no one's waiting. It's already happened. A lot of car manufacturers are way-y-y behind the curve. And the hackers have been warning them about it. They've breached core systems—entertainment systems, air bags, brakes, steering. Including, apparently, yours."

Vail spaced out for a moment: the mention of operating systems, lines of computer code, and hacking brought her back to her conversation with Lansford. *Is he behind this? Impossible—he's still in custody. But Kerwin. Shit!*

"You okay?" Meadows asked.

"Yeah. Yeah. Sorry. What you're saying makes sense."

"You admit that?"

"Tim, I never ignore what you tell me. It just seems that way."

"Thanks . . . I think."

"Okay, I'll run with this, Tim. Nice work."

"So much praise at one time," Meadows said as he parted the curtain and walked out. "Not sure I can handle it . . ."

46

Taurus-Littrow Valley
The Moon

Carson and Uzi were the first to debark from the Raptor. They entered the airlock, donned their white EVA pressure suits, and then opened the door to the lunar "atmosphere."

Carson descended the twelve-step ladder first and unceremoniously jumped down onto the surface, his boots making noticeable impressions in the fine dirt.

Uzi followed, but paused at the top of the lander to take in the view. It was at once spectacular, Twilight Zone-spooky, and, well, otherworldly. Off to his right, maybe a football field away, stood the Apollo 17 descent stage and to his left the abandoned lunar rover. *This place is like a museum.*

Uzi turned and headed down to meet Carson, who was on his way to examine the engines. Uzi had not experienced any claustrophobia and was getting used to being wrapped up tightly in the pressure suit. Moving in one-sixth gravity was an odd sensation, however. He had to hop, sometimes skip and lift his legs in odd ways to get around—while keeping his balance. The simulator had helped give him a sense of what to expect, but it was nevertheless different from being tethered to a crane in a controlled environment.

Unlike the Apollo missions, there would be no ceremonial driving of the American flag into the soil. The Raptor did not even have a flag decal plastered on its side—it had been removed in keeping with the covert nature of the op. However, because only a limited number of nations were capable of sending them to do what they had just done, there would be little doubt regarding who owned this spacecraft.

"Uh . . . shit."

It was Carson's voice.

"What's up, Digger?" Stroud asked.

"Fuel tank's way down."

"We know," Stroud said. "We fell the last ten f—"

"No, not the descent engine. We've only got about five thousand pounds in the *ascent* stage engine. It's half empty."

"Half empty? As in—"

"As in we've got no way to get off this rock once we've completed the mission."

Because of the weight issue, a rocket engine carried very little extra fuel than needed—leaving almost no margin for error.

Uzi sidled over to Carson. "How can that be?"

"Maybe it's a false reading," Stroud said. "Check out the thruster nozzles. I'll look over the computer system, run a diagnostic. CAPCOM, you getting this?"

"We are," Maddox said. "Telemetry is not showing what you're seeing. I'm conferring with our team. Stand by."

A moment later, Carson gestured Uzi closer. He was standing beneath the bottom of the lander, to the left of the ascent engine cone. "Everything looks intact. No evidence of a leak. But see that?"

"There's a residue on the edges of the ejection valve. I obviously can't take off my helmet to sniff it, but I'm betting it's fu—"

"It's fuel, all right," Carson said. "We apparently jettisoned our fuel on descent."

"Why would we do that?" DeSantos asked. "It's suicide."

"That's the thing," Uzi said. "We *wouldn't* have done that, not knowingly. Opening the ascent valve on *de*scent is—well, it's just not done. An alarm should've sounded and it didn't. More malware." Uzi looked up at the fuel tank, directly above his head. "Whoever screwed around with the avionics didn't want us getting off the surface, if we actually managed to land."

"Their failsafe," DeSantos said. "In case we survived all the other malware-induced glitches, this one was designed to strand us."

"Right," Uzi said. "We weren't seeing the correct readings, so when we thought we were doing X, we were really doing Y. We actually caused a problem that didn't exist—even though we were made to believe it did. If we look at what's happened since liftoff, that's been their plan all along. Much easier to dupe us into doing something stupid by sabotaging the operating system than sabotaging hardware like engines or fuel tanks."

"Even though we recovered," Carson said, "I think that when I fired the steering thrusters, I jettisoned half the ascent engine fuel. So I thought I was stabilizing the Raptor but what I was actually doing was dumping our critical fuel supply."

"Only bright spot," Stroud said, "is that Digger's exceptional flight skills saved us. Most other astronauts probably would've crashed this thing."

"Little consolation," Carson said. "Unless we find a way to blast off with half the fuel we need to rendezvous with Patriot, I only delayed our deaths by three days. And since there's no gas station on the Moon, we've got a big problem."

"You made it possible for us to try to complete the important part of the mission. We'll worry about getting off this rock later."

"Boychick," DeSantos said. "Malware? How?"

Uzi sighed. "It probably reinstalled itself."

"But you checked everything out."

"First, I'm not a cryptographer. Malware keeps getting more sophisticated. If you don't keep up on this shit daily, you miss new trends and concepts. So I can hack and put up a good defense against most kinds of attacks, but not something this sophisticated, in a matter of hours. Second, the person who did this is very, very good. My best guess is that this is beyond a single individual's scope."

"Meaning?" DeSantos asked.

"A well-funded army of people. Possibly even a state sponsor."

"What states have this capability?" Carson asked.

"Iran has upped their game in recent years—they've attacked the highest levels of the US government—successfully. Russia, obviously, and China, also obviously. Oh, and North Korea, maybe. But both China and Russia are infiltrating our government networks on a daily basis. That's not a secret. And it's also not a secret that China's got a lander a couple of miles from here and the Russians are on the way."

"How sure are you of this?" Stroud asked. "The level of sophistication."

Uzi thought a moment. "If it was done by a development team, and I think that's likely, then they coded it so it can be modified and recompiled. I read something about this in the materials Eisenbach gave me on the tablet. It was just a mention in a footnote, but we apparently do this kind of coding on purpose, on our planetary probes. These people made a binary injection. I patched around it—which was not easy—but I'm guessing they inserted a piece of code to monitor *that* area of code, so it self-repaired—basically, it repatched itself. It activated another, similar piece of malware to restore the attack's functionality. The fix that I thought I made with the patch worked initially, but in reality the attack was relaunched later by another piece of malware."

"I hate this shit," DeSantos said. "Technology sucks."

"Technology just put four people on the Moon," Carson said. "It's bad guys who *pervert* technology that suck."

"So what are we looking at here?" Stroud asked.

Uzi turned around and faced the desolate lunar surface. "Best I can say right here, with what we've got, is that it was a sophisticated attack. Likely by an organized group. State sponsored or not, I can't say. We'd need a forensic examination, more than I can do here—or have *time* to do here. That transmit chip will probably give us some clues."

Carson moved away from the engine. "Assuming we make it home."

"So now what the hell do we do?" DeSantos said.

"First things first," Stroud said. "We have a mission to carry out. CAPCOM, how long till the Russians arrive?"

"Eleven hours."

"That's it?" DeSantos asked.

"That's it."

"Then we have to rethink our mission," Uzi said. "And we have to do it fast."

47

Virginia Presbyterian Hospital

Alex Rusakov was fine following the accident—except for a minor hairline fracture of her left index finger, which was tandem taped to the adjacent digit.

When Rusakov joined Vail, Vail's arm was in a removable air splint and a sling was wrapped around her neck.

"Sticks and stones—and car accidents—can break our bones," Vail said, "but names . . . guess that doesn't really apply. They just broke our bones."

"You know that's a Russian saying. The literal, non-Americanized version is, 'The scolding won't hang on one's collar.'"

"I'm familiar with it. No offense, but the American version is catchier."

Rusakov pushed through the door and they emerged by the hospital's front entrance. "Well, I'm glad we came out of it with only a couple of broken bones. Could've been much worse."

"Yeah, as in we could be in the process of being laid to rest about now, six feet underground. When I find out who did this to us, I'm gonna rip him or her a new one."

"Only if you get there first."

Vail grinned. She could grow to like Rusakov.

"Knox is sending a car. He got us an old GMC SUV with very few computer chips and no internet connectivity."

"Closing the barn doors after the horses escape. Government Standard Operating Procedure 101."

They arrived at the industrial park twenty minutes later and entered to find the brain trust gathered in the conference room. The place had been cleaned up and workers were replacing the door and surrounding masonry.

"Glad to see you two are still with us," McNamara said, eyeing Vail's sling and Rusakov's splinted index finger.

"It was certainly an . . . interesting experience," Vail said. "One I don't ever want to repeat."

"Yes," Knox said. "We're taking steps to make sure that doesn't happen. In fact, it's triggered a top-to-bottom review of all Bureau vehicles. It'll then be expanded to all intelligence agencies and their vehicles, here and abroad. A bit like trying to put the toothpaste back in the tube, but at least it served as a wakeup call."

I like my horses and barn analogy better. But that's just me.

"We've gotten some more intel on Lansford. We sent a covert team into Kerwin's house in Rockville right after you grabbed her up. They found an encrypted laptop that's taking a while to break."

CIA director Earl Tasset pushed the glasses up his nose. "I'm told they still hope to get more off the hard drive, but it looks like Kerwin was involved with the people who planted the router in your house, Agent Vail. It also seems like she was in communication with someone in China. We're working on identifying who and why."

"And," McNamara said, "Lansford was not being truthful with you. He wasn't *given* code to insert into the Orion operating system. He co-wrote it."

"So he knows more than he told us," Rusakov said.

"That's an understatement," Knox said as he handed iPads to Vail and Rusakov. "We were in the ballpark regarding what was going on, but we were wrong about some very important things. Read what we've assembled, then get in there and talk with him, see what he'll tell you."

Vail set the iPad on the table and swiped with her good hand, skimming the document first to get an overview before reading it again more carefully. When she had committed the facts to memory, she pushed the tablet aside. "I'd like to take a crack at him first."

Rusakov shrugged. "You seem to have a better rapport with him. I'm better off being the evil bitch who can't wait to zap his balls with a million volts."

I'm still not convinced she wouldn't do it.

A moment later Vail entered the interrogation room. Lansford lifted his chin and gave Vail a pleading look—get on with it or execute him and get it over with. She was not sure which emotion he was projecting. He was once again hooked up to the polygraph.

"You don't look so good, Jason."

"Neither do you."

"Would you like some news on your wife and kids?"

His features softened. "Yes."

Vail nodded. "After you answer my questions, if you answer them honestly, I'll give you an update."

His shoulders drooped slightly but he recovered quickly.

"We had a chat with Jessie Kerwin."

His eyes widened—genuine surprise.

"Yeah, we found her," Vail said with a chuckle. "That's how I ended up with this." She gestured toward her sling. "And Jessie told us some really interesting things. Like your real name." Vail stopped and studied his face. No reaction. "Ivan Lantsov."

"Oh, yeah, nice heart rate, galvanic reaction," Jones said in her ear.

Vail smiled tightly. "Jessie says that you were born in St. Petersburg. Russia, not Florida. Your father was Russian but your mother was Taiwanese, which explains why your facial features have a slight Asian appearance." Vail stopped and studied him. "Was Jessie telling the truth?"

Lansford did not respond for five, ten, fifteen seconds. Then he nodded—slightly, reluctantly.

"You worked at a foundry that manufactured the communications chips for a company that assembled the Deep Space Network antennas. Your younger brother, Garry, was a techie too, and you got him a job at an antivirus company in Moscow. How am I doing so far? Jessie give us reliable info?"

Lansford looked at the ground.

"Still in an excited state," Jones said.

"I'll take that as a yes," Vail said. "But Garry screwed things up, didn't he?" Vail bent over, trying to get a look at Lansford's face. "He used his spare time to run an activist website that was critical of the Russian Federation for the way it treats homosexuals—which, we all know, is pretty shitty. Isn't it?"

Lansford nodded but did not lift his gaze.

"The Federation discovered Garry was behind the site because, well, Garry is good but he's no match for the army of hackers the government employs. So they arrested him. But it didn't end there. Because of his exceptional programming skills, they held onto him and grabbed you up. They leveraged you, made you a proposition. Spy for them and they won't make your younger brother disappear."

"He was such an idiot," Lansford said under his breath. "I warned him. I *warned* him."

"Siblings can cause a lot of problems for us, can't they?" *Boy, ain't that the truth?*

"Yeah."

"So they sent you to the United States, arranged a new identity for you: Ivan Lantsov became Jason Lansford. And they built an impressive backstory. You got hired at Aerospace Engineering as a software engineer. You had that gig for two years and did well. But Jessie created an opening at NASA in its space shuttle program by arranging an untimely death for one of its software engineers. And you submitted your application at a fortuitous time.

"You were hired and worked there for three years. But when the shuttle was discontinued, with no seniority, you were out of a job. So you went back to Aerospace Engineering. Your NASA experience got you an even better position there as head of software development for a program NASA was starting—which became the space launch system rocket and Orion crew exploration vehicle. How am I doing?"

Lansford swallowed noticeably. "Good."

"And you weren't *given* software code to insert into the avionics. You wrote it."

"I had help. But yes." He looked up at the ceiling. "Aerospace Engineering also made the mainboards and tested them."

"Ask him," Knox cut in, "if he arranged for Aerospace Engineering to get the transmit chips from China."

Vail posed the question.

"That was the riskiest part of the operation. We had to use a redundant chip on the board. It was so tiny the feeling was that no one would notice. And even if they did notice, it'd be a Chinese chip, not a Russian component. So fingers would be pointed at China. I thought it was a big gamble, but I did as I was told."

Vail sat down across from Lansford. "You said you had help writing the code."

"A team in Russia. I couldn't have done it myself."

"Were there other spies working with you? Here in the US."

"We had someone on the hardware side, to get the chip installed on the board. But I never had any direct contact with him. Or her. Jessie coordinated it all. She said it was safer that way."

"Just one?"

"I assumed one, but I really don't know."

"*Appears to be telling the truth,*" Jones said.

"And because you'd proven your worth to Russia, they released Garry from custody and sent him to China to spy for them—and to serve as a plausibly deniable reason for you to go to China . . . when in fact you were flying on to Moscow to report to Russian officials. Yes?"

"No."

Vail drew back. *Damn, I was doing so well.* "What do you mean, no?"

"You don't know what you think you know."

"Then enlighten us."

Lansford did not speak, did not move.

"We'll give you one chance to be honest with us. You get it wrong this time, the deal for your family is off."

Lansford squirmed in his seat. "What else are you going to give me?"

Vail chewed on that a moment. "A sit-down with your children. Not your wife—you could pass her a code word. Less likely with your kids. And it would be supervised. You'll be cut off if you appear to be passing information to them."

Lansford sat there, head bowed, as he thought it through.

"There's really nothing to think about, Jason. Veronika's ready to rip up our agreement." *Not to mention what she wants to do with that battery.* "And frankly, I'm worried about Renata, Kathy, and Zack. I don't give a shit about you. But them, they're innocents."

No response.

"You've got thirty seconds," Vail said, consulting her watch, "and then I leave. And once I walk out, we're done. I won't be back."

Ten seconds passed, then another five. He lifted his head, made eye contact with Vail, and nodded.

"Okay then, let's have it. And don't leave anything out. No more bullshit."

"It's not the Russian government that's behind the spying, but Ronck Mining Robotics, a Russian company hired by the Chinese Space Agency that built their robotic rover. They pioneered specialized mining equipment for drilling into various depths of the lunar surface to sample, test, and secure the caesarium. Ronck is the only company with this technology."

"How do you know this?"

"It was need to know, and I needed to know."

"Because of what you did to the software? The malware?" Vail asked.

"Yes. And no. Originally they wanted me to sabotage the operating system of the Orion rover. But their plans changed."

"So who's behind all this? China? Russia?"

"Yes."

"Which?"

"I can only tell you what I know. I suggest you look into Ronck Mining. You may find something of interest."

"No more games. You know something, now's the time to tell us."

Lansford shifted his jaw. "One of the main people involved with Ronck has a history. With the KGB."

"Give me a name."

He sighed, hesitated, then said, "Mikhail Uglov."

Vail pulled out her encrypted OPSIG phone and plugged in the name. *Well that can't be right.* "Not sure I spelled it correctly."

Lansford chuckled.

Then again, maybe I did. "Uglov is a Russian diplomat?"

"And the second largest shareholder of Ronck Mining."

Vail turned and looked at the two-way glass and nodded at Rusakov. She—or Knox or Tasset or someone at OPSIG—would be digging into Mikhail Uglov's background. If they weren't already.

And if this diplomat was involved with Ronck Mining Robotics, they might be on the cusp of getting some answers.

48

Taurus-Littrow Valley

Gavin Stroud and DeSantos joined Uzi and Carson in front of the rover, which they had deployed down the long ramp from inside the storage bay beneath the crew cabin.

"Here are our priorities," Stroud said. "I'll secure a sample of caesarium and run the designated tests, then transmit the data to ground control. We've now got a fuel issue, so I'm putting Uzi and DeSantos on that. And we've got the other mission objective—to prevent the Chang'e 5 from getting off this surface or prevent their robotic rover from obtaining the caesarium. Our option. Need be, we've got C-4 and timers, but I'd rather keep it low tech and avoid explosives if we can. Digger, that part of the mission hasn't changed, so you've still got that."

"And let's not forget the new task on our plate," DeSantos said. "The Russians."

"Right," Stroud said. "We don't know their intentions, but we can guess—they want to bring caesarium back to Earth—which we can't allow. So soon as they arrive, that becomes our primary mission objective—so let's try to get these others taken care of in the next eight hours."

"We've got another problem." Uzi turned to the rover. "The mining equipment you'll need to locate the caesarium, drill it out of the ground, and run the tests, is built into the Spider. Which means no one's going anywhere we can't walk. Because you'll have the rover. We can't do everything simultaneously. That wasn't an issue before, but the situation's changed. And time is tight."

Stroud walked toward the Spider's suit port, a type of airlock that enabled them to remove their pressure suits and enter the cabin of the rover relatively quickly—and then be able to carry out their duties free of the encumbrance of the bulky gear and large primary life support system backpack. "You guys work on that while I start scouting out the caesarium. Need be, you can walk—or hop—the two miles to the Chang'e."

"Unless . . ." Uzi stopped.

"Unless what?" Carson asked.

"We've got a used vehicle gathering Moon dust, waiting for a new owner. The Apollo 17 LRV," he said, referring to the lunar roving vehicle. "The Moon buggy."

DeSantos looked at Carson. It was difficult to make out his expression through the glass of the visor—which reflected the lunar surface as well as the black of space—but it was clear he was thinking the same thing: he was not sure he heard correctly.

"Did you just suggest we try to resurrect a forty-six-year-old convertible?" DeSantos asked. "I know a thing or two about old cars and—"

"Less than ideal, I know. But it's there, we need it, and every problem has potential solutions."

"Uzi," Carson said, "it was an electric vehicle and the batteries are long dead."

"So what?" Uzi asked. "We've got solar arrays on the Chang'e—both the rover and the lander. We should be able to use them, wire them into the LRV. What I don't know is what kind of battery they've got."

"And a battery is necessary?" DeSantos asked.

"My technologically challenged friend . . . yes. A direct-to-motor solar-load is theoretically possible, but very challenging. The solar array captures the sunlight and converts that energy into electricity. But then what?"

"It gets used."

"Not that simple. Without a battery, you have no way of storing that energy. So you'd need constant sunlight or the rover would stop. And the array would have to be able to turn to face the sun and move up and down for the same reason. In case you haven't noticed, the Moon's hilly and mountainous, so we could easily move out of direct line of sight of the sun. And the motor loads will be constantly changing because the terrain is so uneven—we'll need more, or less, power as we move from one area to another, from low ground to high ground. We'll have no way of storing the excess if we don't need it at that moment. Over the course of starting, accelerating, stopping, climbing, and turning, the battery gives and takes for instantaneous demand while balancing the amount of total energy generated with total energy used."

"So we really need a battery."

"We really need a battery. And a charge controller."

"Oh," DeSantos said. "Of course. I knew that."

Uzi laughed. "I didn't realize you knew what a charge controller does."

"Boychick, how ignorant do you think I am?"

"Really want me to answer that? Let's just say that using a solar array is not like plugging an appliance into a 120-volt wall outlet. When you plug into an outlet, you get standard voltage and frequency—doesn't matter if you're pulling a small amount of power to recharge your cell phone or a large amount for a hair dryer, table saw, or oven. Because the voltage and current production of a solar array change with the amount of power you're pulling, how efficient you are at pointing the array at the sun, and how hot its operating temperature is, you need a charge controller to keep the power draw constant. But you knew that. Right?"

"Like I said."

Carson tapped the mic button on his helmet. "Hey CAPCOM."

"Go, Raptor," Maddox said.

He explained what Uzi had suggested. "Not that I don't trust Uzi, but we're tight on time and if it's not going to work, we need to know. And if it's feasible we're gonna need some help."

"Stand by, Digger. I'll talk with the engineers. I'm sure we have the old LRV specs on file. And I can probably reach one of the guys at Boeing who designed the thing. Doesn't look like much, but it's a well-built, complex machine. In today's dollars, it cost a quarter billion dollars to develop and build."

"Cowboy," Uzi said. "Drop us at the Chang'e, then you can come back here and start mining. I'm almost positive we can make those solar panels work."

Stroud was now seated in the pressurized cabin at the front of the Spider, minus his suit. "Ten-four. But you're not driving."

Wise guy.

Carson, Uzi, and DeSantos jumped onto the Spider's small rear platform, which was designed to transport astronauts on short trips across a planetary surface. This was significantly more efficient than having them remove their suits, only to don them again moments later.

"I'll give you a rundown of the LRV while you're en route," Maddox said, "in case Uzi's right about the solar power. I've got the spec sheet in front of me. The buggy had two 36-volt batteries and four 1/4-horsepower drive motors. One for each wheel."

"True four wheel drive," DeSantos said. "How fast could it go?"

"If I remember right, about ten—no, check that, max speed was nine miles per hour. It could go forward or reverse, and drive over objects about a foot high. You'll be able to cross crevasses about two feet wide, but I wouldn't push it. It can climb and descend moderate slopes, but that'll probably depend on how much power you can generate from the solar array."

"Roger that," Uzi said.

"And there's no steering wheel. It's got a main center console and a hand controller, so it'll take some getting used to."

"Hang on a second," DeSantos said. "Boychick, you see what I see?"

"Hey, Cowboy, slow down, we want to get a look at this."

"The Apollo 17 descent stage," Carson said.

"Exactly what it is," Stroud said. He slowed, and then stopped, the Spider a dozen feet from the metal framework, which stood stately by, untouched, and ungazed upon, by humanity in several decades.

Uzi, DeSantos, and Carson hopped off the rover and made their way over to the structure. On the side was a stainless steel plaque, roughly eight inches by ten, fastened to the lander's third and fourth ladder rungs. Uzi dusted off the curved surface with his gloved right hand. An engraved Moon and Earth were at the top, followed by the words,

Here Man completed his first explorations of
the Moon, December 1972 AD.
May the spirit of peace in which we came be
reflected in the lives of all mankind.

It was signed by the three Apollo 17 astronauts Cernan, Schmitt, and Evans, as well as by President Richard Nixon.

"Well that's kind of ironic," Uzi said. "Different circumstances, but in a weird kind of way, we came today with the same goal."

"What is all this?" DeSantos asked. He was standing beside a heap of what looked like junk, piled a few feet high and scattered over a five foot radius.

Carson came up alongside him. "After their last EVA, Cernan and Schmitt had to dump all sorts of stuff out of the lunar module to get their weight down. Every ounce counted. They actually used a fishing scale to weigh everything and dump whatever wasn't essential so they could get off the surface."

Uzi gestured to the pile. "All sorts of equipment." He put a hand on DeSantos's shoulder for stability and used his toe to move some of the stuff aside. "MREs!" Uzi said, using the military term for meals ready to eat. "Can you believe that?"

Carson carefully bent forward for a better look. "I don't think they're MREs. Same concept, but a whole lot more sophisticated to withstand the rigors of space flight. Can't remember what they had with them, but dehydrated cream of mushroom soup sticks in my mind."

"Can you imagine what that must taste like all these years later?"

Carson laughed. "Probably not a whole lot worse than it tasted when it was fresh."

"Be glad you'll never find out," DeSantos said.

"Guys," Stroud said over their headsets, "we're on a tight schedule. Bus leaving in T-minus ten seconds."

"My fault." Uzi grabbed the metal handle on the rear of the Spider. "I'm a history buff, especially space history. And instead of a replica in the National Air and Space Museum, I'm on the Moon looking at the actual thing. Mind blowing."

"Blow your mind some other time. We're shoving off. Hang on." Stroud accelerated and drove a couple hundred feet, where the LRV was parked.

The rover was angled toward the descent stage, facing it. The tires were large and made of what looked to be some kind of metal mesh. The seats were crude and had crisscrossing straps, making them resemble old style lawn chairs.

"Pull over," Uzi said. "I want to take a look, see what power connections I'm dealing with."

Stroud stopped a dozen feet away. DeSantos got off the Spider and led the way to the primitive looking four-wheel vehicle.

"CAPCOM," DeSantos said, "we're taking a quick detour at the LRV."

"Roger. Meantime, I'm sending Cowboy the location and heading for the Chang'e. Keep in mind that assuming you get the solar array wired into the Spider, you might need to charge it up for a while, so factor that into your plans."

"Why'd they park the rover so far away from the lunar module?" Carson asked.

"The LRV had a movie camera mounted on it," Maddox said. "Gene Cernan put the rover where it is to get far enough back to film the ascent stage liftoff and beam it back to Earth."

"Copy that," Uzi said. "I see the camera." He carefully lowered himself to his knees, switched on his helmet spotlight, and peered under the rover. "CAPCOM, you think you can get hold of some specs on the Chang'e solar array and battery? And maybe someone who can tell me how long it'd take to get it up and running on the LRV?"

"Already on it," Maddox said. "I think I've got someone for you. I can multitask."

"Hey, there are letters here carved into the dirt," Carson said, standing beside the driver's seat. "T, D, and C."

"Cernan's daughter's initials," Uzi said. "Leave them be."

"Bob," DeSantos said, "what's that big box mounted between the two seats?"

"I've been paging through the old LRV manual. That box is the control console I mentioned before. Are you sitting in the rover?"

Uzi pulled himself up and gestured to DeSantos. "Give us a sec." They climbed in and DeSantos used his glove to brush away a thin layer of Moon dust. "We see the panel."

"Okay, good. The speed and heading gauges are self-explanatory. Obviously, once you've got the solar array hooked up and charging the batteries, you'll have to pay attention to the power/temperature monitor, which is right in the middle. Those will be a guide to the motor on each wheel."

"I see it," Uzi said.

"Directly below that, there's drive power, drive enable, and steering. BUS A and BUS B, for each of the wheels, need to be set to on. Same with the main power switches on the left, for the two batteries."

DeSantos pointed. "We got it."

"And that big white T-shaped joystick in the middle is the controller, your steering wheel. I've heard it took some getting used to because it's in the middle rather than in front of you, and you can only use one hand to steer. It doesn't use pressure sensitive touch control like a fighter jet, so you physically have to move it side to side. Uzi, uh . . . you're not going to be driving it, are you?"

"Oh my god, Bob. You too? I'm not gonna crash the thing. I'm a good driver, really."

DeSantos heard some chuckling over the radio. The ground control guys were listening in and having a good time with this—at Uzi's expense.

"You move the stick forward to go forward," Maddox continued. "Left and right turns it left or right. But pulling the controller backward toward you activates the brakes. If you flip a switch on the handle *before* pulling back, the LRV goes in reverse. But if you pull the thing all the way back, you'll set the parking brake."

"Wait," Uzi said, "just want to make sure I've got this straight: moving the controller to the right makes us go *left*?"

"Very funny," Maddox said. "Last thing is the system reset button. When you've got enough charge, you'll need to hit that. And then you're ready to go."

"Ten-four," DeSantos said.

"And the batteries?" Uzi asked. "I couldn't see them."

"There are two and they're between the front wheels, hidden underneath dust covers, an insulation blanket, and a gyro thermal strap."

Uzi's sigh was audible over the radio. "This transplant is gonna take awhile. Cowboy, where's the toolbox?"

"Open the rear door to the suit lock and in the left wall—"

"Yeah, yeah, I remember." Uzi shuffled over to the Spider and pulled on the rear door handle.

"Oh, one other thing," Maddox said. "During the Apollo 17 mission, Gene Cernan accidentally knocked off the right rear fender extension. They replaced it with EVA maps, duct tape, and lunar module clamps. But when they left they needed the clamps for launch so they removed the maps—"

"Those maps are on display in the Air and Space Museum in DC," Uzi said. "I've seen them."

"Correct. And as a result, you're gonna get a lot of dust kicked up. If you have time, see if you can find a solution. Otherwise, prepare to get filthy. Put the dust covers back on the batteries after you replace them and obviously make sure the solar panel surfaces stay clean."

"Copy that," Uzi said.

"Guys," Stroud said, "climb back on. We've gotta get over to the Chang'e in case the solar conversion will work."

"How much longer till we have some answers on that?" DeSantos asked as he hopped onto the back of the Spider.

"Right now. I've got Sarah Neville here, a power system lead. Normally only the CAPCOM talks to you guys, but Sarah knows the deep distinctions of solar arrays, batteries, radioisotope thermoelectric generators, charge controllers, regulators, and the wiring you'll encounter. She was on her way out but I had someone tackle her before she could leave the building and explain what you need to do."

"Okay gentlemen," Neville said, "it may sound simple to pull out a few solar panels and hook 'em up to the LRV, but any time you mix electronics, solar panels, 1960s technology, foreign components, and batteries, it gets a little complicated."

"A little?" DeSantos said.

"Sarah, this is Uzi. I'm gonna be taking the lead here. Main thing is, can we do this?"

"Yes. And even though my stomach is growling something fierce, I'll help you through it. I'm familiar with the LRV and I've got my trusty calculator in front of me. I'm calling up the original Boeing operations handbook right now."

The Spider lurched and DeSantos, Uzi, and Carson bumped into one another—but hung on.

"So I'm extrapolating a bit since we've got a little more info on the older Chang'e 3 and 4, but the 5 shouldn't be too different. Should be four arrays, two larger ones on the lander and two smaller ones on the rover. The largest are likely a little over a square meter each. Round down the raw solar power flux to 1,300 watts per square meter and assume 25 percent cell efficiency and 85 percent fill factor, since there's a nonworking area in the noncell portion of an array. Each lander array can produce . . . hang on while I punch this in . . . okay, 276 watts. So we'll say 250 watts per square meter of panel. That assumes it's pointing right at the sun. You'd probably get 100 watts each on the rover's panels. You with me so far?"

"This is DeSantos. I lost you as soon as you said 'power flux' and 'watts per square meter.'"

"I'm the geek here," Uzi said. "And I'm with you. So that's the supply side. How about the demand side?"

"I was getting to that," Neville said. "Your buggy weighs 463 pounds. The large golf carts that carry tour groups weigh around 3,000 pounds and need about 415 watts—so the 500 watts those two Chang'e arrays generate will work just fine."

Stroud swerved a bit left and they nearly went flying. "Sorry about that, guys."

"And we take the batteries too," DeSantos said. "Right? I mean, those are essential because they'll store the power the panels generate."

Uzi gave him a look. DeSantos winked back.

"Yes, very good. You're absolutely right. The batteries will make it a whole lot easier for you. And if you need to use the LRV in shadows or darkness, you'll be able to."

"How much time will it take us to remove the solar stuff from the Chang'e and install it in the LRV?" DeSantos asked.

"Figure on at least three hours," Neville said. "You'll be working in pressure suits with thick, clumsy gloves. You won't have the mobility, flexibility, and dexterity you're used to. Not to mention the lander wasn't designed to be user serviceable. Add it all up, it won't be quick."

"Three hours," Stroud said. "Jesus. At least when we disconnect the lander's power source, we might be able to cross off one of our mission objectives. I doubt the Chang'e can make the journey back without its power pack."

"I'll try to get you an answer on that as well," Maddox said. "But to be safe, disable it completely."

"That all we need to know?" Stroud asked.

Neville laughed.

"I didn't mean that as a joke."

"But it was funny. No, that's not it, not by a long shot. I'll have to look up your latitude and calculate how high you'll need to mount the panels. I don't know if this is possible, but it'd be best to have a movable mount so you can position it toward the sun if you change direction. Pain in the ass—much easier if you had a two-motor pan tilt so you can point right at the sun without having to manually do it, but we can't be picky when you're on another celestial body and using decades-old tech."

"We'll make it work," Uzi said.

"Last thing," Neville said. "Power usage. If we assume you'll be traveling three to ten kilometers per hour and on slopes no more than ten degrees—both of which seem reasonable given where you are—the buggy will use about 108 to 216 watt-hours per kilometer. The LRV's got a 36 volt battery. But the power draw is more per kilometer if you're going slower because it takes longer to drive that same distance."

"Now that," DeSantos said, "is something I understand. Driving faster is better."

"Spoken by the guy who drives a Corvette," Uzi said.

"When you're ready to start, let me know. Assuming someone can bring me some chow, I'll hang around here on standby. I'm sure you'll have questions."

"No doubt," Uzi said. "Thanks Sarah."

"It's me again, boys," Maddox said. "We've been tracking the Russian spacecraft and I need to amend our previous ETA. They're approximately six hours off your position."

"On that note, gentlemen," Stroud said as he slowed, "our tour bus is now pulling up alongside the Chang'e 5. This is our last stop. All passengers must exit the train."

Uzi, DeSantos, and Carson climbed down from the Spider and off they went.

49

Black Site

Alex Rusakov looked from Vail to Knox. "So let me get this straight. Evgeny Kirilenko, the guy whose latent was on the router antenna in Karen's garage, not only was he former KGB and FSB but he now works for Ronck, the Russian company whose former CEO is Mikhail Uglov, the Russian diplomat, who *also* used to work for the KGB?"

"Sounds like you've got it right," Knox said.

"Things are starting to come together," Tasset said. "But the lines are intersecting and leading to some disturbing conclusions."

"And," McNamara said, "I checked in with Homeland Security and the Diplomatic Security Service. Uglov's print and facial recognition algorithm matches the ones we have on file for the Russian diplomat of the same name, so they're the same person. Just to be sure, I asked for confirmation."

Vail elbowed Rusakov. "We need to talk with this guy."

"I'll see if I can set something up," Knox said. "He's a diplomat. A Russian diplomat. Not gonna be easy."

Tasset frowned. "I'd say there's zero chance he talks with us."

"Might be possible to corner him. I'll ask Diplomatic Security where and when he eats or gets coffee, and you two can happen to be there."

"See what you can do," McNamara said. "This guy could be a key to what's been going on."

Tasset's phone rang. He listened a moment then angled the handset away from his mouth. "Uglov's at Dulles, booked on a flight due to leave for Russia in forty minutes."

"Jesus," Vail said as she backed toward the door. "I know he's a diplomat, but do whatever you gotta do . . . just delay that flight until we can get there."

50

Taurus-Littrow Valley

DeSantos watched as Uzi and Carson removed panels, pried off access doors, and cursed as they fought one obstacle after another. Neville was not kidding when she said the Chang'e was not designed to be "user serviceable."

While they worked on the solar array, DeSantos conferred with Maddox on a solution for their lack of fuel.

"I know you don't want to hear this, Hector, but there's no way to fill up your tank. I've got a team working on it and they've discussed asking the Russians if it'd be possible for them to take you up with them when they lift off, but I don't have to tell you what the price would be."

"Caesarium."

"As a starting point. They'd have a list of demands, from lifting sanctions, to Syria, to removing our missile shield in eastern Europe. Not to mention NATO. And we'd be in no position to negotiate."

"So that's obviously off the list," DeSantos said. "Are we—are we missing an obvious solution? We've got a Chinese spacecraft right in front of us filled with fuel. Why don't we just siphon it off?"

Maddox laughed. "Sorry. I realize you're serious and that seems like a logical solution, but you don't siphon fuel from a rocket engine the way you do from a car. These fuels are not only highly flammable but really nasty chemicals, the kind you don't want to have *any* contact with."

"So I guess that was a stupid question."

"Uninformed," Maddox said. "But not stupid. Another major obstacle is the fittings. I doubt they're compatible."

"Fittings?"

"When these rockets are fueled with propellant, it's done in a high-tech facility with all sorts of ground support equipment. They hook up the tanks through a fill/drain valve and pump up the tank. Then they button down the spacecraft. They'd de-tank, or offload, the fuel, if they had to, through that same valve. And here's the rub—the valve, the fitting, would need to be compatible. I doubt the Chinese and Americans use the same coupling. And because the boiling point of NTO—nitrogen tetroxide—is around seventy degrees Fahrenheit, you need a closed system rather than a siphon. Otherwise, propellant would boil away in the heat of the sunshine on the Moon."

Uzi leaned away from the solar array, screwdriver in hand. "Bob, we've got a 3D printer on board the Raptor. Why can't you upload a design and we'll print it and use that as the coupler?"

"Well, that's a good question and I'm in way over my head so I don't have an answer. Give me a few minutes to get a rocket guy in here."

Three minutes later, Maddox was introducing Issachar Makonnen.

"Bob's given me a quick and dirty rundown of what you're facing," Issachar said. "I think it's possible this could work, but I've gotta be honest with you. The odds are long."

"The odds of survival are zero if this doesn't work," Uzi said.

"Long odds may not sound so good to you. But to us any odds are better than the alternative."

"Ten-four. We'll try to design a coupler that'll enable you to transfer the Chang'e fuel. We'll need some decent photos of the fitting, multiple angles—and include something of consistent scale if you don't have a ruler."

"I'm on it," DeSantos said.

"You're also going to need some kind of pump and a way to power it. You could use one of the drive motors on the Chang'e rover to provide the cranking, but the pump's another story. It'll have to be manufactured by the printer too. Don't worry about it, we'll take care of that. But—there are a few other things you need to be aware of—full disclosure."

"Uh-oh," DeSantos said. "Never good when you start with, 'full disclosure.'"

"There are a lot of different propellant blends used in rocketry. Propellants are the combinations of fuel and the oxidizers needed to burn it. Kerosene's a typical fuel used for first stage boosters because of its high density and good performance when combined with liquid oxygen. For orbits or landing on the Moon, hypergolic propellants are used. These are liquids that automatically ignite when mixed together. So you'd have some form of hydrazine fuel, like MMH, and nitrogen tetroxide, NTO, as the oxidizer. The Raptor uses MMH and NTO. We think the Chang'e 3 used UDMH and NTO."

"So they're not compatible?" Carson asked.

Issachar chuckled. "Best answer is maybe yes, maybe no. An engine designed for MMH *could* work with UDMH, but I'm not sure that's ever been attempted. Rocket engines are highly engineered machines, designed to mix the fuel and oxidizer at precise ratios under tight pressure and temperature constraints. Putting a different fuel in could easily result in burn-through of components not designed to handle the higher temperatures that might result. But, hey, beats getting stuck on the Moon."

Yeah, DeSantos thought, *sure beats that.*

"The Chang'e NTO would be the same as what our engine uses," Carson said, "so maybe it won't be an issue."

"I'll do my best to get you some answers. But if it's never been done, there may not be any to get."

"Understood," Carson said. "But we're bumping up against a bit of a deadline. Won't it take awhile to print metal parts like that, assuming it's possible?"

"Couple of days, best guess."

"Man," DeSantos said, "that's gonna be tight."

"And there's one more issue. You're likely talking about thousands of pounds worth of liquids, or several hundred gallons. You've got to get it from one vehicle to the other. Are the two close to each other?"

"Not at all," Uzi said. "Put it on our list of things to figure out."

"That's *our* job," Maddox said. "We'll sharpen our pencils and see if we can come up with a solution."

"Then here's one more thing to put on your list," Uzi said. "The difference in the ship's mass. The Chang'e 5 was designed to lift off with a payload of rocks. We've got eight hundred pounds between the four of us, plus all the supplies and equipment that goes with keeping a four-man crew alive—"

"Understood," Maddox said. "You'll have to dump a lot of stuff, for sure. We'll do the math and get back to you."

Uzi removed the solar panel and took it in his hands. "Thanks for your help, Issachar. The sooner you can get us some answers, the better."

DeSantos came up behind them and watched Uzi gently place the device on the ground. "Great idea about the 3D printer, Boychick. But what if it takes two days to print that fitting and something's not quite right? If we need to start over again . . . we've only got four days of food, water, and oxygen."

"Can this get any worse?" Carson asked.

For sure, DeSantos thought. *Just wait till the Russians land.*

51

Dulles International Airport

Vail and Rusakov arrived at Dulles thirty minutes later. Rodman met them at security and handed them two carry-on suitcases containing packets with new identification, passports, coach tickets for the flight to Russia, and a kit for them to carry out their op.

With Uglov having diplomatic immunity, there was no legal way for them to arrest or detain him. It had to be done on foreign soil, with classic black, deniable methods.

Before leaving their car, they removed wigs from their go-bags and colored contact lenses. Because of Vail's cast, Rusakov had to assist with her transformation.

Their "disguises" would not defeat facial recognition cameras, but they would help with face-to-face eyewitness identification. Rusakov, however, had a pair of glasses in her kit constructed with a prism designed to fool the computer algorithms. Vail had used the technology during a previous case in England and made a mental note to ask McNamara for a pair to keep in her go-bag.

Vail's injury was less than well-timed, but as Rusakov had noted on the drive over, with a cast and sling, no one was going to suspect her of being a spy or foreign agent. Unless, of course, the idea was to fake a broken arm, Vail pointed out. Rusakov told her any situation could be overanalyzed and that every op, mission, and maneuver presented risks and handicaps. She should just be flexible, go along with whatever transpired, and be quick and creative with solutions. Vail's injury was an indisputable fact and was not going to change. She should use it to her advantage if the situation presented itself.

They boarded separately, after a forty-five-minute delay due to "mechanical issues" that made for a grumpy group of travelers who were facing a long flight to begin with. They were informed that it turned out to be a faulty light on an air traffic controller's panel, not a problem with the aircraft.

Vail overheard a flight attendant tell her colleague that she did not quite understand the explanation for the delay, but whatever—they were cleared for takeoff and with the padded schedules and jet stream, they would likely make up most of the time.

As they started to button down the aircraft, Vail's phone vibrated. She fished it out and saw it was Troy Rodman. She debated whether or not to answer—she had to be very careful not to let anything slip out on her end of the conversation.

"Hey. Can't really talk."

"You're gonna want to hear this."

Vail glanced up, cradling the phone out of sight in case the flight attendants told them to put their devices in airplane mode. "Go."

"We looked into your man there. A thorough backgrounder, ran it through everything we've got. And Interpol got a hit. Kind of weird because it goes back to a real old case in France. A twenty-five-year-old named Arkady Barndyk set a charge off in a radio station that was critical of the Soviet Union's attempted economic reforms and their plan to combat rampant alcoholism in the country by significantly raising the price of booze."

"Okay." *Is Barndyk now known as Uglov?* She wanted to ask, but would not dare utter those names. "What's the relevance of that story?" She saw a flight attendant headed her way. "Quickly."

"Uglov is Arkady Barndyk and France has had a warrant out for his arrest for thirty years. FBI too because four Americans were killed in the blast. Confirmed by latent prints and facial recognition of photos we gave them. This Russian diplomat is not who he says he is."

"Right. That could be very helpful."

"One more thing. Barndyk had a colleague at the time in the KGB. Name of Evgeny Kirilenko. Ring a bell?"

The guy who built the wireless router they found in my garage. "Sure does."

"Miss, we're pushing back from the gate. You need to end your call."

"Gotta go," she told Rodman. After switching off her phone, she took out a Kindle, which had been preloaded to a book she had no interest in reading. In reality, it was there for show—to give her something commonplace and unremarkable to do for the first two and a half hours of the flight. Meantime, while staring at the screen, she tried to piece together what Rodman had told her—and figure out how she could use it.

Just prior to arriving at the airport, McNamara had laid out the particulars of the plan: Vail was going to get close to Uglov and give him a fast-acting drug that would simulate a heart attack. How she accomplished that was left up to her.

She was provided with four methods of administering it—an intramuscular injection; a patch with microscopic needles invisible to the human eye; a chemical placed in the palm of her hand that would take a bit longer to have its effect but would largely be undetectable; or a small vial of clear, tasteless liquid that could be emptied into his drink.

Rusakov had the identical kit in case Vail was unable to complete her mission.

Given her injury, there was one method that Vail considered easiest to deploy. She would take Rusakov's advice and use the cast to her advantage.

Two hours and thirty minutes into the flight, over the Atlantic and in international waters, with Iceland approaching in the distance, Vail got ready to execute her plan. She waited until the two first class flight attendants were busy with passengers, then rose from her seat and passed Uglov on the way to the restroom. Being a commoner from coach, she was not permitted to use this lavatory, but there was no staff in the vicinity at the moment to notice or object.

She flushed the toilet and walked out. En route to her seat, she suddenly lurched left and tripped forward, into Uglov's chest. He was watching a movie and did not know what hit him—it was the air splint, square in the chest.

He locked eyes with Vail and she, flustered, apologized profusely for bothering him. "I tripped and . . . again, I'm so sorry, sir. This broken arm, I couldn't stop myself from falling."

She extended her right hand to shake and he took it. She held it there while she blabbered something about no one was going to believe this at the office—it never would've happened if they'd bought her a first class ticket instead of coach, like they did for him—and maybe next time he could put in a good word for her.

She was talking fast and figured he had no idea what she was going on about, but he was probably not even listening to what this attractive woman was saying to him. Then she headed back to her seat, twenty-three rows back, and the next phase was set in motion.

Moments later, two hours and forty-two minutes into the flight, Uglov was shifting about uncomfortably and tugging on his shirt collar. He tried to stand but only got halfway out of his seat. He fell and landed in the aisle.

Vail could not hear it—the white noise rush of air and the distance from his seat made it impossible—but despite the first class divider she caught glimpses of the commotion.

Rusakov was at Uglov's side. The plan was for her to inform the flight attendant that she was a physician and offer her services. As a former combat surgeon, Rusakov was well accustomed to the role—no playacting required.

They apparently accepted Rusakov's assistance because she was taking Uglov's pulse, then opening the unconscious diplomat's shirt and removing a stethoscope from her carry-on. She listened a moment, then started talking to the woman, telling her that the passenger was having a heart attack and that he required immediate medical attention or he was going to die. Vail went over and explained that she was Mr. Uglov's assistant at the embassy and demanded to know what was wrong.

A stocky man in his thirties walked over and leaned on the seatback. "Anything I can help with here?"

Vail glanced up and instantly identified him as a federal air marshal. She knew there were four of them on international flights, and that they would need permission from their team leader to render, or offer, assistance. But they had no formal medical training other than basic first aid. And they would not blow their cover in a situation like this—meaning they would not identify themselves. If Vail and Rusakov played this right, the marshal would have nothing to do and, to avoid calling attention to himself, return to his seat.

"Are you a doctor?" Vail asked.

"Uh, no, ma'am. Just wanted to see if there was anything I could do."

"We're good here," Rusakov said. "I'm a physician. We've got it under control."

The marshal hung around another moment, then left. Vail glanced back to see where he was headed. She would need to keep an eye on him until they had successfully deplaned.

Although it was unlikely the marshals were informed that a diplomat was onboard, the flight attendant staff had probably been notified. If so, it could make Vail's and Rusakov's job easier because the airline would not want to be responsible for failing to take appropriate action while presiding over the medical emergency of a high-ranking Russian representative.

Vail again lamented that her boss had not bought her a first class ticket and instead stuck her in coach—otherwise she could've prevented his collapse. Rusakov told Vail that was not the case, that her boss was having a heart attack and that they needed to get him immediate medical attention in a hospital if they were to save his life. Vail created a bogus medical history of prior heart trouble and started rattling off details of his previous treatment.

"Save it for the hospital," Rusakov said. "The cardiologist will need to know all that."

The male flight attendant who had been hovering behind Rusakov's shoulder moved off and grabbed a phone, presumably to talk with the captain.

Minutes later, the plane noticeably banked left.

The steward returned and informed Rusakov that they were altering course to land in Iceland. An ambulance would be standing by to transport Uglov to the hospital in Reykjanes. He told Vail she had to return to her seat.

"I can't leave him," Vail said.

Rusakov placed a hand on Vail's, displaying a warmth Vail did not know the tough beauty queen black operative possessed. "I'll stay right by his side, no need to worry. I'll make sure he gets all the care he needs as soon as we land."

Vail looked uncertain. "Can I go with him, doctor? I should. I should go with him. You said it's important."

Rusakov squeezed her hand. "Of course."

Getting no objections from the attendant, and with the assurance she "needed," Vail returned to her row, glancing at the air marshal on the way. A moment later, she saw a couple of passengers help Uglov back into his seat. Rusakov settled in across the aisle from him to better monitor his vitals.

With the plan in motion, Vail removed the "makeup kit" that contained the remaining mission materials and made for the rear restroom where she would flush the biodegradable items she no longer needed down the toilet. The syringe would remain in her bag, posing as an insulin kit, if anyone asked—but the vials of medication were emptied and rinsed in the sink.

A knock on the door startled her. "Please return to your seat. Captain has turned on the seatbelt sign. We're on our approach."

Vail did as instructed and had just fastened her restraint when the pilot started his announcement.

"Ladies and gentlemen, uh, this is Captain Simmons. We have a medical issue on board with a passenger and we'll be diverting momentarily to the Keflavik International Airport in Iceland to make sure he gets adequate attention. I apologize for this delay, but we don't anticipate it taking very long. We'll get you back in the air as soon as possible. Thank you for understanding. At least, uh, you'll be able to tell people you visited Iceland, the most sparsely populated country in Europe. We'll be touching down in ten minutes. Flight attendants, prepare for landing."

After the wheels hit the tarmac, within thirty seconds the plane came to a stop at the gate. Vail rushed forward as Rusakov put on her stethoscope and placed it against Uglov's hairy chest.

"Is he going to be okay?" Vail asked frantically, doing her best to sell it.

"If we get him proper care, he should survive." Rusakov turned to the flight attendant. "It'd be best if I go with him to the hospital."

The attendant furrowed her brow. "I have no idea when there'll be a flight to Russia from Iceland. Certainly not tonight."

"That's the least of my concerns. Need be, I'll go back to DC and start all over again. But this man is in grave danger. My oath as a physician is more important than what's easiest for me."

The attendant was hardly in a position to argue as Vail and Rusakov deplaned with their carry-ons, the air marshal and his team keeping their buttocks firmly planted in their seats—with no reason to suspect foul play.

52

Taurus-Littrow Valley

Gavin Stroud positioned the Spider over an area where he estimated Eugene Cernan and Jack Schmitt first noticed the elevated radiation levels forty-six years ago. There was no GPS in those days, so the exact spot was unknown. Recently the lunar reconnaissance orbiter, or LRO, circled the Moon and took high resolution images to map the entire surface. Attempts were then made to match up the Apollo mission discoveries with more precise locations.

Stroud was working off those calculations, but he figured he would be spending some time trying to find the right area. Geologists did not know where the caesarium had come from, whether it was extralunar—comets or meteorites—or if it originated from within—a less likely scenario because it had not, as yet, been discovered on Earth.

As a result, it was difficult to say how much of it existed on the Moon. If it was in a narrow vein, he could stick his coring drill into one spot, get nothing, then move over a few inches and poke another hole. He was hoping that would not be the case because if he hit a streak of bad luck, he could be doing this for weeks before he located it.

As the Spider's powerful mechanism spun and cut through the layers of rock, he hit the designated depth and reversed the bit, watching it through the windshield as the basalt dust flew in all directions.

A red light blinked on his control panel and he quickly tapped the button to put the drill in neutral. All activity stopped. The dust swirled outside and he had to wait a moment for the cloud to settle.

He examined his instrumentation and concluded that the mechanism had jammed. "Just what I need." He rebooted the software and the mobile lab came to life. Stroud threw a couple of switches and the computer performed an in situ analysis of the sample he had extracted. The breakdown was not unlike the 838 pounds of lunar rock and soil the Apollo missions had brought back: oxygen, silicon, iron, magnesium, calcium, aluminum, manganese, and titanium. Not a trace of caesarium. He figured as much—what were the odds he would find it on the first hole he poked?

But he had a bigger problem. He donned his pressure suit and climbed out of the rover, moved to its front, and examined the drill with the assistance of his helmet light.

As he cursed under his breath, Carson raised him on the radio.

"How's it going there, Cowboy?"

"Not too good, man. First hole and the goddamn thing locked up on me."

"Malware?"

"Don't know. May just be fine basalt dust getting in the gearbox and jamming up the mechanism. Not sure."

"Can you fix it?"

"Gotta talk with ground, see what they can tell me. Problem is this thing has lots of small parts and gears, and if I've gotta take it apart . . . I can't see doing that with these gloves on, this bubble on my head, racing against time before we've gotta leave. Not to mention the Russians . . ."

"Take a breath and talk with Bob. We've got a whole team down there."

"How's it going on your end?"

"We've got the solar arrays and batteries pulled from Chang'e and we're almost done wiring it all up in the LRV."

"At least something's going right. Took me forever to get this rig ready for drilling, and then on the first stinkin' hole—"

"Call Bob."

"Yeah. Cowboy out."

CARSON TURNED AWAY FROM THE LRV and activated his radio. "We read you, CAPCOM. By the way, did you speak with Cowboy?"

"We did and we're working on it. We're getting ready to run a simulation here and see if we can reproduce some of the readings Cowboy sent us. SITREP?"

"We've got the LRV wired up with the solar panels and batteries in place. Hector's been cleaning off the rover, doing some maintenance. Apparently he enjoys working on old cars."

"Damn straight," DeSantos said. "This one's in decent shape, considering the fact it wasn't garaged and has been sitting out in extreme cold and extreme hot for decades. Thing was built like a tank."

"Yes it was," Maddox said. "But a lightweight tank."

"We just have to get the mounts right and we'll be ready to test it out. Uzi thinks the Chang'e batteries should have a pretty decent charge."

"Keep me posted. Meantime, we have something for you on the coupler parts for the fuel tank. The printed valve may or may not work. Lacking the female fitting here to examine and take precise measurements made it near-impossible to design something with a reasonable certainty of working."

Uzi lowered his arms from a vertical metal rod they had attached to the LRV's chassis. "I sense a 'but.'"

"But it appears they're using the same type of engine the Soyuz used although that's—"

"A guess?" DeSantos asked.

"An educated guess. NASA and the military have been working on an adjustable fitting for their new launch engine to replace the Russian engine we've been buying for the United Launch Alliance. It's so new Issachar didn't even know about it. Problem is, it hasn't been field-tested. Just computer modeling. They haven't even built a prototype."

"Given China's propensity for copying intellectual property," Carson said, "it's not surprising that it'd resemble the Soyuz."

"Our thoughts as well. So we ran with that assumption and together with the photos you sent us, we modified that adjustable valve coupler. No need to get into specifics, but let's just say the female end has the ability to expand half an inch in diameter to allow for a margin of error. If that doesn't work, we can upload something larger or smaller—you'd have to let us know which and by how much. The only problem is that—"

"It'll take two days to print and assemble the parts," Uzi said, "and if it doesn't work, there's probably not gonna be enough time for a second stab at it."

Maddox did not reply. He did not need to.

"So," Carson said, "let's hope it works."

"It's been uploaded to the printer and it's in process, but I promised the guys here I'd give you the caveat: they did their best but there was some engineering guesswork."

"I didn't think there was such a thing," Uzi said.

"How's that?" DeSantos asked.

Uzi chuckled. "Engineers don't like to guess. They deal in data and facts."

"Bull's-eye," Maddox said. "Good luck, gentlemen."

53

En Route to
Health Suðurnesja Hospital
Reykjanesbær, Reykjanes,
Iceland

When they climbed into the back of the ambulance, Vail rode in the front and Rusakov in the rear with Uglov and the medic.

As soon as Vail powered up her sat phone, she called OPSIG. Zheng Wei answered.

"Checking in, sir. Mr. Uglov has taken ill—they think it's a heart attack—and I'm in an ambulance on the way to the hospital."

"You can't talk," Zheng said.

"No." She glanced at the driver, unsure if he understood English—but either way, she could not chance it.

"We've been in contact with our asset in Iceland," Zheng said, "and alerted him to be on the road that leads from Keflavik International Airport to Health Suðurnesja Hospital. It's not a busy area and Garðskagavegur is the only road there, so once you get out of the airport, he'll be by the side of the street in a brown Peugeot sedan. Make sure you stop for him. The hospital is only three miles away so this needs to happen quickly."

It was raining and dark, so she was hoping the Peugeot would be visible far enough in advance for her to get the driver to stop. "Just cleared the airport. And . . ." She struggled to see a sign. "Looks like your route is right."

"Asset goes by Zero."

"Really?"

"Really. Standing by."

"Right." Vail disconnected the call and turned to the man beside her. "You speak English?"

He looked at her and shrugged.

In that moment, she swung her gaze back to the road and saw a brown Peugeot by the side of the road with its hazard lights on. A man dressed in a jacket and wool cap was frantically waving his hands at them.

"He needs help," Vail yelled, pointing at Zero. "Stop."

The driver looked at her—English speaker or not, "help" was a fairly universal word, as was "stop." The man seemed surprised she would want to delay their trip given they had a medical emergency in the back. He shook his head and turned back—

But Vail reached over and slapped the steering wheel with her right hand, then again gestured at Zero. "Stop!"

His brow furrowed but he did not slow.

Vail had no handgun, so body language, vocal urgency, and physical antagonism were the only weapons at her disposal.

She grabbed the wheel and pulled it gently toward the curb. Judging by the driver's wide eyes, he was shocked at her aggression. "Stop. Now!"

He pushed on the brake and guided the ambulance behind Zero's Peugeot.

Their asset was at the driver's side door immediately—and Vail hit the unlock button. Zero yanked it open and he did have a pistol, which he kept low but made sure his victim saw.

The window to the rear compartment slid aside and Rusakov poked her face through. "All secure back here. Threat neutralized." She handed a syringe to Zero and he held it up to the driver. He said something in a foreign language, which Vail assumed was Icelandic. She imagined it was something like, "This won't hurt. Once you wake up, we'll be gone."

Then again, for all she knew, it could've been, "You've had a good life. Now it's over. Resistance is futile."

Zero stuck the needle into his thigh and in fifteen seconds, the man's eyes closed. Vail helped move him into the passenger seat then climbed behind the wheel and followed Zero as he drove his Peugeot to a darker, secluded area.

She figured the hospital would be expecting their patient momentarily, so they did not have much time before the police would be notified of their missing medical transport. They had to work quickly.

Zero parked and joined them in the rear compartment. A young man was slumped in a corner and Uglov was on a gurney, strapped down. "Let's wheel him over to my car and offload him into the backseat. I don't want to be anywhere near the ambulance in case they come looking for him."

"What do we do with the medic?"

"I've dosed him pretty well with BetaSomnol," Rusakov said. "He won't be waking up for a while. And I added a dose of Midazolam, so he won't have much of a recollection of what happened. Hopefully we'll be long gone by then."

Three minutes later they were back on the road and a short time after that they were entering a light industrial area.

They parked in a loading bay and brought Uglov into a nondescript bathroom at the back of a warehouse. There was no writing, signs, or posters—no distinguishing marks of any kind, other than the robust odor of ammonia and the telltale spray of urine around the toilet. This was obviously a men's room.

They sat him up on the commode and Rusakov administered another injection to counteract the initial drug Vail had given him with the handshake on the plane. Aside from the BetaSomnol, Vail had no idea what these pharmaceuticals were. All she was concerned about was that they worked as intended.

And, in fact, Uglov was regaining consciousness. He opened his eyes and his gaze moved from Vail to Rusakov to Zero. Then his face took on a greater degree of awareness as he glanced around the room. “Who are you people?”

Zero said a few words in Icelandic to him, just to disorient the man.

“I—I don’t understand. Where am I? Why am I here?”

Rusakov spoke next, in Russian.

Vail got into the act and spoke a few words in Arabic. Rusakov replied in Arabic, several full sentences—and Vail nodded, as if she understood and agreed. She did not, so she could not . . . but Uglov did not know that.

This was intended to further confuse Uglov, and it worked. His lips parted slightly and he turned from Vail to Rusakov to Zero, and back. “What do you people want?” He turned to Rusakov and spoke Russian.

She babbled back, then said, “Let’s talk in English.”

“You want English? I want answers!”

“That’s good,” Vail said. “So do we.”

Zero walked out, the door swinging shut behind him.

“I’m Russian diplomat, I have diplomatic immunity. I don’t tell you anything.”

“Save it,” Rusakov said. “We’re not in the United States and we’re not the police.”

“Now, Mikhail,” Vail said, “we’re gonna have a chat. And you’re gonna tell us what we want to know.”

“I—I have nothing to say.”

"Sure you do." Vail leaned her left shoulder against the wall and cradled her sling with the other hand. "See, we found a fingerprint on the inside of a wireless router that was planted in someone's house near Washington, DC. That print came up as belonging to Evgeny Kirilenko. Kirilenko is . . . well, let's just say he's another person of interest for us. You know Kirilenko?"

Uglov stared straight ahead.

"That's okay," Vail said. "We already know you do."

"But something also came up when we were doing our homework. A very old Interpol case that had to be searched manually because it hadn't been digitized into the database. It traces back to thirty years ago. Do you know what I'm talking about?"

"This? This is what we talk about? Something long time ago?"

"That's where we're going to start," Rusakov said.

The door opened and Zero entered with three folding metal chairs. He set them out against the back wall of the moderate-size bathroom, a couple of feet from Uglov's knees.

Vail watched as Zero sat down. "The police found a fingerprint in that bombing. It belongs to Arkady Barndyk, a twenty-five-year-old Russian who, back in the mid-eighties, was working for the KGB."

"I do not know this name."

"Not only do you know this name, but you *are* this name." Vail paused. "Arkady was wanted for questioning in connection with an unsolved 1986 bombing in Nice. Apparently he left his fingerprint on a bomb component. Just as Kirilenko did. Nasty habit you two have. One might think it's a clever way of signing your work. Or just carelessness. Which is it?"

He worked his jaw and turned away.

"I know what you're thinking," Rusakov said. "Years ago the KGB would've cleansed that case of any connection you had to the bombing and destroyed that latent print. But that piece of evidence was never made public. And the records were not digitized back then, so there was no way for the KGB to know it existed."

"You *are* Arkady," Vail said. "And you may remember that four Americans were also killed in that bombing. The French have been looking for you. So has the FBI. They've been waiting for this moment for over thirty years."

"I tell you, I have diplomatic immunity."

Vail laughed. "No you don't. Mikhail Uglov has immunity. But Mikhail Uglov does not exist. It's a fictitious name. You're Arkady Barndyk, and we've got a copy of your birth certificate to prove it." *Not really. But he doesn't know that.*

"Arkady Barndyk does not have diplomatic immunity," Rusakov said. "Besides, Russia's got enough problems with the international community right now. They're not gonna want to fight for a fugitive who killed scores of people." Rusakov pulled out her sat phone and held it up. "One call to France's General Directorate for Internal Security or the FBI and your life is over." Rusakov looked at Vail. "Which would *you* prefer? Tough choice. Terrorism trial in France or the United States?"

Uglov studied their faces. "What do you want?"

"Answers," Vail said.

"I don't know about this bombing."

"That's not what we want to know about," Vail said. "We want to talk about Ronck."

"I am no longer CEO."

"But you *are* the second largest shareholder."

"This I will not deny."

Vail laughed. "Well, I guess we're making progress."

Rusakov shifted her seat closer so that her left knee was against his right. "So here's the deal, Arkady. You're in deep shit. You can tell us what we want to know and we leave. You'll have to find a way to Russia because your flight's left. But you'll go free and no one will be the wiser. Or you refuse to cooperate—and if we don't kill you, we'll make a call and turn you over to the French or the Americans for a death penalty trial. And with the forensics we've got on you, I'm sure either agency will have no problem convincing the jury to return a guilty verdict—especially when they flash photos of the victims and their families on a big screen."

"I talk to you, it *is* death sentence. Without jury."

"We're not cops, so there's no way anyone would know the information came from you."

"You ask me to put trust in you."

"No," Rusakov said, "we're asking you to give us the information we want and we'll make sure you're taken care of. We'll even put you back in the ambulance and call the police, tell them the ambulance has a flat tire and has been sitting on the side of the road."

"What ambulance?"

"For the apparent heart attack you had on the plane."

Uglov's mouth dropped open.

"We'll inject some ethyl alcohol into the driver's bloodstream," Rusakov said, "and sprinkle a little vodka on his shirt collar. The police will take you to the hospital and you'll have your tests and they'll pronounce you fit to travel and you'll go home."

"Fit? So no heart attack?"

Vail rolled her eyes. "No, you didn't really have a heart attack. We gave you a drug."

Uglov processed this a moment, then nodded understanding. "Very good, you people. But ambulance driver. He know about you, will tell—"

Rusakov waved him off. "They won't remember what happened when they wake up."

"For this to work," Vail said, "you have to start talking—because the more time that passes, the less believable it'll be that you got delayed by a flat tire and a drunken ambulance driver who passed out behind the wheel."

Uglov put both hands on his face and rubbed hard. He moaned and leaned back. "What you want to know?"

"Ronck has been working with the Chinese on mining equipment for the Moon," Vail said.

Uglov nodded. "What about it?"

"We know why China launched the Chang'e 5. But Russia also launched a mission to the Moon. Why?"

"They want what Chinese want. The element."

"How did Russia know about this element?"

Uglov shifted on the toilet. "We have people. In important places."

"You know we're not going to accept that. Who's 'we'? What places?"

Uglov hung his head. "This is . . . how you say? Complicated."

"Try us," Vail said. "We're intelligent people. I'm sure we'll grasp the concept."

Uglov lifted his chin. "I cut deal with President Pervak. We know each other from KGB days. He is first deputy chairman when I . . . work for them. We get to know each other. He trust me. When KGB no more, we stay friends."

"And President Pervak—what's his stake in this?"

"I give Yaroslav 2 million shares of Ronck. Trade for help. He get funding, get us engineers. We need lot of engineers. We were new business. But Yaroslav, he get us good talent."

Vail nodded. "And Ronck did . . . what, exactly?"

"We make special equipment. For deep water mining. Exxon Mobil try to cut deal with Roseneft to develop major fields. But Yaroslav thought we could keep profits in house, in mother Russia. So he help us, help Ronck make oil rig technology to drill deep holes in hard places. Miles underwater. Ronck use that technology to make special drills that work on Moon. We make it small. Mini—mini—"

"Miniature?" Rusakov asked.

"Yes. Very small. To put on robot Moon rover. We take knowledge we get from deep water mining for drilling on Moon."

"So Russia's spacecraft is fitted with this new mining equipment?"

Uglov bobbed his head. "No, China. China buy this to build its robot lander. For Chang'e 5. The mining drill is on their rover, not Russia's. That is what China sent to the Moon."

"So," Zero said, "the Chang'e 5 has specialized mining equipment, miniaturized to reduce the size and weight. And China paid Ronck for this? A contract?"

"Yes."

"We believe," Rusakov said, "that Russia has spies in the US, embedded in corporations, contractors working with NASA, to sabotage the US Moon mission."

Uglov bit his lip.

"We're running out of time," Vail said. "Don't start playing games."

He started to perspire. "Yes."

"And what is Ronck's role, beyond building this robotic rover?"

"China goes to bring back this element, caesarium, for military. Ronck build mining equipment and rover."

"Right," Vail said, "but Russia has a bigger stake."

"*Ronck* has bigger stake. My company wants to . . ." He shrugged. "We have to make sure US mission fail. If drill work, if Chinese get caesarium, Ronck make money."

"How much?"

Uglov leaned toward Vail, as if he were sharing a secret. "We get $5 billion US." He lifted his brow and nodded in pride.

"Billion?" Vail shared a look with Rusakov. "When you said 'we,' did you mean Ronck? Or—"

"Ronck. But . . ." Uglov laughed. "Remember I tell you who own 2 million shares."

"Yaroslav Pervak," Rusakov said.

Uglov smiled out of the right side of his mouth. "But if rover not work, not bring caesarium back, we only get $15 million China already pay us." He turned his head left and spat on the floor. "Cost us year of research, $250 million US. To design, build, test very expensive. We have motivation to make it work."

"So Ronck is highly incentivized to prevent the US from stopping the Chinese," Vail said. "If China brings back the element, Ronck gets paid $5 billion—a financial windfall." *There's more to it than that. But what?*

"Why did it cost so much to build and test this equipment? Just because it was being used on the Moon?"

"We had to make parts small. Mini. Everything small. Small weigh less. China had drill, but big—very big—too heavy to get to Moon with their rockets. They think to launch two separate spaceships, put together in space and fly to Moon. But US would know. No good. We had solution."

"So Ronck's technology helped them a great deal," Vail said.

"And if it work way we say, Ronck get into S&P 500."

"The stock index?" Zero asked.

"Yes. Index committee say we need market cap of $4 billion US. We get win with China, they pay and put us . . . how do they say? Over the top. China use our drill technology for Moon and Mars. To build colonies. This news will drive rally in stock."

"So that's your motivation?" Vail asked. "Money?"

"Money, yes, yes. But more. Yaroslav wants Russia to get this caesarium too. He think it very important to Russia. Be a superpower again."

"But he wouldn't want to risk the $5 billion payoff from China," Vail said. "Because his 2 million shares would skyrocket when the deal was announced."

"This, yes, is true," Uglov said.

"So the Russian rocket that launched a few days ago, that also has Ronck's mining equipment on board?"

"No, deal with China say only they have the mini technology for one year. So Russia mission has small drill. Not as small as drill we make for China. But," he said with a toothy smile, "small enough. We have big rocket. Our cosmonauts stay on Moon till China gets caesarium and go home. They pay us $5 billion. *Then* cosmonauts come home. With caesarium." He smiled again.

"How long are the cosmonauts prepared to stay up there?" Rusakov said.

"Third part of mission. To stay there for a week, two, three. Can stay a month."

"A month?" Vail asked. "On the Moon?"

"Russia want to colonize Moon but we never land a man there. This prove we can do it. Many Russians upset when American beat us to Moon in 1960s. We give up. Now America busy with space station. Take lots of time to build fancy new spaceship. Spend lots of money. For what? Just fly tests. Test this, test that. Two times, three times, they test. By time you finish tests, technology old. Russia," he said with a proud nod of his head, "we go to Moon and build colony. Make base, go to Mars and do the same."

"Do you have people in the US spying for you?" Rusakov asked.

"For me? No. I no longer CEO. They do their plans, they ask me things to help fix problems. But rest up to them. They decide."

Vail was not so sure he was being truthful, but at this point, he had little incentive to deceive them.

"Russia plan mission to Moon for summer, same time China say they will send Chang'e. But Russian spy, person who work for Ronck, saw plans that US was making lasers for Moon orbit. We tell Chinese Space Agency."

"Because if the US turned on these lasers," Rusakov said, "the Chang'e 5 wouldn't be able to land, and the Ronck rover wouldn't be deployed. So Ronck engaged in industrial espionage and used its spy at the defense contractor to write malware for the spacecraft operating system to prevent the Americans from stopping the Chinese mission to mine the caesarium."

Uglov nodded. "China say they have problem with drill bit. Want fix in forty-eight hours. Ha ha, I laugh." He shrugged. "But we send team. Team says Chinese rover already loaded into rocket fairing! And rocket on launch pad. They were launching much sooner than they tell us."

"Because of the lasers?"

"I think this is true."

"So Russia also moved up its timetable."

"I tell Roscosmos—the Russian Space Agency—you rush, you make shortcuts, you not have good safety precautions." He shook his head. "They tell me I worry for nothing. They can do it because they have lots of practice with the space station launches. Give Russia much experience, training, lots of cosmonauts."

"So Ronck had a lot at stake to make sure the Chinese mission succeeded," Vail said.

"Money. *Lots* of money. Money king in Russia. And China, they also have much to gain."

"But if China's spacecraft doesn't bring back caesarium," Vail said, "Ronck misses its $5 billion payday."

Uglov pursed his lips and nodded admiration. "I see it not so complicated for you."

"And China?" Rusakov said. "It wants the caesarium for what?"

Uglov shrugged. "You know China. Their goal is world domination. Global . . . what is word? Hedge?"

Not like Russia doesn't have similar ambitions.

Rusakov frowned. "Hegemony."

"Yes," Uglov said with a smile. "Not so complicated for you at all."

54

Taurus-Littrow Valley

"We show the Russian craft in lunar orbit," Maddox said. "I've got General Eisenbach and Captain Kirmani here. Stand by."

DeSantos and Uzi, who were at the Chang'e 5 looking over the fuel tank, stopped what they were doing.

"Gentlemen," Eisenbach said, "Give me a SITREP."

Stroud recapped the issues they were dealing with and gave him an update on each. "We're gonna try to remove the Chang'e lander's ascent stage fuel to use in our engine, which I'm sure you've been briefed on."

"We have," Kirmani said. "I believe CAPCOM has an answer for you regarding that, but first we have Russia to discuss. General."

"We've been in meetings for several hours. I don't have to tell you that this Russian landing creates a number of problems—both here on Earth for us and on the Moon for you."

"Do we know what their intentions are?" Carson asked.

"Our operatives have apprehended a Russian diplomat who's been intimately involved in the effort to embed one or more spies at key contractors." He went through the details Vail, Rusakov, and Zero had obtained from Uglov and Lansford.

"We didn't expect much from the Russians going the diplomatic route, especially since we couldn't let them know that we're aware of what their own diplomat's been involved in. And given President Pervak's huge financial stake in Ronck, we could only ask about the launch and request an explanation of their intentions."

"Needless to say," Kirmani said, "they were less than forthcoming—'mapping the surface, scientific research,' you get the idea. Not surprising, but it didn't help us a lick."

"So we've been left to draw our own conclusions," Eisenbach said. "Director Tasset put a team of analysts on it and their assessment jibes with what Vail, Rusakov, and Zero were told: Russia is there to secure caesarium. It's not definitive confirmation, but given the extreme circumstances we have a high degree of confidence in that assessment."

DeSantos and Uzi shared a look of unease.

"Do we have a sense of how aggressive they'll be?" DeSantos asked.

"It's our belief that the Russians are there to secure the element—for themselves *and* for China if the Chang'e mission fails. They will not leave the surface without achieving mission success. In short, they will bring it home or die trying."

"And that puts you in a disadvantaged position," Kirmani said. "Which is a failure of our intelligence since we had no indications the Russians were on the cusp of launching a Moon shot."

"But apologies will be of no benefit to you," Eisenbach said, "so we're suggesting you prepare for an inevitable confrontation. That said, the president has directed us to be extremely conservative and nonconfrontational. You are not to trigger an international incident because it's also possible the Russians will be all bluster and no action. They don't know that we didn't know. So while we did not equip you properly relative to weapons, we have no indications they're aware of that fact."

"So we'll have to bluff," DeSantos said.

"Word is that you're a skilled poker player," Eisenbach said.

"I don't usually play for such high stakes."

"Look," Kirmani said, "these are the types of situations you four have trained for. You know the deal. Complete your mission and, God willing, return home safely."

"If you fail and the Russians secure caesarium," Eisenbach said, "we'll deal with it. The Pentagon is drawing up contingency plans for preventing their craft from safely returning to Earth. That will obviously trigger a conflict here, if not outright war. How far the Russians are willing to take it, no one knows. Not to mention China. Because of Ronck's business deal, Russia will definitely tell them we were behind the loss of their spacecraft and rover. We're in uncharted waters. And we're counting on you to get the job done."

"FUBAR," DeSantos said. Military lingo for *fucked up beyond all recognition.*

"Yes sir," Stroud said, taking the high road. "We won't let you down."

"We're turning comms back over to the CAPCOM."

"Is the LRV up and running?" Maddox asked.

"It is," Uzi said. "We brought Digger back to the Raptor to gather whatever weapons we have. Digger?"

"We've got our survival pistols," Carson said. "We can't fire them on the Moon because we can't remove our gloves and the trigger guards are in the way."

"Can a gun even be fired on the Moon?" DeSantos asked.

"It can," Maddox said. "With some caveats. Ammo contains its own oxidizer to trigger the explosion of gunpowder, so the lack of oxygen is not a problem. The bullet will have the same initial velocity on the Moon as it does on the Earth. Basically, it exits the barrel at the same speed. But there's no air resistance and little friction, so it can maintain its speed longer than on Earth.

And it'll travel at least six times farther on the Moon. And that's without even factoring in the one-sixth gravity. It won't lose its trajectory as quickly because there's less pull toward the ground."

"But there'll be a problem with the guy firing it," Uzi said.

"Correct. Remember, just as when you push against something in your pressure suits, for every action there's an equal and opposite reaction. After you shoot, the recoil will be six times greater on the Moon. So one pound of push would be six pounds back against you. At the very least, it'll knock the shooter on his ass. Not life threatening—well, unless he fires while standing in front of a huge boulder and cracks his helmet open—but it'd be violent enough to make the shooter think twice."

"We should expect the Russians to be armed," Stroud said.

"There's precedent for that," Maddox said. "The Soviets launched a Salyut space station with a 30-millimeter Nudelman cannon. And the standard survival pack for Russian cosmonauts has always included a gun, an all-in-one weapon with three barrels and a folding stock that doubled as a shovel and a swing-out machete. Idea was to help them survive in case they had to make an emergency landing in a treacherous region back on Earth. But we can assume they've got something more conventional for use on the lunar surface."

"Other than the Glocks," Carson said, "we've got our tactical knives, which might just be our best weapon because they can be used with these ridiculous gloves on. You pierce a guy's pressure suit, he's a dead duck. Obviously it means you've gotta get up close and personal. I wouldn't try throwing it on the Moon without substantial practice."

"So we made the mistake of bringing knives to a gunfight," Uzi quipped.

"You have some answers on the fuel situation?" Stroud asked.

"You'll need an empty vessel of some sort," Maddox said, "to offload the fuel into so you can get it back to the Raptor. One idea being discussed is using the old fuel tank from the Apollo 17 descent stage. You'd obviously have to disconnect it somehow, without ruining the valve, but the fitting we uploaded to the printer will have one of those adjustable couplers on each end. I've got Issachar Makonnen here because there are a few things he needs to review with you."

"Good evening, gentlemen. As Bob said, we've been looking into your empty vessel needs. We researched the size of the Apollo descent stage propellant tanks. These tanks carried basically the same hypergolic fuels we think you'll get off the Chang'e. The descent stage carried about 7,500 pounds of MMH fuel, split between two tanks, each about 500 gallons of volume. So liberating one MMH tank from the lunar module would give you a nice vessel to transport fuel in. We also found a reference indicating that Apollo 17 had about 455 pounds, or 60 gallons, of fuel left when it landed."

"Would it still be there after fifty years?" Uzi asked.

DeSantos laughed. "I remember what my lawn mower's fuel tank looked like after not using it for a couple years. My guess would be no, but that was on Earth. And, well, I know shit about rocket fuel, subzero temperatures, and one-sixth gravity."

"I only point it out in case you need it," Issachar said. "It might be there. Might not."

"Got it," Carson said.

"We did some computations and the Apollo ascent stage carried 1,962 pounds, or 267 gallons, of fuel—enough to lift a very lightweight spacecraft, a couple of astronauts, and some rocks. You've got four people and a bigger craft, so you're going to need at least that amount of fuel—even the full 500 pounds—unless you slim down and drop lots of weight."

"Is there enough on the Chang'e?" Uzi asked.

"The Agency found a Chang'e 5 listed on China's slate of future launches," Eisenbach said. "Director Tasset warned it's old intel so it's no longer accurate. Chang'e was originally slated to return just 30 grams of lunar sample, so the ascent stage wasn't going to be carrying much fuel. But once they changed their mission objectives to bring back caesarium, they would've reengineered things and significantly increased their payload capabilities."

"Added to what you've got left in the Raptor tank," Issachar said, "you might have enough fuel. I just wanted you to get a sense of how much we're talking about. And that things are going to be very tight. Start planning to dump equipment from the Raptor."

"Thanks," Stroud said. "We'd be in a bad way without your help."

"Standing by. Good luck, gentlemen."

"Digger," Stroud said, "I'm putting you in charge of the empty vessel issue."

"Suiting up to get back outside. I'll take a look, see what's involved. CAPCOM, you have any info on that?"

"One of the engineers drew up a diagram. Sending it through to your suit now. Look it over on the helmet's heads-up display and let me know if you have any questions."

"Uh, we may want to postpone that," DeSantos said.

"Shit," Uzi said.

"What's going on?" Maddox asked.

"We have visual of the Russian spacecraft. It's firing its descent stage engine. Pretty cool sight—if they weren't coming to kill us."

"Fall back," Stroud said. "Give them room. Let's assess their actions before we jump to any conclusions. We've gotta complete those parts of the mission we're able to. Once we interact with the Russians, we'll have a better sense of what we're dealing with."

"Meet me back at the Raptor so you can pick up your side arms," Carson said.

DeSantos maneuvered the LRV in a tight arc and drove back toward the Raptor.

"Copy that," Uzi said. "On our way."

55

KEFLAVIK, ICELAND

Vail and Rusakov bid good-bye to Zero, who helped them hold up their part of the bargain by bringing Uglov back to the ambulance, injecting the driver with ethyl alcohol, and calling the police to report the suspicious ambulance.

They had asked Uglov what he knew about Lukas DeSantos, and he provided nonspecific information on the man and his career. He gave no indication that he had knowledge of the kidnapping. They informed Uglov the general was missing, that he was likely snatched by Russian security forces, or men hired by them, and that they would check back with him in twenty-four hours to see what he could find out.

Uglov had become a CIA asset. In the near future, they would again contact him, surreptitiously, for more assistance. This time it would involve forward-looking intel on President Yuroslav Pervak's intentions *before* he carried them out.

If Uglov refused to cooperate, two anonymous packages would be delivered to the FBI and France's General Directorate for Internal Security, reporting Uglov's true identity and providing the forensic evidence relative to the bombing. How the law enforcement agencies would proceed was unimportant—the threat that hung over Uglov's head was what mattered. It would be his motivation for cooperating. In the spy business, this was a time-honored method of recruitment.

Vail and Rusakov drove to the US naval base in Keflavik, where Boeing P-8 Poseidon antisubmarine jets were stationed. The base, shuttered in 2006, was resurrected ten years later when the Icelandic government, whose military consisted of only its coast guard, grew concerned by increasing Russian flyovers and circumnavigation of the isolated island as well as sudden patrols of the North Atlantic by Russian submarines.

Vail and Rusakov did not board a Poseidon because its maximum flight distance was not great enough to reach Washington. Instead, McNamara had a nondescript 737 leave Andrews Air Force Base at the same time Vail and Rusakov boarded the flight to Russia. Since Boeing had modified its standard 737 to create the militarized—and renamed—P-8 Poseidon aircraft, no one would question a gray 737 bearing the same external appearance as its sister P-8 flying into the naval base at night.

Vail and Rusakov touched down at Andrews six hours later—having caught up on their sleep—in time to start their workday after a quick shower and change of clothes.

They entered a secure room in the black site at the industrial park to be debriefed by McNamara, director of Central Intelligence Laurence Bolton, and CIA director Earl Tasset. As the meeting got underway, Douglas Knox arrived. Eisenbach was conferenced in on an encrypted video chat.

"We now have a pretty clear idea of what's going on and why," Tasset said. "China doesn't appear to be a malevolent player here—their only goal appears to be securing the caesarium before we have the ability to cut off access to the Moon. Still, their goals are incongruous with ours—and, one might argue, an obstacle to long-term peace on this planet. So the portion of our mission dealing with China remains unchanged."

"Russia, however, is another matter," Knox said. "Ronck is clearly the perpetrator of corporate espionage, but the close ties between President Pervak and Ronck are undeniable. Not to mention Russia is also trying to obtain the caesarium—and is likely going to use force, if necessary, to bring it back home should we intervene."

"And I think it's safe to assume," Tasset added, "that they'll realize our men have disabled the Chang'e. So the only way for Ronck—and Pervak—to get their $5 billion payday is for Russia to bring back caesarium and deliver it to China."

"And then there's the matter of General DeSantos's kidnapping," Bolten said.

"We hope to have some information from our source by this evening," Tasset said. "Meantime, we have to follow leads and conduct a standard missing persons case investigation."

"There's nothing standard about this case," Vail said.

"Right now this is our only avenue," McNamara said. "Standard or not, you are the best investigator we have. You and Alexandra will get on this trail and stay on it like fucking bloodhounds until you end up at the general's front door—wherever that may be." The artery in his temple began pulsing. "Is that clear?"

"Yes sir," Rusakov said.

McNamara looked at them. "Then what the hell are you waiting for? Get to it."

56

Taurus-Littrow Valley

Cowboy," Carson said. "We've got company."

Stroud, DeSantos, and Uzi ambled over to Carson, who was standing near a strut of the Raptor.

On the ridge a few hundred feet away was the tip of the front of a rover and two men in pressure suits: cosmonauts. They were standing there, unmoving, facing the Raptor.

"What the hell are they doing?" Carson asked.

"Assessing their enemy," Stroud said. "Rule number one: see what you're up against. Are their hearts in this? How well trained are they? How many of them are there? Are they armed?"

"Or they're getting their lay of the land," Uzi said. "Like where they think they need to drill for caesarium." He pressed a button and a heads-up display appeared on the inside of his visor showing a zoomed image. "Could be taking readings. Who knows what kind of equipment they've got."

Stroud pressed the button on the side of his helmet to activate his own display. "They're just . . . standing there. Could be another one or two behind the ridge. Hard to tell."

"They could be assessing how aggressive we're willing to get," Carson said.

Uzi twisted toward Carson. In the suit he needed to turn his entire torso. "Good point. So how aggressive *should* we get?"

DeSantos moved around behind Uzi, trying to get a different angle, stopping a dozen feet to his right.

"Our mission calls for us to prevent China and Russia from securing caesarium," Stroud said, "without triggering an international incident. Show resolve so they don't think they can push us around—but don't cross the line."

"Puff out our chests but don't throw the first punch," DeSantos said.

"This is getting awkward," Carson said, "them looking at us and us looking at them. Makes us look weak."

"Let's start walking toward them," Uzi said as he zoomed his helmet display to maximum. "Subtle show of force."

"Agreed." Stroud started forward, followed by DeSantos. "Just heading that way will be interpreted as a threatening move. We should know in a few steps how they're going to respond."

Seconds later, the two cosmonauts turned and disappeared from the ridge.

Stroud stopped. "Interesting."

DeSantos kept walking another ten feet. "Still don't know what the hell that was about."

"Doesn't matter," Uzi said. "We sent the right message. And I'm sure we'll be seeing more of them."

TWO HOURS LATER, as DeSantos, Uzi, and Carson unhooked Apollo 17's spent fuel tank, two cosmonauts drove up in a rover that looked like a cross between the old LRV and the Spider: not as large and not enclosed, but it featured six wheels and three axles, and a flat platform on the back that sported a telescoping arm. It was difficult to see more than that because of the angle of their approach.

They stopped a hundred yards short of the Raptor and sat there.

"Uh, guys?" DeSantos said. "Our friends are back."

The others turned in unison.

"Is it me, or is this a little creepy?" Carson asked.

"We should see what they're up to."

Uzi faced Stroud. "You mean just walk over and ask them?"

"Aside from the fact that we can't exactly speak to them with these suits on—and we've got no idea if they speak English—yeah. Something like that."

DeSantos grunted. "What's the point? We know why they're here."

"Détente," Uzi said. "If we had some vodka, we could offer to break the ice, bond."

"Dream on, Boychick."

The rover started moving again, making a tight circle and heading back the way they came.

"So much for that," Uzi said.

"Let's follow them," DeSantos said, walking toward the LRV.

"I've gotta get back to taking core samples," Stroud said, "see if I can locate caesarium."

"Fine," DeSantos said, not bothering to turn around. "Digger, Uzi, you're with me."

DESANTOS AND UZI TOOK THE TWO FRONT SEATS and Carson climbed onto the rear payload interface and stowage area, which they had cleared of equipment while Uzi was wiring in the solar arrays.

"Hang on," DeSantos said as he drove forward. "Are the panels pointed at the sun?"

"We're good," Uzi said. "Batteries are charged too. System's working fine."

"At least something is going as planned."

They arrived at the Russian spacecraft thirty-five minutes later. It was slightly larger than the Raptor but roughly similar in appearance: utilitarian piping, fuel tanks, struts, and a long ladder to a rectangular main cabin that was mounted near the top. Two cosmonauts were standing outside at the rear of the rover doing something with the telescoping arm.

"I think that's their drill," Uzi said. "For mining."

"Your eyes go to the science and technology," DeSantos said. "And mine go to weapons systems. "He's packing a side arm."

"Sure is," Carson said.

One of the men noticed them and stopped, elbowed his colleague. They turned and looked at the Americans.

"Here we go again with the awkward stares," Carson said. He got off the back of the rover and started toward the cosmonauts. They put down their tools and took steps in their direction.

DeSantos activated his heads-up display. "I think we're about to make first contact."

"Copy that," Carson said.

The two Russians and three Americans stopped a few feet from one another.

DeSantos got a better look at the large pistol on the Russian's hip. DeSantos had one too—except his was a bluff rather than a functional weapon. By design it was buried in his pocket to hide the trigger guard, which was a dead giveaway to the fact that there would be no way for him to fire it.

He was playing a high stakes poker game—with a losing hand.

"Keep away from your Glocks," DeSantos said. "If we don't draw, maybe they won't. Because once we do, game's over."

One of the cosmonauts stepped in front of his partner and motioned for the Americans to lift their sun visors. It was unnerving looking at a reflective surface. You could not see your opponent's face, and facial expressions were an indication of what the individual was thinking.

DeSantos understood. He lifted his and gestured for the Russian to do likewise.

The cosmonaut did as requested. He stepped to his right, moving awkwardly as he made eye contact with each of them. He tapped DeSantos on the chest, then gestured with his head for him to follow. DeSantos—and Uzi—started toward the ladder.

The man held up a hand: STOP. Only DeSantos would be permitted inside for their chat.

"I'll be back." DeSantos shuffled toward the Russian lander.

"Where do you think you're going?" Carson asked.

"It's the only way we can talk," DeSantos said. "We go inside their ship, pressurize, and remove our helmets."

"Just you?" Uzi said. "I don't like it."

"It's a small craft, Boychick. Plus, I don't think they're gonna do anything to me. Be a shitty way to introduce yourself."

"If you're not out in five minutes, we're gonna assume there's a problem."

"Give me ten," DeSantos said as the Russian ascended the ladder. DeSantos waited a moment then grabbed hold of the metal rung and pulled himself up, an infinitely easier task than it would've been in Earth's gravity.

The man was waiting for him in the cabin. DeSantos stepped in and pulled the hatch shut. The cosmonaut reached over and yanked down on a handle then spun a medium-size wheel. He pressed a black button on the wall to his left and a dial indicated increasing pressure in millimeters of Mercury.

As the gauge hit 350, the Russian removed his helmet. DeSantos did the same.

UZI AND CARSON WAITED OUTSIDE. Another cosmonaut appeared from behind a hill and joined his comrade. The five men stood there staring at each other, hands on their hips.

"What do you think, Digger? This gonna be trouble?"

"At the moment, not sure. But in ten minutes, I'll be able to give you a better answer."

"Smart ass."

"I HOPE YOU SPEAK ENGLISH," DeSantos said. "Or this is gonna be a short conversation." DeSantos did speak some Russian, but felt more comfortable—and in more control—with English.

"I speak English. Good enough. Welcome to the Resurs. Bigger than yours. Nice ship, eh?"

"Yes, very nice ship." DeSantos gave a glance around—which he had wanted to do anyway. Now he had an excuse to do so without having to hide it. "Since you speak English, you can tell me why you're here."

"I am here for same reason you are here."

DeSantos cocked his head. "I don't think so, comrade."

"Do not matter. I am glad you came to me."

"Is that right?"

"Yes, Mr. DeSantos. I have to come look for you. This much more easier."

DeSantos could not hide the surprise that likely registered on his face. His identity was a fairly well kept secret—not to mention his presence on this mission, which was a tightly guarded fact. "Since you know who I am, who are you?"

"Oleg. And that is Andrei, Boris, and Viktor outside watching over your friends."

"Oleg, Andrei, Boris, and Viktor. Those your real names?"

"We no have things to hide. I am just cosmonaut who study geology. Rocks."

"I know what geology is, thanks." And he knew one other thing: Oleg was no ordinary space explorer.

"Now, Mr. DeSantos. Let us stop dancing, yes?"

DeSantos glanced around the lander's interior, taking in everything, soaking in the details. "I'm not a very good dancer. At least that's what my ex-girlfriend used to say." They may know who he was, but they likely did not know his personal details—and he was not about to disclose anything.

"You no need to play game. We know."

DeSantos took in the layout, the instrumentation, the number of hammocks they used for sleeping. "Know what?"

"There is no point to deny this. We are here to take our rocks and leave."

"No offense," DeSantos said, making eye contact, "but we can't let you do that."

"America not own Moon. It belong to everyone."

"I can't argue with you, Oleg. I agree. But this isn't about ownership. It's about being the police officer at the drug cartel meeting."

Oleg's brow scrunched. "I do not understand this."

"Russian aggression is well-documented. I'll sum it up in one word: Crimea. Ukraine. Georgia. Okay, well, that was three words. But you get the idea. Your close military and economic relationship with Iran is also well-documented. So we can't let you have this—this thing you want to take back."

"Caesarium. Why so hard for you to say?" He smiled, no doubt enjoying the reaction on DeSantos's face. "I tell you before. We know."

"We can't let you have it. It's as simple as that."

"Not yours to give or not give."

"No, but we're the police."

Oleg clenched his jaw. "You cry about Russian aggression. What about American aggression? You want to extend your reach over the world. The caesarium will give you that ability. You here to take for yourself."

"That's not our mission."

"I do not believe you."

"If we wanted to take it for ourselves, we would've come and taken it a long time ago. We knew about it back in the 1970s."

"Maybe you already have it, then."

"If that were true, something tells me the FSB and SVR would know," DeSantos said. "We're only here to make sure no one gets it—not you, not the Chinese, the North Koreans, or the Iranians. And not us."

Oleg stared at DeSantos a long moment. "You have your orders. I have mine."

"I figured that'd be your position." DeSantos shifted the helmet to his hands and prepared to lift it back over his head. "I guess we're done here."

"Not so fast, my friend."

DeSantos tensed—prepared for anything. Was he going to pull out a knife and puncture his suit—a move that would, essentially, make him a prisoner there—or worse, kill him?

Oleg smiled out of the left side of his mouth. "There is something we have. It may interest you. And it may . . . how do I say . . . impact your decision."

"It's not *my* decision," DeSantos said. "I have my orders, just like you."

"Yes, well. Orders can be . . . changed, hmm?"

"I can't be bought. Money is not going to—"

"Oh, no money, Mr. DeSantos." Oleg laughed. "More valuable than money." He turned to his instrument panel and called up a looping video image of a man sitting on a squalid floor, large soldiers with submachine guns standing over him, at each side. His face was bruised, one eye swollen shut. "You know this person, yes?"

DeSantos knew that person all right. His father. He looked at Oleg.

"He has not been harmed. And he will not be harmed. If." He held up an index finger. "If you change mind. About the caesarium."

DeSantos glared at him. "Not been harmed? Look at—"

"We do not want fight," Oleg said, as if his offer was completely reasonable. "But if need to, we fight. And we win. Much easier if you . . . you know, what is saying? Turn the other way."

DeSantos ground his molars. "I *can't* look the other way. I don't know how else to say this, Oleg. I have my orders." Truth be told, he wanted to reach back and slug the man. Pound his face into the sharp metal protrusions that lined the interior. And then toss him outside without his helmet.

"We will see, no?" Oleg smiled. "You know where I be when you change mind. But do not take too long. We leave when we have what we come for."

DeSantos shoved the helmet over his head and pressurized the suit. Once the cabin was depressurized, he opened the hatch and climbed out.

Uzi and Carson were where DeSantos had left them, standing ten paces away from their counterparts, who now numbered three: Andrei, Boris, and Viktor.

"How'd it go?" Carson asked.

"About what I expected."

"Waste of time?"

"We now have an understanding."

DeSantos hopped over to them, stopping for a second to steady himself in the low gravity. He kept his gaze on the three Russians as he passed.

"An understanding?" Uzi asked.

"Their lander is called the Resurs. His name's Oleg and these comrades here," he said as he shuffled by them, "are Andrei, Boris, and Viktor." And he wanted to put a bullet in each of their brains.

"Santa. You hear me? Is that it? Are there four of them?"

"Sorry." DeSantos turned away from the cosmonauts. "Best I could see, four hammocks."

"Four of them, four of us."

"Good to see the lower gravity hasn't eroded your math skills, Boychick."

Uzi looked at him. His friend's visor was still up, so he could see DeSantos's eyes. "You okay?"

If there was someone who knew him well, it was Uzi. DeSantos did his best to shrug it off as he climbed back into the rover. "Oleg told me he's under orders to bring the caesarium back. And I told him we can't allow that."

DeSantos wanted to tell them that the Russians had kidnapped his father. He knew he should. But something was telling him not to. Why? Because they would cut him out of vital parts of the mission to eliminate any conflict of interest. Was there a conflict? If he was objective, he would acknowledge there had to be. He prided himself on being able to compartmentalize things in such situations, but could he simply ignore the fact that they had kidnapped his dad and go about things as if it did not matter?

"So," Carson said, "what do we do about it?"

DeSantos looked over at the Resurs.

"Not sure there's anything we can do to stop them from finding it and bringing it back to their ship. But one thing I am sure of is that if they do find it, we're not going to let the Resurs leave the surface."

STROUD MANUALLY WITHDREW THE HOLLOW CORE BIT from the freshly drilled hole and transferred the haul into the rover's front bin. He pressed a button and waited for the analysis to be completed.

He glanced around at the barren landscape surrounding him. The Raptor was not visible, as he had ventured around the eastern edge of the South Massif to Bear Mountain. The Taurus-Littrow valley was located on the edge of Mare Serenitatis, along a ring of mountains formed billions of years ago when a large object impacted the Moon, pushing extensive areas of rock upward. Though the entire valley showed promise for caesarium, they had assembled a list of places in descending order that he should poke full of holes. And the location where Stroud now stood was one the geologists had prioritized. Somewhere nearby was where Cernan and Schmitt found the caesarium traces that touched off years of planning—and hand-wringing.

Thus far, all he had found was feldspar-rich breccia in the massifs surrounding the valley and regolith and basalt on the valley floor. Of course, none of this mattered if they got into an escalated conflict with the Russians.

Stroud turned back to the Spider and saw a green light on the spectrometer. His pulse began thumping in his ears.

Holy shit. I found it?

Stroud looked around to make sure no one was there, then pulled on the Velcro closure of the front pocket of his pressure suit. He extracted a thin lead-shielded receptacle and popped it open, then scooped the rock and soil that had tested positive into its small cavity. He set it down, removed his handheld Geiger counter, and took a reading as confirmation. Satisfied that it was, indeed, caesarium, he closed the container and slipped it back into his pouch.

He went around to the back of the Spider and entered the suit lock, then deleted the location and geologic data from the computer.

"Digger," he said, "give me a SITREP. How'd it go with the Russians?"

"As expected. They say they're not leaving without caesarium. Speaking of which, how about you? Find anything?"

"Just basalt and breccia. But I'm not giving up."

"We're heading back, see if we can finish removing that fuel tank. Then we have to swap out our O2 tanks."

"Roger that. Meet you there in half an hour."

57

WASHINGTON, DC

Where do you want to start?" Rusakov asked.

"Back at the general's house." Vail walked outside, where the old black Suburban was parked. "Gotta make sure we didn't miss anything. We also need to look at his life, phone records, emails, texts, letters, men and women he served with and under, foreign governments he had conflicts with, terror suspects he may've had a public discourse with, employees he may've had a beef with, and—"

"Karen," Rusakov said as she pulled open her door. "This is all great for a couple detectives investigating a crime. But we don't, and can't, have that kind of help. It's just you and me. And we don't have time to do all that stuff."

"No we don't. And we don't even have Hector as a resource for insight into his dad's life. So we need to be smart about it. If we can find the relevant tip of the iceberg, we can dive deeper and find the answers. And right now, there are three priorities—his home, his office, and Jessie Kerwin."

"We can't talk with Kerwin until we find her."

"I've got someone working on that. So we'll start at Lukas's home, spend a couple of hours, and then drop by his office."

Rusakov groaned.

"There are no magical shortcuts, Alex. Crimes don't solve themselves. It's the result of grind-it-out police work. That, my dear covert operative, is why cops earn their paychecks."

THEY ARRIVED AT LUKAS DESANTOS'S HOME, which was still under military guard.

They spent the next two hours going through his office desk, file cabinets, and safe room. They looked for hidden compartments, threatening notes, and seemingly harmless photos of the general with troops and foreigners that could be evaluated by CIA analysts. They scanned documents, pictures, notes, written communications—and uploaded it all to OPSIG for analysis.

Everyone had to be looked at—a seemingly insurmountable task, as Rusakov had pointed out, except for one thing: there appeared to be Russian involvement in his capture.

"Even if we had an army of agents, we wouldn't be able to look at all possibilities," Vail said. "So we have to cut away the distractions and focus on the most likely things, things that are related to what the Russians and Chinese are after—and anyone who might benefit from that."

"Like Ronck. Its shareholders. President Pervak, or even our favorite mass murderer-turned-diplomat, Mikhail Uglov."

"Even Uglov. I asked Hot Rod to keep looking into his background and to check out the info he gave us. Seemed like we got the truth from him, but who knows. He could've given us 60 percent of the truth and left out key facts—like maybe *he* was the one who engineered the general's kidnapping."

"As the second largest shareholder, Uglov's got a lot of money riding on the rover's success in bringing back the caesarium."

"Bit of an understatement." Vail placed her right hand on her hip. "We should move on to his office. Anything else you need to look at here?"

Rusakov indicated she was done as well, so they left the premises and headed to the corporate headquarters of DDI.

DESANTOS DEFENSE INDUSTRIES was the third largest defense contractor in the United States, fifth in the world—but no one would know it from the appearance of its facility. Utilitarian and generic in its construction, there was nothing grand in its design or materials. And that was how the general wanted it. He preferred business to come to him and clients to hire him because he and his employees did a fine job, not because their marketing department produced glossy brochures and flashy websites or networked relentlessly in Washington.

Vail and Rusakov entered the building and checked in with the security guard at the front. After he scanned their faux IDs, he gave them each a barcode-enabled pass that hung from a lanyard they slung around their necks.

They rode the elevator up to the fifth floor and were met by a man who brought them to the office of Cynthia Meyers, the chief operating officer. Meyers was a well-kept fifty-year-old professional, dressed in a black dress and heels.

"Thanks for meeting with us on such short notice," Vail said.

"And thank you for taking this seriously. I'm really concerned about him."

"Any idea who may be involved in this?" Rusakov asked.

Meyers sat down behind her large desk, which was orderly yet stacked with work: files to the left and a humongous HP monitor in the center. She pressed a button and the screen folded down into the desktop, out of the way.

"I've been going through old cases," she said, resting her left hand atop the pile of folders. "And there are a handful of potentials, though nothing that stands out as an obvious lead. I was about to call Douglas but since you're here . . ."

Douglas? First name basis with the FBI director?

"Probably best for us to determine what's a lead and what isn't. There are things we know that you don't."

"Of course," Meyers said. "I'm used to being in charge. I didn't mean any disrespect. Douglas said he was sending his best. He obviously thinks a lot of you two."

Fishing for brownie points or did Knox really say that?

Vail's phone rang. She excused herself and walked into the hallway. "Vail."

"It's Hot Rod. Got something here I thought you should know about, in case it's important."

"Whatever you've got, I'll take it."

"One of the photos you sent us from the general's house. By the way, you happen to know? Last name is same as—"

"It's Hector's dad, yeah."

"Well, shit. Does Hector know?"

"No, and he's not supposed to. Direct orders."

"Not like I have a way of contacting him. He's on the friggin' Moon."

"What'd you find? That photo?"

"Sorry—we identified all the people in the pictures you sent over, except one of them. But there's a guy who served under the general. Bill Tait. After being discharged from the military, he started an executive protection, security, and investigation firm—Tait Protection Services. Looks like DDI used Tait on several jobs each year."

"So what's the problem?"

"Don't know there *is* a problem. Just looking for connections."

"I'll run with it, see where it takes us." Vail returned to the office and apologized for the interruption. "What do you know about Bill Tait?"

"Bill served under Lukas," Meyers said, "looked up to him. They developed a deep relationship over the years. When Bill got out and started up his company, the general was one of his early investors. Lent him half a million dollars seed money."

"Did Tait pay him back?"

"He made his last payment six months ago."

"Any bad blood between them?" Rusakov asked.

"None I'm aware of. They're good friends, like a mentor relationship. Almost . . ."

"Almost what?"

"Well," Meyers said, "kind of like father-son."

Wonder how Hector feels about that.

"I called him soon as I realized Lukas was missing. He's out of the country but he said he'd put some people on it and let me know if they dug anything up."

"Does your company have any ties with Russia? Or Russians?"

Meyers cocked her head left. "Why?"

Vail smiled.

"Right," Meyers said. "Just answer the questions. I get it." She lifted her brow. "We've done business with a number of Russian companies. And anytime we've shipped weapons overseas to Moscow, we've always gotten the appropriate foreign military sales State Department approval and coordinated it with the Department of Defense. Of course, that was before the sanctions."

"Has the general had any direct dealings with Yaroslav Pervak?" Rusakov asked.

"Well, there's some complicated history there. The two don't like each other much, but they've had a working relationship. Enough to get things done. But they won't be playing eighteen holes anytime soon."

"Any reason to think Russia, or Russians, could have anything to do with the general's disappearance?"

"There's a Russian deal I've pulled, actually. One of the cases I was going to pass on to Douglas." She handed the file to

Rusakov, who opened it and thumbed through it, then passed it to Vail.

Rusakov continued asking Meyers questions—until something caught Vail's eye.

"Wait, the general knew Mikhail Uglov?"

Meyers stopped talking and turned to Vail. "They've known each other since the late eighties."

"When Uglov was KGB?"

"Yes." She hesitated, then said, "Lukas knew something about Mr. Uglov that complicated their relationship."

"Such as?" Vail asked.

"He never said. He didn't like talking about it."

Probably the bombing. And he likely knew Uglov's real name. Vail turned her attention back to the file. "Looks like this was one of those cases where DDI threw some business to Tait Protection." She looked at Meyers.

"Right. That was the only time Bill and Lukas had words."

"About what?"

Meyers sighed. "He wouldn't say. You think that's got something to do with his disappearance?"

"We don't know enough to draw that conclusion," Vail said. "But it's piqued my interest. There's something there, but I'm not sure what. May be nothing, but it may lead to some answers. Keep thinking on Tait, the Russians, Uglov, and the general. You come across anything, let us know immediately."

"There was someone at Tait the general didn't like. Guy was involved in something shady."

"Shady?" Rusakov asked. "In what way?"

"Not sure. The general came back to the office after a meeting with him and said, 'I *really* don't like this guy.' I sensed there was a history there, but I never pressed him about it. There were things he told me and things he didn't want to discuss. And I could usually tell when it was something he didn't want to discuss."

"But you figured it out," Vail said. "Didn't you?"

Meyers drew her chin back. "Why do you say that?"

"I'm good at reading people."

Meyers's lips pursed in appreciation. "I think he was into something that the general disapproved of."

Vail leaned forward. "Like what?"

"Like maybe he was an assassin, a hired gun for unsavory types. Dictators, strongmen, criminals, organized crime figures."

"You *think*?" Rusakov said. "Or you're pretty sure? Intuition?"

"More than intuition. I heard the general talking with someone."

"And this guy's name is?"

"Dirk Patrone."

"You have a file on Patrone?" Rusakov asked.

Meyers hesitated. "I'd have to check. Maybe some informal notes."

"Anything you give us would be helpful," Vail said. "And an address on Patrone if you've got it. Contact info on Bill Tait too."

"Give me a few minutes," Meyers said as she pressed a button. The HP monitor rose out of the desk and came to rest facing her. She started pecking away at the keys and a few moments later the printer whirred behind her desk and several sheets emerged. "Here's all we've got."

Vail took the papers and thanked Cynthia.

"The general's an American hero," Meyers said. "One of a kind. Please find him. Alive."

58

Taurus-Littrow Valley

"What the fuck?"

DeSantos, Uzi, and Carson heard the expletive over the radio.

"Cowboy?" DeSantos said. "What's up? We're a minute out."

"I—shit. It's gone."

"What's gone? Where are you?"

"It's not here," Stroud said. After a pause, he said, "I'm in the Raptor. Main cabin."

Uzi steadied himself by grabbing the metal handle on the right side of his seat, and leaned forward to scan the control panel's labels and switches. "Can this thing go any faster?"

"Believe me," DeSantos said, "if it could, I'd be putting pedal to the metal. So to speak."

"Almost there," Carson said from the back stowage area.

The Raptor got larger as they neared. DeSantos pulled up in front and Uzi got to the ladder first.

"Coming up," Carson said. "Wanna tell us what's going on, Cowboy?"

"Our food. All our food's gone."

"What do you mean?" Uzi said as he reached the top of the ladder. "What do you mean by 'gone'?"

"I mean, it's not here."

DeSantos, one rung behind Uzi, said, "How can that be? You had the Raptor in your sight the whole time, right?"

"Yeah, of course. Well, there might've been a few minutes where I wasn't watching. Twenty at most, but—"

"Jesus Christ, Cowboy," DeSantos huffed, his visor fogging.

"It's not like they put locks on these spacecraft," Stroud said. "I mean, who thinks someone's gonna go in and loot your food or equipment? You land on a planet, you're the only ones there." The frustration was evident in his voice.

They got into the airlock and pressurized, then moved through the metal door and saw Stroud kneeling on all fours.

"Asymmetrical warfare," DeSantos said. "Simple, effective. Brilliant, actually."

Carson checked various compartments in the cabin. "But why steal our food? Why not destroy our engines—or even the whole ship?"

"Because taking our food is easy. And it's smart. It forces us to leave the Moon, but in and of itself it wouldn't be deadly because we've got more supplies in our crew module. If they destroyed the Raptor, we'd be stranded—and our only way to survive would be to forcefully take the Russian ship. This is the least confrontational approach—but it accomplishes exactly what they want."

"Without food," Uzi said, "we could survive by leaving—which is what the Russians want anyway. And they'd get it without starting a war."

DeSantos nodded. "We'd be angry and pissed off, but not desperate. Desperate soldiers have nothing to lose and would go after them with a vengeance. We'd be dying anyway, so why not try to take their ship—and their food? If we can't, we die trying. Much more preferable to starving to death. Or we could merely leave and eat all the food we want in the Patriot."

"They outsmarted us." Stroud pounded his fist into the bulkhead.

"Yeah they did," Carson said. "Let's make sure that doesn't happen again. We're at war, gentlemen, and it's a battle that won't end well—either for them or for us. I'm gonna be a little selfish here, but I'd like it to be them."

"Sorry to be the one to point this out," Uzi said, "but there's a problem with the Russians' thinking."

DeSantos turned to Uzi. "And what's that?"

"They thought we could survive by leaving." Uzi leaned back against the bulkhead. "But we can't. We don't have any fuel."

"And that brings us back to the fact that we don't have any food. And the red elephant in the cabin." DeSantos turned slowly to Stroud. "You said the Raptor was out of your sight for twenty minutes? Where the hell were you?"

"I didn't find caesarium nearby so I went to one of the prioritized locations, not far from where the DOD believes Schmitt and Cernan found it. I was . . . looking around and exploring. I got too far away."

DeSantos's voice rose an octave. "Looking around and exploring?"

"Hey, we've got a limited number of hours here. I didn't want to regret not spending a few minutes to take it in, experience the fact I was on the fucking Moon. C'mon, don't tell me you don't know what I'm talking about." He made eye contact with each of them but was not getting a sympathetic look in return. "I didn't think it'd be a problem."

"You didn't *think*," DeSantos said. "*That's* the problem. What the hell's the matter with you? We have a mission. You're a skilled operator. Our enemy's now a few miles away. Don't do shit like that again."

"I'm the mission commander," Stroud said firmly, jamming a finger into the instrument panel. "You don't have the right to talk to me like that."

DeSantos snorted. "After the poor judgment you just showed, you *deserve* to be talked to like that. And if I could, I'd relieve you of command. We're all dependent on one another. This is a team. You put the team at risk for no good reason."

"So you still haven't even found any caesarium?" Carson asked.

"No. I've got two dozen other potential sites to check. It takes a lot longer because I have to drill manually."

"I may have a solution to our food problem," Uzi said, staring out the window to his left. "Well, not a solution, but something that'll keep us on the surface until we can complete our mission."

DeSantos tore his gaze away from Stroud. "Go."

"Those Apollo 17 food packs we found. They're dehydrated and—"

"They're decades old," Carson said. "I mean, they were made shelf-stable and some of it was treated with gamma radiation to sterilize it before it was packaged. But still, I'm sure they didn't give any thought to it lasting for so long."

"Hopefully they still have enough calories to sustain us for three days. Rationed, obviously."

DeSantos looked at Stroud. "Your screw up may end up killing us. We have no fuel to lift off and no food."

"I told you w—"

"Shut up. Just shut up." DeSantos clenched his jaw. "I don't see a choice. Let's go take a look at those food packets."

"From what I remember," Uzi said, "they mixed the contents of the packet with water and they had their meals. They also had hard nutrition bars. Chemically stabilized to last a long time. Not decades, but . . . maybe we'll be pleasantly surprised."

"Can't wait." Carson grabbed his helmet. "Look, we're in a bad way here. Uzi's got a reasonable solution. We'll make the best of it, make it work. Right?"

They all made eye contact and nodded, except for Stroud—who kept his gaze on his feet.

"Cowboy, you stay here, keep watch over the Raptor," DeSantos said. "You think you can handle that?"

"You're not in charge here."

"Tough. Consider it a mutiny. I'm giving the orders now."

Stroud looked at Carson, who turned away. Uzi, however, was staring Stroud down.

"Fine. I'll stay behind. Go. You're wasting time."

After pressurizing the airlock and donning their helmets, they descended the ladder and headed to the rover.

"UV exposure of the packing materials will be a problem," Uzi said. "We're talking direct exposure to the sun's mostly unfiltered ultraviolet rays. My biggest concern is that the radiation could cause the packaging material to fail. Then you've got the temperature swings. Heat, then cold, then heat, then cold . . . and so on, for a really long time."

"Let's go look," Carson said. "No sense in guessing. We'll have an answer inside of thirty minutes."

DESANTOS PARKED THE ROVER a dozen feet from the landing pod of the Apollo 17 descent stage. Lying in a heap was the collection of discarded equipment they had seen before, including a couple of the large, rectangular-shaped portable life support system backpacks.

They got out and circled the graveyard, then knelt down carefully in their bulky suits. Carson started with the eighty-four-pound PLSS backpack and lifted it up—fairly easy in the Moon's one-sixth gravity—and examined it. "Jack Schmitt's PLSS from 1972. How cool is that?"

"Hey, over here." DeSantos lifted a thick panel and unceremoniously tossed it aside. "A whole bunch of those high-density food bars. They're labeled."

Uzi knelt beside him and helped sift through tightly wrapped plastic laminate packs. "Tubed ham sandwich spread. Oh, that sounds . . . just. Plain. Gross."

"We can't afford to get sick," DeSantos said, "so we'll stay away from meat and dairy products if possible. My guess is those are the most likely to have gone bad. What else we got?"

"Strawberry cubes," Carson said. "That should be fairly safe."

"And date fruit cake," Uzi said, "which should also be good to eat. Well, not good. But edible. Uh, we'll pass on the beef sandwiches and—" He held up a cloudy, white/grayish bag—"I'm not even sure what this is." He turned it over. "Oh yuck. Butterscotch pudding."

Carson chuckled. "Yeah, a few decades ago. Now, it's . . . maybe the first microbes on the Moon in a millennium."

"I think we'll be safe from microbes if we stick to sealed packages," Uzi said.

"Just kidding," Carson said. "NASA never found organisms of any kind on the Moon. And the food was packed and sealed to ensure it was free of bacteria and viruses. We should be okay."

Uzi examined a couple of clear bags. "Dehydrated peas. Yum. And . . . this one's cocoa." He held it up in front of his helmet. "Looks like they've got some kind of a spring-loaded valve in the corner. You add water, shake, and then stick a straw in. Worth a try."

Carson held up another pack. "I've got a chocolate bar. And brownies. Boy, the Apollo astronauts liked their sweets."

"Graham crackers look to be intact," DeSantos said. "Sealed. And probably pretty stable." He discarded pouches marked "beef and gravy," "white bread," and "scrambled eggs."

"Surprised how much this stuff looks to be in decent condition," Carson said.

"That thick metal thing landed on top of some of the food," Uzi said. "At Intel we had to deal with thermal radiation, heat generation, and energy loss. Thermal radiation is the least efficient form of heat transfer, and objects heat up more slowly in a vacuum than in an atmosphere. Some of these food packs were protected by the reflective metal and constant shade, so it wasn't exposed to the damaging heat. It just stayed frozen. Stuff that wasn't underneath probably doesn't have any nutrients left, even if it is palatable, which I doubt."

"None of it looks palatable," Carson said.

"Survival 101," DeSantos said. "Eat to sustain, not for enjoyment."

"That's the point." Carson laughed. "Survival's the key. You willing to put that stuff in your body?"

Uzi opened his suit's Velcro pouches and started stuffing the food packs inside. "If we were in the jungle, we'd be eating grasshoppers and deer and insects and nuts and snakes and anything else we could find. This is no different. We have a mission to execute and we're not leaving here until we've done just that. Between the malware and the food, the Russians complicated that mission by a factor of a thousand."

DeSantos scooped some nutrition bars and slipped them into his pockets. "Let's get to it. I'm starving."

"I lost my appetite," Carson said. "But I'll get it down. Somehow."

"As soon as we re-dock with Patriot we'll be fine," Uzi said. "We just have to survive until then. This should supply the minimum number of calories we need. Good news is we're all gonna lose weight, which will help with liftoff."

DeSantos gathered up the remaining packs. "We can market it when we get home. Call it the Moon Survival Diet. What do you think?"

Uzi stood up and gave DeSantos a look. "Don't quit your day job."

59

Potomac, Maryland

With Bill Tait out of the country, they went to the next best source for information, Dirk Patrone. They arrived at his home an hour later—though calling this a home was a gross understatement. Although Patrone's mansion, unlike DeSantos's, did not sit on a park-size plot of land, it was still impressive, with two tall brick chimneys jutting skyward, rising above the sharply sloped gray tile roof. A smaller guest house sat to the east.

"Looks like a castle," Vail said, peering out the windshield as they approached along the gravel driveway. She looked down at her phone as the real estate webpage loaded. "Whoa. Only cost $7 million. Guess the mercenary-for-hire business pays well."

"I can tell you it does."

Vail cocked her head. "Personal experience?"

"No comment."

Probably best that I don't know. Vail drew her fingers apart and zoomed in on the screen. "Got a floorplan. It'll have to do on short notice. Besides, we're just going to talk to the guy, not invade." Vail flashed back to her last case, where she and a bunch of cops on her task force visited a home—and were met with a barrage of fully automatic assault rifle fire.

"Send the address to Hot Rod, just in case."

Just in case . . . what?

"I don't expect any trouble," Rusakov said. "This guy's got too much at stake to come out aggressively. He's got a good life—and unless we have hard evidence of criminal activity, we're no threat to him. And if we had hard evidence, we'd be showing up with a warrant and a tactical unit."

"I'll buy that."

They got out of the car and walked up to the eight-foot-tall cherry wood door. Rusakov knocked and a moment later a man appeared, about thirty-five and wearing a sport coat and an open collared dress shirt.

"Mr. Patrone?" Vail asked. She held up Department of Defense creds. "I'm Kathryn Vega. This is my partner. We're hoping you can help us out with an investigation."

"Me?"

"Yeah. Just a few minutes. If you don't mind."

"Um, okay." He shrugged. "Why don't you come in?" He stepped aside and they entered the residence, which featured slate floors and expensive art on the walls—Vail estimated the frames alone ran thousands of dollars apiece. There were even a couple of well-known paintings she remembered studying as part of her art history major.

He took them into a sitting room that had floor-to-ceiling windows across the entire twenty foot wall. It provided a view of the guest house and a massive hill in the yard—probably artificial—that was meticulously landscaped with a dry creek, footbridge, outdoor kitchen, and fire pit.

"Beautiful home," Vail said. "Sorry, didn't mean to insult you by calling it a home."

"It *is* a home. A home is what you make of it, right? But if you're referring to the structure, thank you. A friend of mine, who's an architect, designed it to my specs."

They took a seat on the buttery soft tan leather sofas. Vail took the angle facing the windows because she could not take her eyes off the view. *And that guest house. Something about it. But what?* "Just love the landscaping."

"Thanks," Patrone said. "But you didn't come here to compliment me on my choice of architecture and design."

"True," Rusakov said. "We're looking for some help with a case involving Lukas DeSantos. Do you know him?"

"Never met him. But I know *of* him. Everyone in this industry does. Hell, even if you're not in the industry you've probably come across his name at some point in the media. I think I heard something about him getting some kind of medal from the president in a couple of weeks."

Hmm. Cynthia Meyers said Lukas had talked with him. They had an argument. Why's he lying? "You sure you never met him? Never had a chat with him?"

"Never."

"How about your boss, Bill Tait? Doesn't he know General DeSantos?"

"Bill served under him. The general provided seed money for his business. Why?"

"We've been told you guys do a significant amount of work with Russia."

Patrone nodded thoughtfully. No surprise, no concern registered.

"The Russians contract with Tait for a variety of things, sometimes when diplomats need added protection or if they've got a dignitary or celebrity."

"And what's your position with the company?" Rusakov asked.

"Enforcement."

He said it without flinching. To Dirk Patrone, enforcement was a euphemism for murder. Or just a more politically correct term?

He laughed. "It pays well."

Vail laughed too—and tried to make it sound genuine.

While Rusakov continued questioning Patrone, Vail's gaze kept coming back to the guest house just beyond the large wall of windows. All its windows were locked down, the shades were drawn, and the shutters were closed. *Why?*

"Just curious," Vail said. "That guest house. You rent it out?"

"Rent it out?" Patrone chortled, as if that were a ridiculous question—which, of course, it was.

"No, it's for friends and family, when they visit."

"Is it decked out like the main house?"

"Pretty much, yeah. The decorator and art broker did both structures at the same time."

"You know—that would—I'd love to see it. I'm a student of art and I couldn't help but admire the Degas and Cézanne in your living room."

Patrone narrowed his eyes and cocked his head to the side. "You want to see my guest house?"

"Yeah, if you don't mind."

"It's a mess. My brother and his kids stayed there last week and I haven't had time to get the cleaners in."

Vail waved a hand. "I just want to see the artwork. I'm not going to pass judgment on your cleanliness."

Patrone chortled—a bit unevenly for Vail's liking. Then he got serious. "I agreed to answer some question on your case, but I don't think I'm obligated to give you a tour of my residences." He stood up. "Now, I guess we're done. But I do thank you for all the lovely compliments on my home and my taste in art."

Without waiting for an objection, he led the way to the front door and whipped it open in one swift motion. The cool air brushed against Vail's face.

"Thanks for inviting us in," Rusakov said.

"Yeah. And what was your name? Other than 'her partner.'"

"Viktoria Hawkins." She pulled out her creds and held them up for Patrone to see.

And with that, they left, trudging along the gravel path toward their car.

"You weren't really interested in seeing the paintings in the guest house," Rusakov said.

"I *am* a student of art history. But no. Something's not right with that place. Couldn't put my finger on it. Then I realized all the windows are shuttered. The place is buttoned up."

"So? Maybe he likes his privacy."

"The wall of windows had no shades, drapes, blinds, coverings of any kind. A guy like that, if he's not gonna worry about people looking in on his main house, why would he do the opposite for a guest house?"

"Because it's a mess." She held up a hand to keep Vail from responding. "Just kidding. Okay, so what do you want to do about this mysterious house that has all its curtains drawn?"

"You're mocking me."

"Maybe a little bit."

"I think he's hiding something."

"Like what?"

Vail pulled out her keys as they reached the SUV. "Don't know. Lukas DeSantos? He lied at least once that we know of. I'm betting there's more. He's very polished."

Rusakov opened the door and sat down on the cold seat.

"We need a warrant."

"Whoa," Rusakov said with a laugh. "Okay."

"What?"

"Didn't realize we had enough to get a warrant."

Vail chuckled. "We don't. I'm surprised you know about that stuff."

"Saw it on TV."

Did she just say that?

Rusakov spread her hands. "So if we don't have enough to get a warrant, why'd you say we needed one?"

"If we were following police procedure, we'd *need* a warrant. I didn't say we'd actually *get* one."

Rusakov motioned for Vail to finish the sentence. "But . . ."

"But we're not here as police officers. We're here as non-law-abiding covert operatives."

Rusakov buckled her belt. "See? You're getting the hang of this."

60

Taurus-Littrow Valley

They spent the night sleeping in four-hour shifts, guarding the Raptor with two men posted on the outside and two on the inside. This used up their oxygen supply faster, but they did not have a choice.

The Russians had already proven that they had no compunction about entering their lander. At least inside, without their gloves and pressure suits on, the OPSIG operators would be able to use their pistols. But if the cosmonauts got that far where they had penetrated the exterior perimeter, two of their team would have already perished.

The Apollo 17 food was worse than they anticipated. The bars were not only tasteless but hard as concrete. They resorted to soaking them in water to rehydrate them to the point they were at least chewable. How much nutritional value there was left was unknown, but they satiated their hunger and provided some calories, allowing them to continue working.

They each had an energy bar in their pressure suit pocket, and two in the Spider. They rationed these out as well, and supplemented their cement foodstuffs to give them at least some fiber, nutrients, and protein.

The mission was originally drawn up to last three days, a maximum of four if need be. With their food gone, however, and consuming oxygen at a greater rate, the only commodity they had in sufficient quantity was water. But on a hostile planetary body, all three resources were essential. Remove one part of that equation and life was not sustainable for any significant amount of time.

Bottom line, they estimated that tomorrow "night" they would need to leave the Moon, which meant that they would have to have the 3D printed parts finished and usable, the fuel offloaded from the Chang'e into the Raptor, the Russians neutralized, and the tests run on the caesarium.

They all knew the odds were not with them, but they chose to remain focused on their tasks.

When the time came to get back to work, they drafted a course of action: Uzi and Carson finished removing the fuel tank from the Apollo 17 descent stage and prepared it for transport to the Chang'e 5 as soon as the pump and coupling parts were finished printing. They would then use the Spider to tow it over to the Chang'e, load the vessel with fuel, and haul it back to the Raptor with the LRV.

As soon as Uzi and Carson completed their task, Uzi dropped him at the Raptor and picked up DeSantos. They drove the LRV to the Resurs and parked fifty yards away.

"Close enough to let them know we're watching, but not so close that we're a threat," DeSantos said.

Uzi shifted his bulky suit in the rover's barebones seat. "This has got to be the strangest stakeout I've ever done."

"We should take turns sleeping. No reason for us both to stare into space. So to speak."

"Nah, I'm okay."

"Bullshit. You didn't get a whole lot on the flight out here because you were reading endless lines of computer code. We take the z's where and when we can. I've got the first shift. Promise to wake you if the cosmonauts all of a sudden start dancing the jig."

DeSantos sat there a moment watching the Russian lander, replaying that video loop Oleg showed him inside the cabin. He couldn't stop thinking about his father, picturing his beaten face, the proud general reduced to a drooling prisoner. Humiliated. "Have you talked with your dad since we went to visit him?"

"Nope."

"Boychick. You should."

Uzi swung his helmet, and the top of his torso, toward DeSantos. "Why? I mean, I know *why*. But why are you bringing it up?"

"My mind started to wander. I remember playing football with my dad at an Army base in Germany. We lived there for a couple of years. Pretty fun, actually. Got in some good skiing. He taught me how to ski without breaking my neck." DeSantos laughed. "It was one of the only times when I didn't feel like I had to live up to his standards. He wasn't a very good skier. He knew how, but he just wasn't very coordinated. I think he had a hard time with the concept of being out of control, sliding on slick, hard-packed snow down a mountainside, without brakes. He's a control guy. There aren't many things that humble him. But that was one of them."

"You never told me much about him. Just that he was career military."

DeSantos sat there in silence for a long moment. "I've spent my life trying to live up to his legend. He was a highly decorated general."

Uzi processed that for a moment, then shifted his body to fully face his friend. "Wait. Your dad's not *General* Lukas DeSantos."

"Now you know why I haven't mentioned him."

"That's something to be proud of. He served his country with distinction."

"So did *your* dad."

Uzi turned away. "You got me there."

"I've had . . . issues trying to live up to his reputation, trying to be what he wanted me to be. Not sure that makes much sense—I mean, I guess it does, but it's not really rational."

"C'mon. That's normal, Santa. We all—well, lots of boys look up to their fathers. That's why it's tough for a kid to grow up without a male influence—a father *figure*, if not a father. That doesn't mean everyone's relationship is always healthy. Some have better experiences than others. Mine was pretty good growing up. He always had my back. I knew I could count on him. Do you guys have a good relationship?"

"Not sure how to answer that." DeSantos chewed on it a moment. "Yes. But no. It's artificial, almost like he says and does things he thinks a father's supposed to say and do." He thought of a million examples, but none were the kind he wanted to get into. Besides, he needed to keep focused on the Russians. "We haven't talked a whole lot the past few years. I don't think he respects what I do because there's no military decorum. No uniform, no conventional chain of command, little discipline."

Uzi yawned. "Did he tell you that?"

"Just a feeling I have. I know he was disappointed when I left the Army. He wanted me to follow in his footsteps. I think he'd used some capital with the brain trust to pave the way for me. But I didn't want that."

"You wanted to do it on your own. Earn it."

"It wasn't that. I don't have a problem taking gifts, because something may be given to you but you have to run with it. The quarterback can shove the ball in your stomach during a handoff. It's what you do with the rock in that split second that defines you—not that he gave you the ball. So that wasn't the problem. I didn't want to be an administrator. I wanted to save lives, do things few people can. Make a difference. When I told him that, I think I inadvertently insulted him."

"But you are making a difference. And saving lives. Remember? You have to add, 'On the Moon.'"

DeSantos laughed. "On the Moon."

Uzi yawned again. "See, it works."

DeSantos fell silent a long minute. "I used to look up at the Moon when I was a kid and wonder what it was like up here."

"But now you're actually here," Uzi said, his voice getting slower, almost as if he was buzzed. "Only twelve walked the surface before we got here . . ."

"I do feel privileged. But there's no time for that, you know?"

Uzi did not reply. DeSantos heard his breathing over the radio and realized his friend had fallen asleep. He stared out at the Resurs and tried to clear his mind . . . but all he could think about was skiing in the Alps with his father.

His father.

He wondered what the Russians were doing to him this very moment.

61

POTOMAC, MARYLAND

It was dark in the neighborhood where Dirk Patrone lived. OPSIG had put a bird in the air with infrared surveillance to monitor his movements and make sure he did not enter the guest house. If he did, Vail and Rusakov, who were parked half a mile down the road off a side street, would intervene. They now had reason to believe the general was not in the residence, but they did not want Patrone erasing any evidence if it did, in fact, have any relevance to Lukas's disappearance.

An hour after the sun set, Patrone drove off in his Bentley and the OPSIG team, wearing black tactical uniforms, moved in silently and breached the guest house front door. Vail and Rusakov trailed behind Troy Rodman, Zheng Wei, and six other operators skilled in covert entries.

Vail was there to look for evidence—not for prosecution but for clues that could give them an indication as to what happened to the general and where he was being kept.

They cleared the residence as Vail wandered the main floor. She had followed the team as they went through their infrared-goggled incursion, but once they declared a room safe, she went to work.

Vail had covered almost the entire downstairs when her boot caught on a wood plank as she left the study. She knelt down and shined her flashlight across the floor and determined it was an artificially created seam. "Got something," she said in her mic.

Zheng and Rusakov were first in the room.

"Looks like there may be a lower level here. But you guys are gonna have to lift this."

Zheng pulled out a tactical knife and pried the flooring up. He and Rusakov grabbed the edge and swung the large trap door back against the wall.

"Lights," Vail said.

They illuminated the opening and shared a look. A wooden ladder led down. Weapon drawn, Zheng descended the steps.

Fifteen seconds passed. "All clear," he said over the radio.

Vail went down, followed by Rodman, who had just entered the study, and Rusakov.

"Looks like our mercenary has a torture chamber all his own, right in his backyard," Zheng said.

Vail crouched in front of a knife that had been tossed to the floor. "I see bloodstains."

"On this too," Rusakov said, holding up a saw.

"Gross." Vail recoiled. "I don't want to know what he did with that. But we do need to know *who* he did it to. We need an evidence response team here to test for DNA. I'm sure we can get an exemplar on the general. And if not, I know where Hector lives. That'll give us a close enough match if there's a match to be had."

"I'm on it," Rusakov said. She pulled out her encrypted radio and went back up the ladder.

"So how do we handle this?" Vail asked. "We've got no idea when Patrone will be back."

"Actually, we do. He was booked on a flight to Houston due to leave in—" Rodman consulted his watch—"one hour. We had agents follow him to Dulles. He's at the gate. Once we know for sure he's boarded and the jet's gone wheels up, we'll be fine. We've got a quiet presence posted at the mouth of the street, the only access point to this property. Anyone goes past him, the team will be notified and we'll deal with it."

Very efficient. I should've expected nothing less.

"Meantime, keep looking around, see if anything else looks out of the ordinary."

"Down here? Nothing is *in* the ordinary."

Rodman gave her a stern look.

"Right," Vail said. "I'll get back to it."

62

Taurus-Littrow Valley

DeSantos gave Uzi's shoulder a nudge. "Time to wake up."

Uzi opened his eyes and appeared disoriented for a second until his brain registered and identified the interior of his helmet. "Right. The Moon." He sat up. "I was dreaming. Dena and Maya."

"Sorry Boychick. I know that wound never heals."

"It scars over." Uzi stretched his arms out as far as he could with the suit on. "But the pain remains."

"At least the memories are still there."

"I may've lost my girls, but I'll never lose the memories." He figured that at some point he would have told Maya about this mission. How could a dad not tell his little girl that he walked on the Moon, that bright disk in the sky that appeared nearly every night—unlike her father, who was off working missions instead of being at home for family dinners.

And his wife . . . could he keep such a secret from her? Would Dena believe him? "Hey, you think you'll ever tell Maggie you went to the Moon?"

"That's a rhetorical question, right?"

"Right." Uzi's empty stomach rumbled, contracting hard. "I'm so friggin' hungry."

DeSantos chuckled. “We’ve got some delicious blocks of concrete waiting for you at the Raptor.”

“Can’t wait.” He looked out at the Resurs. “How’s everything been?”

“Quiet. Too quiet. Two of them returned to the lander without their rover, which might mean you were right. Their drill is built into the rover like the Spider. But whether or not they’ve found caesarium yet . . . no way of knowing.”

“We need to get closer so that the Geiger counter can pick up the caesarium if they get hold of it.”

“And how close is that?”

Uzi shrugged. “Pretty close. We’ve gotta figure out a way to plant one of our handheld Geiger counters on their spacecraft so that when they return with it, if they find it, the sensor will set off an alarm remotely. I think I can rig something up.”

“We also need a contingency plan for what we’re going to do if they do find it.”

“Hang on.” Uzi raised Carson and Stroud on the radio and said, “We’ve all had time to think. We need to make some decisions.”

“No way around it,” Stroud said. “The Russians can’t leave here with caesarium. Digger and I have run it through the scenarios and the only option is to blow up their ship. Our ascent stage can’t lift eight men—even if we could fit everyone, which I don’t think we can. But we’re pushing the weight limit for four. Even if we dump equipment so it’s just a shell with a flight computer and engine, there’s no way we can clear another eight hundred pounds. And that’s assuming the fuel transfer works.”

“So if we destroy their ship,” Uzi said, “we’re essentially stranding the Russians here. We’re killing them.”

They were silent.

Carson cleared his throat. “It’s us or them. I don’t think they’d hesitate if the situation were reversed. In fact, we should check the Raptor, make sure they didn't plant an IED when they took our food. I'll get right on that."

"If we do blow their ship," DeSantos said, "won't the explosion be detected on Earth?"

"Doubt it," Carson said. "The Apollo astronauts placed seismometers at their landing sites around the Moon. The instruments radioed data back to Earth until they were switched off in '77."

"Switched off," Uzi said. "So our answer is probably not."

"I think that's fairly safe to say."

"Probably and fairly," DeSantos said. "Not confidence-inducing assessments."

"Our mission is to stop them," Stroud said. "If the Russians find out what happened, which they may anyway, it's not our job to figure out what to do about it. The Pentagon will be cleaning up the mess back on Earth."

"Fine," DeSantos said. "So how do we stop them? How do we blow up the Resurs?"

Stroud chortled. "Space vehicles are incredibly fragile things, since they need to be very light. So a C-4 charge should easily do the job, even if it doesn't ignite the fuel. Remember the SpaceX explosion that happened while they were just fueling on the pad? No bombs necessary."

"We need to be sure," Uzi said. "There won't be any do-overs. And just in case they find the charge, we should have a backup that can do the job."

"One thing," Stroud said. "We can't destroy the ship until we lift off because the Raptor's too close. Shrapnel would carry farther than on Earth. It could damage *our* ascent stage."

"So we do it as we lift off," Uzi said. "Once we're high enough, we blow it. I'll need to rig up a remote."

"What kind of range will it have?" DeSantos asked.

Uzi shrugged. "Not a whole lot. We've got to be sure it'll work or we're screwed. Once we're out of range, I'm not sure what else we could do. Short of crashing our ship into theirs. A suicide mission. If we could even maneuver like that."

"Obviously, it's not something we ever did in the simulator," Stroud said. "I could probably pull it off, but a kamikaze mission wouldn't be my first choice."

DeSantos turned off his heads-up display. "So where should we place these charges?"

"One inside, one outside," Uzi said.

"How the hell are we gonna get a bomb on board a Russian ship?" Stroud said. "They've stolen our food, tried to kill us. Why would they let any of us onboard again?"

DeSantos knew the answer to that but chose not to share it. "I'll figure something out."

"The charges are small," Uzi said, "and magnetic. Almost everything in the interior of the spacecraft is made of metal or a metallic alloy. Anywhere we put that thing inside the crew compartment would work. Except if it's aluminum."

"Which it could be," Carson said.

"A chance we'll have to take. But you'll feel it as soon as the magnet grabs hold. If it doesn't, find another place."

"So we definitely have to get inside their crew cabin again," Stroud said. "Without them knowing."

"Better chances of hitting the lottery," Uzi said. "They've had a guy posted there 24/7."

DeSantos cocked his head. "The Russians are paranoid, cunning, and very careful. But I might be able to get inside by confronting Oleg about the missing food. We can only talk inside the spacecraft. He'll expect me to accuse him—and he'll deny it, but who cares? I need an excuse to get in, and arguing about the food will divert his attention from what I'm doing."

"I also want to place a Geiger counter close to their craft, if not on it," Uzi said. "They're not as small as the explosive charges, but putting it on one of the landing struts of the Resurs should conceal it."

"We can create a distraction," Carson said. "His men will have to react. During the commotion, you can stick it on the strut. It's likely a magnetic alloy."

"If the altercation is nasty enough, they'll alert Oleg," DeSantos said. "If I haven't already had a chance to place the charge, I'll slap it on something and follow Oleg out so he won't think twice about leaving me alone in their cabin."

"You sure you can get this guy to talk with you?" Stroud asked.

"No," DeSantos said. "Not at all. But I'll do my best."

AN HOUR LATER, Uzi left DeSantos on point and took the LRV back to the Raptor to pick up the materials Carson and Stroud had assembled. Forty-five minutes after that, Uzi returned to their stakeout location with Carson beside him.

"Your timing's good," DeSantos said. "They're all back at the Resurs."

Uzi and Carson showed DeSantos what they had—a small, handheld Geiger counter pilfered from a panel in the Raptor and a compact explosive, both fitted with a strong magnetic backing.

"And this thing is guaranteed to go off?" DeSantos asked as he examined the square of C-4, which was half the size of his palm.

"Not counting bizarre, unforeseen circumstances," Carson said, "yes."

DeSantos groaned. "I've never been a fan of bizarre, unforeseen circumstances."

"That's why we have two charges," Uzi said.

"Try to place it somewhere close to their fuel tank," Carson said. "Or near the avionics panel."

"Why don't I put it right *on* the fuel tank?"

Carson held up a hand. "Only telling you what would be best."

"May not be necessary," Uzi said. "I'm going to try to put this secondary charge onto one of their struts. Even if it doesn't ignite the fuel, knocking off one of the legs should do the job. They won't be able to lift off."

"You clear on how you're going to approach Oleg?" Carson asked.

"It's all about the food. I've got it. What about you guys?"

"Gonna be a little harder for us. Uzi and I have something planned. We can talk between us and they can't hear us, so that's an advantage. But we can't converse with the cosmonauts. So we have to antagonize them without getting so crazy that they pull their guns. Because if they fire, even a minor flesh wound would depressurize our suits and kill us instantly."

"Okay then." Uzi got back in the rover. "On that happy note, let's do this."

UZI DROVE THE LRV right up to the Resurs, allowing him to position it very close to the side strut of the large lander. DeSantos got out, striding—as best he could in one-sixth gravity—toward the men.

Carson followed, creating some anxiety. Even in their bulky pressure suits Uzi could see the cosmonauts' postures change, ready for confrontation.

DeSantos looked into each of their helmets to see which was Oleg. They raised their sun visors and DeSantos pointed to the forward hatch, indicating that he wanted to talk with him.

Oleg obliged, climbing the twelve rungs up to the egress platform. He spun the wheel and pulled open the access panel.

A MINUTE LATER, the cabin was pressurized and they removed their helmets.

"You came to accept offer," Oleg said.

"Offer? What offer?"

Oleg contorted his mouth, as if it should have been obvious. "Deal. For your father."

"Where are our food packs?"

"Food? What food? Do not know what you say."

"C'mon, Oleg. There are eight people on this entire planet. Four of them need that food to survive. The other four . . . well, life would be a lot easier for them if those four had to leave prematurely, wouldn't it?"

"You have—how do you say? Active imagination."

"Do I?" DeSantos glanced around the small cabin, looking for a good place to stick the charge. He turned his torso and reached down—and in that instant, he placed it under a control panel. "I don't believe you," he said angrily as he felt the device grab the metal surface. He continued moving his hands around the interior. "I know it's here somewhere. Where'd you put it?" he said, his voice rising.

"I tell you. We do not take food."

DeSantos swung around. "It's not here, is it? He examined Oleg's gaze. "No. You wouldn't bring it back here. You'd dump it someplace we'd never find it."

Oleg appeared to be suppressing a grin. "We here for caesarium. That is all. Well, we also come to keep United States from getting it." The left corner of his mouth lifted noticeably this time—a devious smile.

"I told you," DeSantos said, looking deep into his eyes. "We're not here to bring caesarium back with us. If we'd wanted to do that, we would've come years ago. Before Russia or anyone else knew about it."

Oleg spread his hands. "Then there not be problem. We not want a war with—"

"No," DeSantos said. "I'm sure you don't. Except for one thing. You've kidnapped my father."

Oleg shrugged. "He be well cared for."

"Really? He didn't look so well cared for in that video."

"You worry much. He is fine. And he is released once we have caesarium safely in Russia. If caesarium not get to Russia . . ." Oleg sighed. "Well, no need to spell out meaning."

"You have a father, Oleg?"

"Everyone has father. Some know who he is, some do not."

"You care about yours?"

"This about you. Not me."

"It *is* about you. As a human being."

"No, my friend. This bigger. Me, you? We just players in game. But," he said, his gaze boring into DeSantos's, "you not careful, this become war." He tapped his temple with an index finger. "Think careful."

"You harm my father and I won't stop until you're all dead. That's not a threat, Oleg, it's a promise. Tell your people. He gets returned or you'll be sorry you fucked with me. And my friends back on Earth."

"There is saying you Americans like: 'Good luck with that.'"

DeSantos seated his helmet and turned to the hatch. He took a breath, pushed the anger from his thoughts, and realized there had been no interruption about a commotion outside. Had something gone wrong?

63

POTOMAC, MARYLAND

Vail leaned her air splint against a large piece of plywood—and it nearly fell over. *A divider to a back room?* She moved to the edge where it met the cinderblock wall and squeezed around its edge.

"Alex, in here."

Rusakov joined her. "Well, well, well."

"It wasn't built to pass as a fake room. So what are we looking at here?"

Rusakov pointed. "See that tripod over in the corner? And the walls, how they're painted and decorated?"

"Yeah, so? I'm not seei—"

"It's a movie set. Sort of. But you get the idea—our friendly neighborhood mercenary shoots ransom and proof of life videos down here. Untraceable to a region because there are no identifiable objects in the background. And . . ." Rusakov reached up to the ceiling and poked at it. "Sound proofing. So even if the person screamed, in the basement and with no houses nearby, their pleas would be swallowed up by a soundproofed interior."

And we have no warrant so we can't arrest the bastard. We're technically not even here.

"I know what you're thinking," Rusakov said. "At least he'll be on our radar. And the FBI can keep an eye open so when he does cross the line, they'll be able to come in and take him down."

"A guy like that will know people have been in his house," Vail said, "no matter how careful we are. He'll disappear. Or take his business somewhere else. Another state. Another country."

"You may be right. Meantime, we've gotta stay focused on our task. I know it's hard for you to turn off one part of your brain and switch to the other. But the lab guys will be here in ten minutes and we'll have some answers as to whether or not the general was kept here."

Vail glanced around at the movie backdrop Patrone had created. "That proof of life gif we received will be our quickest indicator. If it matches the setup here, we'll need to look into where Patrone was headed on that flight. You have the video on your phone?"

"I can call it up. Give me a minute."

Vail walked over to the tripod and held up her cell, opened the camera app, framed the shot, and tried to picture where the general was kneeling when the video was filmed.

"Here it is," Rusakov said as she held up the device between them.

They only had a few seconds to work with, but after watching it several times as it looped repeatedly, Vail was able to place where Lukas had been kneeling. "This is where it was shot."

Rusakov looked from the image to the area in front of them. "You sure?"

"Look at the fold in the burlap in the corner. And that torn scrap of paper on the floor. Same as the video." Vail lowered the resolution setting, then pressed record and held it in place for a few seconds. She played it back and compared it to what Rusakov had on her phone.

"You convinced me," Rusakov said. "Now what?"

"Now we track Patrone's movements, where he's been, who he's met with, and where he's going. And we do the same for Bill Tait. He was out of town. Let's find out where. And why."

64

Taurus-Littrow Valley

DeSantos climbed down the long Resurs ladder, scowling at the other three cosmonauts as he passed and giving them the middle finger—at least, that's what he tried to do. In those gloves, it looked more like an Italian salute, conveying, "Up yours."

"Did you do it?" Uzi asked.

"I did. What about you two?"

"Done and done. We didn't even need to start a fight."

"Too bad. Would've been the first one ever on the Moon."

Uzi harrumphed. "I think we've already created enough firsts on this mission."

"While you were cavorting with Oleg," Carson said, "CAPCOM told us the 3D printer's done making the parts. We've gotta get back and see if we can hook them up. Cowboy's on his way with the Spider to the Apollo lander. Hector, you stay here and watch the Geiger remote Uzi set up. Uzi and I will haul the tank over to the Chang'e and try to offload that fuel. One of us will get back here as soon as possible."

"I'll hold down the fort. One against four? No weapons? No problem."

"Wrong, Santa. You have two weapons at your disposal: sharp wit and biting humor."

Carson shook his head at Uzi's joke—an awkward jiggle with a pressure suit on. "God help us."

AFTER UZI AND CARSON TRANSPORTED the Apollo 17 fuel tank to the Chang'e, they spotted the small Chinese rover returning to transfer its find into the lander's onboard laboratory for analysis.

They stuck the back end of a wrench in its rear wheel gear to jam it. The robot attempted to reverse, then drive forward to free the obstruction. Finally it stopped moving and went into sleep mode. They cut the wiring to the solar array, essentially rendering the rover inert.

Carson pried open its payload door and Uzi ran his Geiger counter over it.

"Nope," Uzi said.

"CAPCOM," Carson said, "this is Raptor. Chang'e rover disabled. Ready to install the pump and coupler, then try to offload the Chang'e fuel."

"Roger that, Raptor. Issachar is here standing by."

"Gentlemen," Issachar said, "I want to give you one more thing to watch out for. These engines are pretty simple in that you just mix the fuel and oxygen and it ignites. But those propellants need to be pressurized to make them flow into the engine, since you can't rely on gravity in space. Typically, we use high pressure helium tanks to pressurize the propellant tanks."

"Meaning?" Carson asked. "That the fuel will be under pressure?"

"Yes. Hundreds or thousands of PSI. The pressure can be vented by activating a valve. So when you're ready, let me know and we'll figure out which one it is."

"Don't worry," Uzi said, "we won't be making a move without your input."

It took them forty-five minutes to make the connections and, with Issachar's instructions, find the valve and release the pressure.

"Is the pump working?" Issachar asked.

"It is," Carson said, "and we're ready to load the tank."

"Let her rip. We've all got our fingers crossed here."

"We would do the same, if we didn't have these ridiculous gloves on."

"Starting transfer," Uzi said. He watched and waited, then gave an awkward thumbs up to Carson. "Both couplings are holding. I think it's working."

"Great news," Issachar said. "Just so you know, start to finish, this is going to run about four hours, so you might want to take turns sleeping. It's gonna get mighty boring staring at two fuel tanks."

"Ten-four," Carson said.

Uzi thought of leaving Carson and rejoining DeSantos, but they all felt it was best to maintain two "guards" at the Chang'e. It was their only hope of getting off the surface—and if the Russians somehow got wind of their fuel situation, the Chinese craft would become a prime target.

For the next several hours, DeSantos was on his own.

65

Potomac, Maryland

Vail and Rusakov had gotten to their SUV when Vail's phone rang.

"This is Hodges at headquarters. I've got a couple things for you. The guys decrypting Kerwin's laptop said they found the name of the guy working with Lansford and Kerwin at Aerospace Engineering."

"The one who put the Chinese comms chip on the mainboard?" Vail asked.

"Right. They went to pick him up but looks like he left the country. Kerwin must've gotten word to him his cover was blown. We're trying to figure out where he went. If he's gone underground, we may not find him for a very long time. And if he's fled to a country without extradition . . . well, we should be glad we at least got Lansford."

"And the second thing?"

"A call just came through on Vail's Bureau Samsung. A US marshal, Lewis Hurdle."

Vail lifted her brow. "Can you call him back and patch him through without him seeing my OPSIG caller ID?"

"Give me a few seconds."

She heard a beep, then said, “Hurdle? That you?”

“What the hell’s going on with you, Karen? You got secretaries answering your cell now?”

“Ha. Good one.” *Please let it drop.* “So you have something for me on Jessie Kerwin?”

“Better than that. I’ve got Kerwin.”

“You shitting me? You’re really good, you know that?”

“I told you. The marshals always get their men. And women. So what do you want me to do with her?”

“Turn her over to the FBI. I’ll have you coordinate with the director’s office and—”

“The director’s office? Get outta town. What are you doing working cases with that much weight?”

“Guess they think I’m good at what I do.”

“Yeah, yeah, yeah. Whatever. I stepped into that one.”

“I’ll have someone call you back on this number inside of ten minutes. And two favors. Don’t mention my name to Kerwin and, well, don’t ask her any questions and don’t answer any questions. Let her wonder what the hell’s going on.”

“Well, that’ll make two of us.”

“Just the way I like it. And Hurdle—thanks. Nice work.”

Vail told Rusakov they had identified the other spy at Aerospace Engineering and that they had Kerwin back in custody—which she had already surmised. Then she called Rodman, who had returned to the Pentagon an hour ago.

“How are we doing on the Bill Tait dossier?”

“Got some people on it. Have a call in to NSA.”

“Check the GPS on his car, that’d be helpful too.”

“Consider it done,” Rodman said. “Give us a couple of hours. Anything important, I’ll let you know.”

VAIL AND RUSAKOV DROVE TO THE PENTAGON, using their commute to talk through the pertinent information they had gleaned thus far, including everything they had gotten from, and about, Jason Lansford, Jessie Kerwin, Cynthia Meyers, Mikhail Uglov, Bill Tait, Dirk Patrone, Yaroslav Pervak, and Ronck Mining, then cross-referenced it all with what they knew about Lukas DeSantos.

When they walked into the OPSIG operations center, a group of fifteen men and women sat around an oval conference table, laptops open and keyboards clacking.

Rodman, seated at the head of the room, told Vail and Rusakov to pull up a couple of vacant chairs that were pushed against the far wall.

"I've got a team at Dulles doing a forensic examination of Patrone's car on site," Rodman said. "These things are like sophisticated computers and—"

"Yeah," Rusakov said. "We know."

"And the CSIs are tapping into it and reviewing all the data. They've correlated trip information with Kerwin's car's GPS. Looks like there was periodic contact between Patrone and Kerwin."

"Patrone and Kerwin," Vail said as she took her seat. "That's a relationship that smells like rotten fish."

"There's more," Dykstra said, taking a seat next to Vail. "Page 27 of the PDF I sent over. Don't bother pulling it up. I've got it here." He clicked and his screen changed to an Excel spreadsheet. He pointed to a number of dates. "Uglov had meetings with Tait and Patrone."

"So there's a connection between our players," Vail said.

Rusakov continued examining the document. "Now we just have to see what this has to do with Lukas. I mean, we know he was taken to leverage Hector. But what was Tait's motivation? Money?"

Vail sat back. "Or is someone else behind it and there's a vendetta? Is this about retribution? *If* Tait is mixed up in Lukas's abduction, I'm not sure that makes any sense—given what we know so far. Lukas was a mentor to Tait, seeded his company when he didn't have to."

"*Unless* Lukas had to make that investment," Rusakov said. "A payoff for something that happened years ago and it was hush money to keep Tait quiet. Blackmail. A little more palatable if Lukas gets some shares in Tait Protection."

"Possible, but there's almost nothing to suggest anything like that."

Rodman motioned a couple of people over. "We'll look into it just in case it turns out to be true."

"Could be as simple as greed or a vendetta—Tait's paid to do a job and the money is too good to pass up. Maybe Tait gets a cut of Ronck's profit if China pays up."

Vail stood up and began pacing. "We need to focus on what we already know—facts. Ronck rakes in billions if China gets caesarium. Kerwin is hired to find a way to place someone inside NASA or a defense contractor to make this happen. She puts Jason Lansford into Aerospace Engineering. Lansford plants malware in the US rocket software and a colleague adds a rogue chip to the onboard computer systems."

Rusakov brushed away a speck of dust from her keyboard. "But Lansford pays unexpected dividends because he's able to hack top secret DOD servers and they see that the military is close to launching both a ring of preventive laser satellites and a Moon shot."

"And they hit the jackpot when Lansford discovers that one of the astronauts chosen to replace the two killed in the NBL bombing is DeSantos—whose father is pretty much an American hero."

"There's no time to take out Hector and Uzi," Dykstra said, "so they need to find some other way of protecting their mission."

"Right." Vail stopped pacing. "Leverage. They grab up Lukas—and try to contact Hector directly—to force him to sabotage the mission and clear the way for the Russians to leave the Moon with caesarium."

"But an important part of this," Rodman said, "is that the largest shareholder in Ronck is Yaroslav Pervak, the Russian president."

"Now we need some speculation to connect the remaining dots." Rusakov pushed away from the laptop. "Ronck's done business with Tait, so the company's familiar with him. Through Uglov, Pervak lets it be known that Lukas DeSantos needs to be kidnapped and taken somewhere. And Tait has a guy who's willing to do a job for them off the books."

"Dirk Patrone."

"Yeah. Mercenary extraordinaire." Vail glanced up at the ceiling for a moment. "You think Patrone also took out the NBL employee? The one whose stolen ID was used by Alec Hayder to get into the lab to plant the bomb?"

"I think that's a pretty damn good guess," Ruskaov said.

Dykstra nodded slowly, putting it all together. "So Pervak arranges for Ronck to pay a great deal of money to Tait, which he and Patrone split—or whatever. Patrone has a crew, part of Tait Protection or freelance, that grabs up Lukas."

"Bastard," Rodman said. "Tait served under Lukas. He was his CO. This is—" he curled a fist—"wrong. This is personal. We're gonna get this bastard, wherever he is."

Vail held up a hand. "We don't for sure what went down with Tait. We can't jump to conclusions without facts. Important thing is, if we find Lukas, we might find Patrone. That's now our focus."

66

Taurus-Littrow Valley

DeSantos sat on a boulder watching the Russians. One cosmonaut always remained on station with the Resurs while the other three left on the rover. Thus far, there had been no alarms emanating from the remote Uzi had rigged. He hoped it was working.

Uzi and Carson had been updating him on how things were progressing. The fuel was nearly finished loading into the empty Apollo 17 tank and the unproven valve had performed well.

If Carson was right, they were only going to get 490 pounds. Even added to what they still had in their ascent stage tank, Issachar warned them it was going to be close: it was a delicate balance between amount of required fuel and the total weight of the craft.

They fastened the vessel to the LRV and transported it to the Raptor—which took a lot longer than they had hoped because of its weight. The increased strain on the batteries took its toll and Uzi had to make sure the solar panels were pointed directly at the sun at all times.

They arrived at the Raptor on the morning of their third day, dog tired, famished, and mentally spent. Even Stroud, after a four-hour nap in the cabin, was back in the Spider scouting areas for caesarium. Their deadline was approaching, but DeSantos said that if the time came where their supplies had run out—and that threshold would be exceeded in six hours—they would have to leave without running their tests on the caesarium; that portion of the mission would go unfulfilled.

Eisenbach agreed, though he was not pleased they were discussing this. He had expected them to locate caesarium and have their tests completed by the end of the first day or, at the latest, sometime during the second. But Stroud pointed out that his efforts were hampered considerably by the malfunction of the automated mining apparatus.

Uzi and Carson set about loading the half-filled ascent stage tank with the Chang'e fuel. They held their breath as they hooked up the coupling—but since NASA and the DOD had precise design specs for the Raptor's valve, they had much greater confidence that the joint here would be clean and successful.

It held and the fuel started moving at the expected flow rate.

"Santa, I'm headed back to you," Uzi said. "Be there in forty-five minutes if I push it."

"Push it, Boychick. After several hours of sitting on a boulder, my butt hurts more than the time I spent half a day on a camel."

UZI ARRIVED AS PROMISED. DeSantos, lacking sleep and food, closed his eyes a short time after settling himself into the LRV seat and was off in dreamland.

Three hours later, DeSantos stirred and woke up in time to see the Russian rover approaching, a small cloud of Moon dust surrounding each tire. He blinked a few times and worked his dry tongue, trying to shake off the cobwebs.

"They're coming from a completely different direction," Uzi said.

DeSantos used the handgrip on the side of the LRV's metal frame to reposition himself into a more erect posture. "Maybe they're having a tough time locating caesarium, so they tried another area."

"They seem to be heading right for us."

"Maybe Oleg wants to chat again."

Uzi twisted his torso toward DeSantos. "What's there left to talk about?"

My father.

The rover stopped twenty feet from the LRV and one of the cosmonauts climbed out. As he approached, he lifted his visor. DeSantos did likewise.

It was Oleg. He stopped a few paces away and stared at DeSantos, who sat there and looked right back at him. DeSantos knew he was giving him one last opportunity to accept their demands, and in turn they would release his father.

DeSantos gave no indication of an agreement. An awkward moment later, Oleg turned and walked away, got back into his rover and drove off toward the Resurs.

"What was that about?" Uzi asked.

DeSantos did not answer. He did not like keeping secrets from his friend, but he was reluctant to read Uzi into the situation with his father. Did Knox know what was going on? McNamara? If they knew, there was no way they would tell him. They would be afraid it would jeopardize the mission. In fact, they would specifically not tell Uzi, because it would be nearly impossible for him to keep a secret of that magnitude from DeSantos.

As DeSantos pondered this, the rover parked by the front strut of the Resurs. And the remote Uzi had programmed began vibrating and blinking.

"They've got it," Uzi said. "They found caesarium. Shit."

"Shit is right. Let's get back."

Uzi started the rover, swung a U-turn and headed toward the Raptor. "Assuming they know what they've got, they'll start prepping for liftoff. And since we've gotta be off the surface before they are—if we're gonna blow their ship—we don't have much time."

DeSantos grabbed the metal bar as the rover slid left and right on the loose dirt—which created a cloud in their field of vision because of the missing fender. "They've never seen caesarium before. They may not realize what they've got."

"If I'm them," Uzi said, "I'd run tests to be sure. If they're wrong and they leave, they can't turn around and come back."

DeSantos tapped a button on his helmet and changed the radio frequency. "Digger, Stroud, what's your status?"

"The fuel is loading," Carson said, "and everything's looking good. I've dumped some equipment and taken a weight reading. We're still over."

"How much longer till it's done loading?"

"Issachar says it shouldn't be long. Still not sure this fuel mixture will work. He had the engineers run simulations. One failed and one succeeded."

"How many minutes is 'shouldn't be long'?" Uzi asked.

"Suddenly got some place to be? You sound a little . . . I dunno, desperate."

"They've got caesarium. The Russians. Readings peaked as soon as they got back to their ship. Don't know what their next move is, but once they realize they've got what they came for, no reason to hang around. They'll probably high-tail it into orbit before we can stop them. They have no idea what we have planned."

"And," DeSantos said, "we've gotta lift off before they do."

"Not to mention that the range on our trigger remote isn't that great," Uzi said.

"Roger that. I'll keep you posted. You headed back?"

"ETA twenty-five minutes," Uzi said as he skidded a bit around a large boulder. Be ready to lift off ASAP. Cowboy, stop what you're doing and return to base—whether or not you've found caesarium. Nothing we can do about it. Just ran out of time."

They waited a moment but only the white noise of radio silence came over their headsets.

"Stroud," DeSantos said firmly. "Report."

Nothing.

The rover hit a rut and bottomed out on the hard-packed surface.

"What do you think, Santa?"

"I'm thinking this isn't good. Could be radio failure, but . . . something tells me we've got a problem."

Uzi swerved left to avoid a small crater and DeSantos nearly flew out of the rover—as it was, the journey was full of angles, ditches, and rocks. A paved road it was not. "Hang on, buddy."

DeSantos tapped his helmet to switch the radio channel. "Digger, any idea where Cowboy is?"

"Last location on his list. Around the Massif, Bear Mountain. Can't see him from here."

"But you don't know for sure."

"He's got the rover. Could be anywhere."

"Jesus," DeSantos said under his breath—but it still registered over the radio.

"You want me to go look? I do that, I have to leave the fuel tr—"

"No." DeSantos tapped his helmet again. "CAPCOM, this is Raptor. The Russians have caesarium and we need to lift off before they do. Cowboy's not responding. Last seen driving the Spider. Any way for you to locate the rover?"

"Copy that. Give us a moment."

Seconds felt like minutes when Maddox's voice came through clear and confident. Sending coordinates to your heads-up displays."

"Thanks much, CAPCOM." DeSantos activated the screen on the inside of his visor. "I see it. We're not far. Headed there now." He cut the line and said to Carson, "Finish transferring that fuel. We'll hit those coordinates and see what the problem is with Cowboy. Hopefully he's near the rover."

UZI GESTURED WITH HIS FREE HAND. "Gonna come up alongside the base of the South Massif. Location Bob gave us is consistent with what Digger thought. Bear Mountain, southeast."

Uzi swung by the back side of the foothills and stopped behind the Spider. They got out and skipped/shuffled forward.

"There," DeSantos said. "On the left."

As they approached, Uzi said, "Digger, we've got a visual. Located Cowboy. He's down. Repeat, he's down."

"Down?"

"Not moving," DeSantos said. "On our way."

"You need help?"

"Stay where you are. SITREP on the fuel transfer?"

"Like watching a pot boil."

"Go through our prelaunch checklist, get as much done as you can."

"Already on it," Carson said. "I should be ready to go as soon as we're gassed up."

They neared Stroud, who was lying on his left side facing a rocky outcropping.

"Fuck. His suit's depressurized."

They came up alongside him and DeSantos pulled Stroud onto his back—as best he could because of the thick backpack—and saw a shattered faceplate.

"Oh, man." Uzi turned away.

"You serious?" Carson's voice. "You guys aren't jerking me aro—"

"Digger," Uzi said, "I'm sorry. He's gone."

"And a crappy way to die, at that," DeSantos said.

"How?" Carson asked. "How'd it happen?"

Uzi glanced up and down Stroud's body. He raised his left hand toward DeSantos. "Don't touch anything. Don't move."

"Why?"

"Just listen to me. We've gotta treat this as a crime scene."

"Crime scene? Boychick, forget that FBI bullshit. We've gotta get back."

"I hear you. Go help Digger prep for launch. I need a few minutes. Something's not right."

"Until we know what happened to him, I'd rather not leave you alone while your back is turned. You should have someone on your six," he said, referring to his rear.

"Digger's by himself, he's in the Raptor. Better you check out the lander in case they sabotaged it. Or none of us is gonna get off this rock. If the Russians are responsible for Cowboy, they may not be done."

"I checked for an IED after our food went missing," Carson said. "We're clean."

"You sure?"

"I'm—yeah, I'm sure."

"Hurry up, Boychick. You've got two minutes." DeSantos stood erect, rested his right hand on the useless sidearm.

The suit was clinging tightly to Stroud's body since there was no longer any internal air pressure present. A rectangle of dirt covered Stroud's right thigh pocket. Uzi yanked open the Velcro closure on the pant leg but it was empty. "There was something small, long, and flat in here. Any idea?"

DeSantos stepped closer and took a look. "A box of some kind. The black Moon dirt created an outline in the suit material."

"Hey Digger, there was a flat metal box in Stroud's pocket. Probably eight or nine inches long, three wide, couple inches thick. Give or take."

"No idea."

Uzi checked the bulge in Stroud's other pocket and ripped it open. "Geiger counter."

"Fuel's almost done transferring over," Carson said. "Maybe another ten minutes."

"And that's our cue to finish up, Boychick. For all we know, Stroud just tripped and face planted."

"Yeah, yeah, yeah." Uzi turned on the device and the LEDs glowed brightly. "Shit."

"Caesarium? No way. He would've told us immed—"

"Obviously he found some." Uzi held it over Stroud's body and the readings were strongest in the vicinity of his thigh pocket. "And it looks like he was planning to take it back with us." Uzi leaned forward and looked at the black streaks that originated in the pocket and traversed the white suit material. It was as if someone pulled a dirty box out and dragged it up and across Stroud's body.

He touched the broken face plate, examining the fracture pattern in the glass, then ran his glove over the helmet just above the visor. There was a slight indentation. The surface was abraded and covered in Moon dust.

"We were tasked with running the tests *here*," Carson said, "and specifically told not to bring any back with us."

"Those were the orders." Uzi swiveled around and surveyed the area, then canted his head up the rock face to his right. He stood carefully and stepped around Stroud's body. *Boot tracks.* They were similar to the prints made by US pressure suit footwear, but possessed a key difference: aside from the parallel horizontal lines that ran from toe to heel, the ones he was looking at here had a vertical line down the center. He had seen this once before—at the Resurs. They were Russian.

He followed them: two sets from what he could tell. They were heading toward Stroud's body—as well as away. He skipped several more feet and around the bend and found tire tracks. No doubt the Russian rover.

"Uzi," DeSantos said. "Get back here. We've gotta go. Enough playing detective."

"This was deliberate, Santa. Cowboy was murdered."

"How do you figure?"

"No rocks on the ground near his body, so if he fell, he couldn't have struck his helmet on anything sharp and hard. These visors are made to withstand normal blows, for this very reason. Jack Schmitt fell a number of times on 17. I think someone swung a blunt object of some kind into Cowboy's face, denting the helmet and smashing the visor and faceplate."

"You sure?" Carson said over the radio. "I'm kind of blind here."

"As sure as I can be dressed in a pressure suit in a microgravity environment. On the Moon. Without proper equipment."

"Why not just shoot him?" DeSantos said. "They've got guns. Not like we'd hear it in our pressure suits."

"Because it'd be obvious they did it," Carson said. "And that it wasn't an accidental fall. They staged it to *look* like an accident. This way, even if we suspected them—maybe—we couldn't be sure. Obviously there's no way for them to know about Uzi's FBI background. You and I, we wouldn't have thought twice about it."

"We've gotta get going," DeSantos said. "Examining the crime scene isn't gonna bring him back. But unless we get off this rock soon, we're all gonna die here. Let's get his body onto the Spider."

"Uh, guys? Russian rover's headed for the Raptor. They're a distance away but you better get back here now. Headed straight for us. Looks like they're in a rush."

"How long do we have?" DeSantos asked.

"If you want me to figure their exact position," Carson said, "I have to stop what I'm doing. And right now, lifting off is my priority. But if their rover goes about as fast as the Spider and my guess is they're maybe three miles out right now . . . they'll be here in about eighteen minutes, give or take."

"And it'll take us fifteen to get back to the Raptor," Uzi said. "Get in. No time to get Cowboy's body."

"We can't just leave him h—"

"No time," Uzi said. "And no choice. Digger, fuel done?"

"Maybe another minute."

"This is bullshit," DeSantos said as he started toward the Spider, which was as Stroud had left it.

"No—the LRV's faster."

They got into the Moon buggy and Uzi accelerated. They instantly felt the pull of the vehicle as the four meshwork tires gripped the lunar dirt.

"Digger, how soon can we be airborne?" DeSantos asked.

"I'll get us up as fast as I can," Carson said. "Putting my helmet back on and depressurizing the cabin. But we haven't checked the weight. Or the weight distribution."

"We're two hundred pounds lighter," DeSantos said with disdain.

"I don't even know if this fuel will work. Or if we've got enough to get us into orbit."

"Bad enough they killed him," DeSantos said. "Goes against my core to leave him behind."

Uzi navigated around a crater at top speed, causing a slight lateral slip of their rear wheels.

"We've got no choice," Uzi said. "And we've got no time."

"Are we being cowards?" DeSantos asked. "We should stay, confront them. Stand and fight."

"We don't have usable weapons and they do. We've accomplished almost everything we needed to do here. The charge is set on their ship. We've gotta get off the surface before they do. Nothing to be gained by confronting them, as much as we want to. Assuming things go as planned, we'll have the final word."

"Assuming that, yeah. But what if those charges don't blow?"

Uzi kept his gaze on the path ahead. "Then we fly over their lander and cut our engines. And hope we can steer into the Resurs, destroy it."

A few moments of silence passed as Uzi navigated the landscape.

"Why do you think they killed Stroud?"

Uzi took some time to work it out as he moved the control stick left, then right, avoiding rocks and ruts. "They were going to take us out one or two at a time. Divide and conquer. They don't know what weapons we've got. And since we haven't been in one place at the same time, they can't kill all of us simultaneously. With as many of us out of the way as possible, the greater the chance they accomplish their mission. Nothing we can do to sabotage them. They eliminate the threat. Could be other explanations, but that's my take."

DeSantos was silent for a while, no doubt running that scenario through his filters. Finally he said, "Yeah. Makes sense." Concession in his voice, as if angry at himself for not figuring it out sooner. "Digger, we're two minutes out."

"Roger," Carson said. "Fuel's done. I'm commencing countdown. Computer will fight me because it won't let us open the hatch to let you in. I'll have to override it manually."

Uzi saw their lander ahead—and the cloud of dust being kicked up by the Russians as they approached.

He pulled the LRV in front of the Raptor, beside the ladder. They hopped off and started ascending the rungs, climbing as fast as they could. Uzi's hand slipped off twice and he almost went flying sideways.

Before Uzi squeezed through the hatch, he looked out at the Russian rover and dust cloud, both of which grew in size as they neared. "We'd better hurry."

DESANTOS GAVE UZI A SHOVE into the airlock. He followed a second later and cranked the door closed behind them.

The moment of truth had come. If Uzi was right about what happened with Stroud, the Russians stole the caesarium Stroud had found—so they now had the element. If they let them leave the surface, would Oleg keep his end of the deal and release his father? He chided himself for even entertaining the idea.

"Keep your helmets on," Carson said in their headsets. "Safety precaution against sudden depressurization."

Uzi hit a button and the airlock door slid apart. "You mean if the Russians shoot holes in our cabin?"

"Exactly."

As they entered, Carson was pressing virtual buttons on the control panel, re-securing the room.

DeSantos thought of Stroud—and knew Uzi was right. Given the situation, they didn't have a choice. But the concept of leaving no one behind was not just a hollow phrase. It meant something.

"T-minus three minutes," Carson said.

DeSantos looked out the small window that faced west. "And they're getting close. Too close."

"Soon as they see us lift off," Uzi said, "they've got two options. Shoot at us or return to the Resurs and take off. If I were them and I had the caesarium, I'd get the hell off this rock. But I'm not them."

"Our walls are only a quarter inch thick," Carson said. "Like a piece of glass. It's all about weight and strength. The Apollo LMs were some kind of thin Mylar you could poke a finger through. Ours is carbon fiber—but I've got no idea if can survive gunfire."

"It'd have to be too thick," Uzi said. "And too heavy. They hit us, we could be fucked. It might disperse the force of the round but at the very least it'd crack the shell."

"That's why we've got our suits on," Carson said.

"If they start shooting," Uzi said, "losing our atmosphere would be the least of our problems. Damaging our electronics, hitting the computer or fuel tank—"

"I know the risks," Carson said as he worked the touch screen. "T-minus two minutes," he said, the digits on the LCD rapidly counting down the seconds.

"Longest two minutes of my life," DeSantos said.

"Hopefully it won't be the *last* two minutes of your life."

DeSantos craned his neck again to position his oversize helmet for a look out the window.

"You have the remote control for the charge you planted?" Carson asked.

DeSantos patted the front pocket of his suit but did not answer.

"Santa," Uzi said. "You got it?"

"Got it." He again thought of his dad. If he blew up their ship, if what Oleg had told them was true, he would be killing his father as well.

"T-minus ninety seconds," Carson said. "What are they doing?"

"They're slowing," DeSantos said. "I think they realize we're about to lift off."

Uzi grabbed hold of a metal bar. "Moment of truth."

"Do we know for sure the Russians got the caesarium?"

"The Geiger counter lit up, Santa. They have it. I'm guessing the sample Stroud had in his pocket is what they returned to the Resurs with. That's what set off the alarm we rigged. They'd just come from killing Cowboy. That's why they came from a different direction."

"Even if you're wrong," Carson said, "odds are they'll find it after we leave. We've gotta destroy their ship to prevent them from leaving. We don't have a choice."

I'm beginning to hate that saying, DeSantos thought.

"Fifteen seconds," Carson said. "Secure your harness. Prepare for ignition." The engine rumbled and the vehicle vibrated.

DeSantos hesitated. He did not trust the Russians and—almost on cue—the cosmonauts got off their rover and brought something up in front of them. "Gun!"

The numerals on the red LED clock tumbled lower. "T-minus twelve. Ten. Nine."

A concussive force struck the wall facing the Russian rover. Then a second and a third. It cracked and a chunk broke inward.

"What if they hit our engine?" Uzi asked.

"We've only got one," Carson said. "Pray they miss." He grasped the sides of the control panel and held tight. "We have ignition."

A vibration shook the craft—and DeSantos saw a sparking fire through the new "window" in the Raptor's side.

"Two. One."

DeSantos felt a hard rumble beneath his boots, followed by a forceful upward lift.

They rose rapidly off the surface. The sensation was palpable as if something was exerting tremendous force, pulling them down into the floorboard.

"Forty feet," Carson said. "We'll be clear of the explosion radius in five seconds."

"Do it," Uzi said, turning to DeSantos. "Blow it."

But DeSantos did not move. He continued to stare out the hole in the fuselage.

"Santa. Blow the charges!"

"Yeah, I know."

"What the hell's the problem?" Carson asked. "Do it!"

"They tried to kill us, Santa. We've got our order—"

"I know."

"You keep saying that."

"Fifty-five feet," Carson said.

"We don't know the range of that remote," Uzi said, his speech quickening. "If it doesn't transmit the detonate order, we're fucked."

But what about his father?

Uzi grabbed for the remote, but DeSantos yanked his hand away, closed his eyes, and pushed the button.

A long second later, a concussive force shot skyward, shaking their fragile craft as the engine continued its burn and powered it higher against the Moon's light gravity.

67

616 23rd Street NW
Washington, DC

Vail stole away from her nonstop schedule to have lunch with her son Jonathan at the Potbelly Sandwich Shop on the George Washington University campus.

She had just finished her skinny chicken salad sandwich when her OPSIG phone buzzed.

"You gotta get that?" Jonathan asked.

Vail frowned. "I do. Can you give me a minute?"

"Mind if I get a berry smoothie?"

"Go for it." She handed him her credit card. "And get me an oatmeal chocolate chip cookie."

As Jonathan walked off toward the counter, Vail brought the phone to her ear. "Yeah."

"Sorry to interrupt lunch with your son," Rusakov said, "but I think this is something you'd want to know right away."

"What'd you find?"

"We were running that list of known associates, right? Well, a name showed up in an unexpected place. Seems that Bill Tait employed a guy off the books for some freelance work nine years ago."

Vail glanced around, cognizant of who was around her. In DC, you could be sitting beside just about anyone—a foreign dignitary, a spy, a senator, FBI support personnel, Secret Service agent . . . the list was endless—especially so close to the White House. The "threats," in this case, were many. She guarded her words carefully.

"How'd you find that?"

"Total accident. A note on the margin of the checkbook, a stub about a misspelled name. Otherwise, I doubt we would've known to dig deeper."

"Okay," Vail said. "Sometimes we need breaks like that to solve a case. And that person's name?"

"Gavin Stroud."

Vail almost dropped her phone. "The astr—the um, the guy who's working with our friends right now?"

"Yes."

"Could there be someone else with the same name?"

"Wishful thinking, but no."

Vail swallowed hard. *What does this mean? Maybe nothing. Maybe everything.* She sat there a moment, suddenly numb.

"Mom," Jonathan said. He was standing there holding the smoothie and cellophane wrapped cookie. "You okay?"

Vail looked over at him and realized her jaw was slack. Her mouth was cotton-dry. She forced a smile. "All's good, honey. I'm fine." She felt for the back of her chair and sat down gently.

"I know, that threw me too," Rusakov said.

"Why didn't we know about this?"

"It was off the books. And it was only a few months. When he went to work for OPSIG, he didn't disclose it and they didn't catch it during the vetting process—or they caught it and didn't think it was important. At the time, it probably wasn't—it's only in the context of what we know now that it's significant. It wasn't a red flag."

"Is there a way to get word to our friends?"

"At this point Knox and McNamara think it may make more sense to let things play out and not confront him with it. Good news is that they're now off the surface. I can give you a better SITREP when you're back."

"Sounds good."

"Oh—nothing concrete connecting Tait to Patrone or Stroud. He may be wrapped up in this, but other than speculation, we're not finding anything."

"A guy like that, with a lot to lose, covers his tracks. Even if he's involved on some level, we may never be able to connect him. I'll—" She looked at Jonathan, who was sucking on his straw and watching his mother's face carefully. "I'll be back as soon as I can."

Vail ended the call and tore open the cellophane packaging.

"So," Jonathan said, studying her face. "Unexpected news?"

Vail took a bite of the cookie and laughed nervously. "Playing detective with me?"

Jonathan shrugged. "The best start young. Weren't you like twenty-one?"

Vail rolled her eyes. She had hoped her son would change his mind about going into law enforcement. But that wish had thus far not come true. At the moment, however, she had other things to occupy her concerns.

"I've gotta go, sweetie. You mind?"

"I have to get to class. But thanks for lunch. I'm glad you were able to get away."

"Me too." She gave him a kiss on the cheek, then stuffed the cookie back in the wrapper and handed it to him before she jogged toward her car.

68

Lunar Orbit

You okay?" Uzi asked, studying DeSantos's face through the visor.

"Me? Hell yeah. Mission accomplished."

"Approaching Patriot," Carson said. "Uzi, can you give me a hand with docking?"

"Um . . . yeah." Uzi turned and faced the touch screen beside Carson.

Carson talked him through the process—which was largely automated by the flight computer software and high resolution cameras—but given the malware issues, Carson was not taking any chances. He watched over the instrumentation and made sure the readings were logical and expected. The docking went off without a hitch and they opened the connecting hatch.

"Say good-bye to our home away from home," Uzi said. "Raptor served us well."

"More like a Motel Six," Carson said. "Next time let's go for a Marriott. M Club."

Uzi chuckled. He looked over, expecting to share the laugh with his buddy, but DeSantos was stone faced, as if he had not been paying attention. "That was funny, Santa. You sure you're okay?"

He turned to them. "Doing great. Let's get back inside Patriot and blast this thing to bits. Motel Six is right."

"T-minus nineteen minutes ten seconds," Carson said. "Let's get moving. We don't want to be anywhere near that baby when she blows."

Rather than leaving the Raptor in orbit until its systems shut down over a period of months—sending the dead hulk crashing into the lunar surface—they rigged the Raptor and the descent stage with their remaining explosive charges. The bombs would reduce the former to twisted fragments of space waste and the latter to lunar rubble.

They completed the docking, transferred their backpacks to the crew module, then took their seats and watched the Raptor get smaller as they pulled away.

With Stroud gone, Uzi took the copilot's chair beside Carson, who had assumed the role of mission commander.

They left the Raptor behind as they swung around the Moon, preparing to fire their engine for two and a half minutes while over the far side. This added three thousand feet per second to their velocity and set them on a return course to Earth—a maneuver called TEI, or trans-Earth injection.

Four minutes later, the Raptor served out its useful life by blasting into thousands of tiny pieces.

"T-minus twelve seconds to TEI," Carson said.

The computer set their course and the powerful engine lit up as planned. They felt the push back into their seats as the Gs took hold.

"Pressures are good," Carson said two minutes into the burn. "Total attitude looks good. Standing by for engine off. Five seconds."

"Four . . . three . . . two . . . one," Uzi said. "Engine off."

They were weightless again.

Eleven minutes later, they had passed around the dark side of the Moon and regained comms with mission control.

"Nice to have you back," Bob Maddox said. "Return to Earth trajectory looks real good. Nice work."

"Hector and I would like to take credit," Uzi said, "but we were just passengers on this flight."

"Patriot," Maddox said, "I'm going to turn the mic over to Director Knox."

"Congratulations, gentlemen," Knox said. "We've activated the ring of satellite lasers and the DOD will be test firing them at the Spider. All goes well, there'll be little sign left of our mission footprint."

"Understood," Carson said.

"CAPCOM, I need a moment with the men," Knox said. "Secure channel, please. Just me and the crew."

There was radio silence—leading DeSantos to fear they had lost comms again—until Knox's voice filled the speakers. "Patriot, do you read?"

"Affirmative," Uzi said. "You've got me, Hector, and Digger."

"I'll be brief. Hector, you need to know some news has broken. There's no easy way to say it, so let me just come right out with it. Your father has been kidnapped. We're reasonably certain the Russians are behind it. I believe they did it to leverage you into sabotaging your mission so they could be assured of bringing the caesarium back."

There was silence.

Uzi studied his face.

"Patriot, are you still with me?"

"We are," DeSantos said. "Thank you for telling me, sir. Is he—is my father still alive?"

"We've got reason to believe he is . . ." Static interrupted his sentence. " . . . And trying to . . . but . . ." The remainder of Knox's comments were garbled into incoherence.

Uzi unbuckled and floated down to the seat beside DeSantos. "You knew. How?"

DeSantos kept his gaze ahead, his demeanor steady. "Oleg told me. Just like Knox said, he wanted me to cut a deal. My father's life for the caesarium."

"Are you serious?" Carson asked. "You didn't think that was an important thing to share with us?"

"Why didn't you say something?" Uzi said.

"What good would it have done?" DeSantos's voice was distant, emotionless. "It was irrelevant."

"It was anything but irrelevant, Santa. If you're honest with yourself, you'll know that's true."

"That's why you hesitated during liftoff," Carson said. "You were thinking of not blowing up their ship."

"I was thinking of my dad," DeSantos said. "But I was never seriously considering letting the cosmonauts live. They couldn't. We couldn't let them bring caesarium to Earth. My father's basically a POW. He spent his whole life as a soldier. He knows the deal. I'm sure he'd understand."

"Bullshit. *Sounds* good—and from his point of view, you're probably right. That's exactly what he'd think. But not from your perspective. He's your father."

"Spoken by the guy who doesn't talk to his anymore."

Uzi worked his jaw before composing himself. "If my dad's life was in danger, all that . . . stuff gets tossed aside. I'd do everything I can to help him, to save his life."

DeSantos looked at him. "Including looking the other way, harming your team, your country, the world? Don't lie to me, Uzi. There's no way you'd do that."

Uzi sat there silent for a moment, the very slight movement of the ship—now traveling a mere six thousand feet per second—allowing him to think. "You're right. I wouldn't. But I'd find a way of changing the rules. A way of keeping Russia from getting the caesarium *and* getting your dad back. Alive."

◆ ◆ ◆

"LOST THE SIGNAL AGAIN," Maddox said, studying his screen.

Knox kicked the chair. "Just get me through to them! Can't you people keep a stable conn—"

A command and control technician flinched at the sudden display of anger. "We're being jammed, sir."

"Who's jamming us?"

"Working on it. We'll have an answer for you in a minute."

McNamara lifted the secure phone and made a call. While it rang, he cupped the mouthpiece. "Bob, why don't you just switch to a different antenna?"

"Not sure we can."

Eisenbach and Kirmani entered the room. Knox explained—along with a few not-so-carefully-chosen expletives—what had occurred.

Maddox leaned back in his chair and canted his head toward Knox. "It's the Russians."

Kirmani balled a fist. "Of course it is."

"In three hours we can hand off to our antenna array in Australia, but there's some kind of problem with the transmitter." Maddox leaned forward and made eye contact with an engineer a few seats to his right. "We're trying to figure it out."

Knox ground his jaw. "Any danger to our men?"

Maddox shook his head. "This comms breakdown is on our end, not Patriot's. I think they're okay."

Knox blew air through his lips. "Fine. Just . . . do what you can to reestablish communications."

"Most of the flight is automated from here on out," McNamara said. "Handled by the computer. That should make me feel better. But it doesn't."

"No," Knox said. "It sure doesn't."

69

Space Flight Operations Facility
Vandenberg Air Force Base

The president has been fully briefed?" McNamara asked. He, Eisenbach, Kirmani, Earl Tasset, and Douglas Knox faced the large screen, where director of Central Intelligence Lawrence Bolten, director of the National Security Agency Elliot Stern, and the new White House chief of staff Wilton Adams were appearing via secure video feed.

The Space Flight Ops center was adjacent to mission control—so they were not far away if new information on the Patriot became available.

"And President Nunn is reluctant to take action against Russia?" Eisenbach asked. "Did I understand you right?"

Adams held up a hand and dropped his chin. "Please, gentlemen. I realize this is not what you wanted to hear, b—"

"Wanted to hear?" Eisenbach said. "We've got three men hurtling toward Earth and we can't assist them, let alone coordinate recovery procedures. Or even simply *talk* with them."

"Problem is," Adams said, "that we can't start a conflict with Russia. We're culpable. They're convinced our men killed their cosmonauts, who were on a peaceful, exploratory mission and—"

"Bullshit," McNamara said. "They were there to get caesarium before we restricted access to the Moon. They came armed and they murdered one of our men. Not to mention they used a network of spies to plant dangerous malware on our spacecraft."

"I understand all that."

"Does the president?" Tasset asked.

Adams maintained his composure, which was more than McNamara could say about his own burgeoning temper.

"I assure you," Adams said evenly, "this was all discussed with him."

"Besides," Knox said, "Russia jamming our communication arrays is an act of war in and of itself. Two of those antennas are located inside military installations."

"The president and his advisers feel there's enough blame to go around. No one's innocent here. We were walking a fine line in deploying the lasers in lunar orbit and launching a black op against the Chinese lander. There's no precedent for any of that. And the spy Russia had in place was technically working for a private company, not the government."

"C'mon," Tasset said. "That's bullshit and you know it. The Russian president stood to make a mint on that mission. And he's in charge of the space program. Ronck didn't launch a mission to the Moon. Russia did."

Adams held up a hand. "Yes, Russia intended to bring back the most powerful WMD known to man. The president understands that. But we're not blameless here. And when you live in a glass house, you can't throw stones. And right now, there are wall-to-wall windows all around us."

Eisenbach leaned both palms on the table in front of him. "And he wants us to stand down and not engage them? What the hell are we supposed to do?"

Adams shrugged. "Find some other way of communicating with the Patriot."

Kirmani laughed. "Oh, of course. Why didn't we think of that?" His grin evaporated. "It's easier said than done, Mr. Adams."

"Is there an imminent threat to our astronauts?" Adams asked.

"No," Eisenbach said. "But given the Russian malware they've dealt with, who knows what's coming?"

"Yes," Adams said with a frown. "We certainly don't know what's coming. This entire incident has been an indictment of US intelligence, if not a complete failure. You've left us blind and deaf to what's going on."

Tasset physically took a step back. He opened his mouth to speak but said nothing.

Bolten bowed his head. "Understood. We've already been spanked. But—"

"No buts. Find another way to get in touch with your men or talk with them after they splash down."

"So that's it? We sit on our asses waiting for something to go wrong?" Kirmani asked.

Adams's face went taut. "Think about what will happen if the media gets hold of what really went on up there. We *can't* have a war break out over this—definitely not over jammed communications. It could escalate very quickly."

"I disagree," Tasset said. "Thing is, *nothing* would happen. Both Russia and China suffer from insecurity. They desperately want to be seen as superpowers. So neither would want to publicly acknowledge their lunar missions because they'd both have to admit they ended in failure."

"Not to mention that they were trying to mine nuclear material for a powerful weapon," Bolten added.

"Exactly," Tasset said. "So Russia and China will keep quiet. As will the US. We don't want to confirm the existence of a dangerous element that could wreak havoc in the wrong hands. People would freak out, to say the least. So *we'll* keep quiet. Nothing will be released by anyone even resembling the truth. Meantime, negotiations will begin, quietly, on a new Moon treaty that specifically prohibits mining of caesarium—and creates an independent inspecting body that forensically examines any mission that returns from the Moon."

"I'm glad you both have it all figured out," Adams said. "But things don't always go the way you think they will. The president's made his decision. Thank you for your opinions."

The men were left staring at a blank screen. Finally Eisenbach threw down his remote. "We're wasting time. We need to find a way to reach our men."

70

DEEP SPACE
RETURN TO EARTH

Sixty-one hours passed uneventfully. DeSantos, Uzi, and Carson took turns catching up on their sleep, one remaining awake and working on his classified mission report while monitoring the Patriot's progress as the others sawed wood.

Uzi stretched his arms and took a deep, cleansing breath.

"Good morning," DeSantos said. "Or good evening. I don't know what the hell time it is."

"You just have to check the clock."

"If it mattered, I would have. I've been busy."

Uzi shoved Carson's shoulder.

He moaned, then rubbed his eyes. "My entire body's sore. And my hands are still chapped from those suit gloves."

"What's our status?" Uzi asked as he pulled himself into his seat.

"Still no contact with mission control," DeSantos said. "At 41,000 miles from Earth I entered in our flight correction manually, as you wanted."

"You keyed in hash-65, ENTER, ENGAGE, for an Atlantic splash-down," Carson said. "Right?"

"Correct. 'Command up' to lengthen by 215 nautical miles. I was paying attention."

"And where are we now?" Uzi asked.

"At 13,294 miles. Around 35,000 we started to get more pull from the Earth's gravity."

"I feel it," Uzi said as he floated over to the aft window. "Definitely moving downhill. We'll be in the water before we know it."

"Okay." Carson stood up. "Let's get ready for splashdown and recovery. Everything needs to be stowed. And I want to have our manual checklists in front of us in case something weird happens with avionics. Now is no time for a software glitch—intentional or unintentional."

"Amen to that," DeSantos said.

71

OPSIG Operations Center
The Pentagon

Vail, Rusakov, and Rodman were huddled over a computer terminal as the data came in.

"It's confirmed," Vail said. "Get the SecDef on the line."

Rodman lifted the handset and a moment later was talking with McNamara.

"You've got all of us here," McNamara said. "Directors Knox and Tasset, General Eisenbach, and Captain Bansi Kirmani. Please, Hot Rod . . . tell us you've got something."

"I believe we're close to locating General DeSantos," Rodman said. "We've found evidence of a private jet with a diplomatic call sign leaving a small airport in New York. We've been tracking the transponder."

"How can we trust that data?" Eisenbach said. "Wouldn't they *disable* the transponder so we couldn't do exactly what you just did?"

"I asked the same question," Vail said. "I spoke with the FAA and NORAD and here's the deal. Something bad has to happen for the FAA and NORAD to monitor every flight plan. That 'something' was the kidnapping of a decorated US general. So that's the good news."

"What's the bad news?" Tasset said.

"It's like looking for a needle in a haystack."

"But if they're monitoring every single flight, I don't see how—"

"Let me put it in perspective," Rodman said. "Let's say they took off in a private jet from a small airfield on the East Coast. Small, but not too small. Better to hide in plain sight—because if they turned off their transponder, Canada, the US, the UK, and Iceland air traffic controllers will all get a warning alarm that they just lost an aircraft. But if they keep it on, they're one of 270 airliners in the air . . . 1,300 flights a day, 54 flights per hour."

"The needle in a haystack," Tasset said.

"Right. So if Panorama Flight Service files a flight plan from White Plains, New York, to somewhere in western Europe, like Keflavik, Iceland, that wouldn't raise an alarm. If it'd been White Plains to Russia, the FAA would've notified NORAD. This way, making a stop in Iceland and then filing another flight plan from Iceland to Russia looks benign."

"So is that what they did?" Knox asked.

"Yes," Rodman said. "They took off in an Embraer Legacy 650 at 0300 and arrived in Keflavik around noon, cruising at .85 Mach at an altitude of 45,000 feet. They got handed off from New York Center to Gander Center to Icelandic Center, then Prestwick Center. They landed in Russia—"

"Where in Russia?"

Rodman laughed. "I'm waiting for that information as we speak."

"Soon as you get it, let me know. That's probably where they're holding the general—there or somewhere nearby."

An encrypted message hit Rodman's computer. "Here we go." He drew his chin back. "Interesting." He pointed at the screen and Rusakov nodded.

"Sirs," Rusakov said, "satellite data shows it landed at an airfield one hundred kilometers northwest of St. Petersburg, Russia. Veshevo air base."

"Why is that interesting?"

"Veshevo's an old, abandoned cold war–era airfield. Last I heard, the runways and military buildings were crumbling, overgrown with foliage."

"Good place to bring a prisoner, to hold him without anyone knowing," McNamara said. "You sure about that info?"

"Confirmed with CIA and Air Force satellites," Rusakov said. "The plane landed in Leningrad Oblast. That's where the old abandoned air base is located."

"Give us a minute," McNamara said. He muted the mic, then huddled with Knox, Tasset, and Eisenbach.

A moment later, Knox lifted a phone handset while McNamara pressed the audio button. "Hot Rod, you and Alexandra will go with Team 4 and bring back General DeSantos. Flight leaves Andrews in thirty minutes. Chopper will be hot on the roof in ten."

Rodman rose from his chair. "Yes sir."

"Alive," McNamara said. "We want him back alive. The men holding him . . . don't afford them the same luxury."

THE SPECIALLY OUTFITTED STEALTH BLACK HAWKS, long rumored to exist—called "unicorns" by some because they had never been seen—accidentally made their appearance on the world stage when one crashed during the covert SEAL mission that disposed of Osama bin Laden.

Its newer-generation cousin, boasting high-tech absorbent material to lower its radar signature and sound-suppressing technology to quiet the rotor noise, left Finland air space traveling at its top speed of 151 knots. It traversed Lake Ladoga using very low-altitude nap-of-the-earth flying to minimize detection by ground-based radar, enemy aircraft, and surveillance and control systems. Nine men and one woman fast-roped into a clearing in the dark without incident and began a three-mile hike from the landing zone to their target area.

Two hours ago, a Global Hawk aerial surveillance drone equipped with infrared imagers flew above the Veshevo air base at nearly 60,000 feet. Before returning to Finland to avoid detection—which would tip off the Russians that the US knew where the general was being held—it showed six human signatures moving amongst the structures.

An hour after touching down, the ten OPSIG operators cut through the links of a barbed wire fence and entered the compound. It was overgrown with dense tree cover and poorly maintained—if it was maintained at all.

They advanced through the base systematically, moving toward the location where satellite imagery showed the buildings that were most likely to contain the general and his captors. According to their intel, there were officer houses and apartments, hostels for staff, and administration buildings.

An hour later, they were closing on a crumbling two-story white brick structure painted with green blotches that looked like crude attempts at camouflage. They surrounded it and looked for signs of activity. There was nothing—no interior lights, no voices.

Rodman inserted an optical camera and looked around. The room was empty. He repeated this at regular intervals until he had covered the entire first floor.

He reported his findings, then said, "We're going in. Ready to breach front door on my mark."

They planned to use a stealth approach, since there were other buildings nearby. If they took a bull in a china shop approach, and their tangos were in the adjacent structures, things would escalate quickly—something they very much wanted to avoid.

They rapidly infiltrated the space. A minute later they had cleared the floor and half the team headed up the stairs.

Their SITREP: nothing. It did not look like anyone had been in there in years.

“On to the next building,” Rusakov whispered into her mic.

72

Approach to Earth

DeSantos opened a floor panel and grabbed one of the compact rucksacks to stow it away—but the bag had more weight than expected. "Digger, what've you got in here?"

"Food, Dopp kit, underwear, medical gear, mission checklists from the first leg. Why?"

"Feels heavier than it should. Obviously we're weightless, so it's not heavy per se, but—"

"I know what you mean."

Carson floated over, unzipped it, and peered inside. "What the hell's this?" He reached in and pulled out a flat metal container.

"Looks like a small safe deposit box," Uzi said. "Hang on. That's—that's about the same size and shape as the one that was taken from Cowboy's pocket when he was killed."

DeSantos flipped the four latches around its perimeter and lifted the lid.

They all leaned forward for a look.

"Is that what I think it is?" Carson asked. He felt the sides of the thick box. "It's heavy, so to speak, because it's lead-lined."

Uzi quickly shut the cover. He pulled open another panel, removed his own rucksack, and rooted out a portable Geiger counter. He switched it on and shared a look with each of them. "Caesarium. Digger, what the hell?"

"Don't look at me. I didn't put it there. How would I have gotten hold of it anyway? Cowboy was the only one using the mining equipment."

"So he must've stuck it in your backpack," DeSantos said. "Why?"

"To deflect suspicion from Cowboy to Digger in case it was found," Uzi said.

"Deniability," Carson said. "I get that. But why'd he take it in the first place? We were only supposed to run a battery of tests. We were specifically ordered not to bring it back with us. Cowboy, he just wouldn't disregard orders like that."

"First thought," Uzi said, "is that he was going to sell it to Russia or China. Or North Korea or Iran."

"He was a decorated spec ops soldier," Carson said. "A SEAL. The best of the best. No way would he have done something like that."

"Option two," Uzi said, "is that he was working for someone else."

Carson slammed his hand on the bulkhead. "No fucking way. I'm telling you. I knew the guy real well. I mean, you work with an operator, you know him on the battlefield. What he's made of, how he thinks. But you socialize with him, you hang out together, you get to know his family . . . you know who he *is*. At his core, what's in his heart. Follow me?"

"I do," DeSantos said. "And I agree. A guy like that, no way would he sell out his country. For any amount of money."

Uzi kept his gaze out the windows, where there was nothing but stars and the Earth: a stark, high contrast ball of color set against a background of blackness. "Okay, then not a foreign country. Not an enemy. What about the CIA?"

They looked at one another.

DeSantos cleared his throat. "Regardless of who he was working for, we've got caesarium on board. And we have to deal with it."

Carson laughed. "Deal with it? We'll be splashing down in forty-five minutes. What do you suggest we do?"

"Dump it," DeSantos said. "Soon as we hit the water, we'll open the hatch and drop it in the ocean. It's heavy, it'll sink."

"And how long till we get a leak of radioactive material in the water?" Carson said. "It's shielded but probably not water tight—certainly not at higher pressures. We should turn it over to OPSIG and let them dispose of it responsibly."

"We all know what'll happen," DeSantos said. "We'd be handing the Department of Defense the ability to build the most powerful weapon of all time. It'll be deemed too valuable to get rid of. The best of intentions don't guarantee the best results."

"We can dump it here, now," Uzi said.

"Boychick, we're traveling 25,000 miles per hour. We can't just open the window and toss it out."

"Actually, we can. We make sure everything's secured—which we're doing anyway for reentry. We get our gloves and helmets on and pressurize the pumpkin suits, then depressurize the cabin. Open the hatch, dump it out, seal her up again and repressurize."

DeSantos turned to Carson. "Is he right? Can we do that?"

"It's been done before," Carson said. "Apollo did this during the last few missions. On the way back to Earth, they did an EVA outside the command module to retrieve film and data records from compartments in the service module."

"We don't have a lot of time," Uzi said. "Let's do it."

"There *is* risk," Carson said. "Apollo didn't do it anywhere near this close to Earth. If we can't get the hatch closed, it jams, whatever—we'll be incinerated as soon as we hit the atmosphere."

"Now there's a lovely image," DeSantos said. "Barbecued ribs. And breasts. And thighs, and—"

"But it's got another advantage," Uzi said. "Momentum will carry the box into the atmosphere and it'll burn up. No radioactive space waste. Plus, if it's just floating around in space, it could potentially be retrieved. This way, it's history."

"Might not be that simple," Carson said. "Assuming it's like standard fission material—uranium or plutonium—it'd need to be assembled and compressed to cause an explosion. Obviously this won't happen when it burns up in the atmosphere, but it could spread lots of radioactive material around."

"You mean like a dirty bomb," DeSantos said.

"Potentially. But there's not that much of it, so . . . there's that. Worse case, exposure will be minimal."

"There's no perfect solution," Uzi said, looking down at the box. "Just one that's not as bad as the others."

"If that's our decision," DeSantos said, "we'd better hurry."

They quickly went about getting their helmets and gloves locked in place and the suits pressurized—and made sure everything was secured.

"We've got two minutes to get this done," Carson said.

By design, the crew module was coming in "blunt end forward," meaning the convex, wider undersurface of the vehicle was going to hit the atmosphere first. The ablative heat shield, built to absorb and deflect the intense frictional 5,000 degrees Fahrenheit heat by charring, melting, and expelling dangerous gases, was only located on the bottom of the spacecraft.

"We're ass forward, heading toward the fire. Hurry up and get that thing open."

DeSantos moved to the forward hatch, the one at the nose of the Orion crew module where they had docked with the Raptor, and through which they had climbed after docking. He worked the gears, unlocked it, and swung the door open into space.

Uzi handed him the box and DeSantos pushed it out into the black void. It tumbled wildly end over end, following the Patriot down toward Earth.

"Close it up!" Uzi said.

"Hey Hector." Carson was at his console, working the touch screen—a more difficult task with the gloves on. "You sure you keyed in the correct command?"

"Positive. Hash-65, ENTER, ENGAGE. Command up." DeSantos pulled the hatch closed but it bounced open. "Shit. Uzi, give me a hand. I can't seat it."

Uzi propelled himself alongside DeSantos, grabbed hold of the bulkhead, and reopened the door. He swung it shut again and it struck the coupling lip but did not engage. He grunted, repeated the procedure, and cursed.

"Get that thing closed," Carson said. "Entering outer atmosphere in ten seconds. Nine. Eight. Seven."

Despite the cooling air coming through his suit, DeSantos was perspiring profusely.

Uzi went through the process again and it clicked into place.

"Four. Three."

"Try it now."

DeSantos cranked the hatch mechanism. "Done! Locked down."

Uzi let go and floated backward. "Thank God."

"And not a second too soon," Carson said. "Get your belts on."

The noise level rose dramatically and a colorful light show began outside the windows: a central flare of orange-yellow gave way to outer tinges of purples and blue-greens. Against the black of space, the flames were dramatic.

"Why'd you ask me about the code I entered?" DeSantos said as he turned away from the brilliant display of colors to engage his restraint.

"Because we're not coming down in the Atlantic. Our entry corridor's now the Pacific. And if this data is right—which is obviously a big 'if'—we'll be splashing down not in US waters but in international waters, pretty damn close to China. And Russia's Red Banner Pacific fleet in Vladivostok."

"I'm sure this is part of the training I never got to," DeSantos said, "but why can't we just correct our trajectory back to the Atlantic?"

"We've got eight reaction control system pods on the Patriot," Carson said. "But they're for making all the critical maneuvers *before* we enter the atmosphere, so we hit it at just the right angle. It helps us stay right in the center of our entry corridor, an angle of 6.5 degrees below the horizon. Too shallow, off by tenths of a degree, and we'd skip off the atmosphere. Too steep and we'd burn up."

"So the pods have already fired," Uzi said.

"Right. They've done their job. Our trajectory was set 30,000 miles ago. Too late now. Laws of physics."

"So the command I entered. It got changed? More malware?"

"Looks like it," Uzi said. "It was designed to take the data input—an Atlantic Ocean landing—and change it to a Pacific splashdown, as far north of the equator as possible. Close to China and Russia."

"You think they're coming for us?" DeSantos asked.

"I'd bet one of them is, Santa. And since Russia's the one that developed the malware, my money's on them."

"Oleg was convinced we were bringing caesarium back with us."

"So they think we've got caesarium on board. Since their Moon mission failed, they see this as another shot at getting it."

"That's just terrific," Carson said. "Let's hope the Navy and Air Force know that."

73

Space Flight Operations Facility
Vandenberg Air Force Base

Although the Navy and Air Force had been out of communication with the Patriot, they were tracking its progress utilizing every bit of data they could collect from multiple sources—and there were a lot of them spread across the globe.

Assets that had been deployed to the Atlantic were recalled to base and West Coast vessels were set in motion.

Since the Navy, Air Force, and NASA had practiced the Orion recovery many times in the Pacific during the spacecraft's development, they had perfected the procedure. But what they had not trained for was having to ramp up at a moment's notice. And they had never anticipated having to simultaneously engage, and fend off, the Chinese and/or Russian military.

Fortunately, the United States had run drills every year as part of its war games and strategic readiness for potential incursions by an enemy force.

But as the situation unfolded, it became clear that the Russians—because they had created the malware that sent Patriot off course—knew where the capsule was headed and where it would splash down.

"Status," Eisenbach said as he entered the ops center, which occupied a large, low-lit room adjacent to the Space Flight Operations facility. His gaze immediately found the humongous wall-size display mounted at the front of the room, which showed real-time satellite imagery of the Pacific Ocean.

The Air Force major kept his eyes on his dual-monitor readout. "Russian aircraft carrier Admiral Kuznetsov is now 166 nautical miles from the revised splashdown site, North 8 03.00 by East 159 51.00. The Kuznetsov just launched four Su-33 Flanker fighter jets, which should be on station in seventeen minutes."

Eisenbach leaned forward to get a better look at the major's screen. "Go on."

"We've sent the Reagan Task Force from Johnston Atoll. At 171 miles out, they launched an MV-22 Osprey with divers on board to secure the Patriot. Four F-18s took off three minutes ago and will arrive exactly when the Su-33s arrive. That 4-ship will secure the skies over and around the splashdown site and remain on station above the target for ten to fifteen minutes. Another four F-18s are due to leave the deck in twelve minutes. That second 4-ship will relieve the first and allow retrograde back to the carrier."

Eisenbach rocked back on his heels. "And that'll give the Osprey at least fifteen minutes to drop the divers, orbit/hover over the Patriot while the divers extract the crew, and then egress back to the fleet."

"Yes sir. A third and fourth 4-ship will launch fifteen minutes apart. All four teams will rotate at regular intervals to secure the vacant Patriot crew module until the Reagan arrives on station in six and a half hours. The USS *Anchorage,* which is specially outfitted for towing the crew module into his well deck, is approximately 190 nautical miles out. Seven and a half hours at top speed."

"So we're gonna have a shootout," Kirmani said, coming up behind Eisenbach.

“Looks that way. But why the Russians are so interested in the Patriot escapes me. Retribution? Are they gonna launch missiles? Or do they think we brought back caesarium?”

“We have to be prepared for either scenario,” Kirmani said.

“No worries,” Eisenbach said, not taking his eyes off the screen. “We are.”

74

Over the Pacific Ocean

When the Patriot burst through the other side of the atmosphere, the bright flares of protoplasmic light outside the windows disappeared. The crew module got quiet again—or as quiet as it could be traveling at hundreds of miles per hour.

Carson armed the mortars and controllers for the forward bay cover parachutes at 50,000 feet and deployed them at 26,500. DeSantos heard a muffled pop as the pyrobolts fired and the chutes rushed out with a loud whoosh.

Next up were the drogues, accompanied by the same pop and whoosh as they billowed out and dropped the Patriot's velocity to 242 miles per hour.

At 9,500 feet and 130 miles per hour, the pilot parachutes lifted the red-and-white striped main chutes from the forward bay and reduced the crew module's descent rate to a more manageable thirty feet per second.

The three main parachutes' nylon/Kevlar broadcloth material had a surface area that covered nearly an entire football field and had eighty suspension lines that, when placed end to end, stretched ten miles in length. While this eleven-parachute setup was extensive, it was essential to providing the necessary braking power to slow the crew module before it hit the water.

But this massive amount of material had to fit inside the ports at the top of the module—and they had to deploy properly, on demand. Failure would be catastrophic. The solution was to compress them to the density of oak with a powerful hydraulic device.

"Braking is according to specs," Carson said. "So far, so good."

They had been paying close attention to the altimeter and speedometer, not trusting the automated chute deployment system to run unmonitored. Because of its importance, even without threats of malware, they would be watching to make sure the system worked as engineered.

"We should hit the water at seventeen miles per hour," Carson said. "Exactly as they drew it up."

DeSantos twisted left to look up at Carson. "Except we have no idea what the Russians—or Chinese—are doing. If they're coming for us, we'll be sitting, or bobbing, ducks on the lake. Kind of literally."

"We'll find out in ninety seconds."

The sense of falling continued as Uzi called out updates. "Ten seconds. Five seconds. Two. One."

Even landing in water, Patriot impacted with a powerful jolt.

"Woohoo," Carson yelled. "Welcome home!"

They unbuckled quickly and removed their helmets, then tried to climb over to the windows to get a look outside.

"Damn," DeSantos said. "I feel like a ninety-pound weakling. Hard to stand up."

Carson laughed. "After ten days in space with little to no gravity, it's gonna take a while to adjust."

DeSantos made it over to the window. "Good news. No Russians or Chinese with rifles pointed at us. No gunships and no heat-seeking missiles." He struggled to stand on his seat to reach the top hatch.

Uzi helped release the lock and push open the door. They both fell backward into the lower tier of seats.

"Oh man," Uzi said. "Can't even support my own weight."

In between two large orange nose cone balloon-like floats, a cloudless baby blue expanse stared down at them—but the choppy ocean was tossing them about, bobbing the capsule up and down.

"Never thought I'd be so happy to see something as simple as the sky," Carson said.

"Uh-oh." DeSantos tried to push himself up, but his arms felt like jelly.

"What's up?" Uzi asked.

"Out the forward windows. Two fighter jets approaching from the, uh, northeast . . . and I don't think they're ours. Maybe Flankers."

Carson fumbled to remove a side compartment, where he found a pair of binoculars. "Camouflage blue. Definitely Russian Flankers."

Uzi had his own lenses pressed against his eyes and was looking out the rear windows. "Two—no, four—F-18s coming from the northwest."

DeSantos took the glasses from Carson and located the jets. "They fired—"

A flash of light appeared high overhead, followed by a loud boom. Two more zipped by from the other direction.

"Much lower than they should be," Carson said, "couple thousand feet at most. What's up with that?"

"Ohhh shit," Uzi shouted. One of the missiles struck the lead Flanker. It exploded on impact, scattering black smoke and shrapnel in all directions. "Close the hatch!"

The fiery hulk struck the water as Uzi and Carson struggled to lift themselves up to button down the crew module before any debris hit them.

"Who shot who?" DeSantos asked.

"We hit one of the Flankers," Uzi said, letting go, his boots hitting the floor with a thud.

"Fire in the hole!" Carson said. "Get down."

Another flash—and boom.

"Direct hit," DeSantos yelled. A second Flanker smashed into the water to the north, splintering into dozens of pieces. "Two for two, brutha!"

Uzi and Carson joined DeSantos at the windows as the four F-18s flew a wide circle overhead, securing the airspace.

"Patriot, this is CAPCOM, do you read?"

"This is Patriot," Carson said. "We read. Great to hear your voice, Bob."

"Same here. Welcome home, gentlemen. An MV-22 Osprey is en route and will be over your position in four minutes. Open the hatch and prepare to exfil."

"Roger that," DeSantos said. "Thanks for the air cover."

"I'll pass on your thanks to the men and women flying the sorties. They've got your six. Looking forward to seeing you in a few hours. Standing by."

To lower the risk of a wave flooding the module, Carson had them wait to open the access until the Ospreys were two minutes out. Rather than hand cranking the gearbox to swing the heavy door open, they would use the quicker backup method, blowing the pyrobolts.

As they swung the thick metal panel open, DeSantos felt the downdraft of the Osprey's two powerful rotors as it lowered the Navy divers from the Explosive Ordnance Disposal Mobile Unit into the cold waters of the Pacific.

Three of the men secured a horse collar towing device around the periphery of the Patriot crew module while the others attached a rope to DeSantos, then Uzi, and finally Carson. Moments later, all were onboard the Osprey. Five minutes after that, the divers were back on the MV-22, and the pilots flew a course headed for the USS *Ronald Reagan.*

75

USS Ronald Reagan
The Pacific Ocean

DeSantos, Uzi, and Carson were brought into a small room onboard the USS *Ronald Reagan*. They were briefed by Eisenbach via the VTC, or video teleconference system, which incorporated a large TV screen and camera pumped through a secure remote laptop.

What had transpired in the skies above them was exactly what it looked like—a short-lived fight over the crew module between US and Russian forces.

"Any word on my father?" DeSantos asked.

"I can answer that."

They turned around and saw Karen Vail standing in the doorway. "Welcome home, guys. Well done." She exchanged hugs with DeSantos and Uzi, and was introduced to Digger Carson.

"What'd you do to your arm?" Uzi asked.

"Let's just say that technology and I don't always get along."

Douglas Knox, Richard McNamara, and Earl Tasset entered seconds later. McNamara checked his watch, then gestured at Eisenbach.

"General, patch us through."

A moment later, Eisenbach's face was replaced onscreen by a dark scene with a jumpy, green-hued picture and a digital readout in the right corner.

Operators outfitted in light-absorbing tactical gear and night goggles ran along the tree line of an aged asphalt runway, weeds sprouting from cracks in the pavement. Several mothballed helicopters sat parked along the periphery, rust rendering its airframes non-airworthy. A few were missing their rotor blades.

DeSantos leaned forward, studying the real-time video. "What are we looking at?"

"We followed a string of leads," Vail said, "and found a connection between Russian interests and the computer malware that hit your spacecraft. And—your father. I'll explain in more detail later. Bottom line, the intel led there, to Veshevo air base."

"Veshevo," DeSantos said. "Russia?"

"Leningrad Oblast," McNamara said. "Near St. Petersburg. We sent Team 4."

DeSantos pointed at the screen. "That's Hot Rod. And that's—" He chuckled. "I'd know that body anywhere, even with the gear on. Alex." He turned to Vail. "You found my father?"

Vail placed a hand on his shoulder. "We think he's being held at the abandoned air base."

"So he's alive?"

"We hope so," Tasset said.

"Thank you," DeSantos said, his eyes glazed with tears. "Thank you all. I—"

"We don't have him yet," Tasset said. "We don't even have a visual. Let's not get ahead of ourselves."

"They've systematically searched all the buildings on the base," Knox said. "Most are clustered together in one area. Haven't found him yet—or any obvious indication that anyone's been there recently. They're coming up on the last structure."

"Klaus," McNamara said, "can you get us some audio?"

"Affirm. Audio going live."

They heard chatter over the speakers and tactical commands as the team came upon a brick building and fanned out.

DeSantos found it difficult to stand there and watch—he wanted to be there, leading the way, MP7 in hand and forging ahead. In truth, he wished he could drive automatic rounds through the bodies of the men who had kidnapped and abused his father. On full auto.

Vail squeezed his shoulder. She knew what he was feeling. He put his left arm around her and brought her close—he needed that.

"Steel door," Rodman said. "Can't breach without a charge."

"Copy that. Same around back. Windows welded shut. Set charges. We'll do the same and detonate on your mark."

DeSantos took a deep breath. He felt another body beside his. Uzi brought an arm around both him and Vail as they watched the scene unfold.

Seconds later, the explosives blew the hinges off and they pushed the metal door aside, moving forward into the dilapidated bunker.

The operator with the helmet cam engaged two tangos—and took them out with quick suppressed rounds to the head. He stepped forward and killed another. It was like watching a video of the old shoot house they trained in—except this was no exercise.

The team finished clearing all the rooms.

"What about the second floor?" DeSantos asked. He knew they couldn't hear him, but he could not help himself.

"Single story," Uzi said. "I saw on their approach."

Rodman's voice: "Building's clear. No sign of the general."

DeSantos's shoulders noticeably slumped. Vail brought him closer. "He's gotta be there," DeSantos whispered.

"What about Patrone? Any sign of him?" Vail asked.

Eisenbach relayed the question and Rusakov replied: "Not among the dead. My guess, he's in the wind." She knelt down and moved her hand along the floor. "Hang on. Hey, over here!"

The camera bobbed up and down, left and right as the operator made his way to Rusakov's side. "Give me a hand. Trap door."

Three men came around and covered the opening as Rusakov and Rodman lifted the lid.

On his knees, bound and gagged, looking up at them with a bruised face and swollen left eye, was Lukas DeSantos.

"Touchdown," Rodman said.

"Dad," DeSantos said under his breath.

Uzi and Vail shook him in celebration.

"We got him, Santa. He's safe."

"Thank you," DeSantos said, pointing at the screen. "General Eisenbach, please tell them."

"Already done, Hector. Congratulations."

76

USS RONALD REAGAN

Sir." Two men entered the room and pulled Tasset aside. One spoke by his left ear.

Tasset drew backward. "What do you mean it's not there?" He stepped in front of Carson, who was shaking DeSantos's hand.

"Where the hell is it?"

"Where's what?" DeSantos asked.

Tasset spoke slowly: "A small flat metal box."

"I . . ." DeSantos looked to Uzi and then Carson. "We don't know what you're talking about."

"Don't insult my intelligence."

"That's assuming there's intelligence to insult," Uzi said.

Vail grabbed his arm, well aware of Uzi's rocky history with Tasset.

"Sir," Uzi said, outwardly showing respect but clearly mocking him. "I'm sure you're not talking about caesarium. Because our orders were not to bring it back with us. Isn't that right?"

"Those were the orders," Knox said. "You mind explaining, Earl?"

Tasset looked at Knox, then turned away. "Stroud put a box in his backpack for me. Its contents were classified. CIA business."

"Oh, that." DeSantos glanced at Uzi. "Yeah, we found it when we were getting the cabin ready for reentry. A metal container filled with caesarium. At least that's what the Geiger counter showed."

Knox turned to Tasset. "Tell me this is a joke."

"You instructed Cowboy to bring caesarium back?" McNamara said.

Tasset clenched his jaw but kept his gaze on DeSantos. "Where is that box now?"

"We didn't want to disobey orders," Uzi said, "so we opened the hatch just before we entered the atmosphere and tossed it out. It burned up."

Tasset's face turned beet red and his temporal artery pulsed. "You're fucking lying. Where's that box!"

"Where would we hide it?" DeSantos asked.

Tasset looked away, his lips pursed in anger. "On whose authority did you dispose of it? You had no right. Stroud was mission commander."

"*Was* mission commander," Uzi said.

"He was also a CIA operative," DeSantos said. "Wasn't he?"

Tasset swung his gaze back to DeSantos but he did not reply.

"I think we should take that as a yes," Uzi said.

"The Agency does not answer to you, Agent Uziel. Or to OPSIG. Or to the Department of Defense. We only answer to the director of national intelligence and the president of the United States."

DeSantos jutted his chin back. "The president authorized the recovery of caesarium?"

Tasset ground his molars, then turned to Knox. "I want full access to the crew module as soon as it's towed on board the USS *Anchorage.*"

"No one but the DOD will have access to the Patriot," Eisenbach said on screen. "Once it arrives here at Vandy, it'll be brought to the holding area. Where it'll remain under guard."

"I'll make sure you're given full access to run your tests on whatever trace is in the module," McNamara said. "Once it's brought to Washington at the end of next week."

Tasset pushed the glasses up his nose. "This is completely unacc—"

"I think we're done here," McNamara said.

Tasset narrowed his left eye, then gave DeSantos and Uzi a stern look. "You people don't know what you've done. We're not going to get another chance to secure this element."

"If we do our jobs," Uzi said, "no one will. That was the point."

Tasset gave them all a look of disgust, then walked out.

"You didn't know about this?" DeSantos asked Knox.

"No. And I'm glad you three got rid of it. Thank you for upholding the integrity of the mission. Hector, a moment in the hall."

DESANTOS JOINED KNOX IN THE CORRIDOR.

"You're right," he said in a low voice. "Gavin Stroud was CIA." Knox raised a hand as DeSantos opened his mouth to speak. "I didn't know. That's the truth. Something came up during our investigation and I asked Hoshi Ko to roll up her sleeves. Obviously we couldn't confirm it definitively, but there are, well, let's say there are very strong indicators. And unfortunately the same goes for Digger Carson."

"Digger—" DeSantos swallowed his outburst. "Son of a bitch. So that's how the box got into his backpack. Anything happened to either of them, the other would make sure the caesarium got moved from the Raptor to the Patriot when we docked."

Knox nodded. "Makes sense. But that's not why I wanted to talk with you." He looked down at his shoes. "I'm well aware that you and your father have had issues. Just know that he admires your work with OPSIG, that you put your life on the line, that you're willing to do that with no safety net, no diplomatic, military, or government protection."

"He's never told me that."

Knox brought his gaze up to DeSantos's eyes. "He's an old general, Hector. He's not the best at expressing his emotions, let alone admitting that he was wrong. But he told me. More than once. When I'd gotten a couple of beers into him. Just wanted you to know."

DeSantos thought about that a second. "Think he'll respect my decision to sacrifice him for the good of the mission?"

"For the good of the *country*. And likely, the world. So yeah, I have no doubt he'll respect your decision. He knows better than anyone the sacrifices soldiers sometimes make in a war—that's what this was, by any other name."

"Thank you sir."

"Well, good thing is, because of the fine work of your team, including Vail, Rusakov, Hot Rod, and Zheng, you'll get to discuss it with him yourself."

DESANTOS WALKED UNSTEADILY ONTO THE DECK, where Vail was standing beside Uzi, who was leaning against the railing.

"You guys did stellar work," she said. "Truly exceptional."

"Same goes for you. Means a lot to us, having our backs like that."

"You'd have done the same for me."

Uzi took a long breath of ocean air. "Wonder what the fallout is going to be."

"Russia and China are supposedly thinking of filing a formal protest at the UN," Vail said. "I'm told that, even if they go ahead with it, they don't have a case. We're making them sign this mining treaty with a gun to their heads. So to speak. But tough. Even if they say the US has no right to police the Moon, it's hard to argue that what we did, keeping caesarium off this planet, wasn't for the good of humankind—and in the spirit of this new treaty."

"I'm sure there'll be a . . . robust argument," DeSantos said.

"Maybe," Vail said. "Maybe not. Each of the countries has its reasons for not discussing or disclosing what happened. It may all just fizzle away." Vail turned away from the ocean and leaned her back against the railing. "So what was it like?"

"It was . . ." Uzi stopped and thought a moment. "It was unlike any mission I've ever been on. In some ways, because of the environment, everything we knew about warfare and black ops was thrown out the window. And we were basically unarmed . . . against an armed opponent. Deep down, I wasn't sure we were going to make it home." Uzi turned to DeSantos. "I think it was about as tough a mission as we could've had."

"Amen to that," DeSantos said with a laugh. "Then again, the mission planners could've put us down on the dark side of the Moon. That would've been a whole *lot* more difficult."

"The dark side of the moon is not a place, Santa. It's a thing. A very dangerous thing, an element with the potential to give new meaning to the term 'weapon of mass destruction.' The Moon harbors a dark secret and Apollo 17 unwittingly exposed it." He looked out at the setting sun. "Humanity's got a horrible record with death and destruction. It's in our DNA. Let's hope caesarium stays where it is, a quarter million miles from where we can get our hands on it."

"So you told me what it was *not* like," Vail said. "What was it like?"

Uzi glanced at DeSantos. "What was *what* like? Playing astronaut? Blasting off with the world's most powerful rocket on our backs? Flying to the Moon? Walking on the Moon? Splashing down?"

"All of that. I mean, what you guys did . . . very few have done. It's . . . well, it's every boy's dream."

DeSantos chuckled. "Every man's dream, I think."

"I know some women who share that dream." She studied his face. "I'm still waiting for an answer. I'm more than a little bit curious. And 'every man's dream' doesn't quite cut it."

"It was . . ." Uzi again looked off at the orange blaze reflecting off the rhythmic ocean waves. "Indescribable. Being on another planetary body, a moon . . . It was so desolate. Quiet. I mean, when we landed, there was no one there. No trees. No weeds. No noises. No water, no wind. No squirrels or birds. No bugs. A lifeless world. Everything that we take for granted on Earth, even *color*, none of that was there."

Vail shook her head, processing what Uzi said. "I can't imagine."

"Setting down near Apollo 17's landing site, looking at all the stuff that was left behind by Cernan and Schmitt was, well it was exactly the way they left it decades ago. Kind of creepy."

"Definitely creepy," DeSantos said. "Like visiting a ghost town where the people just up and left one day." He thought a moment. "It was everything Uzi said. And more. Looking up and seeing the sunlight but no blue sky. Seeing the earthrise. The stars were something else—they were everywhere, but there was no atmosphere, so they didn't twinkle."

"Once you've done something like that," Uzi said, "what can top it? I mean, you can hike the Grand Canyon or the Himalayas, and you've got a breathtaking view. Nature at its best. Climb Mt. Everest, hike up Machu Picchu. Beautiful and exhilarating. And yet none of it compares to what we experienced."

Vail thought about that. "Think it'll change you in any way?"

DeSantos turned back to the ocean. He looked up at the nascent Moon rather than the setting sun. "We were definitely changed by it." He studied the darker irregular circles that stood out in relief against its smooth, bright white surface. Somewhere up there were his footprints, preserved in time. "If there's one way to sum it all up, I'd have to say, out of this world. Literally."

77

Langley, Virginia

Earl Tasset and three of his confidantes stood inside a nondescript, secure room at CIA headquarters.

Tasset took a deep breath and held it as he watched the drama unfold on a large screen at the front of the room.

A covert paramilitary operations team from the Agency's Special Activities Division/Special Operations Group–Ground Branch, waited at the rear entrance to Vandenberg Air Force Base storage building F, having taken out the guards with tranquilizer darts.

Much like OPSIG, the CIA unit was a secretive special ops detachment that carried out hostage rescue missions, acts of sabotage that supported US interests, personnel and material recovery, kidnappings of key opposition personnel, and counterterrorism duties.

"Power's down," one of the operators said. "Backup generator's offline. Go, go, go!"

Six black-clad men activated their chronometers and entered the facility. The drugged guards would be under for ten minutes at least, but the operatives needed to be in and out of the facility well before then—because standard operating procedure dictated that when the power went down and the generators did not come on, it triggered an automatic cell-signal based alarm. They activated a jamming device but did not know for certain it would be 100 percent effective.

They had to assume the facility would be swarming with armed personnel within 120 seconds. And since this was an Air Force base, the response would be no-nonsense and forceful.

At thirty seconds in, the operatives had secured the crew module, and fifteen seconds after that, they had removed the communications array. Behind it sat a thin metal container that looked like a small safe deposit box.

The men opened the receptacle and removed a device from their kit. They took a reading, then slammed the lid shut.

"We've got it, sir. Right where Carson put it. Geiger counter confirms. Exfiltrating now."

"Sixty seconds." Tasset looked at the high resolution satellite imagery on his large screen and said, "You've got company. Two klicks out and approaching at sixty miles per hour."

"Affirm," the operator said, slightly out of breath. "Implementing a tactical descent and departure."

Nine seconds later: "Helo's inbound and we are en route to the exfil point."

Tasset dropped his chin and tapped his foot as he waited for the all clear.

"Onboard," the man said, his voice rising in pitch, "but taking hostile fire on the climb and acceleration!"

Tasset turned back to the screen but the angle of the satellite, dense cloud cover, and nighttime darkness made it difficult to see what was transpiring.

As the radio silence ticked by, Tasset put his head back and looked at the ceiling.

Twenty seconds passed. Thirty. Then:

"Dodged the rooftops. We are clear. Repeat, we are clear."

Tasset took a deep breath and removed his glasses. “Excellent work, gentlemen.” He wiped his brow with a sleeve and turned to Bansi Kirmani. “The Agency—the country—owes you a great debt, captain. We couldn’t have done it without you.”

AFTERWORD

I always strive for accuracy in my portrayal of real-world issues and the behind-the-scenes looks at how things work. In the case of *Dark Side of the Moon*, I have grounded my fiction in fact, but I took minor literary license where needed to advance the story or to keep it from getting bogged down in rocket science minutiae and governmental bureaucracy. NASA and the military are two sprawling complexes of acronyms, disparate locations, and compartmentalized functions involving not only their own agencies but corporate contractors. I have simplified it to keep the plot moving. For the dozens of you "in the know," I've compressed, streamlined, or tweaked certain details. (In other instances, I was asked not to include certain information for security reasons.)

Moreover, our world is changing rapidly as threats emerge, some of which are discussed or alluded to in this novel. New entities within the military are created or existing ones are collapsed and merged with others to address such challenges. What I write today may not be referred to in the same way, or organized as such, two years from now. The concepts behind how these things function, however, will likely remain as depicted.

Another layer to all this is the integral role private industry plays in our military and public space endeavors. This has always been the case—going back to pre-Apollo and Gemini days—but perhaps more so now because of the enormous costs and increasing complexity of the technology involved in these missions.

Finally, a note regarding what's real and what's not. Please read my discussion on this at www.alanjacobson.com/moon-hidden-page, but I at least wanted to note here that caesarium is my creation. While the astronauts on various Apollo missions did bring back hundreds of pounds of rock, and Moon rock does contain radioactive materials thorium and uranium, the extraordinary nature of caesarium, as well as Gene Cernan's and Jack Schmitt's comments about it, are fictional.

ACKNOWLEDGMENTS

Dark Side of the Moon forced me to stretch my research muscles because most of what I needed to know for this novel fell well outside my normal sphere of expertise. It was a challenge finding the following esteemed professionals. Some insisted on remaining anonymous, especially those in private corporations, so to those of you not included below, I appreciate the extensive time, explanations, and access you provided me.

First, a hat tip to **Debbie and Josh Sabah** for connecting me with Philip Dumont and José Hernández, respectively. This kicked my knowledge base into high gear and sent me off in exciting directions. Additionally, I would like to thank the following individuals, who gave generously of their time:

Philip Dumont, PhD, scientist, NASA Jet Propulsion Laboratory (JPL), gave me a broad, early overview of what the Moon shot would look like, what issues the team would face, the challenges I had to overcome in getting my people to the Moon—and lined up some of the experts I needed to fill in all those blanks.

José Hernández, NASA Space Shuttle astronaut (STS-128) (ret.), engineer, co-developer of the first full-field digital mammography imaging system at Lawrence Livermore National Laboratory, and currently principal of Tierra Luna Engineering, for all his assistance with astronaut training, NASA procedures, the US x-ray laser project, orientation regarding NASA's SLS/Orion program, the Vandenberg shuttle pad and its utility for covert government missions; the required composition (and training protocol) of astronaut teams for my mission, the Russian space (and Buran shuttle) program, return-to-earth reentry issues and landing options. José has an inspiring story of how he became a shuttle astronaut—not to mention that he co-developed the first full-field digital mammography imaging system. I urge my readers to find out more about José by reading his biography, *Reaching for the Stars*.

Charles Galindo Jr., planetary scientist, lunar processor, and lunar researcher for NASA contractors Lockheed Martin and Northrop Grumman (ret.), and planetary scientist and education outreach professional at Tierra Luna Engineering. Charlie worked with the real Moon rocks brought back on Apollo 17 and educated me on lunar geology, new element discovery and the basics of minerals, the nomenclature of elements, and how the caesarium would be mined/retrieved—as well as its radiation concerns and how they would be addressed by the astronauts. He also helped educate me regarding the former military/NASA collaborations and the potential monitoring organizations, both government and private, that would first observe the Chang'e 5 launch.

Kent Wong, senior manager, system engineering, Aerojet Rocketdyne, for explaining in great detail the way rocket engines work relative to fuel—and how one fuel might be used in a foreign engine, and the risks involved. Kent also assisted me with how to get the Apollo 17 tank to the Chinese lander and the details as to how that fuel transfer would happen, how and what parts would need to be printed, the scenarios in which rockets could malfunction, and the particulars that go along with that. In short, Kent was my go-to resource on rocket engine–related technology, terminology, and how to solve various problems the characters encountered—while keeping it within the realm of that pesky thing known as physics. His review of the space- and rocket-related portion of the manuscript caught many of my scientific flubs. (Any literary license I took to "make things work" is my responsibility.)

Jonathan Adam, lead structures engineer, SpaceX, helped me understand the concepts behind manned space flight and rocket booster launch power; the relationship between payload, rocket capacity, and duration of mission. On personal time, Jon ran the numbers on crew complement and assisted me with the engineering concerns relative to this mission; and he gave me the options of places where the mission should be run, and launched, from. His information regarding the transportation of the Hercules II rocket, and the covert nature of portions of Vandenberg, made it the clear choice—and set up the information I would later learn from Moon Milham, below.

Moon Milham, lieutenant colonel, USAF and Air National Guard, F-16 fighter pilot, F-16 Weapons School graduate, instructor, forward air controller, mission commander, and combat aviator in three conflicts (Desert Storm and Operations Northern Watch and Allied Force)—and a host of other things filling an impressive thirty-three-year military career. For this novel, Moon's first "mission" was assisting me with Uzi's and DeSantos's F-18 training scene. He walked me through the entire process, step by step, of the onboard F-18 malfunction, post-ejection landing and search and rescue procedure, and fighter pilot terminology. Getting it right took weeks. As if that were not enough, Moon helped me understand launch trajectories—important for a Vandenberg launch to the Moon—and abort procedures. Moon also taught me about transponders, satellites, the Deep Space Network, communication jamming protocols and limitations, and private plane tracking through NORAD.

Rich London, physicist, Lawrence Livermore National Laboratory, for information on the proposed laser deployment in lunar orbit; the nuclear properties of caesarium; explosive properties of nuclear weapons; destruction radiuses; transuranic superheavy elements; and the types of radiation detection devices. Although I have a science background, nuclear (and laser) physics is well outside my knowledge base—and what I used to know I've long since forgotten. Rich took pity on me and made sure I understood the nuances of his field—or just enough to tell my story. I stretched the physics of things here and there to make things work—but that reflects on me as storyteller, not on Rich as scientist.

William "Red" Whittaker, Fredkin Professor of Robotics and director of the Field Robotics Center, Robotics Institute, Carnegie Mellon University, for helping me understand how to connect the Chang'e 5 solar panel and battery to the Apollo 17 LRV (rover). As you now know, it's a lot more complex than meets the eye, but Professor Whittaker—who has designed (and built) lunar and Mars rovers—walked me through the procedure like a true educator. When all was said and done, I actually understood everything we discussed.

Heather Jones, PhD, project scientist, Robotics Institute, Carnegie Mellon University, helped me with all of the above, as well as the particulars of the rover battery, solar panel array removal from the Chang'e and installation into the LRV—and the concept of the Moon as a junkyard in space.

Steve Garrett, US Navy Hospital Corpsman senior chief (diver/free fall parachutist/Fleet Marine Force)—also known in military parlance as HMCS (DV/FPJ/FMF) (ret.)—for refining my parachuting techniques (Uzi and DeSantos thank him as well!). Steve also read the entire manuscript and corrected my Special Operations Forces terminology, procedures, and approaches. (Steve and I interviewed each other on www.

the-lineup.com for *The Lost Codex*, OPSIG no. 3, which I recommend checking out. Steve's Spec Ops skill sets are on full display.)

Jason Rubin, captain, United States Marine Corps (ret.) and foreign service officer for the State Department, laid the groundwork as to where the F/A-18 scene had to occur, in what type of jet, and the perils of both ejection and flying over DC's Metropolitan Area Special Flight Rules Area; he also read and edited the chapter for accuracy.

Valerie Neal, PhD, curator and chair, Space History Department, Smithsonian Institution's National Air and Space Museum, for her efforts in getting me the contacts and information I needed to write this novel. Valerie understood what I was trying to accomplish and connected me with planetary geologist Bob Craddock and NASA'S head engineer of the Orion Program at Johnson Space Center, Julie Kramer White.

Julie Kramer White, NASA's head engineer of the Orion Program at Johnson Space Center; engineers **Stuart "Stu" McClung**, **Jeffrey "Jeff" Fox**, **Thomas "Tom" Walker**, **Annette Hasbrook**, and **Gary Cox** for information and explanations regarding the Orion chute deployment and splashdown procedure, the Orion hatch operation, the Orion avionics operating system, the flight software, and vehicle management computer, the Orion service module, and prelaunch sequence.

Barbara Zelon, communications manager, Orion Spacecraft, and **Laura A. Rochon**, public affairs specialist, at NASA Johnson Space Center; **Debbie Sharp**, operations manager/NASA Goddard Space Flight Center, and **Radislav Sinyak**, communications manager, Ares Corporation for making the connections with the aforenoted engineers.

Robert Craddock, PhD, geologist, Center for Earth and Planetary Studies, Smithsonian Institution's National Air and Space Museum, for assistance with questions regarding the procedure and feasibility for opening the Orion hatch prior to reentry.

Matthew Kramer, Lockheed-Martin, and **Allison Rakes**, SLS/Orion at Lockheed-Martin, for helping me get clearance through **Rachel Kraft** at NASA. Rachel then worked on my behalf to obtain answers to my questions.

Tomás Palmer, senior cyber research engineer, for helping me understand and implement my idea of operating system malware. He also assisted me with the communications issues the Patriot encounters and the ways Uzi approached his solution. Tomás has a long-standing knack for helping me get my characters into, and out of, trouble.

Mark Safarik, supervisory special agent and senior FBI profiler with the FBI's Behavioral Analysis Unit (ret.) and principal of Forensic Behavioral Services International, for reading the manuscript and correcting any FBI and/or law enforcement procedural issues I may've mucked up. Mark also helped with identifying and solving a logistical issue I had glossed over.

John P. Cooney, special agent, ATF, for assistance with plastic explosives, Semtex, PETN, and RDX and for reviewing the pertinent excerpts for accuracy.

Jeffrey Jacobson, Esq., former assistant US Attorney, for assistance with certain federal law enforcement procedures.

Jon Kalan, who suggested I contact the National Air and Space Museum. It seems obvious in retrospect, but I had not thought to do it.

Annie Maco, digital diplomacy specialist, Peruvian embassy, for information pertaining to diplomatic fingerprinting and photo identification capture.

After writing professionally for twenty-four years, I've come to realize you may sit in a room alone writing a book for a year, but your success is a team effort. My team includes my agents, **Joel Gotler** and **Frank Curtis**, who makes sure the rights, administrative matters, and contracts are taken care of properly; a big hat tip to **Rachel Levine** in Joel's office, who oversees the details and makes sure everything transpires as it is supposed to; my editor **Kevin Smith**, who helps shape the story and characters; my copyeditor **Chrisona Schmidt**, who catches my grammatical flubs and ensures everything flows well and conforms to CMS standards.

Terri Landreth and **Sandra Soreano**, my two superfans who maintain my Facebook page and stimulate ongoing discussion regarding my novels; and my **readers** and **fans** who make it all possible. Without you, I'd have some impressive looking books on my shelf, but it would be wholly unfulfilling.

Lastly, my wife, **Jill**, who reads my material, edits it, criticizes and praises it, all with the goal of making it the best it can be. When I'm in writing mode and the weeks are long and sleep is short, Jill keeps me sane and grounded.

ABOUT THE AUTHOR

Alan Jacobson is the award-winning, *USA Today*–bestselling author of twelve thrillers, including the FBI profiler Karen Vail series and the OPSIG Team Black novels. His books have been translated internationally and several have been optioned by Hollywood.

Jacobson has spent over twenty years working with the FBI's Behavioral Analysis Unit, the DEA, the US Marshals Service, SWAT, the NYPD, Scotland Yard, local law enforcement, and the US military. This research and the breadth of his contacts help bring depth and realism to his characters and stories.

For video interviews and a free personal safety ebook co-authored by Alan Jacobson and FBI Profiler Mark Safarik, please visit www.AlanJacobson.com.

You can also connect with Jacobson on Twitter (@JacobsonAlan), Facebook (www.Facebook.com/AlanJacobsonFans), Instagram (alan.jacobson), and Goodreads (alan-jacobson).

THE WORKS OF ALAN JACOBSON

Alan Jacobson has established a reputation as one of the most insightful suspense/thriller writers of our time. His exhaustive research, coupled with years of unprecedented access to law enforcement agencies, including the FBI's Behavioral Analysis Unit, bring realism and unique characters to his pages. Following are his current, and forthcoming, releases.

STAND ALONE NOVELS

False Accusations > Dr. Phillip Madison has everything: wealth, power, and an impeccable reputation. But in the predawn hours of a quiet suburb, the revered orthopedic surgeon is charged with double homicide—a cold-blooded hit-and-run that leaves an innocent couple dead. Blood evidence has brought the police to his door. An eyewitness has placed him at the crime scene, and Madison has no alibi. With his family torn apart, his career forever damaged, no way to prove his innocence and facing life in prison, Madison must find the person who has engineered the case against him. Years after reading it, people still talk about his shocking ending. *False Accusations* launched Jacobson's career and became a national bestseller, prompting

CNN to call him, "One of the brightest stars in the publishing industry."

FBI PROFILER KAREN VAIL SERIES

The 7th Victim (Karen Vail #1)> Literary giants Nelson DeMille and James Patterson describe Karen Vail, the first female FBI profiler, as "tough, smart, funny, very believable," and "compelling." In *The 7th Victim*, Vail—with a dry sense of humor and a closet full of skeletons—heads up a task force to find the Dead Eyes Killer, who is murdering young women in Virginia . . . the backyard of the famed FBI Behavioral Analysis Unit. The twists and turns that Karen Vail endures in this tense psychological suspense thriller build to a powerful ending no reader will see coming. Named one of the Top 5 Best Books of the Year (*Library Journal*).

Crush (Karen Vail #2)> In light of the traumatic events of *The 7th Victim*, FBI Profiler Karen Vail is sent to the Napa Valley for a mandatory vacation—but the Crush Killer has other plans. Vail partners with Inspector Roxxann Dixon to track down the architect of death who crushes his victims' windpipes and leaves their bodies in wine caves. However, the killer is unlike anything the profiling unit has ever encountered, and Vail's miscalculations have dire consequences for those she holds dear. *Publishers Weekly* describes *Crush* as "addicting" and *New York Times* bestselling author Steve Martini calls it a thriller that's "Crisply written and meticulously researched," and "rocks from the opening page to the jarring conclusion." (Note: the *Crush* storyline continues in *Velocity*.)

Velocity (Karen Vail #3)> A missing detective. A bold serial killer. And evidence that makes FBI profiler Karen Vail question the loyalty of those she has entrusted her life to. In the shocking conclusion to *Crush*, Karen Vail squares off against foes more dangerous than any she has yet encountered. In the process, shocking personal and professional truths emerge—truths that may be more than Vail can handle. *Velocity* was named to *The Strand Magazine*'s Top 10 Best Books for 2010, *Suspense Magazine*'s Top 4 Best Thrillers of 2010, *Library Journal*'s Top 5 Best Books of the Year, and the *Los Angeles Times*' top picks of the year. Michael Connelly said *Velocity* is "As relentless as a bullet. Karen Vail is my kind of hero and Alan Jacobson is my kind of writer!"

Inmate 1577 (Karen Vail #4)> When an elderly woman is found raped and murdered, Karen Vail heads west to team up with Inspector Lance Burden and Detective Roxxann Dixon. As they follow the killer's trail in and around San Francisco, the offender leaves behind clues that ultimately lead them to the most unlikely of places, a mysterious island ripped from city lore whose long-buried, decades-old secrets hold the key to their case: Alcatraz. The Rock. It's a case that has more twists and turns than the famed Lombard Street. The legendary Clive Cussler calls *Inmate 1577* "a powerful thriller, brilliantly conceived and written." Named one of *The Strand Magazine*'s Top 10 Best Books of the Year.

No Way Out (Karen Vail #5) > Renowned FBI profiler Karen Vail returns in *No Way Out*, a high-stakes thriller set in London. When a high profile art gallery is bombed, Vail is dispatched to England to assist with Scotland Yard's investigation. But what she finds there—a plot to destroy a controversial, recently unearthed 440-year-old manuscript—turns into something much larger, and a whole lot more dangerous, for the UK, the US—and herself. With his trademark spirited dialogue, page-turning scenes, and well drawn characters, National Bestselling author Alan Jacobson ("My kind of writer," per Michael Connelly) has crafted the thriller of the year. Named a top ten "Best thriller of 2013" by both *Suspense Magazine* and *The Strand Magazine*.

Spectrum (Karen Vail #6) > It's 1995 and the NYPD has just graduated a promising new patrol officer named Karen Vail. During the rookie's first day on the job, she finds herself at the crime scene of a woman murdered in an unusual manner. As the years pass and more victims are discovered, Vail's career takes unexpected twists and turns—as does the case that's come to be known as "Hades." Now a skilled FBI profiler, will Vail be in a better position to catch the offender? Or will Hades prove to be Karen Vail's hell on earth? #1 *New York Times* bestseller Richard North Patterson called *Spectrum*, "Compelling and crisp . . . A pleasure to read."

The Darkness of Evil (Karen Vail #7) > Roscoe Lee Marcks, one of history's most notorious serial killers, sits in a maximum security prison serving a life sentence—until he stages a brutal and well-executed escape. Although the US Marshals Service's fugitive task force enlists the help of FBI profiler Karen Vail to launch a no holds barred manhunt, the bright and law enforcement-wise Marcks has other plans—which include killing his daughter. But a retired profiling legend, who was responsible for Marcks's original capture, may just hold the key to stopping him. Perennial #1 *New York Times* bestselling author John Sandford compared *The Darkness of Evil* to *The Girl with the Dragon Tattoo*, calling it "smoothly written, intricately plotted," and "impressive," while fellow *New York Times* bestseller Phillip Margolin said *The Darkness of Evil* is "slick" and "full of very clever twists. Karen Vail is one tough heroine!"

OPSIG TEAM BLACK SERIES

The Hunted (OPSIG Team Black Novel #1) > How well do you know the one you love? How far would you go to find out? When Lauren Chambers' husband Michael disappears, her search reveals his hidden past involving the FBI, international assassins—and government secrets that some will go to great lengths to keep hidden. As *The Hunted* hurtles toward a conclusion mined with turn-on-a-dime twists, no one is who he appears to be and nothing is as it seems. *The Hunted* introduces the dynamic Department of Defense covert operative Hector DeSantos and FBI Director Douglas Knox, characters who return in future OPSIG Team Black novels, as well as the Karen Vail series (*Velocity*, *No Way Out*, and *Spectrum*).

Hard Target (OPSIG Team Black Novel #2)> An explosion pulverizes the president-elect's helicopter on Election Night. The group behind the assassination attempt possesses far greater reach than anything the FBI has yet encountered—and a plot so deeply interwoven in the country's fabric that it threatens to upend America's political system. But as covert operative Hector DeSantos and FBI Agent Aaron "Uzi" Uziel sort out who is behind the bombings, Uzi's personal demons not only jeopardize the investigation but may sit at the heart of a tangle of lies that threaten to trigger an international terrorist attack. Lee Child called *Hard Target*, "Fast, hard, intelligent. A terrific thriller." Note: FBI Profiler Karen Vail plays a key role in the story.

The Lost Codex (OPSIG Team Black Novel #3)> In a novel Jeffery Deaver called "brilliant," two ancient biblical documents stand at the heart of a geopolitical battle between foreign governments and radical extremists, threatening the lives of millions. With the American homeland under siege, the president turns to a team of uniquely trained covert operatives that includes FBI profiler Karen Vail, Special Forces veteran Hector DeSantos, and FBI terrorism expert Aaron Uziel. Their mission: find the stolen documents and capture—or kill—those responsible for unleashing a coordinated and unprecedented attack on US soil. Set in Washington, DC, New York, Paris, England, and Israel, *The Lost Codex* is international historical intrigue at its heart-stopping best.

Dark Side of the Moon (OPSIG Team Black Novel #4)> The Moon's darkest secrets come to light in Alan Jacobson's latest OPSIG Team Black thriller. In 1972, Apollo 17 returned to Earth with 200 pounds of rock—including something more dangerous than they could have imagined. For decades, the military concealed the crew's discovery—until a NASA employee discloses to foreign powers the existence of a material that would disrupt the global balance of power by providing them with the most powerful weapon of mass destruction yet created. While FBI profiler Karen Vail and OPSIG Team Black colleague Alexandra Rusakov go in search of the rogue employee, covert operatives Hector DeSantos and Aaron Uziel find themselves strapped into an Orion spacecraft, rocketing alongside astronauts toward the Moon to avert a war. But what can go wrong does, jeopardizing the mission and threatening to trigger the very conflict they were charged with preventing. *USA Today* bestselling author Alan Jacobson has once again gone behind the scenes to work with industry experts to bring his characters—and their Moon mission—to life. *New York Times* bestselling author Gayle Lynds said *Dark Side of the Moon* is "the thriller ride of a lifetime . . . a non-stop tale of high adventure that puts Tom Clancy to shame. I loved this book!"

SHORT STORIES

"Fatal Twist" > The Park Rapist has murdered his first victim—and FBI profiler Karen Vail is on the case. As Vail races through the streets of Washington, DC to chase down a promising lead that may help her catch the killer, a military-trained sniper takes aim at his target, a wealthy businessman's son. But what brings these two unrelated offenders together is something the nation's capital has never before experienced. "Fatal Twist" provides a taste of Karen Vail that will whet your appetite.

"Double Take" > NYPD detective Ben Dyer awakens from cancer surgery to find his life turned upside down. His fiancée has disappeared and Dyer, determined to find her, embarks on a journey mined with potholes and startling revelations—revelations that have the potential to forever change his life. "Double Take" introduces NYPD Lieutenant Carmine Russo and Detective Ben Dyer, who return to play significant roles in *Spectrum* (Karen Vail #6).

More to come > For a peek at recently released Alan Jacobson novels, interviews, reading group guides, and more, visit www.AlanJacobson.com.

THE OPSIG TEAM BLACK SERIES

FROM OPEN ROAD MEDIA

OPEN ROAD
INTEGRATED MEDIA

CPSIA information can be obtained
at www.ICGtesting.com
Printed in the USA
BVHW04s1940070518
515279BV00001BA/1/P

9 781504 050098